The Eye of Istar

A Romance of the Land of No Return

by

William Le Queux

Double 9
BOOKS

The Eye of Istar
A Romance of the Land of No Return
by William Le Queux

ISBN: 978-93-59950-86-0

Published by

DOUBLE 9 BOOKS

2/13-B, Ansari Road
Daryaganj, New Delhi – 110002
info@double9books.com
www.double9books.com
Tel. 011-40042856

ABOUT THE AUTHOR

Anglo-French journalist and author William Tufnell Le Queux was born on July 2, 1864, and died on October 13, 1927. He was also a diplomat (honorary consul for San Marino), a traveler (in Europe, the Balkans, and North Africa), a fan of flying (he presided over the first British air meeting at Doncaster in 1909), and a wireless pioneer who played music on his own station long before radio was widely available. However, he often exaggerated his own skills and accomplishments. The Great War in England in 1897 (1894), a fantasy about an invasion by France and Russia, and The Invasion of 1910 (1906), a fantasy about an invasion by Germany, are his best-known works. Le Queux was born in the city. The man who raised him was English, and his father was French. He went to school in Europe and learned art in Paris from Ignazio (or Ignace) Spiridon. As a young man, he walked across Europe and then made a living by writing for French newspapers. He moved back to London in the late 1880s and managed the magazines Gossip and Piccadilly. In 1891, he became a parliamentary reporter for The Globe. He stopped working as a reporter in 1893 to focus on writing and traveling.

CONTENTS

Preface

PEACE, O READER! Constant, blessed and abundant salutations.

Of a verity the groves of my hopes have been refreshed by cooling showers from the clouds of Allah's blessing, my rose garden has been weeded of the thorns of despondency, and the tree of my prosperity has become fruit-bearing from the breeze of his bounty. He is the Giver of Gifts, the Source of Liberality, the Sovereign, the dust of whose sandals is deservedly the collyrium of the eyes of mortal men; and I, called by my fellows El-Motardjim, am the servant who, in compliance with the exalted command, have placed my finger of acquiescence on the vision of obedience. During many hopeless nights I waited for the radiation of the sun of the benefits of prosperity, and counted the stars till the rise of dawn, but, by my ill-luck and the machinations of enemies, was deprived of the felicity of penetrating the mystery of the Land Forbidden.

At length, however, on a happy day when the fire of my anguish burned so brightly that it was not easy to extinguish it with the water of patience, the Abolisher of the signs of darkness and aberration invested me with the robe of the favoured, guarded me through the calamities and vicissitudes of fortune during long journeys, directed my footsteps through the mazes of paths untrodden, and revealed unto my dazzled eyes weird and wondrous marvels stranger than men have dreamed.

Therefore, O Reader! wipe the dust of ennui and fatigue from the speculum of thy mind, withdraw the tongue of blame into thy palate, and lend a willing ear to this my Tarik; for, verily, I have elucidated the secret of the mystic Land of the No Return; I have torn the veil that hideth the Great Sin from the eyes of men, and have gazed into the Eye of Istar. "Imsh Allah!"

Chapter One
The Blast of the Onbeia

We were leaving Omdurman, on an expedition to the far west, beyond the high misty mountains of Marran and the great glaring Saharan plains. Our forces, consisting of over fifteen thousand armed warriors, were assembling to parade and receive our Ruler's blessing ere we departed.

Red and fiery the sun rose, the houses shone milk-white against the intense blue of the sky, the monotonous thumping of the *nahas* continued, the yelling of the fanatical multitude increased, and the black silken standard, planted in the centre of the parade-ground, stirred by a breath of hot wind, suddenly spread itself out lazily, revealing its inscription in sprawly Arabic characters of bright yellow. The excited populace, the black-faced warriors of the Tumali, the Tegele and the Fajelu, regarding this as a good omen, shouted themselves hoarse in cursing our enemies, but a few seconds later the sound of loud trumpets echoed across the square, and a silence, sudden and complete, fell upon the multitude. Drawn up in long lines, we were facing in the direction of the Holy City, ranging ourselves in order, attending the commands of Allah and the Khalifa and celebrating the divine praise. From where I sat I had full view of the great arched gate of the Palace, which next second was thrown open as the Khalifa himself, stout, dark-bearded, and hawk-eyed, rode forth, accompanied by his officers and bodyguard. Mounted on a fine camel, and wearing a suit of golden mail armour and a helmet with spotless plume, he was surrounded by about two hundred horsemen also clad in mail, with thick, red turbans around their helmets, their horses all wearing brass head armour to protect them from sword cuts. Four *onbeia* blowers walked in front, and, in turns, sounded the great elephant's tusk, while, headed by the dreaded sable standard and moving very slowly, came the Khalifa, stern, stately, statuesque, with drawn sword. Behind, followed the gaudily-attired *mulazimin*, or body-servants, riding, while his black guards, veritable giants in stature, formed a compact square around him.

The spectacle was brilliant and imposing. In the bright morning sunshine the spears and armour of the cavalcade flashed and glittered, and, as the Khalifa drew up his camel within a few yards of me, his keen black eyes wandered around us, as if in search of absentees. Thrice the deafening plaudits of the multitude rent the air; thrice he bowed an acknowledgment with regal gesture. With one voice the people cried, "Alhamdolillah!"—the pious expression which leaves the lips of True Believers on all occasions of concluding actions—the review began, and the wild enthusiasm and confusion knew no bounds. Remington rifles with ammunition were distributed to us, in addition to the customary three spears and sword, and, amid the endless shouting and recitation of suras from the Korân, with bows and protestations we dashed at a wild gallop hither and thither past the powerful Ruler of the Soudan, raising clouds of white dust. At length, in obedience to a long, loud blast from the *onbeia*, we halted, and the Khalifa— whose custom it was to attend the mosque five times a day and to enforce the presence of all his principal emirs—commenced the second portion of the parade. The review, or *arda*, as it was called, was a religious ceremony, and those who took part in it were supposed to obtain special advantages and blessings.

Gazing slowly around him, with an expression of restlessness and revenge clearly portrayed upon his gross, bloated features, he waved his fat hand, with imperious gesture, exclaiming in a loud, firm voice,—

"Harken unto me, O my people! The believer doth not escape from the chastisement of Allah—whose glory be glorified,—until he leaveth four things—lying, pride, niggardliness and evil-thinking. Paradise desireth four kinds of men: the first of them are they who feed the hungry; the second, they who lend succour unto the naked; the third, they who fast in Ramadan; and the fourth, they who read the Korân. Fear ye Allah in secret, O my people!"

Every head bent low in obedient submission, every voice cried with one accord, "May the peace of Allah cover thee like a cloak, O august Ruler! O Pearl of the conch of Prophecy!"

"Our kingdom is made flourishing through justice, is protected by courage, and ruled by good government," he continued. "Good government is that the gate of the Chief be guarded in the proper time of being guarded, and opened in the proper time of being open, and the gate-keeper friendly. Verily, the One Merciful hath servants whom he distinguisheth with his favours, and whom he rewardeth for fighting for the Faith with great rewards. To go forth into battle against the Sultan of Sokoto is necessary for the well-being of our State, and of our people; therefore, O men-at-arms, gird your loins and sharpen your spears, so that ye may enter the great city of Kano, vanquish your enemies, trample their country underfoot, deliver it over to fire and sword, and return hither to your ease within yonder walls of this, your dwelling-place. In the darkness of night, as in the sunshine of noon, ye carry with ye upon thy wanderings the ever-anxious thoughts of your Khalifa, into whose keeping the welfare of our kingdom was entrusted by the holy Mahdi whom Allah, who liveth in Heaven, hath been pleased to remove from amongst us."

"His name be exalted and praised!" roared the excited, dark-faced multitude. "May it endure as long as time lasts!"

"True, O my people," continued the autocrat, with well-feigned reverence. "May our great Chief, El Mahdi, drink of the stream Al-Cawthar, whiter than milk or silver, and more odoriferous than musk, with as many cups set around it as there are stars in the firmament, of which water whosoever drinketh will thirst no more for ever. May he wander through the groves of Jannat-al-Ferdaws with the glorious Hur-al-oyun, whose dark eyes are a pleasure to beholders, and whose pavilions are as hollow pearls."

Then, after the people had given vent to loud acclamations, he repeated, in a loud voice, two long prayers from the Korân, followed by the *khutba* for days of the Jihad, "Praise be to Allah, the One Merciful, who is the best of helpers; for we say, verily, help us against the Infidel people. He who is dissatisfied with the licentious, we ask Him, 'Do help us against the Infidel people.' Glory to Him who scattereth the strength of the unbelievers; so we say, verily, 'Do help us.' He who surroundeth with His aid His grateful worshippers, help us. He whom Allah sent to give vigour unto the lukewarm, help us. Know ye that Allah, whose name be exalted, has written upon you the Jihad against the wicked. Therefore, exert yourselves and say, 'Help us against the Infidels, and may their place be in Al-Hawiyat.' And be ye patient in the fatigues of the expedition; for, verily, His help maketh bold those who watch. Then say ye, 'Help us against the Infidels. Thou art our Allah. Then help us against the people of the Infidels.'"

This concluded, he delivered a further invocation for the victory of the religion of Al-Islâm, long life for himself, and the continual success of his arms, following it up with a prayer, calling down the vengeance of Allah on all unbelievers and those who had erred from the paths of Mahdiism, especially the enemies we were about to attack, and asking that their wives and children might be given as booty unto us. At the end of the prayers he repeated the *Fatiha*, the whole gigantic assembly joining in the declaration of the Unity, loud, fervent, impressive.

Every head again bowed for a second, then wild yelling, shrill battle-cries and deafening war gongs sounded, mad, enthusiastic confusion becoming general everywhere as the Khalifa Abdullah and his black bodyguard slowly moved back along the Nile bank towards the great white

Palace, the ponderous iron-studded gates of which opened wide to receive them. Men and women, giving vent to cries of "*Sidi! Khalifat el Mahdi!*" and "*Ya Sidi ana mazlum!*" threw themselves upon their faces, craving his blessing as he passed, and some of the more fanatical struggled and fought with his bodyguard of ebon-faced Taisha in a vain endeavour to touch the hem of the garment of the Great Ruler inspired by Allah.

Thus, while the shouting multitude followed our Master, we dismounted, ate the handful of dhurra allotted to each of us, and took leave of our women and relations prior to setting forth on the first stage of an expedition to Kano, the City of the Mirage, which most probably would occupy us many months, and from which many of us would certainly never return.

Chapter Two
Sun and Silence

Headed by the great Raya Zerga, held in awe throughout the Soudan from Assouan even unto Lado, we of the Jihadieh, two hours later, under the heat of the brilliant sun, rode forth from the city gate, amid the vociferous shouting of the women, the frantic beating of war drums, the ear-piercing blast of great *onbeias* and the encouraging yells of old men and children. Then, with a parting war-cry, our gleaming swords flourishing in air, we left the cupolas and minarets of Omdurman behind, and spurred forward in huge compact bodies towards the low, distant hills, half hidden in their mystic haze, but supposed to be the abode of the Jinns, or genii, which our dead lord, the Mahdi, declared always fought in thousands on our side. Some of my comrades-in-arms declared that they had had visions of these strange creatures, but I confess I have never seen one, and am inclined to agree with what one of the White Fathers once told us in El Obeid, that their existence is purely imaginary. But perhaps I am a sceptic. Indeed, my white skin betrayed my Arab parentage, and, because of it, I had long ago been nicknamed by my dark-visaged comrades, "The Unbeliever." Not because I had ever expressed doubt as to the truth of the Mahdist teaching, but my pale face was alone responsible for the epithet which had, in fun, been bestowed upon me.

My personal appearance, as a horseman of the great Khalifa, was, perhaps, not such as would commend itself to the Roumis, the enemies of Allah and His Prophet. My Jibbeh, or Dervish uniform coat, was dirty and patched with multi-coloured strips of cotton; on my head was the white skullcap, called the *takia*, bound by a broad white turban; while I wore a pair of loose cotton unmentionables with a red girdle, and my bare feet were thrust into rough slippers of undressed cowhide. My weapons consisted of a circular shield which bore the deep dints of past combats, two small spears, one long one, a rifle, and a heavy sword with cross hilt strapped up under my left arm.

Light-hearted, laughing among ourselves, and eager for the fray, we crossed the hills, but saw nothing of the mysterious Jinns; then, continuing our ride into the stony, waterless desert of Bayuda, that immense country forgotten of Allah, we halted at sundown for the *maghrib*, and journeyed forward yet another three hours before encamping. The expedition was under the leadership of Ali Wad Helu, chief of the Baggara Arabs, upon whose crimson flag, borne before him, was inscribed in gold in the Arabic character, '*Nekhrib ed Dunia wa nammir el Akher*.' (We shall destroy this, and create the next world). This was his motto. A fierce and fanatical warrior, he had acted a conspicuous and unenviable part in that terrible storm of 1885 which deluged the Soudan with blood, and now thought not of sparing the lives of his men, but urged that, by dying by the sword, we should go direct to the Jannat-al-Ferdaws, where the great lote-tree throws a cool shade, and where the houris have lips of musk and eyes bright and sparkling as stars of night.

Resting during the day, on account of the furnace-heat of sunshine, and travelling during the clear, starlit nights over the sands with our black standard ever waving at our head, the hosts of the Khalifa swept onward through the land of sun and silence, like a great swarm of locusts, bent upon ruthless pillage and destruction. Day by day, week by week, we travelled over the immense plain, always in the crimson track of the dying day. Everywhere spread vast solitudes, an interminable country of desolation and sad monotony, without a plant or a vestige of life—only shifting, brown sand-hills, boundless horizons and a blinding glare of sun. Through Foja and El Fasher we passed, then over the great, bare mountains to Kol-Kol. Three journeys from that place, however, Ali Wad Helu, fearing attack by hostile tribes, sent forward fifty spearmen—of whom I was one—to act as scouts. The orders we received we obeyed promptly, and, heedless of heat and sand storms, we travelled rapidly onward to Abu Guerra, across infinite, mysterious solitudes, where the blazing heat and the loose sand retarded our advance, until, at last, we reached El-Asagga, on the shore of Lake Tsad, exactly one moon after our departure from Omdurman.

Inured as the cavalry of the Khalifa were to the burning breath and silent gloom of the desert, the privations of the march and the fatigue of long travel, we found in this journey that our horses were utterly unfit to negotiate the stony wilderness that lay between ourselves and Kano, known to the desert wanderers as the City of the Mirage by reason of the amazing mirages seen in the vicinity almost daily; therefore, on arrival at the Well of Sabo-n-Gari, four days' journey south from the Lake, and two days' beyond the boundary of the territory of the Sultan of Sokoto, we resolved to encamp under the palms and await our main body in order to utilise the spare camels which they had brought with them in case of need. To attempt to approach nearer to the city we intended to attack would, we knew, result in speedy death.

The last fires had faded from the west; moonless night had fallen. The poison-wind blew in sharp hot gusts, the heat from the sand was reflected into one's face, black clouds hung low and ominous, and the atmosphere, laden with particles of grit, was stifling. We prayed our *isha*, ate our *dhurra*, and leaving three of our comrades on the alert, in case of surprise, stretched ourselves in our tents and endeavoured to snatch a brief repose. The neighbourhood of the well was not a safe place after sundown, for wild beasts came there for water, and we had seen the marks of lions on the sands. Wearied, my eyes at length closed in sleep, and I was dreaming of cool, idle hours at my mountain home in the far-off Aures, and of bygone days amid the civilisation of London, when suddenly I was startled by the quick rattle of musketry, followed by fiendish yells, while, at the same moment, there was a flash of powder as a bullet tore its way through the canvas of my little tent, whistling unpleasantly near my head. Seizing my rifle, I sprang up, and, with my comrades who had been sleeping by my side, rushed forth.

Next second I knew the truth. The place was alive with horsemen, led by a minor sheikh mounted upon a splendid grey. We had fallen into the trap against which our spies had repeatedly warned us, and were evidently being attacked from every side by the Tuaregs. In the Great Desert there are two terrors ever present—the sand and the Tuaregs. The latter are the forbidding-looking pirates of the desert, held in awe from El Fasher to Timbuktu. It is said that ages ago they were compelled to migrate south from the fertile Atlas into the Great Desert, and owing to their eyes being unaccustomed to the terrible glare, nor their lungs to the sand storms, they adopted a head-dress with two veils. One, the *nicab*, is rolled round the temples, hanging down in front to protect the eyes; the other, the *litham*, reaches from the nostrils to the edge of the clothing, completely covering the lower part of the face. Hence they are known to-day, everywhere in the Soudan, as the "Veiled Men of the Desert," while upon all those who do not adopt their mysterious-looking costume they bestow the sobriquet, "mouths for flies." The veils are never removed, even at meal times, and the garb has become so much a part of them that any one, being deprived of it, is unrecognisable to his friends and relatives. If one of their number is killed in battle and divested of his veil, no one can identify him until it has been restored to its place. And this, in spite of the fact that the bridge of the nose and the eyes alone are visible. Their power is felt in nearly every part of the Great Desert, and to such an extent have they carried their depredations that until quite recently almost every town was compelled to pay them tribute. These nomads are thieves of the worst character, travellers and merchants being their principal victims. Their vague form of Islâmism they have reduced to a belief in talismans, and their chest and back are covered with bags of black and yellow, like a cuirass. Ruse is their principal weapon, even though they never show themselves without spear or gun, a sword at their side and a poniard attached to the left arm. We, of the Khalifa's army, had bestowed upon them three epithets which epitomise their psychology— "Thieves, Hyenas, and the Abandoned of Allah."

There had been a deadly feud of long standing between us, and they, learning that a small party of Dervishes was in the vicinity, had apparently come forth to check our advance. But the horsemen of the Khalifa Abdullah, Sultan of the Soudan, know not fear, as their valiant actions at Abu Klea, Berber, El Obeid and Toski had already proved, and now, even though we saw ourselves surrounded by hundreds of yelling "Veiled Men," who poured into us a withering fire from their long-barrelled guns, not a man among us was dismayed although many bit the dust ere reaching cover.

That it must be a struggle to the death we knew, therefore, unable to mount, we obtained what protection we could among the few palm trunks, and replied to the hail of bullets with careful precision, picking off a white-robed figure whenever one showed itself. Behind every rock or tree large enough to shelter a human form a veiled man lurked, and, well-practised in the use of firearms, they proved themselves superior shots. As far as we could discern in the gloom they outnumbered us by about ten to one, and their weapons, aimed deliberately at us from the security of the ambuscade, had already taken deadly effect. On every side white robes fluttered as rifles shed their weird red light, and ere long many of our men, stumbling forward, sank upon the sand and died with fierce curses upon their lips. Unable to approach our opponents sufficiently near to effectively use our long spears we continued our erratic fire, determined to make a stubborn stand until the end. During a quarter-of-an-hour this continued, when suddenly wild piercing yells sounded above the incessant rattle of musketry as, with one accord, about two hundred Tuaregs, their villainous faces encircled by their black veils, and standing in their stirrups, swept down upon us with a ringing shout of triumph. In a moment a fierce hand-to-hand struggle ensued, for horses and riders plunged upon our spears, and dozens of the desert pirates fell impaled, their burnouses dyed with blood. One man, tall and sinewy, his breast loaded with talismans, riding a magnificently-caparisoned horse, and evidently a sheikh, I held in the grip of death, and he fell by my hand. Indeed, so strenuous was our defence that, on glancing round, I felt half inclined to believe that the fierce onslaught would not be repeated; yet, almost before this thought had crossed my mind, another shrill war-cry resounded as an additional force on foot emerged from the dark clump of trees with burnouses flying, eyes blazing, and firing as they ran they rushed together upon us in such numbers as to prove absolutely overwhelming. With rifles held high above their heads, and yelling fiercely, they sped onward, driving us from our cover, and shooting us down, although we slashed, stabbed and hacked like very demons. Prodigies of strength and valour were performed by my comrades, the Dervishes, in their last defence. The struggle inflamed them, as it ever does men courageous by nature and born brave. They sold their lives dearly, but to effectually repulse the attack or to crave for quarter were alike futile. Alas, the soldiers of the Black Standard, who for years had fought long and fearlessly for the holy Mahdi and his successor, were now falling helpless victims to the cunning and rapidity with which the Tuaregs had delivered their terrible onslaught.

Full of breathless anxiety were those fatal moments. Elated by their success and filled with a deadly hatred against us, our enemies were evidently determined to sweep us into eternity. The ground was encumbered with dead and dying. Several of my comrades, believing that the Jinns had deserted us, and therefore resistance was useless, threw down their arms, and falling on their knees, cried, in the name of the *One* for their lives to be spared, but the Veiled Men of the Desert only jeered, and shot them down as ruthlessly as they would slaughter dogs, crying, "Kill the black-faced sons of offal! Let not one escape, or he will give warning unto the hosts of the accursed tyrant, the Khalifa. Kill the dogs! Kill them!" My comrades' death-wail uplifted, and, sharpened in soaring, hung in anguish at its height; then, like hope's expiring sigh, it faltered downward and fell mute.

Escape was hopeless; we had fallen into an ambush. Our enemies had surrounded us by hundreds. Amid the shrieks, the firing, the fiendish, exultant cries of the victors and the fierce, hoarse curses of the dying, I fought on with spear and shield, unhorsing more than one of our deadly foes. My comrades were apparently all being ruthlessly slaughtered, when suddenly a gigantic son of the desert, lithe as a deer, black-veiled, and sitting his white horse as if he were part of it, galloped straight towards me with a loud cry, his whirling blade flourishing in mid-air ready to match me, strength to strength. In a second my spear left my hand, and striking him full in the breast, felled him to earth a corpse, but ere I could draw breath, another piercing yell sounded behind me, and I felt a sharp twinge in the left shoulder. Then a horrible, choking sensation seized me, and I have a vague recollection of a man's dark face, hideously distorted by hatred, and with a black *rawani*, or shawl wrapped around it, within a few inches of mine, so near that I could feel his hot, foetid breath upon my cheek.

A sudden darkness next instant fell upon me, and all consciousness became blotted out.

Of events that immediately followed, or of how long I remained insensible I have no knowledge. Thoughts, strange and confused, grim and pleasant, incongruously mixed flitted through my unbalanced mind, but I had no idea of place, of time, of anything. A darkness, black and impenetrable, had obliterated my senses and held me powerless, until a sharp spasm of pain shot through my limbs, and then I recollected, in a half dreamy manner, that I had fallen in the desperate fight. I tried to repeat the first *sura*, but my lips, cold and clammy, refused to utter sound. The pain increased in intensity until my whole body became racked by a torture so acute and horrible that I believe I must have fainted. Many are the scars I had received in battle, but never had I experienced such suffering. Indeed, the pain was so intense that I felt myself writhing in terrible agony, while the perspiration stood in great beads upon my neck and brow, and the tightness in my chest held me, as in a vice, breathless, with all the horrible pangs of asphyxiation.

An interval of senselessness was followed by a brief period of calm; then gradually, with a feeling that I was struggling hand-to-hand with Azrael, the dreaded Angel of Terrors, I slowly struggled back to consciousness. Blindly enduring, I suffered alternately torments of fire and of ice. Memories haunted me, vivid, voluptuous; scenes of a passionate past recurred. I stood in a magical Hall of Echoes, where every echo seemed the voice it mocked, and through some flaw in each illusion drove the shattering spear of truth.

In the impenetrable darkness my fingers wandered involuntarily to seek the objects around. On either side I stretched forth my hands, but clutched at air. Faint sibilations, like the sound of hushed whispering fell upon my ear, and in that moment filled me with a strange fear. My resting-place seemed soft and comfortable, and as again my hands sought to discover something that would give me a clue to my whereabouts, my finger-tips suddenly came into contact with embroidered satin. I could feel the raised pattern upon the smooth, glossy surface at my side, and became aware that I was not stretched upon the sand, where I had fallen, but upon a divan. I felt the cushion upon which my aching head was pillowed. It was also of satin, soft as down. The air seemed heavy with the sensuous intoxicating odour of attar of rose rising from a perfuming-pan—a subtle scent that still vibrates my memory—and as I touched the pillow I made a further discovery. Raising my hand to wipe my clammy brow, I became aware of the reason of my obscurity of vision.

My forehead and eyes had been bandaged with a folded square of thick black silk.

By frantic movement I endeavoured to tear away the tightly-bound fabric, but failed. It had been dexterously knotted, and no effort of mine could remove it. Again, with words of haste upon my lips, I tried to tear it from my eyes, but did not succeed, for when I tried to lift my left hand to my head I again experienced a spasm of pain that was excruciating.

Suddenly I was conscious of the presence of someone near me, and a voice in low, soft, musical tones, scarcely above a whisper, exclaimed in the Hausa tongue,—

"*Barka, sanu sanu.*"

My acquaintance with this language of the people beyond Lake Tsad was very imperfect, but I nevertheless knew that the words gave me peace, and, being translated, were, "Allah, bless thee. Gently, gently."

"Peace be upon thee, O unknown friend," I answered fervently, in Arabic. "Thou who hast given succour unto the wounded, I beseech of thee allow mine eyes to behold the mirror of thy face."

"Of a verity thine eyes shall ere long witness things that, peradventure, will amaze thee," answered the low voice of the unknown, in tones in which severity and gentleness were strangely mingled.

Soft hands deftly unloosed the double knots at the back of my head, the scarf was drawn away, and on eagerly opening my bewildered eyes they were dazzled by a strange flood of bright light that poured down upon them.

Next second, however, my vision grew accustomed to the extraordinary brilliance, and the scene which met my wondering gaze was so strange and bewildering, so inexplicable and stupendous, so awe-inspiring yet entrancing, that, in sheer amazement, I slowly raised myself upon my arm and gazed aghast in stupefaction, fascinated, open-mouthed, petrified.

Chapter Three
Azala

My transition had been remarkable; the sight that met my eyes was, indeed, sufficient to cause breathless wonderment.

What time had elapsed since, in the darkness of night, I had fallen senseless beneath the palms of the oasis of Sabo-n-Gari, or by what means I had been rescued from the tortures of a lingering death by fever and thirst, I knew not. I had lapsed into unconsciousness at a moment when the last of my brave comrades had been slain, only to awaken and find myself stretched on a divan in a spacious apartment, the walls of which were richly hung with rose-coloured silk. The marble floor was half hidden by the profusion of rugs of beautifully blended hues, while around, near the arched roof, verses and good counsels from the Korân were written in Arabic characters, in long lean letters of gold. There were many dainty coffee-stools of inlaid silver and pearl, and a number of soft divans of gold-coloured silk. The place was windowless, but the sunlight, apparently reflected and intensified by mirrors, was admitted from the roof, and so directed that it fell in a golden bar across my face, presumably for the purpose of bringing me back to consciousness.

At one end of this brilliant apartment was a door with horse-shoe arch, like all the others, leading to a little retreat, the gloom of which was, to me, impenetrable. In a corner, close to me, was a great gold perfuming-pan from which rose sweet odours in a column of thin blue smoke, while two gilded derboukas and a pair of slippers, cast aside upon one of the larger mats, showed that the occupants had indulged in those terpsichorean exercises in which Eastern women delight.

Almost before I could realise the luxury of my surroundings, a soft, cool hand was laid upon my fevered brow, and, turning my head with difficulty, I suddenly beheld a vision of wondrous beauty. Over me there bent a fair face, so perfect in feature that I became entranced. The eyes, dark and large, expressive of the soul that lay behind, held me in fascination, and I gazed, tongue-tied, in amazement.

She was young, not more than twenty, with a countenance white as those of the Englishwomen who come to Algiers at Ramadan; soft brown eyes denoting the mildest, tenderest nature, and a mouth sweetly pursed like the bud of a rose. Tendrils of soft, brown, wavy hair strayed across a fair forehead, hung heavily with strings of golden sequins, the centre of which was formed by a great oval pearl surrounded by diamonds, the finest my eyes had ever beheld, and in her ears were large, delicately-chased rings of gold. Her dress was the gorgeous costume of the harem: the tiny skullcap thickly embroidered with gold and seed pearls, set jauntily upon her head, the zouave of palest amaranth velvet, similarly embroidered, worn over a gauzy, low-necked vest, and the flimsy *serroual* or trousers of pale pink China silk. Her white, delicately-moulded arms were bare, adorned by heavy *mesais* of gold and jingling bangles set with gems, while her feet, likewise uncovered, were thrust into dainty little embroidered slippers of pale green velvet, her *redeefs* being composed of single bands of curiously worked gold set with beautiful jacinths. Her necklets, of which she wore fully a dozen, were of various patterns, several being composed of strings of golden coins, or discs of gold thickly encrusted with rubies and turquoises, her oval perfume bottle, suspended at her breast, being conspicuous on account of the top being formed of a single emerald, while the diamonds set in the ornament itself were of amazing lustre.

My mouth was parched, but she knelt beside me, and supporting me with her left arm, with her right held a goblet to my lips.

How it came about I never knew, but before the draught was finished a change passed over me. Whether it was her soft touch, her strange and fawnlike loveliness, or the tender pity in her eyes matters not, the issue was the same; she struck some chord in my turbulent nature, and in a moment it was filled full with passion for her. I did not for a moment mistake the significance of the flood of feeling that surged through my veins. I have never shirked facts.

"I thank thee," I said; "thine hand is kind."

As she smiled upon me, moving slightly, her sequins tinkled, and the ray of sunlight, streaming full upon her, caused her jewels to flash and gleam with a thousand iridescent fires, producing an effect that was dazzling.

Opening her lips she displayed an even set of beautiful pearly teeth, as she exclaimed, in the soft speech of my mother tongue,—

"Peace, O stranger. May the blessing of the One, whose name be exalted, rest eternally upon thee. Let not fear oppress thee; of a verity thou art with friends."

"Mine eyes are bewildered, O One of Beauty, whose countenance is as the glorious light of day, and whose eyes are brilliant as stars in the desert. Upon thee be perfect peace and the fervent blessings of one who hath approached near unto Certainty," I answered with difficulty. Then, as I raised my hand and it came into contact with bandages about my shoulder, I added "The darkness of unconsciousness hath long obscured my mind, and I know not under whose roof I rest. Allah hath been gracious unto me. Verily, He bestoweth abundant provision on such of His servants as He pleaseth."

"Yea, O stranger," she answered, piously. "Everything shall perish except Himself; unto Him belongeth judgment. Accursed be those who struck thee down, for Allah, Gracious Bestower of abundant benefits, knoweth both the secret malice which their breasts conceal and the open hatred which they discover."

In a fit of renewed weakness, brought about by the turmoil of my blood, I lay back upon the silken pillows watching her face. It almost seemed as though something of what was passing in my mind communicated itself to her.

"Knowest thou mine enemies?" I asked, raising myself, and, to my astonishment, discovering, for the first time, that the loose garments I wore were of finest silk, and that I was veiled and disguised as a woman.

"I know that thou wouldst kill me," she answered briefly, with a curious smile, standing before me with hands behind her back, a veritable houri.

"Kill thee! Why?"

"Because thou art a soldier of the great Khalifa of Omdurman, enemy of my people, and Ruler of the Soudan."

"What name bearest thou?" I asked.

"I am called Azala Fathma."

"Daughter of whom?"

"Daughter of 'Othman, Sultan of Sokoto."

"Thou—Princess of Sokoto!" I gasped, struggling slowly and with difficulty to my feet, scarcely believing my ears. "Where, then, have I taken mine ease?"

"For three days past hast thou been concealed here, in the harem of thine enemy," she answered, in low, placid tones, looking seriously at me. Then, noticing the uneasy glance I cast in the direction of the dark alcove beyond, she added quickly, "Let not apprehension fall upon thee. To this my apartment none dares enter unbidden, therefore thou art safe, even in the midst of those whom thou didst seek to destroy."

"Chastise me not with a scourge of words, O Daughter of the Sultan," I said, apologetically. "Thy servant Zafar-Ben-A'Ziz, Arab of the Chawi, horseman of the Khalifa, armeth not himself against those who give him succour, nor seeketh he the overthrow of the city of thy father."

Leaning gracefully, with her back against the twisted column of polished marble, inlaid with gold, supporting the arched roof, she clasped her hands behind her handsome head and gazed at me. Then, half reproachfully she said, —

"Whoso doth that which is right, doth it to the advantage of his own soul; and whoso doth evil, doth it against the same: hereafter shall we return unto Allah. Thou earnest with scouts to reconnoitre—perchance to enter this our city singly or in company—so that on the advance of the ruthless legions of thy Sultan thou mightest, by treachery, admit them within our walls. But Allah, who hath placed the twelve signs in the heavens, is merciful and knoweth the hearts of men. Thine encampment was discovered and destroyed."

"How was my life spared?" I asked.

"I was present when thou wert forced to bite the dust," she explained. "I had journeyed unto Katsena, where I had lingered one moon, and was returning hither to Kano when my Tuareg guards, warned of thine approach, watched thee by stealth, and in the darkness fell upon thee at a moment when thou wert unprepared. On the rising of the sun I searched the spot, and found that thou alone still lived. Secretly thou wert attired in the haick belonging to one of my handmaidens, and by my orders conveyed hither in a *jakfi* on one of mine own camels. Still dressed as a female slave thou wert able to pass the guards of the outer courts and of the harem, to rest and recover on mine own divan."

"Then to thee, O Azala, Princess of Sokoto, whose beauty is peerless, I owe my life," I answered, fervently. "Truly hast thou snatched me back from the grave, even though I sought to assist in the sacking of this, the palace of thy father, and in the holding of thy people in bondage. Tell me, why shouldst thou interest thyself in my well-being?"

Hesitating, apparently confused at my question, Azala moved uneasily, toying with the silken fringe of her broad girdle.

"Is it not written that we should bear no malice?" she answered, after a pause. "Al-Sijil registereth our deeds."

"Wisdom falleth from thy lips," I said, smiling. "But hadst thou no motive in bringing me into this thine apartment, even at the imminent risk of detection and disgrace?"

"I am not compelled to answer thy question," she replied, with a forced laugh. "Reason underlyeth most of our actions."

"And wilt thou not explain thy reason?"

"No. At present my lips must remain sealed," she answered calmly, her bejewelled breast heaving and falling in a long-drawn sigh. "Peradventure thou mayest learn my motive some day; then will thine eyes open in astonishment, for thou wilt gain knowledge of things undreamed-of and behold marvels amazing."

"Thou speakest in enigmas. When may these secrets be revealed unto me? Of what character are they?"

"Seek not to unloosen my tongue's strings, O mine enemy—"

"Nay, not enemy, friend, grateful and ever devoted," I interrupted.

"Then, if thou art my friend seek not to discover mine innermost thoughts," she said, earnestly. "As the wicked are in Sajin, beneath the seventh heaven, where dwelleth Eblis and his host, so assuredly will those who seek to discover the hidden marvels without mine aid or sanction taste of the bitter fruit of Al-Zakkum."

"But if thou givest unto me a pledge that thou wilt render explanation, I will be content," I said.

"Not only will I, when the time is ripe, explain the strange secret unto thee, but, likewise, shall I seek thine assistance in elucidating a strange and incomprehensible mystery."

"I am thine to command," I answered gallantly, taking her slim, white hand in mine. "When thou desireth me to serve thee, O Azala, thou wilt find me ever ready, for to thee I owe my life; my future is in thine hands."

"To seek the key of the hidden mystery, to vanquish the angel Malec who hath charge of the gates of hell, will require a stout heart and lion's courage," she said slowly, fixing her clear, wonderful eyes upon mine, and allowing her soft bejewelled hand to linger for a second within my grasp.

"When the day dawneth thou wilt not find me wanting in defiance of danger, for, of a verity, I fear nothing with the beauteous daughter of the Sultan 'Othman as my pole-star."

For a second a blush suffused her pale cheeks.

"As thou trusteth me, so also will I trust thee," she said, in deep earnestness. "Even though my position is exalted as Princess of Sokoto; even though I am surrounded by all that is beautiful, with many slaves to do my bidding, yet unhappiness eateth like a canker-worm into my heart."

"Wherefore art thou unhappy?" I asked, sympathetically.

"Ah! the reason none may know," she sighed. "Until I call upon thee to render thine aid in seeking to discover things that are forbidden, thou must necessarily remain in the outer darkness of ignorance. Here, in the palace of my father, thou must remain in hiding until the time for action cometh. Then will I show thee that which will fascinate and astound thee."

"Thy words of mystery arouse curiosity within me," I said. "Canst thou not reveal to me anything now?"

"Nothing. Save to tell thee that thou canst, if thou wilt, shield me from a fate worse than death. A disaster, horrible and complete, threateneth to overwhelm me, and thou alone canst prevent it."

"How?"

"By patience, silence, and passive obedience to my commands."

"I am thine," I said, as, entranced by her marvellous grace and beauty, my arm slowly encircled her slim waist, begirt with dull gold and flashing jewels. I strove to draw her to me, but without any violence of movement, and with the most perfect dignity, she disengaged herself from my embrace. Yet I held her to me and breathed into her ear words of devotion. Then, as her beautiful head at last turned slowly toward me, and her eyes, looking into mine, spoke mutely of reciprocated affection, our lips met in a hot, passionate caress.

I was trembling upon the pinnacle of Al-Araf, that partition that divides pleasure from misery, love from hatred, hell from paradise. She was the proud and handsome daughter of the Sultan 'Othman, the woman, the fame of whose exquisite beauty had long ago reached us even in far-off Omdurman; I, a mere Dervish, without home or property, one of a band paid by the all-powerful Khalifa to plunder, murder and destroy.

What words of tenderness I uttered I scarcely remember. The sensuous fragrance, rising from the perfuming-pan, seemed to induce a sweet, dreamy half-consciousness, but for the first time I experienced the passion of love. I loved her with all the strength of my being, and the only words that impressed themselves upon me in those moments of mad infatuation were those uttered by the woman I adored,—

"Yea, O Zafar, I will place my trust in thee." Resting in my embrace, her bright eyes betrayed her perfect happiness, and as I softly stroked her silky hair and implanted a kiss upon her white, sequin-covered brow she clung to me with her long bare arms clasped tightly around my neck in an ecstasy of joy.

"Never will I forsake thee," I answered, fondly. "With the faithfulness and obedience of a slave will I carry out thy commands, for thou art my queen and I thy devoted bondman."

Tears dimmed her bright, clear eyes; tears of joy she vainly strove to suppress.

"Truly to-day is the dawn of my life's happiness," she said, in a low tone, full of emotion. "To-day Allah hath sent me a friend."

"And, on my part, I pledge myself unto thee with unswerving devotion," I exclaimed, fervently. "In veiled words hast thou spoken of certain solemn secrets. When thou explainest to me my task of elucidation, assuredly wilt thou find me ready and eager to undertake it. In thine hands thou holdest my future, for life or death."

"Upon those who seek to come between us may the wrath of the One Granter of Requests fall like an avenging fire; may they find no patron nor defender, nor may they rest beneath the shadow of the lote-tree," she said. "It is written in the Book of Everlasting Will that Allah, who knoweth all things, joineth man and woman with his bounteous blessing. Therefore may the rose-grove of thy prosperity and good fortune be increased daily in freshness and magnificence, and in what difficulty thou mayest be placed, or into what evil thou mayest peradventure, fall, bear in thy mind my declaration of love, and remember always that, even though deserts of great space and rapid waters may separate us, I am thine and thou art mine alone. I trust to thee to break asunder the invisible bonds that fetter me unto misery."

"But surely we shall not be parted," I exclaimed, the mere suggestion being intolerable.

"Neither sultans nor their kin are capable of ruling events," she said. "Of what the future may have in store none knoweth but the sorceresses and the wise women, who, alas! holdeth their knowledge to themselves."

"True, O Azala, my enchantress. In like manner wilt thou remember always, if we part, that I shall be striving to return unto thee; that the one object of my life henceforward is to break asunder the mysterious fetters of thine unhappiness."

Our hands clasped. She looked straight into my eyes. Hers was no dreamy nature. With her, to resolve was but a preliminary of to execute. No physiognomist would need to have been told that this beautiful woman, so quick in intelligence, so kind in manner, so buoyant and joyous in disposition, was at the same time, in force of character and determination, as firm as adamant.

"And thou wilt not fail to render me assistance in the hour of my need?" she exclaimed.

"May Allah bear witness that I am prepared to strive towards the elucidation of thy mystery while I have breath."

Pressing my hand with lingering tenderness, she said,—

"Thy words give peace unto me, O Zafar. Henceforth shall I rest in the knowledge that the man who is my friend is prepared to risk his life on my behalf."

"Yea," I answered; adding, "of a verity this meeting between enemies hath been a strange one. Hast thou not warned thy father of the approach of the hosts of the Khalifa?"

"Even on the same night as thine encampment was destroyed warning was conveyed unto him, with the result that our troops have been sent forward into the desert with the object of checking the advance of thy tribesmen."

"They are not my clansmen," I answered, quickly. "I am an Arab, a native of the Aures, the mountains far north beyond the Great Desert."

"Then thou art not a Dervish?" she exclaimed, gladly.

"No," I answered, and at the same moment remembering that the Khalifa's troops numbered many thousands, and that it was scarcely likely that they would be turned aside in their onward march by a few squadrons of the Sultan of Sokoto, I asked,—

"Have the horsemen of the Black Standard been routed?"

"I know not. Yesterday I overheard the messengers delivering their report to the Sultan in the Hall of Audience," she replied.

"But if they are still advancing! Think what terrible fate awaiteth thee if the soldiers of the Khalifa loot this thy beautiful palace, and spread death and desolation through thy city with fire and sword!"

"Arrangements have already been made for my secret escape. In case of danger I shall assume thy garments, arms and shield, which I have preserved, and pass as a Dervish."

"Excellent," I said, laughing at her ingenuity. "But let us hope that my comrades will never gain these walls. If they do, it will, alas! be an evil day for Kano."

"The detection and slaughter of thy scouts placed our army upon its guard," she said. "Already the defences of our city have been strengthened, and every man is under arms. If the Dervishes attack us, of a verity will they meet with an opposition long and strenuous, for by our fighting-men the walls of Kano are believed to be impregnable. See!" she added, drawing aside a portion of the silken hangings close to her, and disclosing a small window covered with a quaintly-worked wooden lattice. "Yonder our men are watching. Our principal city gate, the Kofa-n-Dakaina, is strongly guarded by night and day."

Chapter Four
The Mark of the Asps

Stepping to the window, I found that the apartment in which we stood was evidently situated in a tower of the palace—which I had heard was built high on Mount Dala—for the great city, with its white, flat-roofed houses and cupolas, and minarets of mosques, lay stretched beneath us. At the massive gate, in the high frowning walls which surrounded the extensive and wealthy capital of the Empire of Sokoto, the far-famed *entrepôt* of Central Africa, soldiers, attired in bright uniforms of blue and gold, swarmed like flies, while cannon bristled on the walls, and everywhere spears and arms glittered in the sun. She pointed out the Jakara, a wide, deep lake, the great Slave Market crowded with buyers, sellers and human merchandise, the Palace of Ghaladima and the Kofa Mazuger. The city was agog, for the hum of life rose from its crowded streets and busy market-places, mingling now and then with the ominous roll of the war drums, the twanging of *ginkris*, the clashing of cymbals, and the shouts of the eager, ever-watchful troops. By the cloudless, milk-white sky I knew it was about noon, and the sun directly overhead poured down mercilessly upon the immense sandy plain which stretched away eastward and northward until it was lost in the misty haze of the distant horizon. Date palms rose in small clusters near the ornamental lake in the centre of the city; in the square spreading *alleluba-trees* cast their welcome shade, and beautiful *gotuias* unfolded their large, featherlike leaves above slender and undivided stems, but beyond the city walls there was not a tree, not a blade of grass, not a living thing. Out there all was sun, sand and silence.

"Dost thou reside here always?" I asked, as together we gazed down upon the great white city.

"Yes. Seldom are we in Sokoto itself, for of later years its prosperity hath declined, and the palace is of meagre proportions; indeed, it is now half-ruined and almost deserted. The wealth and industry of the empire is centred here in Kano, for our trade extendeth as far north as Mourkouk, Ghat, and even Tripoli; to the west, not only to Timbuktu, but even to the shores of the great sea; to the east, all over Bornu; and to the south, among the Igbira, the Igbo, and among the pagans and ivory hunters of the Congo."

"True," I said, gazing round upon the prosperous capital of one of the most interesting empires in the world. "It is scarcely surprising that my ambitious lord, the Khalifa, should desire to annex the land of the Sultan 'Othman. Even our own cities of Omdurman or Khartoum are not of such extent. How many persons inhabit this, thy palace?"

"In this, the Great Fada, nearly three thousand men and women reside. In the harem alone are four hundred women and six hundred slaves and eunuchs, while the Imperial bodyguard numbers nearly a thousand."

Glancing below, I saw the palace was enclosed by white walls as high and strong as the outer fortifications. It was built within the great Kasba or fortress, a veritable city within a city.

Turning, our eyes met, and pointing to the distant, sun-baked wilderness, I exclaimed,—

"Away there, the vultures would already have stripped my bones hadst thou not taken compassion upon me."

"Speak not again of that," she answered. "Thou wert the only man in whose body the spark of life still burned. It was my duty to rescue thee," she replied, rather evasively.

"Now that we understand and trust each other, now indeed, that we are friends true and faithful, wilt thou not tell me why thou didst convey me hither unto thine apartment?"

She hesitated, gazing away towards the misty line where sky and desert joined, until suddenly she turned, and looking boldly into my face with her clear, trusting eyes, answered,—

"It was in consequence of something that was revealed."

"By whom?"

"By thee."

"What revelation have I made?" I asked, sorely puzzled.

She held her breath, her fingers twitched with nervous excitement, and the colour left her cheeks. She seemed striving to preserve some strange secret, yet, at the same time, half inclined to render me the explanation I sought.

"The astounding truth became unveiled unconsciously," she said.

"My mind faileth to follow the meanderings of thy words," I said. "What truth?"

"Behold!" she cried, and hitching the slim fingers of both her hands in the bodice of cream flimsy silk she wore beneath her zouave, she tore it asunder disclosing, not without a blush of modesty, her white chest.

"Behold!" she cried, hoarsely. "What dost thou recognise?"

With both her hands she held the torn garment apart, and, as she did so, my eyes became riveted in abject amazement. Bending, I examined it closely, assuring myself that I was not dreaming.

"Hast thou never seen its counterpart?" she asked, panting breathlessly.

"Yea," I answered, with bated breath. "Of a verity the coincidence astoundeth me."

The sight caused me to marvel greatly; I was bewildered, for it conjured up a thought that was horrible. In the exact centre of her delicate chest, immediately above her heaving bosom, was a strange, dark red mark of curious shape, deeply branded into the white flesh, as if at some time or other it had been seared by a red-hot iron. The paleness of the flesh and the firm contour of her bosom rendered the indelible mark the more hideous, but its position and its shape dumbfounded me. The strange blemish constituted an inexplicable mystery.

It was unaccountable, incredible. I stood agape, staring at it with wide-open, wondering eyes, convinced that its discovery was precursory of revelations startling and undreamed-of.

The mark, about the length of the little finger, and perfectly defined, was shaped to represent two serpents with heads facing each other, their writhing bodies intertwined in double curves.

In itself this mystic brand was hideous enough, but to me it had a significance deeper and more amazing, for in the centre of my own chest I bore a mark exactly identical in every detail!

For years; nay, ever since I had known myself, the red scar, not so noticeable upon my brown, sun-tanned skin as upon Azala's pale, delicate breast, had been one of the mysteries of my life. Vividly I remembered how, in my early youth, in far El-Manäa I had sought an explanation of my parents, but they would never vouchsafe any satisfactory reply. On what occasion, or for what purpose the mysterious brand had been placed upon me I knew not. Vaguely I believed that it had been impressed as a means of identification at my birth, and until this moment had been fully convinced that I alone bore the strangely-shaped device. Judge, then, my abject astonishment to find a similar mark, evidently impressed by the identical seal, upon the breast of the woman who had thus exerted her ingenuity to save my life—the woman whose grace and marvellous beauty had captivated me, the woman who had admitted that she reciprocated my affection.

In that brief moment I remembered well the strange, ambiguous reply that my mother had given me when, as a lad, my natural curiosity had been aroused,—

"Sufficient for thee to know that the Mark of the Asps is upon thee, O my son. Seek not to discover its significance until thou meetest with its exact counterpart. Then strive night and day to learn the truth, for if thou canst elucidate the mystery, thine ears will listen to strange things, and thine eyes will behold wondrous and undreamed-of marvels."

Since then, twenty long years had elapsed, and I had wandered far and near, in England, in France, in Algeria and across the Great Desert. Both my parents had died with the strange secret still locked in their hearts, for by no amount of ingenious questioning could I succeed in unloosing their tongues. Now, however, my mother's prophetic utterance and counsel, spoken in our white house on the green hillside, came back vividly to my memory, and I gazed in silence at Azala full of apprehensive thoughts.

My mother had more than once assured me that she knew not its meaning, and that, although she had sought explanation of my father, he had refused to reveal to her more than she had told me, and he, too, had died with the secret resolutely preserved. But the exact counterpart of the brand burnt into my own flesh was now before me. What could be the significance of the two asps? how, indeed, came the daughter of the great Sultan 'Othman, whom none dare approach, to be disfigured the same as myself, a free-booter of the Khalifa, a Dervish and an outcast?

"How earnest thou to bear the brand of the serpents?" I asked, when again I found speech. "An identical mark is upon my own breast also."

But ere she could answer my inquiry a stealthy movement behind startled us, and as I turned, two gigantic black eunuchs sprang upon me, while two others appeared from behind the rose silk hangings.

"Behold!" cried a man, whom I knew by his gorgeous dress to be the Aga of the Eunuchs. "It is a man, not a woman! The slave hath not lied. Seize him!"

"May Allah show thee mercy!" gasped Azala, pale and trembling, with clasped hands. "We are betrayed!"

I struggled and fought with all the strength I possessed, but my brutal captors bore me down, and in their sinewy hands I was in a moment helpless as a babe. Then I knew that Azala was, alas! lost to me. Romance, hope, passion, one by one, dropped, emberlike, into the ashes.

Chapter Five
The Black Eunuch

Azala, with blanched face and clasped hands uplifted in supplication, sank upon her knees before the gigantic Chief of the Black Eunuchs, whom she addressed as Khazneh, beseeching him with arguments, persuasive, forcible and passionate, to spare my life.

"All blame be upon my head!" she cried, in earnest appeal. "He fell wounded at the fight of Sabo-n-Gari, and I tended him and brought him hither. Spare him! Let not the keen arrow of sorrow enter the soul of the daughter of thy Master, the Sultan."

"Thy servant hath already received his orders," the high and potent official replied with imperturbable coolness, resting his hand on the bejewelled hilt of his great scimitar, looking down at her upturned and agitated countenance.

"From whom?"

"From my Imperial Master, thine august father."

"May the curse of Eblis rest upon our betrayer!" she cried, with a quick setting of her mouth. "The stranger hath done no harm, but by me, it seemeth, he hath been brought unto his doom."

"He is thy lover. Thou wert suspected two days ago," the eunuch answered gruffly, standing statuesque and immovable while my captors held me, apparently reluctant to move, because they desired to overhear the argument between the beautiful Azala and their master.

"I deny thine accusation," she replied, rising to her feet quite calmly. "Thou, Khazneh, who art powerful here in the harem, shall learn a lesson in politeness thou wilt not easily forget. Lies and insults may fall from thy lips, but they neither injure nor distress the daughter of thy Master, 'Othman."

"Silence, woman!" he cried fiercely, shaking his fat fist in the face of the trembling, indignant girl, and showing his white teeth. "Thinkest thou that thou canst save a man whom thou bringest unto thine apartment in secrecy, dressed in woman's garments?"

"If thou darest remove him hence I will appeal in person unto my father."

"Already his Majesty hath full knowledge of this affair," the great negro eunuch answered, treating her threat with calm indifference. "By his order a watch hath been placed upon thee. We saw the accursed son of offal caress and kiss thee."

"May Allah cut out thy heart! Am I a slave, that spies should be set to report upon my doings?" she asked, her eyes flashing with indignation. Then, turning to the negroes who held me in iron grip, she said, "I, Azala Fathma, Princess of Sokoto, order ye to release him."

"And I, Khazneh, Aga of the Eunuchs, order ye to remove him hence. He is a Dervish from Omdurman, a traitor, and an enemy of thy Sultan. Away with him!" cried the black-faced man with big, blood-shot eyes. His gaze was ever on Azala, unless it were fixed on me with a sullen gleam of hate.

But she rushed across to the heavy silken curtain that hid the secret door, and, standing boldly before it, uplifted her long, white arm, and pointing to the towering eunuch, cried,—

"Zafar-Ben-A'Ziz, whom I have long known by report, is not an enemy, but a firm friend of his Majesty, whose despicable slave thou art. Therefore I forbid thee to lay hands upon him. Even though thou findest him here in the place forbidden; nevertheless, I, as Princess of Sokoto, claim for him the protection of the Sultan."

In silence, unable to extricate myself, I stood while my fate was thus discussed. A spasm wrenched my soul—one of those agonies which leave their trace, mental or physical, forever.

"Knowest thou not the punishment meted out to those who dare to pass the Janissaries and tread the sacred courts of the harem?" asked the Aga, impatiently.

"The punishment is death," she answered. Her thin nostrils palpitated. She crushed her finger-nails against the jewels on her bosom. "But if Zafar, my friend, suffereth the penalty, I warn thee that thine head shall be struck off and thy body be given to the dogs as offal before the going down of the sun."

"Be it so," laughed the hulking brute, insolently, his fingers playing with the long, keen *jambiyah* in his belt. Then, turning to my captors, he said, "Come, away with him quickly."

Next second the hangings were raised, disclosing an open door, through which I was unceremoniously hurried, and as I was dragged out into the dark, inter-mural passage, I heard the Aga of the Eunuchs exclaim tauntingly,—

"Seek his Majesty if thou wilt, but I may tell thee that he set out for Katsena at sunrise, and ere his return thy lover's bones will lie bleaching in the sun."

"Farewell, Azala," I shouted. "Be thou of good cheer. Remember that in my heart the tree of affection hath struck root. I am thy friend always— always—even though our enemies may thus part us."

"We will never part," she cried, rushing across to me; but the Aga, catching her roughly by the arm, dragged her away by sheer brute force.

"Whither he goeth there also will I go," she gasped, struggling to elude his grasp, overturning one of the little mother-of-pearl coffee-stools in her frantic efforts to reach and embrace me.

"Tarry no longer," cried Khazneh, in anger, addressing my captors. "Let the Sultan's will be obeyed."

"Farewell, Azala! Farewell," I cried, paralysed with fury as I saw her bow her head upon her arms and weep.

But she answered not, for, as I was dragged fiercely from her sight, I saw her struggling with the chief eunuch, endeavouring to follow us. With brutal disregard of her sex, the big, gaudily-attired brute had seized her by the throat. Her dress was torn, her hair dishevelled, and her jewels lay scattered and trodden under foot. Suddenly a scream sounded, dull and muffled, and, just as I was dragged away into the dark passage, I witnessed the woman who had entranced me hurled backward. I saw her reel, stagger, and fall senseless upon her divan.

The grinning negroes who held me laughed aloud, and hurried me along the short, close passage, and down flight after flight of broken, time-worn steps, while Khazneh, closing the small, heavy door, barred and bolted it securely. Then he followed us, biting his finger-nails in deep thought. Whither they were conducting me I knew not, neither did I care. Azala and I had, by the treachery of some unknown slave, been torn asunder, perhaps never again to meet. Only death would, I knew, expiate the crime of being found in disguise in the Sultan's harem, and towards the bourne whence none return was I being conveyed.

My anticipations of immediate death were not, however, realised. Deep down into the foundations of the ancient palace the eunuchs conducted me, along a labyrinth of gloomy passages that showed the great extent of the Fada, until we came to a long, subterranean corridor where, on entering, I saw, behind iron bars, the lean, emaciated figure of a man, haggard, unkempt, with the gleam of madness in his eyes. Shaking the bars wildly with the strength of a wild beast, he cried as we passed,—

"Strangers! Have compassion. Have pity. In the name of Allah, who both heareth and knoweth, remove these fetters which for fourteen long years have held me captive."

"*Na'al abuk!*" (Curse thy father) growled Khazneh, lifting his trailing scimitar in its scabbard and striking the wretched prisoner a heavy blow as he passed. But the man tearing at the bars shrieked and howled in his madness,—

"May the venom of vipers consume thy vitals, and may the kisses of thy women poison thee, thou black-faced son of offal! I recognise thee, thou fiend. Thou art the Aga of the Eunuchs; the incarnation of Eblis himself. May thy body be cast upon a dungheap and thy soul be delivered unto the tortures of Al-Hawiyat!"

Leaving the wretched man hurling his horrible imprecations, we passed onward along the dark corridor of filthy dens, each protected with strong bars of iron, several being occupied by men, lean, wild-haired and half-clad, who looked more like animals than human beings crouching on their heaps of dirty, mouldy straw. No sunlight ever penetrated there, and the only air or light admitted entered between the crevices of the massive paving stones of the court above. The walls of this Dantean dungeon were black with damp and age, the floor was encrusted with all kinds of filth, and the air was hot, foetid, and so overpowering that Khazneh himself was compelled to take the corner of his silken robe and hold it to his nostrils.

At length, however, on arrival at the further end of the passage, a small door with an iron grating swung open and I was thrust in and there left, the door being immediately closed and secured. In the almost impenetrable darkness I could distinguish nothing, but when I heard the footsteps of my captors receding, my heart sank within me. Noises sounded weirdly in the cavernous blackness; the groans, curses and prayers of my fellow-prisoners. Who were these emaciated, half-starved wretches? What, I wondered, had been their crimes?

Chapter Six
Rage and Remorse

With my feet upon the heap of dirty, evil-smelling straw, I stood hesitating how to act. Of the size or character of my cell I knew nothing; therefore, after reviewing the situation as calmly as I could, I started to feel the walls and ascertain their exact proportions. The place, I found, was small, horribly small. Its height was only just sufficient to allow me to stand upright, while it was not long enough to allow me to lie down except in a crouching, uncomfortable position, its breadth being just two paces.

When, after making myself acquainted with these details, I stood reflecting upon my position, I heard a slight movement in the straw at my feet, and as I bent to ascertain the cause my hand came into contact with the chill, smooth body of a large snake which I had evidently disturbed.

Its contact thrilled me. I drew my hand away in horror, springing back towards the wall, expecting each moment to feel my leg bitten. Straining my eyes into the darkness I did my utmost to discover the whereabouts of the reptile, believing that if it had its bead-like eyes fixed upon me I could detect their brightness. But though I heard a slow rustling among the straw, my enemy seemed in no mood for attack, and I waited motionless, not daring to stir. To be doomed to live and sleep in company of a snake was certainly one of the most hideous tortures to which a man could be subjected, and was a refinement of cruelty equal to any of the revolting barbarities I had witnessed while serving under the standards of the Mahdi and the Khalifa. But the hours dragged on, and although my fellow occupant of the cell remained silent, apparently content, the dungeon itself was weirdly horrible. The cries of my fellow captives, some of whom were perfectly sane and others palpably mad from torture and long confinement, resounded through the place with startling suddenness, and I could hear those whose minds were unhinged gnashing their teeth and beating their bars in vain, frantic effort to obtain release.

With these horrors about me, the whole of my past seamed to flit through my mind—a panorama of wild free life and exciting adventure. My sudden unconsciousness after my fall at the well of Sabo-n-Gari, my strange awakening, and the vision of incomparable beauty that had risen before my wondering, fevered eyes, all recurred to me in hazy indistinctness, like some weird, half-remembered dream. But the pale, anxious face of Azala, who had fought so hard to save me falling into the merciless clutches of my pitiless captors, came before me—vivid, distinct, entrancing. Her every feature was engraven indelibly upon my memory, and her voice seemed to repeat in soft, musical Arabic those strange, mysterious words that had thrilled and entranced me.

She trusted me, she had said. Would she, I wondered, be successful in releasing me from this horribly maddening captivity? That she would use every endeavour of which she was capable I was confident; nevertheless, I knew well the enormity of my crime, and feared that even her earnest words would not soften the flint heart of the relentless Sultan 'Othman, whose every whim was law within his own extensive kingdom.

Well I knew the manner of living of this dreaded ruler of the Western Soudan. He formed the etiquette of his brilliant court upon that of the Khalifa's, keeping himself strictly invisible to the vulgar gaze. He seldom exposed himself to perish of the evil eye. It was he who compelled the women throughout his empire to lead the life of the Eastern harem, and forbade that any (married or single) should show themselves unveiled, making his own family set the example. People approaching the Sultan in audience covered their heads with dust: he never spoke directly to assemblies nor to the people, but always dealt with them through the medium of a herald. Upon the occasions of his going out, his *cortège* was preceded by musicians, drums, and trumpets, and he rode in solitary state, with his suite at a respectable distance behind. Servants marched surrounding his horse, and holding by turns to his saddle; they were called foot companions, and their headman was the "master of the road." Only one drum was allowed to precede them, and musicians kept silent when in sight of a town in which the Sultan was residing.

She had spoken of strange marvels, of hidden mysteries that require elucidation, of perils, and of her own misery. Why had unhappiness consumed her? Why, indeed, had she concealed so much from me? For hours I pondered over the veiled words she had uttered, seeking in them some explanation, but finding none.

Then I remembered the hideous blemish upon her fair breast—that mystic mark exactly identical with mine. What, I wondered, could these entwined asps denote? The words of my dead mother rang in my ears: "Seek not to discover its significance until thou meetest with its exact counterpart. Then strive night and day to learn the truth, for, if thou canst elucidate the mystery, thine ears will listen unto strange things, and thine eyes behold wondrous marvels."

Upon the breast of Azala, the Princess, I had discovered that which I had sought throughout my eventful life, yet even in that moment evil fortune had befallen me, and now, instead of being free to strive towards solving the enigma, I was held captive in that dismal, evil-smelling dungeon, under sentence of death.

Days dragged by—dull, dismal, dispiriting. Suffering the anguish of separation and lost happiness, my whole life seemed wounded. In the dark, damp cell, surrounded by a thousand horrors, oppressed by a thousand vague regrets and bitter thoughts, I awaited the end. Indeed, as the long hours slowly passed, it surprised me that my captors did not drag me forth to die. Once a day three negro guards, heavily armed, appeared and cast to us a little *dodowa*, or kind of cake made of vegetables, with as little ceremony as if they were giving food to dogs, while a slave filled our earthen vessel with water; but we had no exercise, and were compelled to remain behind our bars like animals entrapped.

My cell had been occupied quite recently by some poor wretch, who, according to the story of a half-starved Arab in captivity near me, had died of fever only a few days before my arrival, and with whom the serpent who made his abode there had apparently been on friendly terms. At first both the reptile and myself were consumed by a mutual fear of one another, but on close acquaintanceship he grew to regard me as harmless, and really performed me a service by clearing the mice and other vermin from my narrow, suffocating den.

Once a loud, piercing shriek escaped one of my half-demented fellow captives, who declared he had been bitten by a scorpion, and, to my dismay, the same reptile found its way through the bars of my cell some hours later, but fortunately I detected it in time, driving it out before it could attack me. Hour by hour, day by day, I crouched, disconsolate and despairing, in the almost impenetrable gloom. Accustomed as I was to the wild life of the plains, confinement amid such loathsome surroundings was doubly irksome and nauseating.

In that Stygian darkness day was like night, and I could keep no count of time; but with the harsh gibberings of idiots always grating on my ears, I grew apprehensive that ere long I, too, must become demented. My respite from death I attributed to the intervention of the fair woman whose wondrous beauty had enmeshed me, and whose words of mystery had aroused in me an intense, unconquerable desire to solve the one great enigma of my life.

Yet as time went on and relief came not, I began to fear that the eunuch had spoken the truth when he informed Azala of the Sultan's absence, and that, fearing to order me to execution, Khazneh had resolved that I should be driven to madness in that foul, foetid dungeon, where so many captives had pined and died. Many times I had heard how the great Sultan 'Othman was ruled almost entirely by harem influence; how the bright-eyed, imperious Sultana of to-day might be a mangled corpse torn to pieces by the yelping jackals at the city gate to-morrow; how a single word whispered by a dark-haired houri into the ear of her lord might either cause a courtier's head to fall, or secure for some menial an exalted office of power, with many slaves and fat emoluments. Indeed, it was notorious throughout the Soudan that in the great Fada of the Sultan of Sokoto none was safe. Wives, courtiers, guards, eunuchs, slaves, all trembled, fearing to arouse the anger of the brutal autocrat, for well were they aware that the keen *doka* of the black executioner was kept ever busy, and none knew whose head next might fall. Black plots and dastardly intrigues were constantly at work within the great Courts of the Harem. The favourite, one day loaded with costly jewels, basking in the smiles of her august master, radiant upon her divan and ruler of the gilded Courts of Enchantment, would assuredly sooner or later fall a victim to the jealousy of her less fortunate sisters, and be compelled to wash the feet of the bright-eyed slave her whilom handmaiden, become the wife of some common soldier, or drink the fatal draught from the golden Cup of Death.

Yet amid such surroundings, continually witnessing the complicated plots and counter-plots engendered by the fiercest feminine hatred, with unceremonious strangling, poisoning or decapitation as the inevitable result, lived Azala, pure as the jasmine-flower, bright as the sunrise on the Great Desert, graceful as the rose bending beneath the evening zephyr, a maiden of absolutely incomparable countenance and entrancing loveliness.

For nearly a whole moon had I remained in my foul, dank kennel, when one morning four gaudily-attired Janissaries released me, and, without deigning to reply to my eager questions, conducted me out of the dungeon and up the worn and broken flight of stairs to the blessed light of day. So long had I been in darkness that the sun's glare blinded me, and keenly apprehensive that Azala's efforts had been unavailing, and that I was at last being led to execution, I walked on between my guards, inert, dejected and despairing.

A dozen Janissaries, each armed with gleaming scimitar and *jambiyah*, joined us, as across one great open courtyard after another was I conducted in procession solemn and funereal. The magnitude and magnificence of those squares, with great plashing fountains, tall palms and colonnades of dead-white horse-shoe arches, astounded me. Evidently they were the outer courts of the palace, for at each gate there stood Janissaries in uniforms of blue and gold, with drawn swords, erect, silent, statuesque. Leaving the Courts of Love, the innermost centre of the great Fada, we crossed the Court of the Grand Vizier, the Court of the Gado (Lord of the Treasury), the Court of the Eunuchs, the Court of the Janissaries, the Court of the Armourers and many others, each larger and more massive in construction, until at length we came to the great, arched outer gate, the only entrance to this sumptuous and gigantic dwelling-place of one of the most powerful potentates of Al-Islâm. Here my heart sank within me, for awaiting us was the executioner, a big, brutal negro, who carried over his shoulder his great *doka*, or keen, curved sword, that had smote off so many heads of men and women.

Instinctively I knew my fate. I was being conducted to the Kaboga, or place of execution, there to die.

As we approached, the ponderous gate opened and with a loud blast from a dozen blatant wind instruments of curious shape there entered a man attired in white, sitting erect on a richly-caparisoned, coal-black Arab horse, and followed by a crowd of mounted attendants and guards on foot.

"May Allah, the One Granter of Requests, envelop our lord the Sultan with the Cloak of Peace," cried the guards, lifting their bass voices with one accord, salaaming before the sharp-eyed man, whose black beard was well trimmed, and in whose crimson turban gleamed a magnificent aigrette of diamonds.

Three loud blasts and the roll of a drum announced the return of the Sultan 'Othman. Each time slaves and guards bent low with reverent genuflexions, and each time they lifted aloud their voices in praise of his Imperial Majesty.

As, tongue-tied in amazement, I gazed upon the brilliant cavalcade of the powerful autocrat whose fame had been carried over the boundless deserts even to Omdurman, his keen glance fell upon me. Upon his dark, sensual face, in which cruelty was strongly marked, there rested for a second a shadow of displeasure, then reining his horse close to me his searching eyes wandered to the executioner and the Janissaries. Scarcely had I sufficient clothes to cover me, and what I wore were ragged and dirty, yet with the pride of my race I drew myself up, facing him boldly.

In deep, stern tones he demanded of his Grand Vizier beside him, whose name was Mahaza, son of Alhan, the nature of the crime for which I was to suffer.

"During thine absence, O Mirror of Virtue, yonder spy, an accursed Dervish from Omdurman, hath been discovered by Khazneh, Aga of the women, attired in a woman's haick, concealed within thy Courts of Enchantment."

"In my harem?" exclaimed the Sultan, whose angry eyes flashed in my direction. "By what means did the dog obtain admission?"

"I know not, O Branch of Honour," answered the Grand Vizier, but at that moment Khazneh, in robes of bright yellow silk, pushed forward, and making a deep obeisance, exclaimed,—

"Give leave unto thy servant to speak, O lord, our Sultan. I found the Dervish spy concealed within the pavilion of thy daughter Azala."

The Sultan 'Othman glared at me with brows contracted, and uttered a fierce and terrible curse upon his enemy the Khalifa. His soul in an instant filled with bitterest rage and hate.

"How camest thou, son of *sebel* to pass the guards of mine innermost court?" he demanded, in wrathful tones that caused all to tremble.

"I, an Arab of the North, was wounded in battle, and thy daughter, upon whom may the blessing of the One Bountiful rest, gave unto me succour. If thou sparest me—"

"Silence, dog!" he roared; then, with a gesture of impatience, turned to his councillor, saying,—

"Let the spy's head be struck off and placed upon the palace gate as a warning."

The eyes of my guards, on hearing this, brightened, and they cried: "Thy will, O Mighty Ruler, is our command," and those holding me pushed me forward so roughly that my ragged jibbeh was torn from the neck to the waist, displaying my chest.

The Sultan, with a parting injunction to my captors to place my head upon the gate and to announce throughout the city that a spy of the Khalifa had been captured and executed, was about to ride away when suddenly I noticed that he again fixed his gaze full upon me and sat for a few seconds perplexed and thoughtful.

"Bring hither thy prisoner. Let him approach me closely," he shouted to the Janissaries, who were at that moment hurrying me away.

Amazed at the Sultan's sudden change of manner, the Aga of the Eunuchs and his menials dragged me back before their ruler, who, with his startled eyes fixed upon my uncovered breast, asked in a tone of awe,—

"Speak, slave! How earnest thou by that mystic mark of the serpents?"

His anger had instantly cooled. He had detected the strange red scar, and for him it evidently had some serious significance, for he had grown pale under his manly bronze, and the bejewelled hand that held the reins trembled slightly.

"Of its origin I have no knowledge," I answered, glancing quickly round and noticing the effect produced by the monarch's sudden change of manner.

"Whence comest thou?" he asked, with eagerness unusual to an autocrat.

"From Omdurman. I am of the Ansar of the Khalifa."

"And thy parentage?"

"I was born in the Mountains of Aures, two days' journey from Batna. My father was the Hadj Yakub Sarraf."

"Yukub Sarraf, the Kaid of El-Manaa?" he inquired quickly, his sinister face betraying an expression of combined surprise and fear.

"Even so, O Sultan."

The excess of his rage was only equalled by the promptness of his remorse.

Bending in his saddle for a moment, he examined closely the puzzling mark upon me, and then, after a few moments' silence, he turned to Khazneh, who had been standing aghast and amazed, and said,—

"Let the spy's life be spared, but let him be expelled from our midst. If thou findest him within the confines of our empire after three suns have set, then let him die. Mount him upon the swiftest *meheri*, and let twenty guards similarly mounted journey with him until he hath passed beyond the boundary of Sokoto. I have ordained it. Let it be done accordingly."

Turning to me he said: "If thou ridest on the wings of haste thy life shall be spared; but enter not again into this my kingdom, or of a verity thine head shall fall." And as he turned to ride forward, he added, in a harsh, strained voice that became softened towards me: "Go, leave my rose-garden of happiness quickly. Go, and may the peace of Allah, the Omniscient, rest upon thee in the hour of thine adversity."

The all-powerful Sultan, with face pale and agitated, moved slowly onward across the great court with bowed head, followed by his wondering councillors and cringing slaves. Next second I was free.

Chapter Seven
The White City

All sounds had gradually died away in the town. A marabout had climbed to the terrace of the great mosque and was crying "Allah is great! Allah is great!" The surrounding terraces were peopled with white forms which stood out against the summits of the palm trees and the green of the baobab. Their backs were turned to the purple splendours of the dying light, for their faces looked towards the already darkened east, lighted for them by that eternal light in which Mecca is to be found. The silence was harshly broken by a brazen sound. It was the tam-tams in the Kasbah sounding the call for prayer.

The plain was now a vast desert phantasmagorically illuminated. Above, the sky flamed into every imaginable colour, and the small water-channel, scarcely visible a moment before, blazed into a reflection of the ardour of the sky, while the rows of ospreys on its banks looked like necklaces of pink pearls. Then all the enchantment was overwhelmed by the sudden twilight that heralds the tropical night.

Well mounted on a swift camel, with water-skin and provision-bag filled, and escorted by my guards, I had ridden through the crowded markets, and passing out of the Kofa-n-Magaidi, or eastern gate, set forth across the wide, sandy plain in the direction of prayer. The brief glimpse I caught of the place as I passed hurriedly through its streets surprised me. The inhabitants seemed to some extent a cultured people, and the women apparently enjoyed considerable personal freedom, although the majority were veiled. The men, despite their bellicose spirit and the chronic state of warfare maintained, were not naturally cruel, and treated their slaves kindly.

The towers, cupolas and high white walls of the great, impregnable palace, wherein dwelt the woman who had enchanted me, stood dark and frowning against the crimson brilliance of the afterglow, and from my exalted position on the back of my *meheri* I turned once to glance at them, wondering if Azala knew of my expulsion. Perhaps from her lattice in the great square tower rising above the city she was watching my departure, but she had given no sign, and sorrowfully I at length turned my back upon the White City of the Sultan 'Othman, and urged my camel onward towards the horizon, which seemed a sea of mirage, with a feeling that Fate had, indeed, laid her hand upon me with undeserved harshness.

In the cooler hours that succeeded, when the light had entirely faded, and the wind, whirling up clouds of find sand into our faces, compelled us to cover them as we rode on, leaving only our eyes visible, Shu'ba, the chief of the black horsemen accompanying me, declared that if we were to reach Kukawa, in Bornu, within three days, we should be compelled to press forward constantly, resting but a few hours during the heat of noon. My guards were heavily armed, each carrying a very keen, straight sword, a dagger suspended from the left wrist, and a spear six feet long, while with several this arsenal was also supplemented by a rifle. Acting no doubt under the Sultan's orders, they treated me with every consideration, and proved themselves light-hearted, genial fellows; yet the long ride through the great, silent wilderness, eternally warm, eternally gloomy, gave me many opportunities for dismal reflections upon the strange turn events had taken. Azala had fascinated, entranced me, and I loved her with all the strength of my being. Yet I had been thus forcibly torn from her, never to return on penalty of death. Each long stride of the animal beneath me took me further from her, yet she trusted in me to save her. From the words uttered by Khazneh in reply to the Sultan, it was evident that the latter had had no knowledge of my capture and imprisonment, and Azala had, on account of her father's absence, been unable to secure my release.

The mysterious symbol that seemed to link me in some inexplicable manner to the woman I loved had apparently produced in the Sultan a feeling of dismay, for when he noticed it a sudden terror had enthralled him. Awe-stricken at its significance, he had instantly rescinded the order for my execution, sending me forth from his empire as if apprehensive that my presence was a harbinger of some dreaded evil.

For a brief space we halted in the date-grove of Maifoura at midnight, eating a little *tiggra* with curdled milk diluted with water, and some *ngaji* or paste of sorghum, and having thus recruited our strength the cry of "*Ala e'dhahar! ala e dhahar!*" (Mount! mount!) sounded, and we resumed our ride over the low hills of Kobiri, and through the great, gloomy forest of Gounel. South of the Lake Tsad the country is fertile, and only here and there are there wide, sandy deserts reminding one of the waterless, sterile regions of Azawagh and Taganet in the Great Sahara, that arid, monotonous, and almost impassable gulf that separates the regions of Sokoto, Bornu, Baguirmi and Gando from the European civilisation of Northern Algeria. Having passed through the forest, the wooded level became interrupted from time to time by bare-naked concavities, or shallow hollows, consisting of black, sedimentary soil, where, during the rainy season, the water collects, and drying up gradually leaves a most fertile sediment for the cultivation of the *masakwa*, a kind of holcus which is the most important article in the agriculture of Sokoto. We saw herds of ostriches, troops of gazelles and many moufflons as, on our forced march, we passed the great ruins of Thaba, grim, grey, time-worn monuments of the Roman occupation, forded the Yoobe river at Ngouroutoua—where my guards told me an English traveller named Richardson had died many years ago—skirted the lagoon of Mouggobi, and continuing for nearly eight hours along narrow, verdant valleys, where, side by side with the diminutive, stunted palms, grew the colossal baobabs, the mastodons of the vegetable kingdom, whose gigantic branches were inhabited by vultures, serpents, bats and lizards. Then at last we passed out upon the great granite plateau of Koyam, dotted over with hillocks and in part strewn with quartz sand, home of the nomad Uled-Delim, "pirates of the desert," a sun-baked, stony wilderness devoid of any living thing. The third day was occupied wholly in crossing this vast solitude, where incessantly we were compelled to shout "*Hai! Hai!*" the ejaculation of caution to our camels, as the beasts, weary and jaded, plodded on until, about an hour after we had knelt to repeat our *majhrib*, while the shadows were lengthening as the sun declined, the tall, white watch-tower at the principal gate of Kukawa rose before us, and beyond lay the waters of Lake Tsad shimmering like liquid gold in the glorious evening light.

When the cry was raised that the town was in sight, my guards held consultation and halted. Then Shu'ba, drawing up his camel close to mine, exclaimed,—

"Thou hast performed the journey within the time stipulated by our lord the Sultan, therefore we now leave thee to continue thy way alone."

"Wilt thou not rest yonder for a while before returning?" I asked, surprised.

"Nay," he answered, shrugging his shoulders significantly. "The people of Bornu are our enemies. We would rather take our ease upon the plains than within the city of those who seek our overthrow"—a speech that was greeted by low, guttural sounds of approbation by the others perched on their camels around. Then, continuing, he said, "It is our Sultan's will that the *meheri* thou ridest shall be given unto thee, together with this rifle, ammunition and *jambiyah*," and as he uttered these words he handed me the gun he carried, together with his pouch and a crooked knife in a silver scabbard he drew from his sash.

"Alone in these regions thou mayest require them," observed a light-hearted young negro, with a broad grin.

"Unto thy Sultan, whose dignity be increased, render thanks in my name. Tell him that Zafar-Ben-A'Ziz is his grateful servant, and that he beareth neither malice nor hatred," I answered.

"Behold, I am also charged with a further duty," said Shu'ba, with a solemnity quite unusual to him. "Before we left the Fada one of the eunuchs of the Courts of Enchantment gave this unto me to deliver into thine hands," and he drew from the breast of his gandoura a small box of delicately-chased gold, securely sealed.

"Whence didst thou obtain it?" I asked, in surprise, taking it in my hands.

"From Hisham, the eunuch. He refused to tell who had given it unto him, but gave me strict command to place it in thine hands at the moment when we parted, with an injunction that it must not be opened until thou art actually within the walls of Kukawa."

"May I not investigate its contents now?" I asked, puzzled.

"Nay, curb thine impatience. Behold, the sun is already declining," he answered, glancing around. "Spur onward, or, of a verity, thou wilt not obtain entrance to yonder city ere its gate is closed."

His prompting influenced me to make hurried adieu, and, as with one accord they gave me "Peace," I sped away in the direction of the town, turning once to wave back a farewell. As I rode forward, four armed horsemen, their white burnouses flying in the wind, sped across the plain to meet me. With rifles held high in air with threatening gesture, they in a few minutes pulled their horses to their haunches before me, loudly demanding whence I came.

"I am Zafar-Ben-A'Ziz of the Ansar of thine ally, the Khalifa of Omdurman," I replied, laughing a moment later at the effect my words had produced.

"From Omdurman?" they gasped. "How earnest thou hither in company with horsemen of the Sultan 'Othman, who fled at our approach?"

Briefly, I told them how I had been held prisoner, and subsequently expelled by the Sultan.

"Allah hath indeed covered thee with the cloak of protection," observed one of the men, "None who descends to the terrible dungeons beneath the Fada of Kano ever comes forth alive."

"Yea, thou hast assuredly narrowly escaped," agreed another, and, as they turned to ride back with me, they related news of how, on the advance of the Khalifa's troops towards Sokoto, the iron cymbals of war had been silenced, for the Dervishes had been attacked and routed by the Kanouri and Tuaregs in the swamps outside Massenya, after which it was believed the survivors had returned in confusion to Omdurman. Thus I found myself in sorry plight, without resources, and with a thousand miles of gloomy forest and burning desert between myself and the Dervish headquarters beside the Nile. With my companions I entered the ponderous gate which was being kept open for our arrival, and, passing the little daily market (the *dyrriya*), which was crowded, we rode along the *deudal*, or promenade, past groups of Arabs and native courtiers in all the finery of their dress and of their brightly-caparisoned horses, until we came to the house of the sheikh, a spacious place with a single *chedia* or caoutchouc-tree in front. But the sand into which we had floundered as if it were a mire pursued us everywhere—in the streets, in the houses. The lounging slaves stared at my ragged attire, but the Sheikh Mohammed Ben Bu-Sad, to whom I was conducted, was very gracious, and after hearing the story of the defeat of my comrades-in-arms, my captivity, and my narrow escape, gave orders that for the present I should be lodged with one of the horsemen who had met me, and whom I discovered was named Lamino (properly El-Amin), his confidential officer. Thus, an hour later, I found myself installed in a small, clay-built house in the *billa gedibe*, or eastern town, and when alone I drew forth the small, golden box Shu'ba had given me. It was square, about the length of the middle finger, covered with quaintly-graven arabesques, and securely sealed with yellow wax.

Chapter Eight
Veiled Men of the Desert

Eagerly I broke the seals and tremblingly opened the lid of the tiny casket, taking out a folded piece of paper covered with lines of Arabic hastily-scrawled in yellow ink. These, in the dim twilight, I deciphered only with difficulty, and found they read as follows:—

"Know, O Stranger, now thou hast escaped from the wrath of our lord the Sultan, that thy presence within the walls of the Fada hath placed Azala, Princess of Sokoto, in deadly Peril. If thou wilt lend her thine aid, return, for thou alone canst solve the mysterious symbol of the asps, rescue her from death, and bring her unto the garden of happiness. Know, O Stranger, that even though she cannot communicate or have speech with thee, that she loveth thee; that each hour of thine enforced absence is as a year, and that the gilded pavilion wherein she dwelleth is but a house of sorrow because of thy departure. Keep the seal of silence ever upon thy lips and obey the command of Azala Fathma quickly, that thine endeavours may be approved. Return unto her speedily in such disguise that thou canst not be recognised; then will she tear aside the veil of secrecy and reveal unto thee strange marvels. Pause not in thine efforts to return, for each day bringeth her nearer unto cruel and ignominious Certainty. May the rose-grove of thy prosperity and good fortune be increased daily in freshness and magnificence, and the foundation of thy belief in the purity of thy One of Beauteous Countenance be more firmly established from hour to hour.—Thy Friend."

After the heat and burden of the long African day the respite at twilight always gives one a sensation of physical solace, yet nevertheless it brings with it a feeling of intense sadness and melancholy.

Again and again I read the curious missive. Evidently at Azala's instigation it had been penned in order to reassure me, and to induce me to return so that I could assist her in solving the mysterious problem to which she had hinted so pointedly when we had been alone. But foreseeing plainly the serious risk I should run if I attempted to re-enter Kano, and the absolute impossibility of obtaining access to the innermost courts of the Fada, I regarded the suggestion as utterly hopeless. Had not the Sultan warned me that if I again set foot within his empire my life would pay the penalty? Might not his dread of the mysterious evil that I might bring upon him cause him to take my life, notwithstanding his daughter's fervent supplications?

Yet Azala was in sore need of help, and sought my aid. Her promise to "tear aside the veil of secrecy" I felt inclined to construe into a pledge to render me explanation of the curious marks that both of us bore. Was it not more than an extraordinary coincidence that with a thousand miles of arid, stony desert, and a similar distance of fertile land separating us at our birth, we should each bear the Brand of the Asps—the mystic symbol the sight of which terrified even the powerful Ruler of Sokoto.

From the demeanour of both the Sultan and his daughter I felt that the strange device was the key of some greater secret underlying it, and the thought of Azala in peril, and trusting in me alone for assistance, urged me to a resolution to obey the injunctions of my anonymous correspondent. I had both a stout heart and a strong arm. My true Bedouin parentage had imparted to me the reckless *nonchalance* of the vagabond adventurer, and my life during the past ten years had been a strange series of nomadic ups and downs, desert wandering, fighting, slave-raiding, trading; in fact, I had picked up a precarious livelihood in the same manner as the majority of Sons of the Desert whose camels are their only wealth, and whose ragged tents their only dwelling-place.

The Mystery of the Asps seemed inexplicable, but in that cool night beneath the stars in the little open court I made solemn determination to return to Kano and seek its solution, even though compelled to risk my life in the attempt.

Until the going down of the sun on the Nahr-el-arba following my arrival at Kukawa was I the guest of Lamino; then, refreshed by rest, I prayed my *Fatiha* in the Great Mosque, and assuming the loose robe of dark blue cotton, wrapping a white litham around my face and twisting some yards of camel's hair around my head, set out upon my *meheri* to accompany a caravan of Buzawe conveying merchandise to El Fasher, whence I intended to travel alone back to Omdurman, there to report the annihilation of my comrades.

In the whole of that vast region from Lake Tsad to El Fasher, comprising thousands of square miles, there is not a single carriage road, not a mile of navigable waters, not a wheeled vehicle, canoe or boat of any kind. There are scarcely any beaten tracks, for most of the routes, though followed for ages without divergence to right or left, are temporarily effaced with every sandstorm, and recovered only by means of the permanent landmarks— wells, prominent dunes, a solitary knoll crowned with a solitary bush, or perchance a ghastly line of bleached bones of men and animals, the remains of slaves, camels, or travellers that may have perished of thirst or exhaustion between the oases. Few venture to travel alone, or even in small parties, which could offer but little resistance to the bands of marauders hovering about all the main lines of traffic. Hence the caravans usually comprise hundreds and even thousands of men and pack animals, all under a *kebir*, or guide, whose word is law. Under him are assistants, armed escorts and scouts to reconnoitre the land in dangerous neighbourhoods, besides notaries to record contracts and agreements, sometimes even public criers, and an *imam* to recite the prescribed prayers.

The caravan, belonging to Abu Talib, a wealthy merchant of Yô, was a small one, consisting of about one hundred camels heavily laden with ivory, kola nuts, spices, and other goods from the far south, destined for the great market at El Fasher, and was guarded by twenty fierce-looking Arabs and a number of negro and Arab drivers, all well-armed, for the country through which we were to pass was infested by the marauding Tuaregs, those black-veiled terrors of the plains, who know nothing of anything but the desert and the implacable sun.

Abu Talib, who accompanied us in person, was an aged, good-hearted man of the tribe of Aulad Hamed, who had spent the greater part of his life trading between In Salah and Timbuktu, or between Yô and Mourkouk, over the boundless Sahara, and in the darkness, as we rode together and our camels with silent tread loomed like phantoms in the midnight air, we told each other of our journeys and adventures. His companions were true sons of the sands, active, vigorous and enterprising, inured to hardships, and with the mental faculties sharpened almost to a preternatural degree by the hard struggle for existence in their arid, rocky homes. In making their way across those trackless solitudes they seemed endowed with that "sense of direction," the existence of which has recently been discussed by students of psychology. In the whole of the Great Sahara no race is more shrewd or cunning than the Buzawe, and their tact and skill enable them to get the better both of Arabs and negroes in the markets of the oases. Greed and harshness were stamped upon their hard features, but nevertheless they treated me, a lonely wanderer, with considerable kindness.

On leaving Kukawa we passed across a great plain, then through a dense forest, afterwards entering a fine, undulating country, covered with a profusion of herbage, with here and there large gamshi-trees with broad, fleshy leaves of brightest green. The moon shone bright as day, and as our file of camels strode on with slow, rhythmic movement under their burdens, the drivers would now and then sing snatches of wild songs of daring in the Hausa tongue.

Thus, resting by day and journeying by night, we moved forward around the marshy shore of Lake Tsad to Missene, thence through the cool, shady forest of Dekena Kreda, enlivened by many birds, along the densely-populated valleys of Boulala to the strange little town of Amm Chererib situate in the hollow formed between four great mountains, at length, when the moon was again at the full, reaching Abecher, at the foot of the hills of Outoulo, without much exciting incident. Halting for one day under the fortified walls to fill our camels' *kewas* with provisions, we again pushed forward unceasingly in order to accomplish the two hundred and fifty miles of barren, waterless land unmercifully scorched and burnt by a devouring sun, that stretches between the capital of Darmaba and El Fasher. This portion of the journey was the most difficult we had encountered, for the rough stones played terrible havoc with the spongy feet of our camels, and the heat was insufferable, even at night, on account of the poison-wind sweeping across us continuously. For five days we pushed forward by short stages only, until at sunrise one day we espied an oasis, and, encamping in the small shade it afforded, Abu Talib decided to give the animals rest. The packs were therefore removed, our tents erected, and having eaten our *dakkwa*, a dry paste made of pounded Guinea-corn with dates and pepper, washed it down with some *giya* made of sorghum, we reclined and slept during the warm, drowsy hours of the siesta.

Some noise had awakened me, and lighting my keef-pipe I was squatting in the shadow cast by one of the camel's packs, deep in my own sad thoughts, when the crack of a rifle startled me. Next second, even before my companions could seize their arms, the whole neighbourhood was alive with yelling Tuaregs on horseback, armed to the teeth, with their draperies floating in the wind. I saw they all wore the black litham about their faces. One, as he advanced on foot, levelled his gun at me and fired, but missed. In a moment I threw myself full length upon the sand behind a camel's pack, and opened fire upon our enemies. With deliberate aim I had picked off three with as many shots, when suddenly I heard old Abu Talib cry,—

"Lost are we! Our enemies are the Aoulemidens!"

Almost before the words died upon his lips a bullet struck the old man full in the breast; he staggered back and fell, within a few yards of me, a corpse. To resist these fierce outlaws, the most relentless tribe of Tuaregs who lived in the depths of that arid, desolate country, with no knowledge of the outside world, was, we knew, hopeless, for there were fully three hundred of them, and as they found our little band disinclined to surrender, they began shooting us down ruthlessly. Already four of our party had been captured and bound, while three were lying dead, nevertheless our rapid fusillade kept at bay those preparing to dash in and seize our camels' packs.

" HAND-TO-HAND WE STRUGGLED."

Fiercely we fought for life. We knew that if we fell into the hands of this brigandish tribe who called themselves "The Breath of the Wind," by which their victims were to understand that they might as well seek the wind as hope to recover their stolen property, we should either be sold at the nearest market, or placed under some horrible and fiendish torture to die a slow, agonising death. Suddenly a wild yell rent the air, and before we were aware of it a troop of some fifty horsemen dashed in among us, so quickly that resistance was impossible. Hand-to-hand we struggled, straining every muscle to evade our enemies, but ere long the obstinate, heroic courage of my companions could no longer blind them to the approach of the inevitable, and we were each secured and bound, captives in the hands of the merciless veiled men of the desert, whose fierce brutality was feared alike by slaves and Sultans throughout the sun-parched land.

Our arms were twisted from our grasp, our camels' packs seized, and, linked together ignominiously by chains around our necks, we were secured to three palm trunks, under a strong guard with loaded rifles, to wait while our captors investigated their booty and reloaded our camels. Nearly two hours this occupied, when at length the grey-bearded, sinister-faced leader of the band of free-booters gave the order to mount, and before long the party, numbering nearly three hundred horsemen armed to the teeth, moved away into the sandy wilderness, compelling us to trudge over the hot, stony ground on foot under the fiery rays of the blazing sun. It was evident that we were to be sold as slaves. One unfortunate camel-driver, who had been wounded, fell from sheer exhaustion within the first hour, and was left to die, for slave-raiders like "The Breath of the Wind" regard the wounded only as an encumbrance, and as they will not sell they are either put out of their misery by a shot, or left to die of thirst and become food for the vultures. Fortunately, with the exception of a slight cut on the left hand received from a *jambiyah* with which one of my captors had slashed at me, I sustained no injury, and with my companions, a little band of silent, despairing men, I plodded wearily onward—onward to be sold into slavery.

Upon all the perpendicular rays of the sun beat down with a heat as burning and intense as that of a fiery furnace, and always—always for a horizon—the desert, the infinite breadth of glaring sands.

Chapter Nine
An Audience of the Khalifa

Those days of burning heat were full of horrors. Treated with scant humanity, we were half-starved, allowed only sufficient water to slake our thirst once a day, and beaten mercilessly with thongs of rhinoceros hide whenever one, more faint and weary than the rest, lagged behind. Eastward we travelled for six days, until, at the well of Lassera Dar Abd-er-Rahman, we were sold for two small bags of gold to some nomad Dasas encamped there. The Tuaregs dare not enter a town in the Eastern Soudan, although, in the West, they are universally dreaded on account of their depredations; therefore they always sell their captives to other slavers, who dispose of their human wares at the nearest trade centre. Hence, by our new masters we were conveyed to Dara, a town one day's journey south of El Fasher, placed in the slave market, and, after considerable haggling, disposed of.

My new master was a well-dressed, keen-eyed, wizen-faced old Arab of the tribe known as Jalin, who, after inspecting me and looking into my mouth as he would a horse, handed payment with ill grace to the black-faced scoundrel who sold me, and ordered me to follow him. Together we passed out of the busy, bustling crowd, when he addressed me, asking my name.

"Art thou an Arab from the North?" he exclaimed in surprise, when I had told him who I was, and the place of my birth. "How earnest thou hither?"

"I fell into the hands of the Tuaregs, upon whom may the curse of Eblis rest!" I answered, hesitating to inform him at present that I was a Dervish.

As we walked to the city gate, where he said his camels were tethered, he told me his name was Shazan, and, judge my extreme satisfaction when he added that he was about to return to Omdurman, where he lived opposite the Beit-el-Amana. Hence, my stroke of ill-fortune turned out advantageous, for within a week I found myself once again within the great walls of the Khalifa's stronghold. Then my new master having treated me harshly, I resolved at last that he should suffer, therefore I applied to the Kaid for release from slavery, on the ground that I was a member of the Ansar of the

Khalifa. Old Shazan, amazed that his latest purchase should turn out to be one of his great ruler's bodyguard, rated me soundly for not informing him at first, but I laughed, telling him that I had desired to get to Omdurman, and kept my own counsel, until such time as it suited me. Knowing that he would lose the money he had paid for me, the close-fisted old merchant refused to comply with the order made by the Kaid for my release, but the rumour of my escape from Kano, coming to the ears of the great Abdullah, the latter one day sent six of his personal attendants with orders to release me, and to bring me before him.

The shadows were lengthening in the marble courts of the "Bab," or great palace of the Mahdi's tyrannical successor, when I was conducted across the outer square, where brightly-dressed guards were lounging on their rifles, or playing *damma* beneath the cool, vine-veiled arches. Never before had I been permitted to set foot inside the court, although many times had I passed under the shadow of the Iron Mosque near by, and gazed with curiosity at the high walls, smeared with red sand, which encircled the marble courts, gilded pavilions and cool gardens of the ruler of the Soudan—the ruler whose only idea was self-aggrandisement. The extent of the palace amazed me, for, even if it was scarcely as luxurious as the wonderful Fada at Kano, it was assuredly quite as large. Through one open, sunlit court after another we passed, until we were challenged by four of the royal bodyguard with drawn swords, but a word propitiated them, and a few seconds later I found myself in the great, marble-built Hall of Audience, in the presence of the stout, sinister-faced man of middle age and kingly bearing, with black, scraggy beard, whose name was a power throughout the Soudan. He wore a robe of bright purple, embroidered with gold, a turban of white silk, and his fat, brown hands were loaded with rings of enormous value.

Beneath a great baldachin of bright yellow silk, with tassels and fringes of gold, surmounted by the standard of the Mahdi, the powerful Abdullah, the ruler before whom all trembled, reclined upon his luxurious silken divan, fanned by black slaves on either side, while a negro lad sat at his feet, ready to hand him a pipe, the mouth-piece of which was studded with diamonds. Around him were grouped his body-servants, the *mulazimin*, and officers, while near him was Abdel Gayum, the chief eunuch, his hand resting upon his sword, and Ali Wad Helu, chief of the Baggara, who had led the ill-fated expedition of which I had been a member.

Conducted by my guides up to the scarlet mat spread before the potentate, who thought himself master of the whole world, I fell upon my knees in obeisance, expressing thanks for my rescue from bondage.

"Let him be seated," the Khalifa ordered, turning to his slaves, and in an instant cushions were brought, and I sat myself, cross-legged, awaiting questions to fall from his lips. "What, I wondered, had I done that I was allowed to sit in the royal presence?"

"So thou art the Arab Zafar-Ben-A'Ziz, the horseman who alone escaped death at the well of Sabo-n-Gari?" exclaimed the vain, cruel, quick-tempered man who ruled the Soudan under the guise of Mahdiism.

"I am, O King," I answered, bowing until my forehead touched the carpet.

"Of a verity will I punish those enemies who attacked my Jehadieh," he cried suddenly, in fiercest rage. "Where be those owls, those oxen of the oxen, those beggars, those cut-off ones, those aliens, those Sons of Flight? Withered be their hands! palsied be their fingers! the foul moustachioed fellows! basest of the Arabs who ever hammered tent-peg! sneaking cats! goats of Al-Akhfash! Truly will I torture them with the torture of oil, the mines of infamy, the cold of countenance! By Allah, and by Allah, and by Allah, we will crush those sons of Ach Chaitan like snakes, and throw their bodies to the dogs!" Then, turning to me in calmer mood, the autocrat of the Soudan exclaimed, "Some of thine adventures have already reached mine ear, and I would hear from thine own lips how thou didst escape and how farest thou in the Fada of 'Othman of Sokoto. Let not thy tongue hurry, but relate carefully in thine own words what things occurred to thee."

"Thy servant is honoured, O Ruler of our Empire," I answered. "Under thy Raya Zerga did I go forth, but returned hither as the slave of the merchant Shazan—"

"Already have we full knowledge of that," the tyrannical monarch interrupted, and turning to one of his officers he added, with an imperious wave of his fat hand, "Let the merchant Shazan, the dog of a Jalin, receive fifty strokes with the bastinado and be fined two bags of gold for purchasing a slave belonging to his Sultan."

Then, as the official hastened out lo do his capricious master's bidding, the Khalifa turned towards me, his thick red lips parted in a smile, lolling back lazily on his divan as he exclaimed,—

"Continue thy story. Our ears are open for information regarding the city of 'Othman, therefore describe in detail all that thou knowest."

Briefly I related how we had been attacked at night by the Tuaregs, how my comrades had been slaughtered fighting till the last, and how I awoke to find myself within the palace of the Sultan 'Othman, when suddenly the injunction contained in the anonymous letter recurred to me: "Keep the seal of silence ever upon thy lips." Therefore I deemed it expedient to omit from my narrative all reference to Azala, making it appear that I had been rescued by a kind-hearted soldier of the palace guard. I knew that Abdullah delighted in listening to calumnies and hearing evil spoken of other people, and for half-an-hour entertained him by describing the situation and aspect of Kano, the dimensions of the Fada, the horrors of my dungeon, and the personal appearance and character of the Sultan 'Othman, to which all listened with breathless attention.

When I had finished he remained silent a moment, as if reflecting, then raising his head he bestowed a few words of commendation upon me, concluding by the declaration, —

"Of a verity thou art a faithful and valiant servant. Henceforward thou shalt be chief of my *mulazimin*, and honoured among men."

I was expressing thanks in flowery speech to the autocrat for this appointment, which, as chief of his Majesty's body-servants, was a position of great honour, with substantial emoluments, when suddenly the silk-robed heralds posted at the entrance to the Hall of Audience sounded three loud blasts upon their shining *onbeias*. Then, as every one's attention was directed towards the great horse-shoe arch from which the curtains of blue silk were ceremoniously drawn aside by black guards, there entered a tall, commanding figure in gorgeous robe, attended by a dozen followers less showily dressed, but all armed, making great show of ostentation. With swaggering gait the stranger strode up the spacious hall, and as the Khalifa motioned me to rise and step aside to allow the new-comer to make obeisance in the royal presence, I was amazed and alarmed to suddenly recognise in him the man I least desired to meet.

It was Khazneh, the brutal Aga of the Eunuchs at the court of 'Othman, Sultan of Sokoto.

Chapter Ten
By Imperial Request

In fear of recognition I held my breath, and, withdrawing among the crowd of guards and courtiers assembled around the royal divan, watched the obsequious homage paid the Khalifa by Khazneh, who I discovered was accompanied by Mahaza, Grand Vizier of Sokoto.

Abdullah, reclining lazily upon his silken cushions, at first paid little heed to their salaams. On his brow was a dark, forbidding look; probably he was thinking of the ill-fated expedition he had dispatched, and the apparent hopelessness of ever conquering his enemy 'Othman. Long ago had he overstepped the dignity of a sovereign, and now coveted the honours of a god. The two ambassadors from the Fada at Kano prostrated themselves, pressing their foreheads to the ground, and assured the powerful head of the Mahdists that they were charged by their Sultan to convey to him most fervent salutations. Yet he affected not to notice their presence.

Surprised at the haughty coolness of his reception, Khazneh, still upon his knees, continued to address the mighty Khalifa.

"Know, O One of Exalted Dignity, Ruler of the Soudan, who holdeth thy servants' destinies in the hollow of thine hand, the object of our journey hither is to spread out the carpet of apologies, to become ennobled by meeting thine exalted person, to regenerate and to refresh the meadow of our expectations by the showers of the fountain-head of thy wisdom, and to see the rosebuds of our hopes opening and smiling from the breeze of thy regard. Our lord the Sultan has sent us to deliver this, therefore command and deal with us as thou listeth," and from the breast of his gorgeous robe he drew forth a sealed letter, which was ceremoniously handed to the reclining potentate by one of the black slaves.

The Khalifa Abdullah, suddenly interested, opened it, and, having read the missive, crushed it in his hand with impatient gesture.

"Behold," added Khazneh, "we are charged to deliver unto thee a few gems for thine acceptance as a peace-offering, and to assure thee of our lord 'Othman's good will and high esteem," and as he uttered the words, the gaudily-dressed members of the mission advanced, and, kneeling, deposited before the royal divan a golden salver heaped with costly jewels.

With a cursory glance at them, the occupant of the divan at length motioned the ambassadors to rise, saying in a deep, impressive voice,—

"The request of the Sultan is granted, and his presents accepted, O messengers. Assure thy lord that the knot of our amity is to-day strengthened by this invitation to travel unto Kano, and that ere many moons have risen we shall have the felicity of conversing with him. At present Allah hath not on the face of the earth a servant more excellent nor wise than he, and we are invested with the robe of being the elect and favoured. May the path of our association never become obstructed."

The dead silence that had fallen upon the Court was broken by rustling movement and low murmurings of approbation.

"Truly thou art wise and generous, O Ruler, upon whom be the blessing of the pardoning Sovereign," exclaimed Mahaza. "Thou, who art distinguished by great possessions, abundant revenues, innumerable quantities of cattle, and multitudes of servants and slaves, showerest upon thy servants copious favours. May the enemies of the threshold of thy dignity and station be overtaken by the deluge of affliction, and may they in the sea of exclusion be drowned by the waves of perdition."

"Verily, if thou comest unto Kano, our lord will receive thee with befitting welcome," added Khazneh.

"Thou, successor to the holy Mahdi who possessest the three greatest blessings, namely, meekness in the time of anger, liberality in the time of dearth, and pardon in a powerful position, wilt find a reception awaiteth thee such as none have hitherto received within the walls of our city. The relation of a king unto his subjects is like the relation of a soul to the body; in the same way as the soul doth not neglect the body for a single instant, so the king must not forget the care of his subjects even during the twinkling of an eye. Thou hast never swerved from the straight path, hence thou art honoured throughout the Soudan, even to the uttermost ends of Sokoto, and if thou wilt deign to visit our Sultan he will offer unto thee and thine officers, guards and slaves, generous entertainment within the Fada, for he desireth an understanding with thee that our countries may unite to defeat and discomfort our mutual enemies."

The reason of the unlooked-for invitation to visit the great White City he had plotted to besiege immediately commended itself to the Khalifa, who, with a benign smile, took from his finger two great emerald rings, and, handing one to each of the Sultan's ambassadors, assured them that the sun of his personal favours shone upon them, adding, in prophetic tones,—

"Take your ease here, for ye must be spent with long travel. I know not the day when I can set forth, for I act according to hidden knowledge, the visible effects of which are ofttimes evil, but the consequences always beneficent and salutary."

Then, as the two men from Kano again pressed their brows to the carpet, renewed laudations and gratitude for blessings received emanated from their lips, and from those assembled there rose panegyrical murmurs that Abdullah had decided to visit the Sultan 'Othman as honoured guest instead of arrogant conqueror.

Thus was the meeting between the two powerful rulers of the Sahara and the Soudan arranged, a meeting destined to mark an epoch in the history of Central Africa. The Khalifa's curiosity to investigate the extent of the wealthy country which acknowledged 'Othman as Sultan probably accounted for his sudden decision to undertake the long and tedious journey. Although the invitation had been sent with a view to effecting an offensive and defensive alliance between the two peoples, yet, in my new office as chief of the Khalifa's body-servants, I had ample means of knowing that he still cherished hopes of eventually overthrowing his whilom ally, and annexing the Empire of Sokoto. Two days after the reception of the envoys, Mahaza left on his return to inform 'Othman of his friend's intended visit, while Khazneh remained to accompany his master's guest. Being permitted as a favoured servant to approach Abdullah closely, I was fortunately enabled to express to him a hope that the Aga of the Sultan's Eunuchs would not be made aware of my identity with the hapless victim of his wrath, and it was with satisfaction I found that in my silk robes of bright crimson and gold and picturesque head-dress my enemy failed to recognise me.

The day was an eventful one in Omdurman when, at first flush of dawn, my royal master seated himself under the thatched *rukuba* and addressed his Ansar, urging upon them the necessity of loyalty and discipline during his absence. Then, after a great review of seventy thousand troops in the square of Abu nga, the Mahdist chieftain, with a portion of his harem, one thousand male slaves and four thousand courtiers and picked horsemen with banners, moved down the Road of the Martyrs on the first stage of the long journey westward. Prayers for the safety of the Khalifa were at that moment being said by nearly one hundred thousand men and women in the Great Mosque—not a mosque in its usual sense, but a huge yard—and their murmurings sounded like a distant roar as, in the cool hour before sunrise, we rode at walking pace along the winding Nile bank towards the misty hills where dwelt the Jinns.

Eager as were my companions to feast their eyes on the glories of Kano, none was so eager as myself lo pass the grim, prison-like portals of the great l'ada and rest beside those cool, ever-plashing fountains within the wonderful labyrinth of wide courts and shady arcades. The wheel of fortune had indeed taken a strange turn and was spinning in my favour, for I was actually returning to Azala in disguise so effectual that even Khazneh could not detect me, and as each day brought me nearer to her I racked my brain in vain to devise some means by which I could, on arrival, inform her of my presence and obtain an interview.

To fathom the hidden secret of the Mark of the Asps I was determined, and on the hot, tedious journey across the dreary, sandy waste, infested by marauders, and known by the ominous name of *Ur immandess*—"He (Allah) hears not;" that is, is deaf to the cry of the waylaid traveller—I served my capricious master with patience and diligence, awaiting such time as I could seek the woman who had entranced me, and learn from her lips the strange things she had promised to reveal.

By day the journey was terribly fatiguing, but in the cool nights, when we encamped for our *kayf*, there was feasting, dancing and merry-making. The night hours were enlivened by *Safk* (clapping of hands) and the loud sounds of songs. There were many groups of dancing-girls, surrounded by crowds of onlookers. Though sometimes they performed Al-Nahl, the Bee dance, their performances were wild in the extreme, resembling rather the hopping of bears than the graceful dances of the harem, and the bystanders joined in the song—an interminable recitative, as usual in the minor key, and so well tuned that it sounded like one voice, with the refrain "La Yayha! La Yayha!" Through the brief, brilliant night always "La Yayha!"

Chapter Eleven
Tiamo the Dwarf

A whole moon passed ere the sun-whitened walls and minarets of Kano became visible. The sandy approaches of the city were strewn with bones and carcasses that had been disinterred by wild beasts, the remains of camels, horses and asses that had fallen and died in the last stages of the journey. The cities of the desert are invariably encircled by their bones, and the roads across the glaring wilderness are lined by their bodies. The sun had risen about four hours when the advance guard of the Ansar spurred hurriedly back to announce that the town was in sight, and very shortly the details of the distant shape grew clearer, and we espied a body of troops, bearing the green-and-gold standard of the Sultan, riding forth to welcome us. They were gaudily-attired in bright blue, and, as they dashed forward, indulged in their La'ab al-Barut (gunpowder play) while their bright shields and unsheathed swords flashed and gleamed in the sun, as now and then the wind parted the cloud of dust and smoke which enveloped them. The faint sound of trumpets and clash of cymbals came from the distant city, enthroned upon the horizon a dark silhouette, large and long, an image of grandeur in immensity, wherein all my hopes were centred, and as we approached we saw that Mahaza, the Grand Vizier, had been sent by the Sultan 'Othman to give us peace and conduct us into the Fada.

My master's retinue, consisting as it did of nearly five thousand persons, was indeed an imposing one, and when an hour later we entered the city gate and passed up the hill to where the well-remembered tower of the Fada stood white against the intensely blue sky, the brass cannon mounted on the walls belched forth thundering salutes, and a cloud of soft white smoke floated up in the still, warm air. Strange it was, I reflected, that the houses of Kano everywhere displayed that essential characteristic of early Egyptian art—the pyramidal form, which represented solidity to those ancient architects. The walls of the oldest constructions had a slight inward inclination, and possessed no windows, or only the roughest sketch of them. Light and air entered through openings cut in the roof. The summits of the dwellings were ornamented by those triangular battlements which may be seen on the palaces of Rameses Meiamoun. The pylon, which is another characteristic of

Egyptian architecture, gave access to the dwellings. In short, the effect of the whole, their harmonious proportions, the symmetrical distribution of their ornamental mottoes, and their massiveness, proclaimed the art of Egypt, bearing out the legend that the people of Sokoto came originally from the far east. The multitude was wild with excitement. In their eagerness to catch a glimpse of the Khalifa, world-famous for his piety and his cruelty, they rendered the streets almost impassable, shouting themselves hoarse in welcome. Blatant tam-tams beat a monotonous accompaniment to the roar of artillery, and as the Sultan's guest, mounted on a magnificent camel at the head of his black Jihadieh, passed onward, the shout of "*Alhahu Akhbar!*" rose from fifty thousand throats, echoing again and again. Progress was slow on account of the immense crowds, and even the Sultan's spearmen, who preceded us, had considerable difficulty in clearing a path. Numbers were bruised, kicked by the horses or fatally injured by the long spears, but they were left unnoticed—a mere remark "*Umru Khalas,*" (It is the end of life) being all the sympathy ever offered. Yet the impetuous populace continued to yell enthusiastic words of welcome, the guns thundered, and the three stately men preceding the Khalifa blew long, piercing blasts on their immense *onbeias* fashioned from elephants' tusks.

At length, on arrival at the great, gloomy portal of the Fada, the iron-studded gates suddenly opened, revealing the Sultan 'Othman clad in golden casque and royal robe of amaranth velvet, with a handsomely-caparisoned, milk-white horse curveting under him, and surrounded by his gaudily-attired bodyguards and mukuddums, who filled the air with their adulations, declaring that their Imperial master was *Ma al-Sama* (the splendour of Heaven).

Alone he came forward wishing his guest "Peace" in a loud voice, then adroitly dismounting, embraced the Khalifa. Abdullah, much pleased at this mark of respect and homage, greeted him warmly and ordered him to remount, but the Sultan remained on foot, uttering some rapid instructions to his emirs, who had also dismounted to stand beside him.

Passing through the archway into the great outer court, the Jihadieh and the Ansar remaining outside, we all dismounted with the exception of my royal master and the ladies of his harem, whose camels were led onward to the inner pavilion that had been set apart for them. As chief of the *mulazimin* I followed my royal master, and as we passed from court to court, Janissaries, eunuchs, slaves and courtiers made salaam and raised their voices in shouts of welcome. The reception was throughout marked by the most frantic enthusiasm, even the two gigantic negro mutes at the gate of the Imperial harem—who usually stood with drawn swords motionless as statues—raising their hands to give peace unto the great Ruler of the Soudan.

The extensive palace echoed with the sounds of feasting and merry-making. The Ansar fraternised with the Janissaries, the Jihadieh with the Sultan's bodyguards, and the slaves of the Sultan 'Othman with those of the Ruler of the Soudan. The Khalifa, as religious head of the Dervishes and successor of the holy Mahdi, stood upon his "farwa" or white sheepskin, under the shadow of an ilex-tree in the Court of the Eunuchs, and conducted prayers in which all joined. Such was the wild fanaticism and enthusiasm that had prevailed during the firing of salutes that several men had dashed up to the very muzzles of the guns on the walls of the palace and were blown to pieces. The souls of these unfortunate people had, the Khalifa assured us, gone straight to Paradise, there to have their abode among lote-trees free from thorns, and fruitful trees of mauz, under an extended shade near a flowing water in gardens of delight, and every word that fell from his lips was regarded as the utterance of a prophet by the people as they murmured and told their beads.

After prayers, when the sura entitled "The Inevitable" had been recited, a great feast was held in the Sultan's sumptuous pavilion. The Khalifa was seated on his Imperial host's right hand, and over five hundred officials and courtiers were present. The dishes upon which the viands were served were of beaten gold, the goblets of chased gold studded with gems, while in the centre of the gilded pavilion a large fountain of crystal diffused a subtle perfume. Behind both the Sultan and his guest stood court tasters, who broke the seal of each dish and ate portions of the food before it was handed to their masters, lest poison should be introduced.

After the meal, jugglers entered and performed clever feats of magic, dancing-girls of every tribe under the Sultan's rule performed in turn various terpsichorean feats upon the great mat spread in the centre of the pavilion, and to the loud thumping of derboukas and the plaintive twanging of curiously-shaped stringed instruments, they danced until they sank upon their cushions from sheer exhaustion. These were followed by snake-charmers, wrestlers of herculean strength and story-tellers—the entertainment, which was on the most lavish scale, being continued until, at the going down of the sun, the clear voice of the *mueddin* was heard droning the *azan*.

The leisure at my disposal when, after the shadows lengthened and declined into the glory and vivid charm of the tropical twilight the Khalifa had retired to his private pavilion, I occupied in exploring those parts of the palace to which I had free access. Its vast proportions and its sumptuous decorations and appointments surprised me. When, on the previous occasion, I had passed through its great arcaded courts I was on my way to execution, therefore little opportunity had been afforded to me of ascertaining the full extent of the buildings; but now, in the cool evening hour, as, alone and thoughtful, I strolled under the dark colonnades and across the great open squares with their tall palms, time-worn fountains and wealth of roses, I noted its magnificence.

Around me on every side were sounds of revelry—barefooted girls were trilling and quavering, accompanied by noisy tambourines and serannel pipes of abominable discordance and the constant beating of derboukas and the clapping of hands; but holding aloof from my companions, I wandered from court to court in order to obtain a view of the great square tower wherein Azala's chamber was situated. At last, on entering the court where dwelt the serving-men of the Grand Vizier Mahaza, the tower rose high in the gathering gloom. From which of its small, closely-barred lattices had the city been revealed to me? Halting in the garden and looking up at its white walls, I tried in vain to recognise the window of the apartment where Azala had nursed me back to consciousness. Had she, I wondered, lonely and sad, watched from behind the lattice the festivities in the courts below? If so, might she not discern me now, gazing up at her chamber, and by some means or other contrive a meeting! Yet to deceive the watchfulness of the Grand Eunuch and his satellites was impossible. The square wherein I stood was almost deserted, for in the court beyond there was feasting and marissa-drinking among the Janissaries and the Jehadieh, and all had been attracted thither. I must have been standing there, oblivious to my surroundings, a considerable time, for it had grown almost dark, when a voice behind me brought me back to a knowledge of things about me.

"Why standest thou here aloof from thy comrades, O friend?" the voice inquired, and on turning quickly I was confronted by a black dwarf, whose face was the most hideous my eyes had ever witnessed, and his crooked stature certainly the smallest. His head, which scarcely reached to my hip, seemed too large for his hump-backed body, while his hands and feet were abnormal. Indeed, his personal appearance was the reverse of prepossessing, even though he was well-dressed in an Arab fez and a robe of bright blue silk with yellow sash. His age was difficult to guess. He might have been any age between thirty and fifty, but his thin, squeaking voice suggested senile weakness. His smile increased his ugliness as, perpetually, his eyes, like flaming fire-lances, darted towards me.

"The cool air of this thy garden is refreshing after the heat of the desert," I replied in Arabic, as he had addressed me in that language.

"But I have been watching thee," the human monstrosity continued, looking up at me as his mouth elongated, showing an even set of white teeth. "While thy fellows have been making merry thou hast been gazing up at yonder lattice? Hast thou seen her?"

"Whom dost thou mean?" I inquired, startled that this ugly imp should be aware of my quest.

"Affect not ignorance," he said, lowering his voice to almost a whisper. "Thou hast knowledge as full as myself that high up yonder there dwelleth the Lalla Azala, the beauteous daughter of his Majesty."

"Well," I said, anxiously, "tell me of her. I know so little."

"She hath rescued thee from death, and for many moons hath awaited thy return. She sendeth thee health and peace," he answered, slowly.

"But how dost thou know my innermost secrets?" I inquired, regarding the strange, unearthly-looking figure with some suspicion.

"Fear not betrayal, O friend," he replied. "I am called Tiamo, *khaddan* (servitor) of the Lalla Azala, and thy devoted servant. By day and night alike hath her bright eyes sought for sign of thee, for she ascertained, through one of our spies in Omdurman, of thy promotion unto the chieftainship of the Khalifa's body-servants, and knew that thou wouldst accompany him hither."

"Art thou bearer of a message from her?" I asked, bending towards him in eagerness.

"Yes. Hers is indeed a joyless life. Through the long day hath she stood at her lattice trying in vain to distinguish thee amid the crowds. Yet even now she is most probably standing there, and hath recognised thee. Yea. Behold!" he cried, excitedly. "See! There is the sign?"

I strained my eyes upward, and could just distinguish in the darkness something white fluttering from a lattice high up near the summit of the tower. It showed for an instant, then disappeared; but it was sufficient to tell me that I was not forgotten.

"Such means of communication are unsafe," the black dwarf growled, as if to himself.

"What message bearest thou?" I asked, turning to him and remarking the frown of displeasure that had overspread his hideous countenance.

"The One of Beauty hath ordered me to tell thee to wait patiently. She is in sore peril, being so zealously watched by eunuchs and harem-guards that at present she cannot have speech with thee. Wait, and she will communicate with thee when it is safe."

"What is the nature of her peril?" I inquired.

But the dwarf frowned, glanced up at the little lattice to assure himself that there was no longer a signal there, sighed, and then replied,—

"I am forbidden to tell thee. Rest in the knowledge that Tiamo, her servant and thine, will render thee what assistance thou requirest."

"Is the Lalla so carefully guarded that none can approach her?" I asked, as together we moved on into the adjoining court, where the fighting-men were making merry.

"Alas!" he answered, "she leadeth a lonely life. Forbidden to enter the great Courts of Enchantment wherein dwell the wives and houris of the Sultan amid every luxury, and where every diversion and gaiety is provided, she is compelled by the Sultan, whom she hath displeased, to live alone with her companions, slaves and waiting-women, in the rooms in yonder tower until such time as she shall be given in marriage."

"And shall I see her?"

"She is striving toward that end," the dwarf answered briefly, adding, "May thine Allah, who hath created seven heavens, and as many different stories of the earth, keep thee in peace and safety."

Gradually I overcame the distrust with which I at first regarded the hideous little pagan. From words he let drop in our subsequent conversation it was evident he was Azala's trusted servant, and was no doubt admitted to her apartments because of his personal deformity and ugliness of countenance. Until near midnight we squatted together in his little den in the Court of the Eunuchs, smoked, drank marissa and chatted; but he was discreet, silent as the Sphinx upon the affairs of his mistress, and to all my questions made the stereotyped reply, "Wait; a message will be conveyed unto thee."

Day by day, amid the round of bountiful entertainment, I waited in patience, glancing ever and anon up at the dwelling-place of the woman who besought my aid. Still no message came. Sometimes after the *isha* had been prayed I met Tiamo, but to all inquiry he remained practically dumb. "The Lalla is still unable to see thee," he always replied, if I expressed surprise that the promised message had not reached me. But he would invariably add a word of hope, expressing regret that circumstances had conspired against us.

One night, after superintending the duties of the *mulazimin*, I was crossing the Court of the Grand Vizier when Tiamo hurriedly approached me. By his face I could see that something had occurred, and as he brushed past me in full view of others about him he whispered, "Come to me one hour after midnight." Then he walked on without waiting for me to reply.

Punctually at the hour appointed I entered his little den with beating heart. The shutter was closed, therefore we were unobserved.

"Hasten. There is but brief space," he exclaimed quickly, and pulling from beneath his divan a blue silk robe and yellow turban similar to those worn by the eunuchs, he added, "Attire thyself in these. The Lalla biddeth thee repair unto her chamber."

I obeyed him without doubt or hesitation.

"Now, come with me," he said, when at last I had buckled on a scimitar and thrust my feet into slippers of crimson leather, and together we went out into the open court.

A deep silence rested on the great palace, broken only by the cool plashing of the fountains in their marble basins. The heavens, blue as a sapphire, were profound and mysterious. Myriads of stars twinkled in the clear depths of the skies, and all objects were defined with a wonderful accuracy in the silver moonlight. The Fada was hushed in sleep. On the marble steps of the Bab-Seadet, the gate of the Imperial harem, the black guards stood on either side, mute, erect, motionless, their naked swords gleaming in the moonbeams. How many scenes of gorgeous festivity had been witnessed beyond that great door of iron! how many terrible and bloody dramas had been enacted within those grim, grey walls—dramas of love and hatred, of ambition, disappointment and revenge, of all the fiercest passions of the human heart! By night and day the bewitching pearls of the harem intrigued, schemed and plotted—themselves, through their Imperial Master, ruling the world outside. Too often, alas! in the history of the Empire of Sokoto it had occurred that some dark eye, some bewitching face masking a beautiful slave's ignorance and cunning, had mastered her irresponsible and irresistible lord, and been the means of striking off the heads of not only her rivals within the harem, but those of even the wisest councillors and the bravest fighting-men outside.

As together we crossed the silent court our echoing footsteps broke the quiet. In the gateway of the harem a single light glimmered yellow in contrast with the white moonbeams; but turning our backs upon it we passed through one court after another, receiving salutes from the guards at each gateway. My disguise as eunuch was complete, and as we strolled onward without apparent haste my confidence grew until, on crossing the

Court of the Armourers and entering the Court of the Pages, we discerned a white-robed figure enveloped in a haick and wearing the ugly baggy trousers which are the out-door garments of Moslem women.

"Behold!" I exclaimed, with bated breath. "The Lalla Azala awaiteth us!"

"No," answered the strange, grotesque being. "It is her mute slave, Ayesha. Place thyself in her hands. She will conduct thee unto her mistress."

As we advanced, the woman, whose face I could not distinguish, raised her hand with commanding gesture, and opening a small door beckoned me to follow. This I did, Tiamo remaining behind. Across many courts and through several doors, which the woman carefully bolted after us, we sped until, skirting a pretty garden where pomegranates, almonds, cypresses and myrtles alternated regularly, and roses in full bloom embowered the long alley, we came to a door in a wall near the tower. Having looked well around to see that nobody remarked us, she introduced me into a passage so small that I was compelled to bend to enter it. Taking up a lamp that had apparently been placed there in readiness, she went on before, and I followed through some intricate wanderings; then, instead of ascending, we began to go down a flight of broken stone steps.

The air became hot and stifling, and foul odours rose from the place into which we were descending. Suddenly a loud, piercing shriek of pain sounded weirdly, followed by another and yet another. Then I recognised the uneven steps as those leading to the foul dungeon with its maniac prisoners.

The rough, exultant laugh of my enemy, Khazneh, reached my ears from below, mingled with the imploring cry of some unfortunate wretch who was undergoing torture. Next second a suspicion flashed across my mind that I had been betrayed.

Chapter Twelve
Mysteries of Eblis

My mute conductress halted, listened intently, then placed her finger significantly on her lips. As she turned her half-veiled face towards me I saw in the flickering lamplight that her tattooed forehead was brown and wizened, that her dark, gleaming eyes were deeply sunken, and that her hand holding the lamp was thin, brown and bony.

The sounds that alarmed us ceased, and, after waiting a few moments, scarce daring to breathe, she descended several more stairs to a turn in the flight, and I found myself before a small, black door, which she quickly opened and closed again after we had passed through. Raising her finger to command silence, she moved along a narrow passage and then there commenced a toilsome ascent over great, roughly-hewn steps that I well remembered descending when, in the clutches of my captors, I had been roughly dragged from the apartment of my enchantress. With a nimbleness that showed a familiarity with their unevenness, she mounted, while I stumbled on behind, nearly coming to grief once or twice, and being compelled to save myself with my hands. In my eagerness to meet the woman who had entranced me, upward I toiled, until my breath came and went in short, quick gasps, and I was forced to rest a moment, while she also halted, smiling and turning the lamp towards me. The intricacies of these secret passages were puzzling and fatiguing, and I was anxious to pass into the well-remembered room wherein the Sultan's daughter had, during so many weary moons, awaited me.

At last we stood before a door secured by a large iron bar, so heavy that old Ayesha could not draw it from its socket, but quickly I removed the barrier. The slave who had acted as my guide opened the door, drew aside the heavy curtain, and then stepping forward I found myself once again before the bright-eyed girl who desired my aid.

The place was dimly illumined by great hanging lamps of gold, which shed a soft and dubious light through cut crystals of green and crimson, and the air was sweetly scented by the odours of musk and cinnamon rising from the perfuming-pans. Azala, pale and beautiful, in her gorgeous harem dress, with arms, ankles and neck laden with jewels, was reclining with languorous grace upon her divan of light blue satin fringed with gold, that was placed in the alcove at the end of the apartment, her wealth of dark hair straying in profusion over the great, tasselled cushion of yellow silk. Her feet, tiny and well-formed, were bare, her pearl-embroidered slippers having been kicked aside, her pipe stood near, and upon a coffee-stool of ebony and gold stood a large silver dish of rare fruit, while kneeling beside her was a black female slave cooling her slowly with a fan of peacock's feathers. Unnoticed by her, I stood for a few seconds, bewitched by her loveliness as she lay there in graceful abandon, her body saturated with perfumes, her soul filled with prayers.

"Welcome, O Zafar! Allah favoureth us!" she cried excitedly, springing to her feet the instant she recognised me, and, rushing across, grasping both my hands. "Thou hast brought happiness with thee."

"At last, Azala," I said, clasping her soft hands tenderly, and gazing into those brilliant black eyes that seemed to delight in the anxious curiosity which they aroused in my features. "Of a verity Allah is all-powerful and all-merciful. Our destinies are written in the Book, and therefore what is there left but to submit? For many moons have I striven to seek thee, to redeem the pledge I made unto thee, and now at last is our meeting accomplished."

Noticing that I looked askance at the presence of Ayesha and the young negress, she waved her hand to them to retire. Then, when the curtains had fallen behind them, she led me slowly to her divan, saying in serious tones, "Come hither, O Zafar, I would have long and serious speech with thee."

She having ensconced herself comfortably among her rich, downy cushions, I seated myself beside her, and as one arm stole around her slim waist, encircled by its bejewelled girdle, I drew her tenderly towards me with the intention of imprinting on her white, sequin-covered brow a passionate caress. Gently but firmly she disengaged herself from my embrace. At first the marvellous beauty of my divinity held me spellbound, but fortified by her smile I found courage to pour out a rhapsody of love and admiration, to which she listened, blushing deeply.

Thus, in the bliss of whispering love, we forgot the heavy sorrows oppressing us, and put aside all apprehension for the present and all care for the future.

After a recital of my adventures on being torn from her presence, I told her how wearily the hours had passed and of my mad desire to be again at her side, to which she answered, —

"In thee, O Zafar, have I placed my trust. The sun of the favour of the One Merciful shineth upon us, therefore let us abandon all fear."

"The firmament possesseth but one sun, and the Empire of Sokoto but one Princess. That life, light, joy and prosperity may attend thee is my most fervent desire."

"May perfect peace attend thee in the rose-grove of thine happiness," she answered, turning towards me the most beautiful face that Allah had ever formed. "For many moons have I waited at yonder lattice for thy coming, knowing full well that thou art ready to serve me."

"Ay, ready to serve thee, O Pearl of Sokoto," I said fervently. "I love only thee, and am thy slave."

She was toying in hesitation with her broad gold armlet that contained a talisman. Spells and charms are believed in as strongly by the ladies of Kano as those of Omdurman. The eye and knuckle-bone of a fox hung upon the neck of a boy gives him courage; its fat rubbed on a woman will convert her husband's love into indifference. The dried liver of a cat is believed to bring back the love of a desired object to the person who possesses it; the skin of its nose, if worn on the ankle, is a preventive against murder by poison; while its ashes, if taken internally, will give all the shrewd, cunning qualities of the cat. The one Azala wore was the *kus kaftar*—a portion of the dried skin of a female leopard one moon old, which always bears the greatest price in the seraglios, because, if worn on the arm, it is believed to conciliate the affections of all to its wearer; and as she fingered it she uttered some kind of incantation that I failed to understand.

Her head had fallen back upon the great gold-tasselled pillow, and with her white arm thrown out above she looked up smiling into my face, uttering words of courage, declaring that I was the only man she had ever asked to perform a service.

"But," she added, suddenly raising herself into a sitting position and gazing straight into my eyes, "how little—how very little we are thinking of the deadly peril which threateneth us! Both of us are confident in each other's love; but, alas! no safety can there be until the Great Secret be solved."

"What secret?" I asked, endeavouring to read her story in her brilliant eyes.

"The Secret of the Asps," she answered, in a calm, low tone. "The secret of the strange, mysterious mark that is upon my breast and thine. When it is solved, then only may peace be ours."

"Tell me all thou knowest regarding the curious imprint," I said eagerly, lifting her bejewelled hand and pressing it tenderly. "Now that I am thy best beloved, ready to serve thee blindly and implicitly, surely I may know the secret of things concerning both of us," I argued.

But with a sigh she answered, "No. Some knowledge hath been conveyed to me upon condition that I should preserve its secret until such time as the mystery shall be elucidated. Suffice it to thee to know that thou art the person to whom the truth may be revealed if thou hast forbearance and courage."

"Will any act of mine place about thee the walls of security and the stillness of peace?" I inquired, with eagerness.

"Already have I told thee that, if thou wilt, thou canst save me."

"From what destiny?"

"From one unknown, yet horrible—undecided, yet terrible," she answered, hoarsely.

"Then I am thine to command, O Azala," I answered. "In Zafar thou hast a servant who will serve thee with faith and fearlessness, unto even the uttermost ends of the earth."

"When the dawn cometh we shall be compelled to part, for full well thou knowest what fate awaiteth thee if thou wert discovered by Khazneh or his brutal myrmidons," she said, slowly. "But ere we bid each other farewell we have much to arrange, for upon the success of our plans dependeth whether our hands again clasp in welcome, or our lips meet in salutation. In receiving thee here I have run many risks in common with thee. If our enemies conveyed word unto the Sultan, assuredly would the vials of his wrath be poured out upon me, and he would execute his threat of giving me in marriage to some common soldier of the palace guard."

"Has his Majesty given utterance to such a threat?"

"Yea. Because I fell into the displeasure of Khadidja, the scheming slave who now ruleth the harem as his chief wife, I became banished from the Courts of Enchantment. Indeed, only by the intercession of mine own mother, who hath long ago been deposed from her position of Sultana, and is now a mere slave, compelled to wash the feet of many who once served her, was I spared the indignity of being cast out from the palace and given as drudge to one of the horsemen who guard the Kofa-n-Kura. Indeed, the hand of misfortune hath fallen heavily upon me," and she drew a long sigh, as in deep thought her pointed chin rested in her dainty palm.

"What was the nature of thine offence?" I inquired, interested.

"Involuntarily I acted as eavesdropper. One morning, lying in my hammock in a corner of the harem-garden where the rose-bushes grow thickly, I suddenly heard voices beyond. One I recognised as that of Khadidja, and the two others those of Shekerleb and Leilah, Arab slaves. Listening, I heard them discuss in detail an ingenious plot they had arranged to poison my mother, myself and three others, for Khadidja expressed herself determined to be supreme mistress of the seraglio. Appalled by this bold scheme of wholesale revenge, I lay silent, scarce daring to breathe, but when they had left I went straightway to the Sultan and in my mother's presence explained all to him. The woman Khadidja was brought before him, but denied the accusation, swore on the Korân that she had not walked into the garden that morning, and brought Shekerleb and Leilah to corroborate her false statement. My father was convinced of her innocence, and believed also her allegation that a plot hatched by my mother was on foot to encompass her death. He grew angry, degraded my unfortunate mother from her position of Sultana to the meanest slavery, and subsequently banished me to the loneliness of this high abode."

"Of a verity thy lot, O beloved, hath been an unhappy one, but let us now look forward to the dawn of a joyous day, to a noonday of prosperity, and to a sunset of peace. Azala, I love thee," and as our lips met for the first time in a hot, passionate kiss, her bare, scented chest, with its profusion of jewels, rose and fell with an emotion she was unable to suppress.

In the dead, unbroken silence that followed, the distant roll of a drum, and the cry of the sentinels on the watch-towers at the city gates came up through the silk-curtained lattice, announcing that another hour had passed.

"Harken," she cried quickly, springing to her feet, clutching me by the arm, and looking earnestly into my face. "We have but brief space wherein to plan our emancipation. Fearest thou to investigate the mysteries of Eblis, or to serve his handmaiden?"

"Fear dwelleth not in mine heart when the Pearl of Sokoto is nigh," I answered gallantly, bending to kiss her hand.

"Even though thy Pearl may be daughter of the Evil One, and able to accomplish things superhuman?" she asked, in a strange, harsh voice.

"He who believeth in the one Allah and in his Prophet, holdeth in his hand a two-edged sword against the Ghul (Devil) and all the evil spirits of Al-Hawiyat," I replied, surprised at this latter speech, and at the strange, haggard look that had suddenly overspread her beautiful countenance. "At the moment before our enemy Khazneh laid hands upon me, thou didst promise to reveal unto me some hidden marvel, the nature of which thou wouldst not disclose. For that purpose have I come hither, and now await the fulfilment of thy promise."

Grasping my right wrist and looking into my face with eyes that seemed to emit fire, so strangely brilliant were they, she said,—

"Hast thou no fear of the future, or of the power of the Evil Eye?"

"The curse of Eblis himself shall not deter me from seeking to fathom the Mystery of the Asps. A voice that is dead hath commanded me, and I shall obey, even though I am compelled to engage Azrael in single combat. There is some strange secret in the mystic links that bind our existence—a secret I intend to discover at any hazard."

"Bravely spoken, O Zafar," she answered, her cheeks flushing with excitement and her sequins tinkling musically as she moved. "Thine heart is true as thy trusty Masser blade. May it be the will of Allah, who made the earth for a carpet, that thy courage never fail thee in thine attempt to rescue me from the plots that encompass me, and to penetrate the veil that hath so long hidden the truth of the entwined serpents." She raised her face with a fond, wistful look.

Our lips met, and with her arms about my neck she clung to me, trembling, as if in fear. Then, fortifying herself for an effort, she slowly withdrew from my embrace, and led me across to the heavily-curtained door of the inner chamber, saying,—

"Thou hast declared thyself fearless and undaunted in the coming fight to possess the secret which none may know, even though it is imperative that thou shouldst pass barriers hitherto considered by all insurmountable. Truly thou art worthy a woman's love."

"Thou knowest how the unquenchable fire of love burneth within me, O light of mine eyes," I answered, in fervent adoration. "With thee as the sun of my firmament, and with a stout heart within me, I am not afraid."

For answer she turned, and with her hand upon the curtain, said,—

"Come hither. As a preliminary to thine encounter with the Invisible, I will reveal unto thee an undreamed-of marvel that will cause thine eyes to open wide in wonderment, and thine heart to cease its beating. Fear abideth not within thee. Enter therefore this portal whereat Malec, powerful yet invisible, mounteth guard, and learn the means by which the Mystery of the Asps may be unravelled."

Chapter Thirteen
The Prism of Destiny

With sudden movement she drew aside the silken curtain, and we stepped into a small, dark, stone chamber, almost a cell. Then with a word of warning she guided my footsteps to a narrow flight of stairs, which she descended with caution, her golden anklets jingling as she went. As I followed, there clung about her soft draperies those sweet perfumes of the harem, the fragrance of which had intoxicated me.

Again she flung back a second heavy curtain that barred a horse-shoe arch at the foot of the stairs, when instantly my eyes were blinded by a flood of brilliant light. Under my feet I felt a carpet so thick that my slipper sank deep into it, and gradually as my dazzled vision grew accustomed to the unusual glare, I realised that I was in a chamber about the size of the one we had just quitted, but decorated entirely in bright green, the hue of which, reflected into Azala's anxious countenance, gave her a complexion pallid and ghastly. The walls and ceiling were painted green, with good counsels from the Korân in long, lean letters of darker shade, the divans and cushions were of green silk, the stools of malachite, the large alcoves at the end fashioned from dark green marble, beautifully carved, while a malachite table, shaped like a crescent, near the end of the apartment, was studded with huge green crystals that glittered in the light like emeralds. The effect was weird and startling, for the bright white light came from a thousand lamps cunningly arranged overhead, while screens of glass, the colour of the deep sea, shot from the walls slanting beams of brilliant green.

The place was luxurious, yet, as I gazed around it, I could not repress a shudder.

"Go! Take thine ease upon yonder divan," Azala said in a strange voice, pointing to the great couch within the alcove, and as I obeyed her, she took from her arm the gold band with its talisman of leopard's skin and handed it to me. Apparently she dare not wear it there.

Standing in the centre of the curious chamber, she clapped her hands loudly, and instantly a curtain opposite was drawn aside, and there appeared the ugly, hunchbacked form of the grinning dwarf, Tiamo, followed by two female Arab slaves handsomely dressed in tissue of white and gold, and wearing long strings of talismans, and embroidered bags containing mysterious powders, cabalistic figures, and prayers in the language of Maghrib.

The trio, advancing, knelt before their mistress, and with a murmured blessing kissed her feet, prostrating themselves before her.

"Rise," she commanded, almost breathless with excitement. "Know ye that in one brief hour the dawn will show in the direction of the holy city. Speed therefore on the wings of haste and execute my will."

"We, thy slaves, obey thee, O Mistress," they answered with one accord, and, rising, disappeared for a few moments. The two girls presently came forth bearing between them a huge golden bowl full of some sweet yet pungent perfume, which they set on a tripod upon the table of green malachite while Tiamo produced a small golden brazier which he lit and placed beneath the bowl. Then the girls produced green-painted derboukas, and seating themselves upon the mats at the horns of the crescent-shaped table, commenced a monotonous thumping on their drums, while the hideous dwarf, grinning from ear to ear, beat a rapid tattoo upon a double tambourine or *kalango*, all three chanting a weirdly-intoned accompaniment.

The curious spectacle held me on the tiptoe of expectation, for while the music was continued with a regularity that quickly became monotonous, Azala stood with her bejewelled hands outstretched over the bowl, repeating some words in the Hausa tongue which I could not understand. Her face had now grown deathly pale; surrounding her eyes were large, dark rings that betrayed the terrible anxiety at her heart. As the golden bowl became heated, the colourless liquid perfume gave off a vapour so pungent that it caused water to well in my eyes and my head to swim as if I had drunk marissa too freely. I was afraid to rise to my feet lest I should stagger and fall, so upon the edge of the divan I sat entranced and fascinated. The brighter the brazier grew the more dimly burned the lamps above until the brilliant light vanished and we remained in a semi-darkness, made brighter now and then by the uncertain flicker of the fire. Emerald crystals everywhere in ceiling and walls flashed like jewels with a bright green brilliance each time the flames shot up, producing a weird and dazzling effect, while in the shadow Azala prostrated herself, uttering an appeal to some power unseen.

Eagerly I watched the next development of this remarkable experiment. Suddenly the woman I loved struggled to her feet and with her right forefinger touched the edge of the steaming bowl. As she did this, a bright flash, blinding as lightning, shot through the chamber, causing the music to cease and the slaves, awe-stricken, to bow their heads until their brows touched the carpet.

"AS SHE DID THIS A BRIGHT FLASH, BLINDING AS LIGHTNING, SHOT THROUGH THE CHAMBER."

"Malec, iron-hearted Janitor of Hell, hath been overthrown!" they exclaimed, in voices hushed in fear.

Again was the flash repeated as Azala's hand touched the edge of the bowl of repoussé gold, and the slaves gasped in Arabic, —

"Lo! the Guardian of Al-Hawiyat is vanquished by the sword of Eblis!"

Then, a third time my eyes became dazzled by the sudden brilliance which apparently proceeded from the great basin of perfume, and the slaves lifted their voices, saying, —

"The Pillars of Hell have indeed fallen! — the sword of Eblis is sheathed, and Malec, trembling, hath hidden his dog's face before the incomparable beauty of her Highness, the Lalla Azala!"

Tiamo, whom Azala addressed as El-Sadic (the Sincere), rose at the bidding of his mistress. With her hand pressed to her heart, as if to stay its wild beating, she stood close to me with her face upturned and her lips moving as if invoking the aid of some unseen power.

"Behold!" she cried, with a suddenness that caused me to start. "Behold, the Prism of Destiny!" And as the words fell from her white, trembling lips, there was a wild noise like the rushing of great waters, and a circular portion of the wall of the chamber directly opposite appeared to fall asunder, disclosing a huge gold ring, within which, placed perpendicularly, was a large crystal prism, the length of a man's body, which, as it revolved in its setting, showed all the gorgeous hues of the spectrum with a rapidity that was bewildering.

Azala, standing motionless, gazed at it, while the slaves remained kneeling with eyes riveted upon it in fear and expectation. Propelled by some unseen agency, it revolved noiselessly within its golden circle, emitting shafts of multi-coloured light that illumined parts of the strange chamber, leaving the remainder in deepest shadow. Gradually, however, the speed with which the great crystal turned slackened, and Azala, advancing towards me, placed her hand lightly upon my shoulder, exclaiming in a low, intense tone,—

"Lo! that which we sought is revealed! Behold! before us is the forbidden Prism of Destiny, into which none may gaze without incurring the displeasure of the One Merciful, and the curse of Eblis the Terrible."

The lights flashing full upon my face seemed to enthral my senses, for her words sounded distant, discordant and indistinct. But a sudden exclamation of hers aroused me.

"See!" she cried, pointing to the three-sided crystal. "Its motion steadies! It mirrors life in its wondrous depths, but those who dare discern their future ofttimes pay the penalty of their folly by being struck with blindness, and ignominy attendeth them. Allah, though merciful, is just, and it is written in the Book of Everlasting Will that we may know nought of the hereafter, save what holy writ teacheth us."

"But how is the extraordinary effect produced?" I asked, marvelling greatly at the curious chimera, for though it appeared but a phantom, the prism actually revolved, and the illusion could not be caused by reflected light, as I at first had been inclined to believe.

"By offering sacrifice to Eblis," she answered, looking into my eyes, an intoxicating gaze of promise, triumph, tenderness. On her lips dawned a smile which was pledge of the future—the future all light, all hope, all love.

Then, pointing to the boiling bowl, she said, "He giveth sight of it to those of his slaves and handmaidens who invoke his aid."

"Art thou actually one of his handmaidens?" I gasped in fear, amazed to observe that her beauty seemed to gradually fade, leaving her face yellow, care-lined and withered.

"I am," she answered in a deep, discordant voice. "Once before, after thou wert taken from me, the Prism of Destiny made its revelation. The temptation to gaze therein proved too great, and, alas! I fell."

"What didst thou discern?" I eagerly inquired, my eyes still fixed in fascination upon the mysterious, rotating crystal, my senses gradually becoming more than ever confused.

"I pierced the impenetrable veil of futurity."

"And what manner of things were revealed?"

"I beheld many marvels," she answered, in a slow, impressive voice. "Marvels that thou, too, canst behold if thou darest brave the wrath."

She spoke so earnestly, fixing her searching eyes upon me, that I felt my courage failing. The constant flashing of brilliant colours in my eyes seemed to unnerve me, throwing me into a kind of helpless stupor, in which my senses became frozen by the ghastly mysteries practised before me. It was this feeling of helplessness that caused my heart to sink.

"Didst thou not declare thou wouldst engage Malec in single combat in thine endeavour to fathom the Secret of the Asps?" she observed, half reproachfully. "Yet thine hand quivereth like the aspen, and thou carest not to seek the displeasure consequent upon such an action."

Erect, almost statuesque, she stood before me, pale and of incomparable beauty, holding my sun-browned hand in hers.

"Hearken, O Azala," I cried, struggling with difficulty to my feet, and passing my hand across my aching brow to steady the balance of my brain. "No man hath yet accused Zafar-Ben-A'Ziz of cowardice. If, in order to seek the key to the mystery of the strange marks we both bear, it is imperative that I should gaze into yonder crystal, then I fear nought."

"It is imperative," she stammered. "If it were not, I, of all persons, would not endeavour to induce thee to invoke the curse upon thyself."

"Then let me gaze," I said, and with uneven steps went forward, my hand in hers, to where the great prism had so miraculously appeared. It was moving very slowly, the only light in the chamber being that emitted from its triangular surfaces, and as I halted before it my head reeled with a strange sensation of dizziness I had never before experienced.

Aloud the prostrate slaves cried,—

"O Malec, Angel of Terror, vanquished by a woman's beauty, let the eyes of this friend of thy conqueror witness the sight which is forbidden, so that he may drink of the fountain of truth, and repose in the radiance of her countenance." Tiamo was thumping his *kalango* and grinning hideously.

Bewildered, and only half-conscious of my surroundings, I felt Azala dragging me forward. Though the objects swam around me and I had a curious sensation as if I were treading on air, I advanced to within an arm's length of the slowly-moving prism. My eyes were cast down to the green carpet, for in the sudden terror that had seized me I feared to look.

"Speak!" cried Azala, in a voice that seemed afar off. "What beholdest thou?"

But no answer passed my lips.

"Gaze long and earnestly, O Zafar, so that the image of things revealed may be graven upon the tablets of thy memory for use for our well-being hereafter," she urged in a voice sounding like the distant cry of a night-bird.

The thought of her peril flashed in an instant across my unbalanced mind. Her appeal, I remembered, was for our mutual benefit, in order that I should be enabled to elucidate the Mystery of the Asps and bring peace upon her. What, I wondered, was the nature of this strange revelation which she herself had already witnessed.

Ashamed at this terror that branded me as coward, and determined to strive towards the solution of the remarkable mystery that bound me in a bond of love to the beautiful daughter of the Sultan, I held my breath and slowly raised my head.

Next second my heart stood still as, fascinated in amazement and aghast in horror, I gazed deep into the prism's crystal depths, where an omination, wondrous and entrancing, met my eyes.

There was indeed revealed unto me a marvel of which I had not dreamed.

Chapter Fourteen
A Sign Afar

The movement of the huge crystal was so slow as to be almost imperceptible, but the kaleidoscope of life and movement it presented held me spellbound.

By this strange combination of dactyliomancy with christallomantia, an effect was produced so amazing and unaccountable that my wondering vision became riveted upon it, as gradually my mind cleared of the chaotic impression it had received.

The reflecting surfaces, turned at various angles to my line of sight, presented in their unsullied transparency a specular inversion of figures and scenes that, ere they took clearly-delineated shape, dissolved and faded, to be succeeded by others of a totally different character. Objects and persons with whom I seemed to have been familiar in my youth in the far-off Aures passed before my gaze in bewildering confusion. Ere I could recognise them, however, they disappeared, phantom-like, giving place to a series of pictures of the terrors of battle, so vividly portrayed that they held me overawed. The first showed a beautiful court, evidently the private pavilion of some potentate, with cool arcades, plashing fountains, tall palms and trailing vines. But the place had been assaulted and ignominiously fallen. The courts sacred to the women were full of armed, dark-skinned men, who, with brutal ruthlessness, were tearing from the "pearls of the harem" their jewels, and with wanton cruelty massacring them even as I gazed. Over the pavements of polished jasper, blood flowed, trickling into the great basin of the fountain, and as one after another the houris fell and died, a fierce red light shone in the sky, showing that the barbarous conquerors, intoxicated with blood and loot, had fired the palace. Then in the dense smoke that curled from out the arcades as they were enveloped and destroyed, the scene of merciless slaughter and ruthless destruction was lost, and there gradually evolved scenes of burning desert, of welcome oases, of great and wonderful cities, all of which grew slowly and were quickly lost. Just at that moment, however, a sound behind me caused me to start, and turning, I saw that the dwarf, who had risen noiselessly, had witnessed the magic pictures as well as ourselves.

On seeing that his inquisitiveness had been detected, he turned quickly, rejoined his fellow-slaves, and fell again upon his knees, raising his voice in the strange incantation the girls continued to repeat. Apparently Azala did not notice him; too engrossed was she in the revelations of the prism, for when I again gazed into the crystal, objects and persons were passing in rapid confusion, and she was vainly endeavouring to decipher their mysterious import.

For a second we saw the face of a beautiful woman with hair like golden sheen, and were both amazed to discover that in place of rows of sequins she wore a single ornament suspended upon her white, unfurrowed brow. Apparently it was carved from a single diamond of enormous size and exceeding lustre, but its shape puzzled us; it was fashioned to represent a curious device of arrowheads. Quickly the mysteriously-beautiful face dissolved, and from its remains there came in rapid succession pictures of a mighty city, of a great plain, of running water, of a seething populace, and of a cool garden rich in flowers and fruit. Then there appeared a vision so ghastly and gruesome that I drew back in horror.

It represented a pavement of polished marble, whereon a woman was stretched dead, mutilated by the keen scimitar of a black eunuch of giant stature, who with his foot upon the lifeless body gazed down, grinning with satisfaction at his own brutality.

The face of the man startled me. The hideous countenance, on which revenge was so strongly depicted, was that of our mutual enemy, Khazneh, Chief of the Black Eunuchs of his Imperial Majesty!

"Enough!" cried Azala, horrified at what seemed a revolting augury of her own end. "See! the brute hath struck off her head!" And shuddering, she gazed around the apartment with a look of abject terror, her haggard features in that moment becoming paler and more drawn.

"Heed it not as ill-potent," I said, smoothing her hair tenderly, and endeavouring to remove from her mind the horrifying thought that she might fall under the *doka* of the Grand Eunuch. "The mystic Prism of Destiny showeth much that is grim, distorted and fantastic. The eventuality is only resolved so that we may arm ourselves against the Destroyer."

But, apprehensive of her fate, she shook her head sorrowfully, saying in low, harsh tones, "When on the previous occasion I gazed into the prism a similar scene was conjured up before me, only the woman was then at his knees imploring mercy, while he, with *doka* uplifted, laughed her to scorn. Now, see the end! Her head hath fallen!"

Again I turned to ascertain what next might be shown in the revolving crystal, the mystery of which was ever-increasing, but it had ceased to move. Eagerly I bent, gazing into its green, transparent depths in order to discover whether the strange scenes were mere optical illusions. Only for a second was I permitted to gaze, but in that brief moment suspicion seized me that I had been imposed upon. Whether Azala actually believed that forecasts of the future could be witnessed in the crystal, or whether she was only striving to impress me by regaling me with an exhibition of the mystical, in which all women of her race delight, I know not; but I was sceptical and became convinced that the pictures had been conjured up by mechanical contrivance, and that the illusions—probably the stock-in-trade of some court necromancer—were performed by ingenious but hidden paintings or tableaux.

By this discovery I was much perturbed, for it was remarkable that, on witnessing the scenes, Azala's surprise and agitation were natural and unfeigned, and this act led me to the conclusion that, believing in spells and amulets, she was also ready to place faith in any extraordinary marvel that she might gaze upon.

It was common knowledge, I remembered, that the women of Sokoto were extremely superstitious, believing as implicitly in the sayings of their astrologers as we, of the North, believe in the efficacy of representations of the hand of Fathma of Algiers nailed over our doors to avert the Evil Eye. Was this chamber the sanctum of some seer whose duty it was to forecast the good or evil fortune of the doves of the harem?

I turned, and was about to address to her some question directed towards fathoming the secrets of this cunningly-contrived instrument of psychomancy, when suddenly she drew aside the curtain from a lattice near, uttering an exclamation of mingled surprise and dismay.

Rushing towards her, I looked out, and the sight riveted my gaze in abject amazement.

The dawn had already spread with delicate tints of pink and rose, but in the northern sky a strange, inverted picture was presented with such clearness and vividness of outline that every detail is still as fresh in my mind as it was at the moment I witnessed it.

The picture was produced not by the chicanery of any necromancer, but by Nature herself. It was that strange, puzzling illusion—the mirage. So weird and wonderful was it that, even though I had seen many similar pictures in the heavens during my journeys over the plains, I gave an involuntary exclamation of amazement.

As we gazed away beyond the city, across the sandy desert, the aerial tableaux mirrored above appeared to be the reflection of a flat, black rock of colossal dimensions, rising high and inaccessible like a wall, and descending sheer into dark, deep water, upon the surface of which its gloomy image was reflected as in a mirror. The spot, weird and lonely, was devoid of every vestige of herbage or any living thing, and as I looked upon it in wonderment, impressed by its weirdness, Azala suddenly grasped my arm, exclaiming excitedly, —

"Behold! that black pool! See, it is the Lake of the Accursed! Many times hath its image been revealed unto us in the sky. Remark it carefully, for of a verity am I convinced that in this vision we have a key to the Secret. At that spot must thou search if thou desirest to fathom the mystery."

My eyes took in every detail of the ineffably dismal picture, the great, inhospitable face of dark granite seemingly so smooth that an eagle could scarce obtain a foothold, its rugged summit with one pointed crag, like a man's forefinger, pointing higher than the rest towards the dark, lowering clouds that seemed to hang about it, and the Stygian blackness of the stagnant water at its gigantic base. But its sight told me nothing, for it was the reflected image of a scene I had never before gazed upon, a scene so unutterably dismal and dispiriting that I doubted whether any clue could there be found.

Cloud-pictures are of such frequent occurrence at Kano that it is known among the desert tribes as "The City of the Mirage."

For a few moments the sky remained the mirror of this mystic picture; then gradually it faded into air. When it had entirely disappeared, Azala, uttering no word, drew the curtain again before the lattice as at the same instant Tiamo and the two slaves rose, bowing before their mistress. With quick, impatient gesture she motioned to them to leave, and I, marvelling greatly at the strange religio-magic and extraordinary mirage I had witnessed, followed her through the open curtain and up the stairs back to her own sweetly perfumed apartment.

But in that moment there occurred to me the solemn declaration I had so often heard in the mosque: "Whoso taketh Eblis for his patron beside Allah, shall surely perish with a manifest destruction."

Chapter Fifteen
Tales of the Story-Tellers

In her own chamber, Azala, tottering towards her divan, sank upon it exhausted, while I, grasping her hand, stood by in rigid silence, not daring to speak.

As upon her cushion she was lying, one arm beneath her head, I watched the flush of health mount to her countenance, and her beauty gradually return. She opened her eyes, and as she gazed into mine long and steadily, I told myself that she was nothing like any other daughter of man. Those glorious orbs under their great curved brows shone upon me like suns under triumphal arches. The idea of holding her in my arms brought me a fury of rapture; she held me bound by an unseen chain. It seemed as though she had become my very soul, and yet for all that there flowed between us the invisible waves of an ocean without bounds. She, the daughter of the Sultan, was remote and inaccessible. The splendour of her beauty diffused around her a nebula of light, and I found myself believing at moments that she was not before me—that she did not really exist—that it was all a dream.

She moved, the diamonds on her heaving bosom shining resplendently, and raising herself slowly to a sitting posture, asked in a low, intense tone,—

"Now that thou hast gazed into the Prism of Destiny and witnessed the sign in the heavens, fearest thou to penetrate further the veil of evil that surroundeth us?"

"Already have I spoken, O Pearl among Women. I fear not to speak the truth," I answered, yet half inclined to scoff at the pictures shown in the prism. Yet the distinctness of the gloomy mirage had impressed me, and I refrained from saying anything to give her pain.

"Then thou must of necessity seek the spot, the image of which hath been revealed," she said, and motioning me to a cushion near her, added, "Take thine ease for short space, and lend me thine ear."

Drawing the cushion closer to her, I seated myself, my hand still clasping hers; then, with a slight sigh, she gazed into my face with a look of earnest passion and continued,—

"The great rock and the black water in combination answereth with exactness to the description of the Lake of the Accursed which none has found, but which existeth in the legends of our people, and hath long been discussed by our wise men. It is said that the Rock of the Great Sin, rising sheer and inaccessible from the unfathomable waters, formeth the gate of the Land of the No Return, the unknown country which none can enter nor leave, and upon which human eyes have never gazed. Our story-tellers oft repeat the popular belief that the Lake of the Accursed hideth an unknown, but amazing wonder, although for centuries our armies and our caravans have travelled far and wide over the face of the earth, yet none has discovered it. By the fact of its image being thrice revealed in the sky, I am convinced that if its whereabouts could be discovered, we should find that which we seek."

"But apparently it existeth only in the sayings of thy wise men," I observed, dubiously.

"The descriptions of it all agree, even though the versions, which the story-tellers relate as to its origin, may differ," she answered, her eyes appearing to penetrate far away in the distance beyond terrestrial space. "Those of the tribe of Zamfara assert that ages ago, in the face of the Rock of the Great Sin, there was a large and deep cavern whence issued a black and unwholesome vapour, and men feared to approach because it was the gate of the Land of the No Return. It was the continual resort of a huge serpent, whose bite was fatal, who zealously guarded the gloomy portals of the forbidden land, and who swallowed his victims; but once a man of lion courage dared to escape while the serpent slept, and successfully got away, while, in the heat of noon, the Great Devourer closed his eyes. The serpent, however, awoke in time to see the adventurer flying across the desert, but too late to kill him. Then, in a paroxysm of rage that mortal man should have eluded his vigilance, he smote the rock thrice with his tail, when, with a noise like thunder, the cavern closed, and about it was formed the deep, black pool known as the Lake of the Accursed, which has ever since rendered it unapproachable. Such is the story most popular among our people, although there are some others, notably that of the Kanouri, who declare that, far back in the dim ages, before the days of the Prophet, a great host of one of the Pagan conquerors of Ethiopia was on its way to penetrate into an unknown region where the presence of man had already been forbidden by the gods. When, having crossed the desert many days, they were at last about to enter the fruitful land to despoil it, the earth suddenly opened and devoured them, leaving in their place the Accursed Lake with the great rock as a terrible warning to future generations who might be seized with a desire to gain knowledge and riches withheld from them."

"Do all the versions agree that the Rock of the Great Sin is the gate of a region unknown?" I asked, intensely interested in these quaint beliefs of the storytellers.

"Yes. In the harem ofttimes have I heard slaves of the tribes of Zara, Boulgouda and of Digguera each relate their version, and all coincide that the rock was at one period a gate which gave entrance to a forbidden land. Some say there lieth behind the rock Al-Hotama, (an apartment in hell, so called because it will break into pieces whatever is thrown into it), where the kindled fire of Allah mounteth above the hearts of those cast therein, the dreaded place which the Korân telleth us is as an arched vault on columns of vast extent wherein the dwellers have garments of fire fitted unto them. Others believe that beyond the Lake of the Accursed there lieth the gardens into which Allah introduceth those who believe and act righteously, the Land of Paradise through which rivers flow, where the great lote-tree flourisheth, and where the dwellers are adorned with bracelets of gold and pearls, and their vestures are of silk. All are in accord that the land beyond is the Land of the No Return."

"And thou desireth me to set forth in search of this legendary spot which no man hath yet discovered?" I said.

"To elucidate the mystery of the marks we bear will be to thine own benefit, as well as to mine," she answered, gazing into my eyes with a look of affection. "Thou, an Arab by birth but a Dervish by compulsion, art the enemy of my race, and peradventure had thy companions not been slaughtered by my guards thine hosts would have ere this occupied Kano and looted this our palace. Yet we love each other, though I am a disgraced outcast from the harem, in peril of my life—"

"Why art thou in such deadly peril? Thou has not explained to me," I interrupted.

"My death or marriage would secure the position of Khadidja, my mother's rival, as Sultana. Therefore there are intrigues on foot to take my life by violent but secret means."

"Or peradventure thy marriage?" I suggested.

"Alas!" she said quickly, smiling with sadness. "Didst thou not witness in the prism the decree of Fate? Sooner or later I shall fall beneath the sword of my secret enemy."

The Eye of Istar | 91

"Nay, nay," I said, entwining my arm about her white neck and drawing her towards me. "Anticipate not foul assassination, but seek Allah's aid, and bear courage while I strive."

"I trust thee, Zafar," she murmured, in a soft voice, with tears in her eyes. "I trust in thee to extricate me from the perils that surround me like a cloud on every side."

"Lovest thou me fondly enough to marry?" I asked in intense earnestness, holding both her hands and looking into her clear, bright orbs.

"Of a verity I do," she answered, blushing.

"Then how can we wed?" I asked. "I am, alas! but poor, and to ask of the Sultan for thee would only be the smiting off of mine own head, for already hath he forbidden me to set foot within his Empire on pain of instant death."

"It is but little I know concerning the Mystery of the Asps, beyond the legend that the key to the secret lieth hidden at the Rock of the Great Sin, the whereabouts of which no man knoweth; nevertheless, I am convinced that if thou canst penetrate its true meaning thou wilt not find the Sultan implacable."

"His Majesty feareth the sight of the mark upon me," I said, reflectively. "Knowest thou the reason?" She hesitated for a few moments, as if reluctant to explain, then replied,—

"I know not."

"Dost thou promise to wed me if I am successful in my search after the truth?" I asked, pressing her tiny hand in mine.

"Zafar," she answered, in a low tone, full of tenderness, as she clung to me, "I love no other man but thee. My father's hatred standeth between us, therefore we must wait, and if in the meantime thine efforts to obtain knowledge of the meaning of the marks upon our breasts are successful, then most assuredly will the Sultan give me unto thee in marriage and rejoice thee with abundant favours."

Raising my right hand, I answered, "It is written upon the stone that Allah is the living one. If a man prove obstinate, woe unto him. I swear upon our Book of Everlasting Will to strive while I have breath towards the elucidation of the mystery."

Tightening her grasp upon my hand with her bejewelled fingers, she said, "I also take oath that during thine absence no man shall enter my presence. Whithersoever thou goest there shall also accompany thee my blessing, which shall be as a torch in the darkness of night, and thy guide in the brightness of day. Strive on with fearless determination; strive on, ever remembering that one woman's life is at stake, and that that woman is Azala, thy Beloved. Peace be upon thee."

"By mine eyes I am thy slave," I said. "My ear is in thine hand; whatever thou ordainest I am bound to obey without doubt or hesitation. No other word need be said. I will go wherever thou commandest, were it even to fetch Malec himself from the innermost chambers of the world beneath."

"Be it so," she exclaimed, smiling, fingering her necklet of charms. "When thou hast discovered that which thou seekest, then, misfortune will take its leave, and a new chapter in the book of thy life will open. Of a verity thy thirst shall be slaked by cooling draughts of the waters of Zemzem, thou shalt become clothed in the burnouse of honour, armed with the hand of power, and mounted on the steed of splendour."

"And become the husband of the Pearl of Sokoto," I added, caressing her with passionate fondness in the ecstasy of love.

She laughed, glancing at me with roguish raillery, her finger at her lips. Then she answered, "That is the summit of earthly happiness towards which I am striving." But her scented bosom rose and fell in a long sigh as she added: "Without thee the days are dull and dreary, and the nights interminable. From my lattice I gaze upon the palace courts and the great city full of life and movement, in which I am not permitted to participate, and think of thy freedom; for though daughter of the Sultan, I am as much a prisoner as any unfortunate wretch in the dungeons deep below. Thou art free, free to travel over the deserts and the mountains in search of a key to the strange enigma; free to strive towards my rescue and the fulfilment of my heart's desire; free to gain that knowledge which, peradventure, may make thee honoured and esteemed among men. Here will I await thy coming, and each day while thou art absent, at the going down of the sun will I pray unto Allah, who setteth his sign in the heavens, to shield thee with his cloak, and place in thine hands the two-edged sword of conquest."

"Assuredly will I speed on the wings of haste to do thy bidding," I answered, looking deep into the depths of her wonderful eyes as I knelt beside her with one arm around her neck and her fair head pillowed upon my breast. "At the *maghrib* each day will I think of thee, and whether in the desert or the forest, in the oasis or the city, I will send unto thee a message of love and peace upon the sunset zephyr."

"My lattice shall be opened always at the call of the *mueddin*," she said, "and thy words of comfort will be borne in unto me by the desert wind. I shall know that, wherever thou art, thou thinkest at that hour of me, and we will thus exchange mute, invisible confidences in each other's love."

I looked at her a moment, dazed, then, rising slowly to my feet, seized her hands, asking, "When shall I set forth?"

"Thy journey must be prosecuted with all dispatch. Tarry not, or misfortune may overtake us both," she answered, raising herself, and sitting upon her divan with her tiny feet and gold-bangled ankles stretched out against the lion's skin spread upon the floor of polished porphyry. "Ere the sun appeareth above the Hills of Guetzaoua thou must pass out of the Kofa-n-Kura on the first stage of thy journey. Outside the city gate thou wilt find a swift camel with its bags ready packed, awaiting thee in charge of one of my male slaves. Mount, and hasten from the city lest thy departure be detected."

"As chief of the Khalifa's *mulazimin* I am liable to be overtaken and brought back," I said. "Therefore I must speed quickly away, avoiding the route of the caravans, for if I am missed I shall assuredly be tracked. In what direction shall I prosecute my quest!"

"Alas! I cannot tell," she answered, shaking her head with sorrow. "The Zamfara declare that the Rock of the Great Sin lieth far beyond the land of the rising sun, while the Boulgouda contend that the gloomy spot is situate away in the deep regions of the afterglow. But Allah directeth not the unjust. Towards the pole-star it cannot be, for already our fighting-men have spread themselves over the land and have not discovered it, whereas on the other hand our wise men say it must be beyond the impenetrable forests of the far-distant south. Travel, therefore, not towards the north, but cross the great desert into the distant lands, and make diligent inquiry among the Pagan dwellers in the regions unknown, for by trusting unto Fortune thou mayest find that for which thou searchest. Necessity is as a strong rider with stirrups like razors, who maketh the sorry jade do that which the strong horse sometimes will not do, therefore be of good cheer, and by recourse to thine own ingenuity endeavour to gain swiftly the grim portals of the Land of the No Return."

"Then thou canst give me absolutely no clue to its position?" I said, puzzled, for I had expected that at least she would be able to tell me in which direction the finger of popular belief pointed.

"No. The different versions held by the story-tellers are all conflicting, regarding its position. Its whereabouts is an absolute mystery." Then, placing her hand beneath the silken cushion whereon she had been reclining, she drew forth a bag of gold, adding, "Take this, for assuredly thou wilt require to give backsheesh unto the people of the far-distant lands thou wilt visit."

But I motioned her to keep the money, saying, —

"Thanks to the liberality of my master, the Khalifa, I have at present enough for my wants, and some to spare, concealed within my belt. If, on my return, I am unsuccessful and penurious then will I borrow of thee."

"To show me favour, wilt thou not accept it, in order to pay those who perform service for thee?" she asked with a sweet, winning smile.

"Nay," I replied, with pride. "What payments I make, I shall willingly bear myself. Keep thy gold until we again meet, which, if Allah be merciful, will be ere many moons have faded. Let thy life be happy, thou, who art all in all to me! dawn of my day! star of my night! sweet one rose of my summer!"

"Assuredly thou art brave and true, O Zafar," she said, tossing the bag of gold aside, and looking up at me. "Thou hast, in blind confidence of me, undertaken without fear a task which through ages men have continued to prosecute without success. Sages have long ago relinquished their efforts as futile, yet thou darest to face Malec himself, nay, even to fight Eblis, because thou lovest me and desirest that I should become thy wife. If thine heart retainest its lion's courage, then I have presage that thine efforts will ultimately lead thee unto the rose-garden of happiness."

"With thoughts of thee, O Azala, nought can daunt me. Those who offer me opposition will I crush even like vipers," I said gallantly, and as she rose with slow grace to her feet, I clasped her in fond embrace. "If I falter," I continued, "drown my soul in the vapour of thy breath; let my lips be crushed in kissing thine hands."

But she answered, "I love thee, O Zafar; I will marry only thee," pressing her hot lips to mine fiercely. My arm was about her slim, gold-begirt waist, and the contact shook me to the depths of my soul. We murmured vague speeches, lighter than breezes, and savoury as kisses. In this parting I became impelled towards her, and with dilated nostrils inhaled the sweet perfumes exhaled from her breast, from which rose an indefinable emanation of musk, jasmine and roses, which filled my senses and held me entranced.

In silence we stood locked in each other's arms. Upon her soft white cheek I rained kisses, as she cast her arms about my neck, sobbing her fill upon my breast. I tried to utter words of comfort, but they refused to pass my lips; my heart was too full for mere words. Thus we stood together, each bearing the strange imprint, the mystic meaning of which it had been the desire of all our lives to elucidate, each determined to fathom a mystery mentioned by wise men only with bated breath, and each fearing failure, knowing, alas! too well its inevitable result would be unhappiness and death.

"Fear and hope have sent me mad," I said. "Sweet, sweetest, dry those tears—let me kiss them away—smile again; thou art the sun that lights my world. Think! I have dreamed of thee as winter dreams of spring! Think, my love and thine idea have grown like leaf and flower."

At last, with supreme effort, she stifled her sobs and dried her eyes, remaining in silence and murmuring now and then fervent blessings upon me. For some moments the quiet had been unbroken, when, like a funeral wail, the sound of distant voices came up through the lattice, followed by the dismal howling of a hundred dogs.

"Hearken!" she gasped in sudden fear, disengaging herself from my embrace, as, dashing across to the window, she drew the hangings quickly aside, admitting the morning sun. "The *mueddin* have announced the sunrise! Already hast thou tarried too long. It is imperative that thou shouldst fly, lest our plans be thwarted by thine arrest. Fly! Remember what the Korân saith. Whatever is in heaven and earth singeth praise unto Allah; and he is mighty and wise. He is the first and the last, the manifest and the hidden; and he knoweth all things. He is with thee wheresoever thou art; for Allah seeth that which thou doest."

I placed my arms about her and again clasped her to my breast in final embrace, uttering a passionate declaration of love, and drinking her whole soul through her lips as sunlight drinks the dew. Her great beauty intoxicated me; I stood in an invincible torpor as if I had partaken of some strange potion. How long we remained thus I know not, but at length an alarming sound caused us both to listen breathlessly.

Next second the voices of men, loud and deep, greeted our startled ears as the curtains concealing the door by which I had entered stirred, as if some persons were there concealed.

"May Allah have mercy!" gasped the woman I loved, her face blanched to the lips. "The eunuchs are making their first round. Thou art lost—lost. And I am doomed to die!"

Then I knew that a fatality encompassed me.

Chapter Sixteen
A Secret of State

From behind the curtain the dumb slave Ayesha emerged a second later, and, with fear betrayed upon every feature of her dark countenance, motioned me to follow her.

"Fly! Go in peace! Speed upon the wings of haste and save thyself!" Azala urged, in a low whisper, clinging to me for an instant while I kissed her white brow, half covered by its golden sequins. "Fly, and may the One Guide direct thy footsteps in the right path, and guard thee through all perils of thy quest."

"May Allah envelop thee with the cloak of his protection," I said, fervently. "Farewell, O Beloved! I go to seek to penetrate a mystery that none has solved. Having thy blessing, I fear nought. *Slama. Allah iselemeck.*"

As I released her, her eyes became suffused, but with a gesture of fear she pushed me from her gently, and Ayesha, grasping my arm, led me through the alcove, and as I passed from the sight of the woman I loved she murmured a last fond farewell. Then we descended the stairs to the chamber wherein I had gazed into the Prism of Destiny, and passed through the door by which the Arab slaves had entered, just at the moment we heard men's deep voices in Azala's apartment above. Silently we crept out upon the staircase by which my mute guide had taken me to Azala's chamber, and then descending by many intricate ways we at last crossed the garden and entered the Court of the Pages, where Ayesha left me abruptly without word, gesture or sign. Crossing the paved court where figs and oranges grew in great abundance, I entered the Court of the Janissaries. Here some of the *mulazimin* quartered there, surprised at seeing me in the attire of an eunuch, rose to salute me. Impatiently I passed on, acknowledging their salaams with scant courtesy, until I came to the handsome Court of the Grand Vizier. As I passed the statuesque sentries at the gate I heard men conversing in low tones beyond the screen of thick papaya bushes placed before the entrance to afford shadow for the guards. In an instant it occurred to me that if seen by the slaves of Mahaza attired in eunuch's dress some awkward inquiries might be instituted, therefore I concealed myself in the bushes, scarce daring to breathe.

Peering through the foliage to ascertain who was astir so early, I was amazed to recognise that the two men in earnest conversation were none other than my master the Khalifa Abdullah, and Khazneh, the Aga of the Black Eunuchs of the Sultan.

Quite involuntarily I played the part of eavesdropper, for fearing detection and impatient to get out of the Fada to the spot where Azala's camel awaited me, I stood motionless. The words that fell upon my ears amazed me. At first I imagined that I must be dreaming, but quickly I found that the scene I was witnessing was a stern reality.

The Khalifa, plainly dressed in a robe similar to that worn by his body-servants, in order, no doubt, to avoid being recognised by the soldiers and slaves, stood leaning against one of the marble columns supporting the colonnade that ran around three sides of the great court; his brow was heavy and thoughtful, and his dark eyes fixed upon his companion. Khazneh, with arms folded and chin upon his breast, remained in an attitude of deep meditation.

Suddenly he asked in a low, hoarse tone, first glancing round to assure himself that he was not overheard, —

"And in such case, what sayest thou should be my reward?"

"Thou wilt gain wealth and power," the Khalifa answered. "Think, what art thou now? A mere harem slave of thy Sultan. If thou renderest me the assistance I have suggested, thou canst rise to be first in the land."

"Thou, O Khalifa, art above all," the Aga interrupted, as the complacent smile on Abdullah's gross face told him that he was amenable to flattery. But a second later the expression of satisfaction gave place to a keen, crafty look, a glance, the significance of which I knew well, as he said, —

"Behold! Already the sun hath risen, and we must not tarry. The slaves will see us together and suspect. A single word whispered into the ear of thy Lord 'Othman would ruin our plan. Thou must choose now. Art thou ready to adopt my suggestion?"

In hesitation the Aga bit his finger-nails, hitched his silken robe about his shoulders, and gazed steadfastly down at the marble pavement. "Thou hast, as yet, made no definite promise as to the profits I should gain," he muttered.

"Then give ear unto me," said the Khalifa, in a low, earnest tone. "Thou hast admitted that we have both much to gain by the downfall of thy Sultan, therefore we must act together carefully, with perfect trust in one another. My suggestion is that exactly four moons from to-day my fighting-men, to the number of sixteen thousand, shall encamp at various points two days distant, ready to converge upon this city. On thy part, thou wilt invent some grievance against the Sultan to stir up discontent among the guards, Janissaries and slaves, and let the dissatisfaction spread to the army itself. Then, when they are ripe for revolt, an announcement will be made that the Dervishes are already in force at the city gates, and that if they are prepared to live under better conditions, with thyself as ruler under the Khalifa, they must throw down their arms. This they will assuredly do, and my Ansar will enter the city and the Fada as conquerors. They will have orders to kill the Sultan at once, and to secure his daughter Azala, of whose wondrous beauty I have heard much, for my harem. In the meantime, Katsena and Sokoto will be immediately subdued by my horsemen, and before sundown I shall be proclaimed ruler throughout the Empire. Assuredly, I shall not forget thee, and thy gains will be large. This palace, with the whole of the harem and half the treasure it containeth, shall be given unto thee, and thou wilt continue to reside here and rule on my behalf. Under my suzerainty thy power will be absolute, and with the army of the Soudan at thy back thou wilt fear none."

"Thou temptest me, O Khalifa," the Aga said, still undecided to turn traitor to the monarch who reposed in him the utmost confidence. "But even if thou gavest unto me this palace I should not have the means to keep it up. Of a verity I am a poor man, and—"

"Do my bidding and thou shalt be wealthy," Abdullah exclaimed, impatiently. "As Governor of Sokoto thine expenses will come from the Treasury, therefore trouble thyself not upon that score. Stir up the revolt, and take precaution that the life of the Princess Azala is preserved; leave the rest unto me."

"The daughter of the Sultan hath already a lover," Khazneh said suddenly, his words causing my heart to beat so quickly that I could distinctly hear it.

"A lover!" cried the Khalifa. "Who dareth to gaze upon her with thoughts of affection?"

"A spy from thy camp."

"From my camp?" he repeated, puzzled.

"I had intended that he should lose his head, but the Sultan himself pardoned him because he feared the consequence of some strange symbol the spy bore upon his breast."

"Was he the Arab horseman captured at the well of Sabo-n-Gari?" asked the Khalifa, with knit brows, evidently recollecting the description I had given of the attack.

"The same. The Lalla Azala saved his life, and declared to me that she loved him."

"Then I, the Khalifa, have a rival in Zafar, the chief of my body-servants!" my master cried angrily, between his teeth. "I will give orders to-day for his removal."

"Send his head to her as a present," suggested the Aga, with a brutal laugh. "The sight of it will break her spirit."

"Thy lips utter words of wisdom. I will send it to thee, that thou mayest convey it to her."

Thus I stood, hearing my fate being discussed, not daring to move a muscle, for so close was I to the pair, that I could have struck them dead with the keen *jambiyah* I carried in my sash.

"Then it is thine intention to annex Sokoto unto thine already extensive domains," the Aga exclaimed, in a few moments.

The Khalifa nodded an affirmative, adding, "Hesitate no longer, but give thy decision. If thou wilt open the gates of Kano for the admission of my Ansar, thou shalt, as reward, occupy the highest and most lucrative post in the Empire. If not—" And he shrugged his shoulders significantly.

"And if not?" the Aga asked, slowly.

"If not, then every man in Omdurman capable of bearing arms shall come forth unto this thy city, and take it by assault. Then assuredly will little mercy be shown those who have defied the Ruler of the Soudan," and his brow darkened. "The Empire, as thou hast said, is badly governed. Men are appointed to all offices who are unfit, war languishes, thine enemies rejoice, the leaders of thy troops prefer their harems to their camps, and from the cadis the people obtain no justice. Therefore give me the promise of thine assistance, and let us together gather the reins of office in our hands. Thou hast no power now outside the Courts of Enchantment, and no wealth beyond thine emoluments, but it is within thy reach to acquire both wealth and greatness."

"But if, while I sought to alienate the guards and soldiers against the Sultan, my seditious words should be whispered into his ear? Assuredly my head would fall beneath the *doka* of the executioner."

"Fear not," answered the head of the Mahdists. "If thou art willing to carry out my suggestion, I shall make an excuse for remaining as guest of thy Sultan, by continuing the negotiations for the defensive treaty against those dogs of English. At sundown to-night a trusty messenger will leave, bearing orders to my emirs to assemble the troops and speed hither with all haste, and while the Sultan is unsuspecting, his doom will fast approach. What craft cannot effect, gold may perchance accomplish. If thy treasonable practices are detected, then will I intercede for thee, and he cannot act in direct opposition to the entreaty of his guest. But hearken! Some one is astir!"

The patter of bare feet upon the polished pavement broke the silence as intently we listened. A black slave was approaching.

"Come, give me thine answer quickly, and before sundown our written undertakings under seal shall be secretly exchanged."

Khazneh hesitated. Apparently he was distrustful of the Khalifa's true intentions, although the generous reward promised for his services in securing the entry of the Dervishes without opposition was a tempting bait. His fingers toyed nervously with the jewelled hilt of his sword—the keen, curved weapon that had struck off so many fair heads within the brilliant Courts of Enchantment—and again he bit his uneven finger-nails.

"Think! Thou hast much to gain, with naught to lose," urged the Khalifa. "Under me thou wilt occupy the same position as thine Imperial Master. Come, speak; and let us part ere we are remarked."

"I—I will assist thee," the Aga stammered at last, in a low, half-frightened whisper. "At sundown let our secret compact be concluded."

My astute master well knew that the temptation to secure wealth and power would induce the scheming Aga of the Women to become his catspaw. He had not approached his accomplice without thoroughly fathoming his character, and noting his weaknesses. I could detect from his face that from the first he had been confident of success.

"Then upon thee be perfect peace, even until the day of Al-Jassasa," answered the Khalifa, with a sinister smile of satisfaction, and without further speech the two men parted, walking in different directions, and leaving me, excited and apprehensive, to my own reflections.

Chapter Seventeen
Flight

Allah took me into his keeping. I made a solitude and called it peace. Half-an-hour later I succeeded in escaping unrecognised from the Fada, and passing out by the great gate, hurried breathlessly through the slave market, already alive with Arabs, negroes and herds of half-starved slaves, through the Yaalewa quarter, past the Palace of Ghaladima, and down many quaint and narrow streets of square, flat-roofed houses, their walls intensely white against the bright, unclouded blue, with passages from the Korân inscribed over the doors. The great market presented a most animated scene, for business is transacted in Kano before the sun becomes powerful. All the idioms of the Sahara, Soudan and Northern Africa, from the blue Mediterranean and grey Atlantic to Lake Tsad, were to be heard there, and beneath the white turban or red fez were all the different types of negro races—Berber, Songhoi, Bambara, Toucoulem, Malinka, among the blacks; and Foulbes, Moors, Tuaregs, and Tripolitans among the whites. Rows of shops bordered three sides of the market, and the fourth opened upon the Mosque, as if in reminder that honesty and good faith should preside over all its transactions. Sitting surrounded by calabashes and potteries, the women, with neatly-plaited black hair, sold vegetables, milk, manioc, incense, baobab flour, karita, spices, soap and fagots of wood. In the centre of the market were three shops in which were sold the choicer goods—native and European textiles principally, Manchester calicoes and Lyons silks, with salt, kola nuts, slippers, mirrors, pearls, knives, etc. The money-changer was also stationed there, with his black face showing out from between his little mountain of cowries. For native gold (in rings like the money of the Pharaohs) he gave and took hundreds and thousands of the little shells, grinning broadly the while. Further on, amid a perfect babel of tongues, magic roots, gold dust, emeralds, pearls and amber, provisions dried in the sun, hair torn from the heads of dead negresses, old Korâns, gongs, poniards, ancient jewellery, ginkris, flint guns, and amulets, were bought and sold, while everywhere beggars, ragged and dirty, and lepers, rendered hideous by their horrible white ulcers, held forth lean, talon-like hands, crying aloud in the name of the One Allah for alms.

The people who crowded the narrow thoroughfares beyond the market were of every variety of national form—the olive-coloured Arab, the dark Kanouri with his wide nostrils, the tall, stately, black-veiled Tuareg, the small-featured, light and slender ba-Fellenchi, the broad-faced ba-Wangara, the stout, masculine-looking Nupe female, and the comely ba-Haushe woman. But I sped onward, thinking only of the dastardly plot by which the Sultan was to be overthrown, and the woman I loved spirited away to the great harem in far-off Omdurman. Assuredly the register of the actions of the wicked is in Sejjin, the book distinctly written, which cannot be denied as a falsehood.

At first I had felt impelled to seek an audience of the Sultan, but on reflection I saw that such a course would achieve no purpose. Already he had forbidden me to set foot within his Empire, and it was not likely that he would believe my statement if flatly contradicted by both the Khalifa and the villainous Khazneh, as undoubtedly it would be.

I strove to invent some means of acquainting the Sultan 'Othman of his impending doom, but could devise none. As I crossed the Zat Nakhl (Place of Palm Trees), I reflected that my secret assassination would probably be the only result of my exposure of the plot. Four months must elapse ere the Dervishes could reach Kano, therefore I resolved to preserve silence, and go forth to fulfil my promise to Azala to try and elucidate the mystery.

At a little distance outside the Kofa-n-Kura, I found, as she had stated, two camels kneeling, with their bags ready packed, in charge of the dwarf Tiamo, who, when he saw me, ran forward, greeting me effusively, and urging me to hasten, so that we might leave the city ere our absence from the Fada was discovered. This advice I followed, and a few minutes later we were seated on the animals, speeding quickly away over the loose sand, leaving the gigantic white walls of Kano behind.

Once I turned to gaze upon the tower of the Fada that stood out clear and white, knowing that from behind one of those small lattices Azala was watching our departure with anxious, tearful eyes. Raising my hand I waved her a last farewell, then, with face set doggedly towards the west, I rode forward with my queer companion, in quest of the undiscovered spot that had so many times been reflected with such clearness of detail upon the sky.

On over the arid sands we journeyed, pausing not even during the blazing heat of noon, but pursuing our way with rapidity in order to put as great a distance as possible between ourselves and the city by sundown. Instead of taking the caravan route to Kaoura we had turned off in a south-westerly direction over a confused agglomeration of *aghrud*, or high sand-hills, almost impassable, in order to baffle our pursuers in case we were followed.

Just before sundown we paused at a spot where the light shadows of the palms, tamarisk, alfa and mimosa rested on the dry, parched thirst-land, and decided to halt for the night. Unloading and tethering our camels, I knelt to my two-bow prayer and repeated my *dua*, after which the dwarf became communicative. He was a pagan and believed not in Allah, or the Prophet. During the day he had apparently been too much concerned regarding my personal safety to speak much, but now we ate and took our *Cayf* in the blue and purple haze, sitting silent and still, listening to the monotonous melody of the oasis, the soft evening breeze wandering through the brilliant sky and tufted trees with a voice of melancholy meaning, lounging in pleasant languor and dreamy tranquillity. Briefly my impish companion told me how his mistress had entrusted him with the arrangements for our journey, and had given him instructions to accompany me as servant.

I smoked my *shisha* (travelling pipe), listening to the croaking voice of this strange being with his large, ugly head and small body, in whom Azala reposed such confidence; then I questioned him regarding his past. It always pleased him if I addressed him by the soubriquet El-Sadic that Azala had bestowed upon him. His eyes grew brighter, his grin more hideous, and he fingered his numberless heathen amulets as he related to me the exciting story of how he had been captured by Arab slave-raiders at his home in the forest of Kar, beside the Serbeouel river in Baguirmi, and taken to Kano, where he was purchased by the Grand Vizier, and afterwards given to the Lalla Azala. As he spoke the mouth of this human monstrosity widened, displaying a hideous row of teeth, and this, combined with his croaking voice, rendered him a weird and altogether extraordinary companion. Yet his strength seemed almost double mine, for he had unloaded the camels without an effort, carrying with perfect ease packages that would have made me pant.

Sitting together on the mat we had spread, watching the sun sinking on the misty horizon, and the bright crescent moon slowly rising, I asked him whether he was aware of the nature of my quest.

"The Lalla Azala hath explained to me, O master, that thou seekest the Rock of the Great Sin," he answered.

"What knowest thou of the rock?" I inquired.

"Only that which hath been related by the story-tellers," he answered. "As in Kano, so we away on the Serbeouel river believe in its existence, though none has discovered its whereabouts. By my people, the negroes of Baguirmi, it is believed to be the entrance to the sacred land to which those who die valiantly in battle are transported, while those who betray cowardice are thrown into the Lake of the Accursed, wherein dwell crocodiles of great size, water-snakes who live on human flesh, and all kinds of venomous reptiles. The story-tellers of our tribe say that the reason none has found it is because there is emitted, from the Lake of the Accursed, vapours so deadly as to prevent any one from approaching the rock sufficiently near to distinguish its outline. It is the abode of the Death-god."

"Art thou not afraid to accompany me in this search?" I asked, knowing how superstitious are the negroes.

"It is the Lalla's will," he answered, simply. "Thou, an Arab from the North and my lady's friend, art seeking to deliver her from bondage, therefore where thou goest, there also will I bear thee company."

"Bravely spoken," I said, and after a pause told him of the conspiracy that had been formed against the Sultan. With breathless interest he listened while I related how I had discovered its existence; then, when I had finished, he half rose, saying, —

"But the Lalla shall never grace the harem of the cruel, brutal Khalifa. I myself will save her."

"I cannot give her warning, for I dare not again approach her," I pointed out, with sorrow.

"Shall I go back and tell her, while thou remainest here until my return?" he suggested.

"No," I answered, on reflection. "Silence is best at present. For four months, at least, Kano is safe. If the Sultan is warned within that time, his enemies may be overthrown."

"The dastardly plot of the abuser of the salt, the vile offspring of Shimr, shall be thwarted," he cried, fiercely. "The heads of its originators shall rot upon the city gate, and none shall enter the presence of the Lalla, with whose beauty none can compare."

"Act not rashly," I said. "We know the secret of the conspirators, therefore we may be able to thwart them so neatly that they fall victims to their own plot. Let us act with care and discretion, that the Empire may be saved from falling into the hands of the wild-haired fanatics of Omdurman, who, although my comrades-in-arms, are not my tribesmen."

"Be it even as thou commandest," he answered. "My life is equally at thy service to secure the undoing of the traitor, as for the diligent search we are about to make for the Rock of the Great Sin," and the claw-like fingers of the dwarf slowly grasped his pipe-stem, as he smoked on thoughtfully.

In the deep silence of the desert, under the pale light of the moon, that rose from the direction of the city from which we were fleeing, I sat, plunged in reverie, wondering whether my search would prove successful. My head ached, my lips were parched, and I felt spent with long travel, therefore, scooping a hole in the sand, I threw myself down to snatch a few hours' repose, as we had decided to be moving again before sunrise.

Sleep must have come to my eyes quickly, for I was suddenly awakened by the dwarf shaking me, and saying in a low whisper, as he placed his quick ear to the sand, —

"Hearken! Canst thou not hear the thud of horses' hoofs? Thine absence hath been detected, and we are pursued!"

And, as I strained my ears, I could distinctly detect the regular, monotonous thud of a horse urged across the desert at terrific pace; and, as I knelt upon the sand, I grasped the rifle that I had found packed on the camel, and held it loaded in readiness—prepared to defend myself, an example which Tiamo immediately followed. In the desert no law is recognised but that of the strong arm and the keen blade.

Chapter Eighteen
The Alarm

Rapidly the solitary horseman drew near, galloping as if for life. Being alone, it seemed probable that he had been sent forward by our pursuers to endeavour to obtain traces of us, and as the fleet Arab steed approached, Tiamo, stretched upon the ground, took careful and deliberate aim, ready to fire as soon as he approached within range.

Our camels lazily raised their heads to survey the new-comer, stirred uneasily as if they had presage of danger, and as on the alert we awaited the approach of the mysterious rider, we discerned to our dismay that he wore a white burnouse.

"Behold!" whispered the dwarf, "it is one of our Zamfara, who always act as scouts! He must die if we intend to escape."

It seemed that he had not discovered us, but was on his way to the well to water his horse, therefore I answered, —

"Take not his life unless the circumstances demand extreme measures. At least let him approach and have speech with us ere thou firest."

"Conquest lieth with those who strike the first blow," he replied, a sinister grin upon his ugly visage as again he covered the approaching figure with his rifle and carefully took aim. At that moment, however, the galloping *ngirma* emerged into the moonlight, revealing a strange awkwardness in its white-robed rider's manner that struck me as remarkable, and as it dashed forward and became more distinct, the truth flashed upon me.

"By my beard!" I cried aloud, knocking, with sudden impulse, the rifle from Tiamo's hand. "By my beard! It's a woman!"

The rifle exploded, but the bullet went wide. The rider, startled at the shot, and thinking she had been fired at, pulled her horse instantly upon its haunches, and sat peering in our direction, motionless, in fear.

"Advance, and fear not, O friend!" I shouted to her, rising to my feet, but my peaceful declarations had to be thrice-repeated ere she summoned courage to move forward to us, the bridle trembling in her hands. On approaching, however, she slipped quickly from the saddle of the foam-flecked animal, and tearing her haick from her face, bounded over the sand towards us.

Her appearance struck us speechless with amazement.

The mysterious rider whom we had feared, and who had so very narrowly escaped death by our hand, was Ayesha, the dumb slave of Azala.

With one accord we both eagerly inquired the object of her wild ride in the lonely desert so far from Kano at that hour, but she merely shook her head indicative of her inability to reply, and pressed her brown hand to her side, being compelled to halt for a moment to recover breath. In the moonlight we could see the look of fear and excitement in her dark eyes, with their kohl-marked brows, but although she gesticulated wildly, we failed to catch her meaning.

"Her mouth refuseth to utter sound," observed the dwarf. "Yet she seemeth to have followed us with some important object. No halt hath she made since leaving Kano, judging by the dust about her and the spent condition of her horse, which, by the way, belongeth to the Aga of the Janissaries, and one of the fleetest that the Sultan possesseth."

He spoke rapidly in Arabic, and the slave, unacquainted with any but her native Hausa tongue, gazed in embarrassment from Tiamo's face to mine.

"Cannot she write?" I asked.

"Alas! no," answered my hideous little companion. "So carefully hath she studied the Lalla that she anticipated her wishes by the looks in her eyes."

While thus in conversation, wondering how we could obtain the truth from her, she rushed towards her horse, and seizing its bridle, brought it towards us. Then, with a smile of triumph upon her brown, wrinkled face, she inserted her thin hand beneath the leather of the saddle, and produced therefrom a letter folded small, and addressed in Arabic to myself.

The sprawly characters I recognised instantly as Azala's, and on tearing it open I found it bore the seal of her ancient signet-ring, shaped like an Egyptian scarab. Tiamo El-Sadic, anticipating my requirements, quickly kindled a piece of paper, and by its uncertain light I was enabled to decipher the hasty message from the woman I loved, which read as follows:—

"Fly instantly to the city of Sokoto, O Zafar, my Beloved. Thine enemies seek thy life, and are already in search of thee. Three hours after I had watched thy departure from my lattice my father came unto me, and although I denied thy visit

in order to shield thee, it was apparent that thou hast been betrayed, for he is aware of thy return. As thou hast truly said, he feareth thee because thou bearest the Mark of the Asps, for he compelled me to uncover the mark I bear, so that he might gaze upon it and compare it with thine. Before me upon the Korân he hath sworn that thou shalt die. Already two troops of one hundred horsemen each have left the Kofa-n-Kura and have scattered over the desert in search of thee. Fly! Halt not, for my sake, so that thou reachest the city of Sokoto ere news of the Sultan's wrath can be conveyed thither. When thou reachest the city, seek at once the dyer Mohammed el-Arewa, who liveth in the Gazubi quarter, and deliver unto him the message Ayesha beareth thee. He will conduct thee into the Mountains of Kambari, where thou canst escape the vigilance of spies and continue thy journey unmolested. Halt not, but speed on, for thine enemies are closely following thy camels tracks. My haste causeth my hand to tremble, but Ayesha hath confidence in overtaking thee. Fly, and may Allah favour thee, and protect thee with the invulnerable shield of his blessing. Peace."

Looking into the face of the dark-eyed slave who had so devotedly served her mistress, and undertaken a journey that few women could have accomplished, I stretched forth my hand for the second letter, which she gave me. It bore Azala's seal, and was addressed to Mohammed el-Arewa.

"Lift, O master, from thy servant's heart, the anxiety oppressing it, by telling him what news the mute hath brought," Tiamo said.

"We must travel at once to Sokoto," I answered, briefly. "Let us replace the camels' packs, for sleep must not come again to our eyes ere we enter the city."

"Do our enemies pursue us?" he inquired, eagerly.

"Yes. To reach Sokoto, and gain the assistance of one Mohammed el-Arewa, is our only chance of escape."

"Let us set forth," he said promptly, walking towards where the camels were kneeling. Then turning, he added, "Hast thou forgotten thou still wearest the silk robe of a eunuch? Assuredly it will attract the eyes of all men. Remove it and attire thyself in these," and rummaging in one of the camels' packs, he produced the white haick and burnouse of an Arab, together with the rope of brown twisted camel's hair to wind around the head, so as to keep the haick in place.

While he loaded our camels I carried out his suggestion, quickly transforming myself from a eunuch of the Sultan of Sokoto to a plain wanderer of the desert. With Ayesha we could only converse by gesticulation, rendering her thanks for conveying the message unto us.

Having no writing materials, I cut from my camel's trappings a piece of soft goatskin, and with the point of a knife traced roughly in Arabic the words,—

"*Verily a plot is on foot to encompass the overthrow of thy dynasty. Warn thy father, the Sultan, of the conspiracy between the Khalifa Abdullah and his Grand Eunuch Khazneh. This message Ayesha beareth from thy friend, Zafar.*"

On giving it to the slave to convey to her mistress, she concealed it next her tattooed breast. From our little store we gave her some dates, and as she motioned her intention of remaining to rest, and returning to Kano at dawn, we tethered her horse for her. Then, mounting our camels, we gave her "peace," and rode out again upon the silent, boundless plain.

The moon no longer shed her light; an intense darkness had fallen—that darkness which is invariably precursory of the sandstorm. Without even a star by which to guide ourselves we trusted that by good fortune we were travelling in the right direction. The dwarf, who had once before been over the ground, was searching for a landmark, and, to our mutual satisfaction, half-an-hour after dawn he discovered it.

"Lo!" he cried excitedly, shouting back to me and pointing to where, far away on the grey, misty horizon, a large hill appeared. "We are not mistaken, for we have struck the caravan route. Yonder is the Rock of Mikia, and behind it, the village of Dsafe. Before noon we shall enter the valley through which windeth a river, and continuing along its bank, we shall be within the gate of Sokoto ere it closeth at sunset."

Chapter Nineteen
Mohammed El-Arewa

After halting to refresh ourselves, during which time I snatched a few moments to perform my *sujdah,* we remounted, and through the whole day, regardless of the sun's fiery rays, which struck down upon us like tongues of fire, we pushed forward over a rough, stony wilderness, devoid of herbage or any living thing except the great, grey vultures circling above with ominous persistency.

Throughout the day, my ugly little negro companion continually fingered his strange amulets, uttering curious pagan incantations in his own tongue, while to myself I repeated the "Kul-ya-ayyuha 'l-Kafiruna," and the "Kul-Huw' Allah," more than once inclined to upbraid my friend as an infidel. But, on reflection, I saw that any words of reproach would pain him to no purpose, therefore I held my peace. His face, black as polished ebony, seemed to grow increasingly ugly as he became more wearied; when he smiled his mouth stretched from ear to ear, and the craning of his neck, as he swayed with the undulating motion of his camel, gave him a weird, grotesque appearance, even in the brilliant glare of noon. The beads, trinkets, pieces of lizard skin, and mysterious scraps of wood and stone strung around his neck, he constantly caressed, while twice he suddenly dismounted, and holding his hands aloft, frisked like an ape, yelling at the sun as if he had taken leave of his senses.

Notwithstanding his extreme ugliness and his strange actions, I nevertheless grew to like him, for he seemed genuinely devoted to me, as a slave should be to his master.

Two hours after high noon, when the sun was beginning to veer round and shine directly into our faces, we entered the Wady al-Ward (the Vale of Flowers) the dwarf had mentioned. Beside the small river—scarcely more than a brook—we journeyed over ground thickly covered with herbage and flowers. For a few minutes we allowed our camels to browse, then urged them on, remembering it was imperative that we should arrive at Sokoto before the gate closed for the night. The shadow cast by the rocks, the cool rippling of the water, and the fertility of the country we appreciated after the arid, sun-baked wilderness. But as we journeyed on we found grim relics of an attack which had evidently been made some months before upon a caravan, for fresh, green garlands of ropeweed and creepers had festooned decayed skulls, and entwined about the bleaching bones of arms and legs, now and then blossoming into brilliant clusters of scarlet or blue flowers.

Through the valleys we wound for many hours, while the sky changed from blue to gold, and from gold to crimson, until at last the sun slowly sank before us with that gorgeous flood of colour only to be witnessed in Central Africa, and the low hills, bristling with mimosa and doum palms, assumed singular forms and uncouth dimensions in the twilight mirage.

In the rapidly-falling gloom our eyes were at last gladdened by the sight of the tall minarets of Sokoto, but the tall, bronzed guards at the city gate are ever wary, and a strange scene was enacted. It appeared that with the people of Sokoto the measures formerly taken to guard against surprise are now observed as a matter of form and etiquette. Hence, as we approached the gate the guards crouched, and throwing their litham over the lower part of their faces in Tuareg fashion, grasped the inseparable spear in the right and the shangermangor in their left hand. This action caused us considerable anxiety, but after these preliminaries they began to inquire our names and places of abode, afterwards giving us "peace," and allowing us to proceed. For a few minutes we halted to gossip, so as not to appear in undue haste, and just as the call for evening prayer was sounding and the guards were beating the great drum to announce the closing of the gate, we passed into the spacious market, wherein a caravan of many camels were taking their ease preparatory to starting for Timbuktu on the morrow.

Riding on through the city—the ancient and now discarded capital of the Sultan 'Othman's empire—we found it very extensive, and although the character of the houses was much more primitive than those of Moorish type in Kano, yet there was manifested everywhere the comfortable, pleasant life led by the inhabitants. Each courtyard was fenced with a "derne" of tall reeds, excluding, to a certain degree, the eyes of the passer-by without securing to the interior absolute secrecy; and each house had, near its entrance, the cool, shady "runfa" or place for the reception of strangers or the transaction of business, with a "shibki" roof, and the whole dwelling shaded by spreading trees.

The people, although of cheerful temperament, appeared more simple in their dress than in Kano. The men wore a wide shirt and trousers of dark colour, with a light cap of cotton cloth, while the female population affected a large cotton cloth of dark blue fastened under or above the breast, their only ornaments being strings of glass beads worn around the neck. Proud, ignorant, bigoted and insolent, the people of Sokoto are all owners of cattle, camels, horses and slaves. These latter, along with the women, generally cultivate some fields of dhurra, or corn, sufficient for their wants. The Arab, in Sokoto, would consider it a disgrace to practice any manual labour. He is essentially a hunter, a robber and a warrior, and, after caring for his cattle, devotes all his energies to slave-hunting and war. The lower classes are simply a rabble of filth, petty mendicancy, gaol-bird physiognomy and cringing hypocrisy.

Passing through several markets crowded by chattering throngs, and up a number of close streets where idle men and women were lounging, and where the heat from the stones reflected into one's face, we at last found the *marina*, or dyeing place, near the city wall. It consisted of a raised platform of clay with a number of holes or pits in which the mixture of indigo was prepared, and the cloths were placed for a certain length of time, according to the colour it was desired they should assume. It was beside one of these holes, working by the light of a rude torch, his arms immersed in the dark blue dye, that we found the Arab we sought.

As we gave him "peace" he rose to his feet with dignity, and dried his stained hands. He was about sixty, tall, with kindly, sharp-cut features, and a long, sweeping beard flecked with grey. Taking Azala's letter, he opened it, read it carefully twice, caressed his patriarchal beard, and placed the paper in a pocket beneath his burnouse. Then turning, he said,—

"Upon thee be perfect peace, O friends. Welcome to the poor hospitality of the roof of Mohammed el-Arewa. Take thine ease to-night, for ere the sun riseth over the blue hills of Salame, we must set forth if thou wouldst escape those who seek thy destruction." Then, after blowing out his torch, he addressed me, saying, "Art thou the friend of the Lalla Azala?"

"She is my friend," I answered, with promptitude.

"Discretion sealeth thy lips," he observed, laughing. "Well, I, too, loved once at thine age. If thou art, as I suspect, the lover of the beauteous Azala, of a verity thou hast chosen well. Happy the man who basketh in the rose-garden of her smiles. To her I owe the freedom of my only child, my daughter, who, captured by the Tuaregs, was sold to the accursed Grand Vizier Mahaza—may Allah burn his vitals!—and only by the intercession of the Lalla was she released. I am Azala Fathma's devoted slave, to do as she commandeth," adding in a lower tone, as if to himself, "Women swallow at one mouthful the lie that flattereth, and drink drop by drop the truth that is bitter. But the Lalla Azala careth not for flattery, and seeketh only to do good. She is a pearl among women."

The Eye of Istar | 113

Then accompanying him to his house close to the principal gate, we were treated as honoured visitors. A guest-dish, sweet as the dates of Al-jauf, was prepared for us, and we ate *fara*, or roasted locusts seasoned with cheese, *tuwo-n-magaria*, or bread made from the fruit of the magaria tree, roasted fowl and dates, washed down with copious draughts of *giya* made of sorghum. After our meal, eight negro girls came forth and gratified our ears with a performance on various instruments. There was the *gauga*, very much like our own Arab *derbouka*, only larger, the long wind instrument, or *pampamnie*, a shorter one like a flute, called the *elgaita*, the double tambourine called the *kalango*, the *koso*, the *jojo*, or small derbouka, and the *kafo*, or small horn, which in unison created an ear-splitting tumult impossible to adequately describe.

The negresses blew, thumped and grinned as if their lives depended upon the amount of sound they obtained from their various instruments, but, worn out by the forced march, I heeded not their well-meant efforts to entertain, and actually fell into a heavy slumber with the mouth-piece of the pipe my host had thoughtfully provided for me still between my lips.

In the night, awakened suddenly by the loud blowing of a horn and frantic shouting, I lay and listened. As it continued I got up and aroused Tiamo, who slept near. For some minutes we strained our ears to ascertain the cause of the hubbub, apparently at the city gate, when suddenly our host burst into the apartment panting.

"Alas!" he cried, in a hoarse whisper. "The soldiers of the Sultan have arrived. Listen!"

The noise continued. Armed men were battering on the great gate that closed at night-fall and never opened till dawn, except to admit an Imperial messenger. We could distinctly hear their voices demanding admittance in the name of the Sultan.

"Already have I bribed the guards of the Kofa with twenty pieces of silver. When questioned, they will deny thine entrance here," the old dyer exclaimed in reassuring tones, as at the same moment there fell upon our ears the answering voices of the sleepy guards, urging them to be patient while the gate was unbarred.

Tiamo and I exchanged uneasy and significant glances in the dim light shed by a hanging lamp of brass.

"Suppose they determine to search for us," the dwarf suggested, in alarm.

"The assurance of the guards will throw them off our scent, and at dawn they will rest after their long journey. Then will the gate be opened, and we shall be enabled to escape. Take thine ease in peace, for of a verity, the way will be long ere thou canst again rest."

And hastily raising the curtain that hung before the arched door, he disappeared.

Feeling myself safe beneath the hospitable roof of one who owed to Azala a deep debt of gratitude, I threw myself again upon my divan, and soon dreamed of the beautiful woman whose countenance fascinated me, and whose glorious hair held me entangled in its silky web. How long I dreamed I cannot tell, for again I was awakened, this time by the ugly dwarf shaking me by the shoulder.

"Rise, O master," cried El-Sadic, in alarm. "We are discovered! Already the soldiers of the Sultan have entered the house!"

As, half dazed, I stood rubbing my eyes in wonderment, Mohammed el-Arewa burst in upon us, gasping in a low tone,—

"Gather thy belongings quickly, and follow me. It is thine only chance."

In less time than it occupies to relate, we snatched up our articles of dress, and hurried after him through several doors, until he came to a double one, whereat was seated a black slave. As we passed quickly through this, the odour of fragrant perfumes greeted our nostrils, and, in the semi-darkness, there was the *frou-frou* of silk, and the sound of hasty, shuffling feet. A second later, we found ourselves in a small apartment, lit more brightly than the others, tastefully decorated in green and gold, and containing many priceless Arab rugs and soft divans.

"Rest here undisturbed," he said, waving his hands in the direction of the inviting-looking lounges, around which were scattered traces of women's occupation. "Within the apartments sacred to my women they will not search for thee. Though I commit an offence against our law, thou art safe in this, my harem. I will shield thee, even with mine own life, for the sake of the Lalla Azala, upon whom may Allah ever shower his blessings! Rest, then, while I go and complete the preparations for our flight."

"We thank thee, O father!" I answered, fervently. "May thy face be ever brightened by the sun of Allah's favour!"

But he was already out of hearing, so suddenly did he leave us.

Within a quarter of an hour, sounds of a loud and fierce altercation reaching us, caused us to stand rigid and silent. So rapidly were the words spoken in the Hausa tongue, that many of them were to me unintelligible, but, glancing at the dwarf, I noticed that his brow was contracted. His eyes glittered with a keen, murderous expression that I had never seen before, as, with unsheathed knife in hand, he stood near the doorway of the harem on the alert, determined not to be taken without a struggle, and to sell his life dearly.

The curtain on the opposite side of our place of concealment stirred, and a fair face peered forth inquisitively, listening as attentively as ourselves, to the heated argument outside. Her great, fathomless eyes were surmounted by two delicately-pencilled arches, and her black, glossy hair fell down her neck, covering her cheeks with its warm shadows.

With a suddenness that startled us, a deep voice, raised louder than the others, expressed a conviction that we were hidden there, and declared his intention of making a thorough search, whereupon approaching footsteps sounded on the paving; the young woman withdrew her head with a slight scream, realising that her privacy was to be intruded upon, and Tiamo and I stood together, dismayed at our base betrayal by the keepers of the city gate.

It was an exciting moment. In desperation, I drew my two-edged *jambiyah*—determined to fight desperately, rather than fall alive into the hands of the Sultan's torturers.

Chapter Twenty
The Father of the Blue Hand

As with bated breath we listened, Mohammed, upon whom Tiamo had bestowed the sobriquet of "The Father of the Blue Hand," spoke in Arabic, denying in clear, indignant tones that any stranger had found succour beneath his roof, and expressing his readiness to assist his Majesty the Sultan in arresting the rascally Dervish spy.

"Proceed no further," he cried, evidently barring their way resolutely. "Lend me thine ears. Though a worker at the dye-pots I have, by diligence and integrity, amassed riches, and am honoured among the men of Sokoto. Desecrate not the quarters of my wives by intruding thy presence upon them. If thou thinkest that I lie when I tell thee that no stranger hath eaten salt with me, ask of the Governor, of the Cadi, of the Hadj Al-Wali, chief imam, whether untruths fall from my lips. By my beard! thou art mistaken. Even though thou art fighting-men of the Sultan 'Othman—whom may Allah enrich and guide to just actions!—his Majesty would never suffer thee to penetrate into his servant's harem."

"He lieth! He lieth!" they all cried, loudly. "The spy came hither, accompanied by a slave of small stature. Own it, or thy lying tongue shall be cut out."

And one of the men added, "His Majesty hath given us orders to bring unto him the head of the Dervish from Omdurman—whom may Allah cast into the pit Al-Hawiyat!—but thine own hoary head will do as well," whereat the others, with one accord, jeered at our protector.

The declaration of my pursuers caused my heart to sink. To be decapitated as a spy was as deplorable an end as to starve to death in the desert. But there was no escape; I resigned myself to the will of Allah.

The altercation increased, Mohammed being assailed with a thousand maledictions, while my ugly companion and myself held our peace in fear and trembling. Although the soldiers alternately threatened and cajoled for a considerable time none entered the apartment wherein we stood, yet our discovery seemed imminent, and looking around for means of escape we could detect none.

Suddenly, however, there was a shuffling of feet upon the flags, and a voice, loud in authority, cried,—

"Back, O men-at-arms! What meanest this? Let not thy feet desecrate the mats of Mohammed el-Arewa's harem, for of a verity he is honest and loyal, a trusty servant of our Imperial Master. By my beard! thy Korân giveth thee no right to intrude upon woman's domestic privacy. Back, I command thee. Back!"

"Who art thou, son of *sebel*, who vouchest for this dyer's loyalty, and darest to give orders unto the emissaries of his Majesty?" asked one of the armed men, evidently their leader.

"My name," cried the new-comer, "my name is Shukri Aga. I am Governor of Sokoto."

Dead silence followed. The men mumbled together in an undertone, while our friend and protector briefly explained the position of affairs, laying stress on the fact that the soldiers had threatened to strike off his head. With one accord the men fell upon their knees before the representative of their Sultan, beseeching forgiveness, declaring that they had been misinformed, and that they had felt assured from the first that a devout man such as our host, would never harbour a dangerous spy.

But the Governor was inexorable. Irritated by the insolent manner in which his right to interfere had been questioned, he turned upon them angrily, saying—

"Get thee gone instantly. To-morrow the cadi shall curb thine excess of zeal, and peradventure a taste of the bastinado will cause thee to remember that a man's harem is sacred. Begone!"

Receding footsteps sounded as the soldiers of the Sultan, trembling and crestfallen, having evoked the wrath of a Governor whose harshness was notorious, filed out without a murmur. Then I thanked Allah for my deliverance, while my pagan companion grinned with satisfaction from ear to ear. The Governor crossed the patio with our host, and remained with him drinking coffee and smoking for a full half-hour, when he departed, and Mohammed hastened to reassure us, exclaiming piously, "*Inshallah bukra*" (Please God, to-morrow), afterwards leaving us in order to conclude his arrangements for our journey.

By what means he succeeded in again silencing the tongues of the two watchmen at the city gate, I know not, nevertheless, when the moon was setting, and the dying moonlight and the first pallor of dawn were mingled in a ghastly half-light, the ponderous gate creaked upon its hinges, and I passed out, accompanied by the dwarf and the dyer. We fled straight on, leaving our path to fate.

As I rode my *meheri* rapidly over the grey, sandy plain, under a sky colourless and cheerless, Mohammed showered upon me a profusion of the finest compliments, pronounced in the most refined and sweet accent of which the Hausa tongue is capable, while I, finding myself again in the desert, after so narrowly escaping my enemies, thanked him sincerely for his strenuous and devoted efforts on our behalf.

"I owe much to the Lalla Azala—whom may Allah refresh with the abundant showers of his blessings—and her friend is likewise mine," he said.

He was showily and picturesquely dressed in a green and white striped robe, wide trousers of a speckled pattern and colour, like the plumage of a Guinea-fowl, with an embroidery of green silk in the front of the legs. Over this he wore a crimson burnouse, while around his fez a red and white turban was wound crosswise in neat and careful manner. A gun was slung over his shoulder by means of thick hangers of red silk ornamented with enormous tassels, and his hands and arms were still stained a deep blue. His mount was a splendid camel, the head and neck of which was fancifully ornamented with a profusion of tassels, bells, and little leathern pockets containing charms.

"The Lalla Azala desireth me to conduct thee south to the border of the land of Al-Islâm, so that thou canst escape thine enemies," he said, when we turned our backs upon the great, sun-whitened walls of the ancient capital of Sokoto. "We must therefore cross the desert and gain the forest with all speed, for doubtless the plains are being scoured by hawk-eyed horsemen, who will not spare thee, now that a price hath been set upon thine head." Then, raising his hand before him, westward, towards the dark, low range of distant hills, he added, "Yonder are the Goulbi-n-Kebbi, while to the left thou seest the caravan route that leadeth to Gando. To venture within towns or villages would be unsafe, therefore we must cross the hills and seek the forest of Tebkis beyond."

"Knowest thou the routes in the forest?" I asked.

"Yes, I learned them years ago when, in my youth, I accompanied the ivory-traders from Agadez far south, even unto the banks of the mighty Congo."

"And the route we are following. Whither will it lead us?"

"To the Niger, where dwell the pagans," he answered. "At the river bank I shall leave thee to return to my home."

"In thy wanderings in the south thou hast, I suppose, witnessed many strange things," I said, knowing the long, tedious journeys performed by ivory caravans.

"For ten weary years I travelled through desert and forest," he answered, "and many strange peoples and strange countries of the pagans have mine eyes beheld."

"Yet, during thy travels, hast thou never discovered the Rock of the Great Sin of which the wise men tell?" I asked. It was evident Azala had not disclosed to him the object of my quest, therefore I was determined to ascertain what he knew regarding the strange legend.

The old man laughed, shaking his head.

"Mine eyes have never been gladdened by its sight, although many are assured that the rock actually existeth, and hideth some wondrous marvel. In twenty lands the conviction is current that the Rock of the Great Sin is more than imaginary. That it existeth, though none can tell where, I have with mine own ears heard from the negroes on the Dua river, as well as those who live in the forests of far Buraka. In Dahomey, in Yorouba, in Foumbina, in the country of Samory, in the desert of the Daza, and in the great swamps of Zoulou beyond Lake Tsad, the same popular conviction existeth as firmly as among our own people. The pagans, while believing as implicitly as we of Al-Islâm that the rock is unapproachable, are also imbued with an idea that the very air in its vicinity is poisonous, and to this attribute the fact that nobody has been able to approach sufficiently near to take observations. In Gourma the negroes declare that the rock is by night and day enveloped in a dense, black smoke which veileth it from all human eyes, for their fire-god resideth there and hideth himself in its wondrous fastnesses. The Bedouins of the Digguera entertain a firm-rooted conviction that the river Al-Cawthar and the paradise of those who fall valiantly in battle lieth beyond the mystic rock; the Bazou of the Marpa Mountains, on the other hand, maintain that the rock is the centre of the earth, that it is hollow, and that those who betray their friends, or who attack their blood-brothers, go therein to dwell in fearful torment, while the Kanouri and the Tuaregs declare it to be the abode of all the prophets, martyrs and saints of Al-Islâm, who, though believed to be dead have been transported thither unseen. They say the faces of the holy men are blooming, their eyes bright, and blood would issue from their bodies if wounded, and further, that the Angel Israfil watcheth over them, ready to sound the great trumpet on the last day. These, and hundreds of such quaint beliefs have been related to me by negroes, wise men and story-tellers in the course of my wanderings, but the Rock of the Great Sin itself no man hath ever set eyes upon, and I should regard as a maniac any person who went forth expecting to discover it."

"Why? Are there not many regions still unknown to men?" I asked.

"Truly, but our perspicuous Book telleth us that what Allah hath hidden man should not seek," he answered, piously. "For centuries many have, out of curiosity, sought the strange rock which pagans believe to the abode of their gods, and some sects of Al-Islâm assert is the dwelling-place of the mighty dead, but none has discovered it. It is Allah's will that mortal eyes shall never rest upon it, therefore bad fortune and violent death overtake those who defy the divine wrath and attempt to penetrate the mystery."

"Always?"

"Always," the old man answered, with solemnity. "Upon the inquisitive, Allah, to whom the knowledge belongeth, setteth the mark of his displeasure with the two-edged sword of Death."

Chapter Twenty One
In the Wilderness

On over the stony hills called the Goulbi-n-Kebbi, where around us stretched, as far as our wearied eyes could penetrate, a trackless waste of yellow, sunlit sand; on across a desert peopled only with echoes, a wilderness where there was nothing but He, and where the hot, violent wind sent blinding clouds of dust into our faces at every step of our beasts; on over the rough rocks, where a little stunted herbage struggled for an existence, we pressed forward, scarcely halting throughout the blazing, breathless day.

Inured as I was to the baking heat and many hardships of desert life, I nevertheless found this journey terribly fatiguing. But Tiamo and I were flying for our lives. To escape south into the unknown Negro-land of Central Africa, beyond the territory of the Sultan 'Othman, was our object, therefore neither of us complained of the pace at which our solemn-faced guide conducted us.

At a small oasis, where we found an encampment of Salameat Arabs, we exchanged our camels for asses, and when the sun sank before us three days later we entered the forest of Tebkis by a track which led due south in serpentine wanderings, and compelled us to proceed in single file. Several times old Mohammed drew my attention to the traces of elephants. We had now passed beyond the boundary of the Sultan's Empire, and had at last entered the little-known Land of the Pagans. As we pushed forward the forest became more dense, but the trees with golden shafts of light glinting through the foliage, cast cool shadows, for which we were thankful. Still we travelled on, until, just as it was time for prayers, we reached the site of what had apparently years ago been a large town.

"There are sad recollections connected with this spot," Mohammed said, in answer to my inquiries. "In my early youth the town of Kousara, which stood here, was an important place, and to it Ibrahim, Sultan of Sokoto, the predecessor of our present ruler, retired after his palace in Sokoto had been sacked by Magajin Haddedu, King of Katsena, which at that time was an independent state. From here he waged unrelenting but unsuccessful war against the bloody-minded enemies of Al-Islâm, and once, indeed, the troops of Haddedu were driven out of the city of Sokoto; but they soon returned with fresh zeal and with a fresh force of fighting-men, and the Sultan Ibrahim was expelled from his ancient capital for ever. Then commenced a campaign against him, in this, his forest retreat, and after several battles this town of Kousara was taken, ransacked and burnt."

A solitary colossal baobab, raising its huge, leafless, smoke-blackened frame from the prickly underwood which thickly overgrew the locality, pointed out the market-place, once teeming with life, a half-charred monument of a fierce and desperate struggle for religious and political independence. But in order to get away from this neighbourhood, so full of melancholy associations, Mohammed, cursing and execrating the memory of Haddedu, pushed forward until we came to a large granitic mass projecting from the ground, which my Arab companion called Korrematse, and stated was once a place of worship of the pagans. Here we dismounted and spread our mats for the *maghrib*, afterwards encamping at the wild, deserted spot until dawn, when we moved off still southward, three hours later obtaining our first glimpse of the broad Niger, glittering in the bright morning sunlight.

At the river bank it became a question for me to decide in which direction I should travel upon my strange quest—the nature of which I had been careful not to impart to Mohammed—and at length, knowing that in the north Gando, Borgu and even the fetish city of Nikki had been well explored by traders of my own race, I decided to continue southward, following the river as far as possible, and then striking in the direction of the sunrise across the unexplored regions in search of any information that would lead me to the spot where was promised an elucidation of the indelible mark I bore, and of a mystery which had puzzled the wise men of Al-Islâm for centuries.

After much parleying and considerable persuasion, Mohammed decided to accompany us through the country of the Nupes, therefore we moved along the river bank through swamps of giant mangroves, those weird trees with gaunt grotesque roots exposed in mid-air that seemed to spend their leisure in forming themselves into living conundrums. To the medley of unsightly tree-forms the contrast of the bank of forest which bordered the river-side when the mangrove swamps were past proved a welcome and pleasing contrast.

Proceeding with difficulty along a track made by the natives, we found the fringe of forest exquisite both in colouring and form. In colouring, because mingled with every tint of green were masses of scarlet, yellow and purple blossoms; in form, because interlaced with the giant mahogany and cotton trees were the waving, fern-like fronds of the oil palm, and the still more beautiful raphia, as well as colossal silk-cotton trees, veritable giants of the forest. Dum and deleb palms, the kigelia with its enormous branches, the shea, or butter-tree, mimosas, euphorbias, gummiferous acacias, and hundreds of varieties of thorny and scrubby plants.

Indeed, as day after day we slowly ascended the river by the narrow winding track, the scene on the opposite side was a panorama of beautiful colour. We met one or two traders of the Franks and many woolly-headed natives, half-clad and wearing strange amulets and curious head-dresses; we passed through many palm-shaded villages, but were unmolested, for being two Arabs travelling alone with a single negro slave we were regarded as traders and not as slave-raiders, or "wicked people," who always appeared suddenly, with an armed band ready to burn, massacre and plunder.

Besides, Mohammed had taken a wise precaution before setting out upon the journey. While Shukri Aga, the Governor of Sokoto, had taken coffee with him on the memorable night prior to our departure, he had obtained from him a letter in Arabic, without which credential we might have been regarded with suspicion by the various chiefs through whose territory we travelled. It read:—

"Praise be unto Allah, Lord of all creatures, and to His Prophet, for the gift of the pen by which we can make known our salutations and our wishes to our friends at a distance. This letter cometh from Shukri Aga, son of Abdul Salami, who was called Kiama, Governor of Sokoto, in the name of the Great Sultan 'Othman, whose actions are directed by the one Allah, with salutations to his friend Mohammed el-Arewa, citizen of Sokoto. Thou art our friend in this affair. Thou art not among the warriors; thou art a traveller in many towns of different people. Look now, he is a traveller on account of buying and selling and of all trades. Thou shouldst hear this. Friendship and respect existeth between us. If he come to you, dismiss him with friendship until he cometh to the end of his journey. Assuredly he is high in favour with the Sultan of our land. Thou shouldst leave this Arab alone. It is trade he requireth of thee; he is not of the wicked people, but peace."

Armed with this letter of introduction we ascended the river, receiving the greatest civility from the industrious people, who, however, were living in daily dread of their lives from the incursions of the wild Borgu raiders.

Until we arrived at the town of Lokoja, at the confluence of the Benue river with the Niger, a journey occupying thirteen days, Mohammed remained with us. Then we parted, he to return home by the route of the ivory caravans which ran due north, through Zozo and Zamfara, we to ascend the Benue river in search of the Rock of the Great Sin. When on the morning he embraced me, sprang into his saddle, and raising his hand wished us farewell, I felt that I was parting from an old friend. To him my dwarfed companion and myself owed our lives; to him we owed our safe conduct beyond the clutches of the Sultan's horsemen; to him we owed the letter from the Governor of Sokoto which now reposed in the pocket of my gandoura; to him we owed the directions that we were about to follow, in order to reach the great, unexplored land.

"May Allah, peace and safety, attend thee. May the One Merciful guide thy footsteps, be generous to thee, and give thee prosperity," he cried, as he turned to leave. "And may the sun of his grace shine upon thee and illuminate the path of thy return to the true-hearted woman thou lovest. At the *isha* each night will I remember thee. Farewell, and peace. *Fi amaniillah.*"

"And upon thee may the Omniscient One ever shower his blessings. May the Prophet be thy protector," I cried in response.

But he had cried, "*Yahh! Yahh!*" to his ass, and the beast, thus urged forward, was jogging rapidly away on the first stage of his long journey northwards.

My pledge to Azala, and her earnest words that recurred to me, alone prompted me to continue my journey. A wanderer in desert and forest, with the soul of the true-born Bedouin, ever restless, ever moving, I had seen much of that half-civilised life led by the people beyond the influence of the Roumis. In London, cooped up amid the so-called civilisation of the English, their streets and shops, their wonderful buildings, and their women with uncovered faces, I cared nought for study, longing always for the free life of the plains that knows not law. Even of Algiers I had tired, and chosen a wandering existence of my own free will, exiling myself even from my Arab clansmen, and becoming a soldier of the great Mahdi, who, with his contemptuous disregard for human life, had spread the terror of his name in letters of blood. Yet through it all the one mystery of my life, the indelible mark upon my breast, had remained unsolved. Nay, its mystic significance had increased, for having looked with love for the first time upon a woman, I had found that she also bore the mystic device.

It was to endeavour to penetrate this mystery, to discover the spot, the reflection of which had appeared often in Kano as a mystic cloud-picture, that I had set out, and I became filled with a determination to strive towards it as long as Allah gave me breath. Forward I would fight my way, and plunge without fear into the trackless, unknown regions of which Mohammed had spoken, and question the people of the various countries eastward, to ascertain if any could direct me to where stood the gloomy Rock of the Great Sin.

Accompanied by the ugly dwarf, whose conversation was always quaint, and who entertained me with tales of the prowess of his people, as numerous and varied as those stored within the brain of a Dervish storyteller, we travelled onward day by day, week by week, up the swiftly-flowing Benue, where manioc, pumpkins, yams, kola nuts, colocasia, rijel, sugar-canes, and the helmia, whose tuberous root resembles the potato in taste and appearance, grew in great abundance through the fertile Foulde country, beneath the high granite crags of Mount Yarita, and at last, leaving the river, a mere stream so small that one could stand with a foot on either bank, we made a long and toilsome ascent, at length finding ourselves upon a great, sandy plateau devoid of herbage. Guiding our course by the sun, we struck one day at dawn due eastward, over great dunes of treacherous shifting sand, into which the feet of our asses sank at every step, rendering progress very slow and extremely difficult.

For a long time we were both silent; it was as much as we could do to advance with our animals halting and turning obstinately at every step. Suddenly I was startled by Tiamo crying aloud in dismay, "*Balek! Elgueubeli!*" (Take care! the sandstorm).

Then, for the first time, I realised that a strange darkness had fallen, that the morning sun had become utterly obscured by a dense, black cloud, and gigantic sand columns were whirling over the plain at furious speed. Next moment, a howling, tearing wind swept upon us with the force of a tornado. As I twisted my ragged haick quickly about my face, to shield my eyes and mouth, my ass, apprehensive of our danger, veered round with his hindquarters to the tempest. I leaned towards the ass's neck, and felt him tremble beneath me.

Then, in an instant, I received a terrific shock; it seemed to me that a camel's pack of sand had fallen all at once upon my head.

Chapter Twenty Two
Zu, the Bird-God

So heavily had I been struck that it was with difficulty I regained my breath and kept my seat. For some minutes the sand whirled about me so thickly that Tiamo, only a leopard's leap away, became obscured in the sudden darkness. With mouth and eyes filled with fine sand I experienced a horrible sensation of being stifled, and clutched frantically at my throat for air, but in a few moments the storm grew less violent, and when I looked for the dwarf he had disappeared.

At first it seemed as though the strong wind had carried him completely away, but in a few seconds I discovered him half buried, and struggling in the great ridge of sand that had been formed behind us. Quickly I hastened to his assistance and extricated him, when with his habitual hideous grin, as if amused by his own words, he told me how, being of small weight, the great wind had lifted him from the back of his ass, and rolling him over, buried him in the loose sand.

His was indeed a narrow escape, but apparently he was little worse for his exciting experience than myself, and even as we spoke the wind abated, the sky cleared, the sandstorm swept northward on its course to Lake Tsad, and the glaring sun shone again in the dead milk-white sky. For half-an-hour we halted to rest, then recommenced with fresh vigour the painful, tedious march over the dreary waste where Nature made a pause.

Four long and wearying days we occupied in traversing that lonely plain, at length descending into a fertile valley, through which a large river ran towards the south-east. This, we learned from a group of dark-skinned natives, who at first threatened us but afterwards became friendly, was known to them as the Ba-bai. The men, savages of coppery hue, were apparently hunters of the Bangbai, a powerful tribe who were constantly carrying carnage and victory far and wide southward, in the direction of the mighty Congo, and who were held in awe by all the neighbouring tribes. Of these Tiamo, who found he could converse with them in his native dialect, inquired whether they had any knowledge of the rock we sought, but with one accord they shook their heads, and replied, raising their bows and spears towards the sky. Their answer, as rendered into Arabic by the dwarf, was,—

"Of the Rock of the Great Sin our fetish-men have told for long ages. It is said to be far away in the sky. It cannot be on the earth, our spearmen have travelled all over the earth, and none has seen it."

So, ever failing to find a clue, we continued our way through the lands of the Gaberi and the Sara, along the bank of the Ba-bai, which sometimes wound through wide, rocky wildernesses, at others through valleys where palms and bananas grew in wondrous profusion, and often through forests and mangrove swamps that occupied us many days in traversing, where there was an equatorial verdure of eternal blossom and the foliage was of brightest green.

All along the bank of the Ba-bai, as we ascended still further, pressing deeper into the country of the pagans, there were forests of uniform breadth, overshadowing warm, inert waters—forests full of poisonous odours and venomous reptiles. This country, as all of the great land of Central Africa, rested under a spell of sombre gloom and appalling silence; yet it was a great relief for the eye, fevered and weary after the glaring monotony of desert sands.

For a whole moon we continued our journey due south along the winding river, until one night we came to a point where the waters broke off in two directions to the north and to the south. Northward, I supposed it would take us away into the desert again, therefore I chose the smaller river running up from the south, and for many days we travelled onward, learning from the natives of a strange little village, who seemed generally well-disposed towards us, that the river was known to them as the Bahar-el-Ardh, and that it had its source in the dense forest where lived the fierce people called the Niam-niam, whose flights of poisoned arrows had killed many of their bravest warriors.

Up this river we journeyed many days, until at length, near its source, we came to a village of conical huts, the denizens of which viewed us with suspicion, and threatened us with their long, razor-edged spears.

When, however, I had assured the chief, who sat before his little hut, that I was not one of the Wara Sura, the soldiers of the dreaded slave-raider, Kabba Rega, who periodically visited their country, devastated their land

and carried off their cattle, and we both became convinced that friendship was possible, the mystery of our presence was explained by Tiamo, that we were only travelling to discover a great rock which was reported to be in their country. Had he ever heard of such a rock?

He answered eagerly: "Meanest thou the Great Rock where dwelleth the bird-god Zu, 'the wise one'?"

"I know not thy gods, for I am a son of Al-Islâm, and follower of the Prophet," I replied, through the dwarf. "Tell me of thy bird-god."

"Zu dwelleth upon the summit of a high rock," he answered. "It was he who stole the tablets of destiny and the secrets of the sun 'god of light,' and brought them down to earth, but he himself was banished to the summit of the Rock of the Great Sin, where he dwelleth alone, and may not descend among us."

"And the rock. Hast thou never seen it?"

"I have heard of it, but mine eyes have never gazed upon it. Our sacred spots are always hidden from us."

"From whom hast thou heard mention of it?" I inquired of this chieftain of the Niam-niam.

"Some men of the Avisibba, who were taken prisoners by me in a fight long ago, made mention that one of their headmen had seen it. They knew not its direction, but thought it was beyond the Forest of Perpetual Night."

"And the Avisibba. Who are they? Where is their country?" I demanded, eagerly.

"Continue up this river for twelve days, until thou comest to a point where three streams diverge. Take the centre one, which in nine days will lead thee through the country of Abarmo to Bangoya, thence, travelling due south for fourteen days, thou wilt reach the great river the Aruwimi, upon the banks of which dwell the man-eaters of the Avisibba."

"Man-eaters!" I gasped. "Do they eat human flesh?"

The chief smiled as Tiamo put my question to him. "Yea," he answered. "They eat their captives, therefore have a care of thine own skin. Mention no word that thou hast seen me, or, being our enemies, thou wilt assuredly die."

I thanked him for his directions, and prepared to resume my weary quest, but he bade me be seated, and his wives prepared a feast for myself and my dark companion. Heartily enough we ate, for the food we had brought with us had given out long ago. One's living in that region, unexplored only by ivory and slave-raiders, was, to say the least, precarious; partaking of a savage's hospitality one day, and the next thanking Allah for a single wood-bean. But through our many hardships Tiamo never grumbled. He fingered his amulets, and presumably prayed to his gods, but no word of dissatisfaction ever fell from his lips. Though gloomy and taciturn, he proved an excellent travelling companion, and his devotion towards his mistress Azala was unequalled. When his mind was made up, he was a man of great nerve, fertile resource, and illimitable daring. At the invitation of the chief of the Niam-niam, we smoked and remained that night within his village, circular and stockaded to keep out the wild animals, then at dawn gave him a piece of cloth and bade him farewell.

Chapter Twenty Three
The Forest of Perpetual Night

Onward, along the track by the river bank, penetrating deeper and deeper into the great, limitless, virgin forest of the Congo—that region absolutely unknown to civilised man—we proceeded by paths very infrequently employed, under dark depths of bush, where our progress was interrupted every few minutes by the tangle. For food, we had tubers of manioc; for drink, the water of the river.

Approaching the native town of Bangoya, I climbed into a tree to view it; but not liking the savage look of the people, we avoided the place, and, acting on the advice we had received, left the river bank and turned towards the great Forest of Perpetual Night, striking due south in search of the Aruwimi river, and the cannibals of the Avisibba, who knew the whereabouts of the Rock of the Great Sin.

As we left the river we commenced to tramp over primeval swamps, almost impenetrable, and low-lying land that had been submerged by the winter flood. We were alone, in a trackless, unexplored land, far from cities and the ways of men. The moon glanced in through the leaf gaps, like a face grown white with fear; the bright-plumaged birds fluttered and chattered, disturbed, and a wind stole through the tree tops, with a sound like the roar of ocean's wrath heard in the calm of ocean's depths. Nor foot of man, nor foot of beast had trodden large areas of those pathless thickets—save, perhaps, some homeless elephant—since the days of an elder creation, and one's imagination could fancy the giant lizards and extinct amphibians without incongruity in such desolate wilds. In parts all Nature was still, in that wide, pestilential swamp that gave entrance to the virgin forest; neither bird nor monkey disturbed the silence, unless it be a crocodile moving slowly in the ooze, a long-legged wader, or a solemn crane. Soon, however, the ground became drier, the trees more thick, and at last we plunged into the wonderful forest of which I had long ago heard so much from negro slaves, even away in far-off Omdurman—the huge, towering forest and jungly undergrowth that covers an area of over three hundred thousand square miles of the centre of the African continent. Here, one can travel for six whole moons, through forest, bush and jungle, without seeing a piece of grassland the size of a praying-mat. Nothing but leagues and leagues—endless leagues of gigantic, gloomy forest, in various stages of growth, and various degrees of altitude, according to the ages of the trees, with varying thickness of undergrowth, according to the character of the foliage, which afforded thicker or slighter shade.

Throughout many days we strode on fast through the mighty trees, and forced our way onward, travelling always southward as near as we could guess, through this primeval forest, a journey fraught with more terrors than any we had previously experienced. The great trunks, gloomy, gaunt and sombre, grew so thickly as to shut out the blessed light of the sun, therefore, even at high noon, there was only twilight, and, for many hours each day, we were in darkness—impenetrable and appalling. Had it not been that I was convinced we should ere long reach the Aruwimi, I should have turned back, but, once having plunged into that trackless forest, there was no returning.

The attacks upon us by insects drove us almost to the verge of madness. By day tiny beetles bored underneath the skin and pricked one like needles; the mellipona bee troubled one's eyes; ticks, small and large, sucked one's blood; wasps in swarms came out to the attack as we passed their haunts; the tiger-slug dropped from the branches and left his poisonous hairs in the pores of the skin; and black ants fell from the trumpet-trees as we passed underneath, and gave us a foretaste of Al-Hawiyat. At night there were frequent storms; trees were struck by the lightning, and the sound of the tempest-torn foliage was like the roar of the breakers on a rocky shore. Snakes, chimpanzees and elephants were among our companions, while the crick of the cricket, the shrill, monotonous piping of the cicada, the perpetual chorus of frogs, the doleful cry of the lemur were among the sounds that rendered night in that lone land hideous and repulsive.

Suffering severely from hunger, without light or sunshine, and compelled to be ever on the alert lest we should be attacked, it was a journey full of terrors. The tribes of the forest were, I knew, the most vicious on the face of the earth, and every noise of breaking twigs, or of the falling of decayed branches, caused us to halt with our rifles in readiness. The legs of our asses had been rendered bare by the myriads of insects, and the centipedes, mammoth beetles and mosquitoes caused us considerable pain, yet that unexplored forest was full of fascinating wonders. Many of the trees, weird and grotesque, were centuries old, and some giants—the teak, the camwood, the mahogany, the green-heart, the stinkwood, the ebony, the copal-wood with its glossy foliage, the arborescent mango, the wild orange with delicate foliage, stately acacias, and silver-boled wild fig towered to enormous heights, and over them, from tree to tree, ran millions of beautiful vines, streaming with countless tendrils, with the bright green of orchid leaves. Great lengths of whip-like calamus lianes twisted like dark serpents, masses of enormous flowering convolvuli and red knots of amoma and crimson dots of phrynia berries were confusedly intertwined and matted until all light from heaven was obscured, except a stray beam here and there which told that the sun was shining and it was day above. The midnight silence of the forest dropped about us like a pall.

As we struggled onward, existing as best we could upon roots and fruit, and with our clothes torn to shreds by the brambles, thoughts of Azala constantly occurred to me. Of time I had kept no count, but already four moons must have passed since I had left Kano. Perhaps the conspiracy between the Khalifa and Khazneh, Aga of the Women, had been carried out, but having sent warning of it by Ayesha to Azala, I felt assured that the woman I loved would place his Majesty on his guard, and the base machinations of the pair of scoundrels would be frustrated, and the Empire saved from those who were seeking its overthrow.

Azala trusted in me to elucidate the mystery. Her deep, earnest request uttered before we parted, rang ever in my ears in that trackless, lonely region, her words stimulated me to strive onward to ascertain from the fierce savages of the Avisibba the whereabouts of the Rock of the Great Sin.

"What time has elapsed since we set forth?" I asked of Tiamo, one day as we plodded doggedly forward.

"Nearly four moons, O master," he answered, promptly. "See! I have notched the days upon my gun's stock," and he held out his gun, showing how he had preserved a record of time. I told him to continue to keep count of each day, then asked him if anxiety or fear possessed him.

"I am the slave of the beauteous Lalla, sent on a quest to bring her peace. Thou art her devoted friend. While thou leadest me I fear not to follow," and mumbling, he fingered his amulets.

"Be it as Allah willeth," I said. "Peradventure he will reward us, and gladden our eyes with a sight of the mystic rock. If it is anywhere on earth it is in these regions, unknown to all but the ivory-raiders who come up from the Congo and return thither."

"Let us search, O master," the dwarf, said encouragingly. "Though our stomachs are empty and our feet sore from long tramping, yet if we continue we shall find the river."

"Bravely spoken, Tiamo," I answered. "Thou art well named El-Sadic. Yea, we will continue our search, for with a light heart and perseverance much can be accomplished. Though of small stature, thou hast indeed a stout heart."

He grinned with satisfaction, and we trudged onward in silence through the falling gloom, resolved to bear our weariness bravely for the sake of the beautiful woman who, imprisoned in the great, far-off palace, was watching and waiting anxiously for our return to release her by solving the secret.

The strange device that seemed to link our lives puzzled me even in that dark forest, and many hours I remained silent, wondering whether I should ever ascertain how we both came to bear marks exactly similar in every detail.

Chapter Twenty Four
A Pagan Land

In that dull, dispiriting gloom I knew not the time of the *maghrib* or the *isha*, nor the direction of the Ka'abah of the Holy City, nevertheless I spread my mat and prayed fervently to Allah, the Compassionate, the Merciful, to allow the light of his blessing to shine upon me and guide my footsteps to where I might obtain the clue I sought. Tiamo stood regarding me with a look which plainly told that he considered my prayers as mere empty forms and ceremonies. One of his peculiarities was that he believed not in Allah nor in his apostle Mohammed, and holding the pious in contempt, he placed faith in spirits, magic and sacrifices to the pagan deities.

Having toiled on in the forest for twenty days and discovering no sign of the Aruwimi, we began seriously to doubt whether we were not penetrating those sunless glades in the wrong direction, and travelling parallel with the river instead of towards its bank. Without sun or star to guide us, we were wandering beneath the giant trees, the foliage and creepers of which had become so dense that now and then further progress in that depressing darkness seemed impossible. Yet ever and anon we found tracks of elephants and hippopotami, which we took, our eyes ever strained before us to behold some welcome gleam of light which would show us where ran the river.

All was dark, gloomy, rayless. Though neither of us admitted it, we both were aware that we were lost amid that primeval mass of tropical vegetation, into the depths of which even the savages themselves dare not venture. We had one day crossed a number of small swamps, and thick, scum-faced quagmires, green with rank weeds, emitting a stench most sickening, and on emerging from the foetid slough into which our feet sank at every step, a dozen black heads suddenly appeared above the undergrowth.

Next second, ere we could recover from our surprise, the weird echoes of the forest were awakened by fiendish yells, as twenty black warriors, veritable companions of the left hand, wearing strange head-dresses with black tufts of feathers, and unclothed save for a piece of bark-cloth around their loins, and a thick pad of goatskin on the left arm to protect it from the bow string, bounded towards us, running long and low, with heads stretched forward and spears trailing, shouting, brandishing their long, broad-headed weapons, and drawing their bows ready to send their poisoned arrows through our bodies.

They had evidently lain in ambush, believing us to be scouts of Kabba Rega, or of Ugarrowwa, Abed bin Salem, or some other ivory-raider from the Congo, and so suddenly did they appear, screaming, threatening and gesticulating, that I deemed it best to throw down my rifle and raised my hands to show I had no hostile intent. Seized quickly by these tall, slim, thick-lipped, monkey-eyed men, who bore quivers full of arrows smeared freshly with a dark, copal-coloured substance, we were dragged onward in triumph for nearly two hours, preceded by a band of leaping, exultant warriors who, from the interest they took in our asses and the close manner in which they all scrutinised them, I judged had never seen such animals before.

One of our captors, snatching my rifle from my grasp, held it aloft in glee, crying, —

"Tippu-tib! Tippu-tib!" whereat his companions laughed and yelled triumphantly.

This incident brought to my memory that the renown of the relentless slave-raider Tippu-Tib had reached Omdurman, and that this name had been bestowed upon him by the natives because the noise made by the rifles of his dreaded band sounded like "tippu-tib." This savage's joy when, a few moments later, on touching the trigger the rifle discharged, was unbounded. The others crowded around him, chattering and gesticulating like apes, then finding they could not cause another explosion they handed it to me, compelling me to reload it. Again it was fired, one of the dusky denizens of the forest narrowly escaping, for the bullet struck his head-dress and carried it away, much to the amusement of his companions.

While this was proceeding our position was exceedingly critical. As prisoners in the hands of these vicious warriors our lives were in greatest danger, and whither they were hurrying us we knew not.

As in sorry plight we were dragged forward, Tiamo addressed a question to one of the sinewy savages who held him. At first it was apparent that their tongue was different to any he knew, but after some questions and replies, the dwarf, in a wail of dismay, cried to me in Arabic, —

"We are lost, O master! We are lost!"

"Keep a stout heart," I answered. "We may yet escape."

"Alas! never," he answered, in despair. "We have fallen into the hands of the ghoulish Avisibba!"

"It is these men of whom we have been in search," I observed.

"Yea, O master! But have we not been told that they kill and eat their captives? Have we not been warned that they are among the fiercest cannibals of the Forest of the Congo?"

The truth of his assertion I could not deny. I glanced at the two half-nude warriors who held me, and saw their white teeth had been filed to points. The distinguishing mark upon their bodies appeared to be double rows of tiny cicatrices across the chest and abdomen; they wore wristlets of polished metal, several small rings in their ears, and around their necks I distinguished in the twilight objects which caused me to shudder in horror. Each wore around his neck a string of human teeth!

Roughly they dragged us onward, until presently we struck a native path tramped by travel to exceeding smoothness and hardness, but so narrow that we were compelled to walk in single file through the dense jungle. The path diverged suddenly at a point where a tree trunk had fallen across it, and this point was avoided by my captors, who, instead of stepping over the obstruction, plunged into the jungle and rejoined the path further on. The reason of this I was not slow in ascertaining. I found that in that fallen tree was one of the defences of the village we were approaching. Just beyond the trunk, where the stranger would place his foot in stepping over it, these crafty forest satyrs had placed a number of sharp skewers smeared with arrow-poison, concealed by dead leaves that had apparently floated down from the trees. Therefore, an enemy approaching would receive a puncture, which in a few minutes would result in death.

Suddenly, through the gnarled boles of the trees before us, we saw a gleam of blue sky, and shortly afterwards found ourselves at a small clearing on the bank of a broad river, which our captors told us was the Nouellie, or, as some termed it, the Aruwimi. At the bank two war-canoes were moored near a small village, and our asses having been carefully tethered we were placed in one of the boats, and, escorted by the remainder of the yelling, exultant cannibals, rowed up the winding river a considerable distance, keeping along the opposite bank.

It was evident we were to be taken to the principal village, being regarded as valuable prizes.

Accustomed as my companion and myself had grown to the perpetual twilight, the sudden sunlight and brilliance of day dazzled us. The waters seemed stagnant and motionless; the sun was at its zenith, and the heat so terrible that even the black rowers, in spite of their exultation at having captured two strangers, ceased rowing for a few moments, keeping in the deep shadows of the mangroves and allowing the canoe to drift. Again they rowed, and the boat, dividing the waters, continued its sinuous course up the river, threading its way quickly between the sombre forests. Upon the banks we could see great blue alligators, stretched lazily in the mud, their slimy mouths agape, as on their backs perched tiny, white birds, resting to plume themselves. On the entwining, interlacing roots of the mangroves, brilliant martin-fishers and curious lizards took their afternoon siesta, while butterflies, with gorgeous wings, flitted here and there, sparkling like jewels in the sunshine.

The scene was brilliant and beautiful after the darkness of the Great Forest, but we had no time to admire the river's charms, for in a few moments our canoe was turned suddenly into a creek, our captors sprang ashore, dragging us out, and while several men ran on in front to announce in the village the arrival of prisoners, the others pushed us forward with scant politeness.

As soon as we came within sight of the village—a large collection of low huts surrounded by a tall palisade, which we learned was called Avisibba— hundreds of yelling savages of both sexes came forth to meet us, and as we were triumphantly dragged along the wide space between the two rows of huts, the crowd pressed around us, heaping curses upon us, and causing a continual and ear-splitting din. Between the village and the Aruwimi was a belt of forest about two gunshots wide. Each house was surrounded by strong, tall palisades of split logs, higher than a man, which rendered the place defensible even against rifles, and as we were marched into the centre of the place with our captors holding up our rifles, exhibiting them to the people, I noticed their threatening expressions.

The populace were urging their warriors to kill us, and I feared the worst. Pondering on the difficulties of the situation, I could discern no ray of hope for the success of my mission.

When, however, our belongings had been thoroughly examined by the people in the centre of the village, the excitement slowly abated, and after every man, woman and child had come to gaze upon us with open-mouthed curiosity, we were lashed securely to two trees opposite one another and left to our own sad thoughts while our savage captors leaped, beat their tam-tams and held great rejoicings within our sight, pointing in our direction and capering gleefully before us.

In the centre of the village we could see men and women busily constructing some kind of platform of roughly-hewn logs. Transfixed with horror, our breath came and went quickly. We knew that these people were fierce cannibals of bad repute, and, bound and helpless, dreaded the worst.

They were erecting a kind of rude altar whereon our life-blood was to be shed, and our hearts torn out and held up to the execration of the dusky, screaming mob.

Chapter Twenty Five
Avisibba

Slowly the shadows lengthened as the fierce, chattering horde ran hither and thither, scattering the goats and fowls in their haste to prepare the platform. Upon a large and malodorous refuse-heap, close to the spot where we were secured, many human skulls and bones had been flung, showing only too plainly that the Avisibba were eaters of human flesh. The sun-blanched skulls, of which there were scores, thrilled us with horror, for their presence spoke mutely of the horrible fate awaiting us. Presently, something white attracted my attention at a little distance beyond the pile of village refuse, and almost at the same moment we both discovered that we were not the only prisoners in the hands of the Avisibba, but that two other men were secured to large stakes at a little distance from us. The white garment that had attracted my attention was a burnouse, and, to my amazement, I saw that its wearer was an Arab, and that his companion in misfortune was a half-clothed savage of a dusky copper hue.

"Hail! Son of Al-Islâm! Whence comest thou?" I shouted in Arabic, endeavouring to attract his attention. But my greeting was lost amid the shrill yells and unceasing chatter of our merciless captors. A group of the black warriors, each wearing a strip of bark-cloth and a necklet of human teeth, noticing my effort to arouse my fellow-prisoner, leaped before me, gesticulating, shouting gleefully, grinning from ear to ear and rubbing their paunches with their hands with lively anticipation.

Again I shouted to my luckless fellow-prisoner, but Tiamo remarked, "See! his chin hath fallen upon his breast. The sun hath stricken him, and he hath lost consciousness. Only his cords save him from falling prone to earth."

The dwarf spoke the truth. No doubt my co-religionist had remained bound to the stake during the whole day, and there being no shade, thirst and heat had consumed him. Whence he came was a complete mystery. I was unaware that any Arab had penetrated the terrible Forest of Perpetual Night, and it suddenly occurred to me that possibly there might be some approach to the Aruwimi from the sunlit land of Al-Islâm other than that we had traversed.

From these fierce, pugnacious savages, who set no value upon human life, I could obtain knowledge of the whereabouts of the Rock of the Great Sin! They were indeed of those who have erred and denied Allah as a falsehood, and who shall eat of the fruit of the tree of Al-Zakkum, and fill their bellies therewith, and shall drink boiling water. I looked upon the strange, weird group dancing around us, ready to take our lives and cast our bones upon the refuse-heap, wondering how I could propitiate them and obtain the knowledge I sought.

"Speak unto them, Tiamo," I cried. "Explain that we are not enemies; that we are only belated wayfarers in search of the Great Rock."

The dwarf addressed them, but apparently they did not catch the meaning of his words, for they only laughed the more.

"A hundred times, O my master, have I told them of our quest," Tiamo answered, dolefully. "But, alas! they will not listen. They declare that we are spies of Kaba Rega; that we shall die."

"Are the others spies?" I inquired.

"I know not. They will not loosen their tongues' strings."

It was evident we were in a very critical position, and I cried unto Allah to place before me the shield of his protection. Years ago I had heard, during my studies at the French Lycée at Algiers, that almost all the races in the Great Forest of the Congo practise cannibalism, although in some parts it is prevented by the presence of white civilisation. An extensive traffic in human flesh prevails in many districts, slaves being kept and sold as articles of food. Contrary to an ignorant yet very generally accepted theory, the negro man-eater never eats flesh raw, and certainly takes human flesh as food purely and simply, and not from religious or superstitious reasons. Among the Avisibba we saw neither grey-haired persons, halt, maimed nor blind, for even parents were eaten by their children on the approach of the least sign of old age.

We saw skulls used as drinking-vessels, and even as we waited, breathlessly apprehensive of our fate, we witnessed our captors piling up a great fire near the platform with dried sticks and leaves. So full of horror was each moment that it seemed an hour. The excitement in the village increased. Men brandishing their spears, and women wearing bunches of freshly-plucked leaves at the back of their loin-cloths in honour of the coming feast, leaped, danced and roared with bull voices. Little black children came and looked at me curiously, no doubt remarking upon the whiteness of my skin in comparison with theirs; then ran away, dancing and clapping their hands, infected with the wild, savage glee of their elders.

The sun sank, the dusk deepened, and as there gathered the shadows of a starless night, the blazing fire in the centre of the village threw a red, lurid glare upon the fantastic-looking huts, the crowds of savages, and the thick foliage of the primeval forest by which we were surrounded. Presently there was a great stir among the warriors, mats were hurriedly spread beneath a sickly dwarf tree near to where we were, the great ivory horns gave forth mellow blares, reminding me of the Khalifa's Court at Omdurman, and from among the excited crowd the chief of the Avisibba, a tall, thin-featured savage, wearing a fine leopard-skin, advanced and seated himself upon the low stool placed for him. The flickering light from the fire showed that beneath the strange square helmet of burnished copper, surmounted by a large bunch of parrot's feathers, was a face full of humour, pleasure and contentment.

When the whole village had assembled before him, pointing towards us, shouting and gesticulating violently, he suddenly turned and spoke briefly and low to his sub-chiefs and satellites. There was an instant's silence until the sub-chiefs spoke. Then wild, piercing yells, truly the war-cry of cannibals, awakened the echoes of the forest as the whole dusky horde rushed off to where our fellow captives were secured.

It was evident they were to be sacrificed first.

A few moments later the bonds that had held the copper-hued negro to the stake were loosened, and he was hurried by a dozen warriors into the presence of their chief, amid a storm of triumphant cries. The courage displayed by the unfortunate captive was indomitable. Folding his arms, he stood before the chief of his enemies, gazing upon him with withering contempt. The onlookers were silent. The chief, squatting upon his low, six-legged stool, uttered some fierce words, apparently interrogating him, to which the doomed man replied with scornful gesture.

Again the tall warrior in the copper helmet gave the victim a quick glance, his eyes gleaming with unearthly glitter in his almost featureless face, and repeated his question; but the proud forest-dweller reared his tall body up, raising his voice until his words reached me. Tiamo was equally startled with myself, for the half-naked savage was speaking in Arabic, apparently ignorant of the tongue of the cannibals.

Standing calmly before the chief, he delivered some terrible curses upon him, while the crowd of savages were silent, striving to understand his meaning.

"Thou art a dog, and a son of a dog," he shouted. "Cursed is he who breaketh his plighted vow; cursed is he who nourisheth secret hate; cursed is he who turneth his back upon his friend; cursed is he who in the day of war turneth his back against his brother; cursed is he who eateth the flesh of his enemies; cursed is he who defileth his mouth with human blood; cursed is he who deviseth evil to his friend whose blood has become one with his own. May sickness waste his strength and his days be narrowed by disease; may his limbs fail him in the day of battle, and may his arms stiffen with cramps; may the adder wait for him by the path, and may the lion meet him on his way; may the itch make him loathsome and the hair of his head be lost by the mange; may the arrow of his enemies pin his entrails, and may the spear of his brother be dyed in his vitals. May a blight fall upon thine accursed land, O Sheikh! May thy wives be seized as slaves by the pigmies of the Wambutti, and may the vengeance of Allah, the One Mighty and Just, descend upon thee. May thy face be rolled in hell-fire, and thy torment be perpetual; may the flame and smoke surround thee like a pavilion, and if thou cravest relief may thy thirst by slacked by the water that shall scald thy countenance like molten brass. I am in thy hands; verily, Allah will punish him who taketh the life of a Believer. Whoever shall have wrought evil shall be thrown on his face into the fire unquenchable." The fierce rabble gazed at each other, puzzled and unable to understand a single syllable.

"Well spoken!" I cried excitedly, in Arabic. "If it is Allah's will that we die, we fear not. It is written that the One Omniscient favoureth the Faithful, and lighteneth his burden."

The captive started at hearing words in the tongue he understood, and turned in my direction; but we were in the shadow, therefore it was evident he could not distinguish us.

The silence was unbroken for a few seconds, save by the ominous crackling of the fire, while the chief consulted with his satellites; then the latter, waving their hands, uttered some words. A big warrior placed the ivory horn to his lips and blew thrice lustily, and in a moment the scene was one of intense excitement. Fifty impatient pairs of hands seized the luckless man, and allowing him no further utterance, hurried him away to the small platform ten yards distant, within full view of us.

Scarce daring to look, I held my breath. The howls of wild beasts were heard in the forest. Yet curiosity prompted me to ascertain in what mode my own life was shortly to be taken, and I gazed, fascinated, at the black figures moving and dancing in the red light thrown by the burning branches, like demons let loose from Al-Hawiyat. Suddenly a shrill scream of agony rent the night air, and sent a thrill of horror through me. Then I could see that our captors had stretched the unfortunate wretch upon his stomach on the planks of the platform, and while twenty pairs of hands held him firmly down, incantations were being uttered by a man shaking pebbles in a magic gourd, while at the same time a black giant was wielding a huge club of black wood, relentlessly breaking the bones of the victim's arms and legs.

I closed my eyes to shut out the sight. With the wild Ansar of the Khalifa I had witnessed many fearful tortures to which prisoners had been subjected, but never before had I seen a man's limbs crushed in so methodical and heartless a manner. The victim's screams and groans grew fainter until they ceased entirely, for he had lost consciousness under the excruciating pain. When again I summoned courage to glance in his direction, I observed that four men had seized him, and were carrying his inanimate form towards the narrow stream that flowed swiftly by on its way to join the Aruwimi. The fire, at that moment stirred by an enthusiast, illumined the village brilliantly, enabling me to watch the subsequent movements of these ghoulish fiends. At first it appeared that they were about to wash or drown their captive, but such proved not to be the case, for three of the men jumped into the stream, and, pulling in the helpless victim, still alive, they tied him to a stake in the water, with his head firmly fixed in a forked stick above the surface, in order to prevent him from committing suicide by drowning on regaining consciousness. Then I remembered that long ago I had heard a rumour that this tribe were in the habit of placing the body, thus mutilated and still living, in water for periods varying from two hours to two or three days, on the supposition that this pre-mortem treatment rendered the flesh more palatable. I shuddered.

Chapter Twenty Six
The Ivory-Raiders

Those moments were full of torments, fears and anxieties. Neither Tiamo nor myself uttered a word. We knew our fate, and awaited it, overwhelmed by misfortune. Assuredly a grievous punishment is prepared for the unjust. For many moons we had toiled onward together, surmounting every obstacle, penetrating the Forest of Perpetual Night, wherein none from the north had ever dared to venture, until our features had become famine-sharpened, and our feet blistered and torn. Yet we had endured the privations, faced the terrors of the dark, dismal forest, and the poisoned arrows of hidden enemies; had fed for weeks upon the flat wood-beans, acid wild fruit and strange fungi, encouraged to strive for existence by the knowledge that here, amid these primitive denizens of the woods, we could obtain a clue to the whereabouts of the mystic rock we sought—the spot where was promised a solution of the one extraordinary mystery of my life. Never once had Tiamo hesitated or failed. He was as true to me as to his mistress, Azala, and ofttimes in the depths of the great, gloomy region he had urged me to look forward with hope to a triumphant return to Kano and to the graceful, true-hearted woman who loved me so dearly.

But having fallen into the hands of the Avisibba all further progress towards the mystic Land of the No Return was arrested. Vainly I had looked about for some mode of escape, but, alas! could discover none. With these fierce warriors all argument and declarations of friendship had proved futile. They were man-eaters, who looked upon all captives as lawful food; and we knew that our fate could not be much longer delayed.

The Arab, who had not yet regained consciousness, was the next victim dragged into the chief's presence. Quickly he was divested of his burnouse, and the chief, rising with imperious gesture, bade his attendants array him in the cloak of his prisoner. As he wrapped it about him with a self-satisfied air, the people raised their voices in admiration, and at a sign dragged the unconscious wretch towards his doom.

Already the pebbles rattled in the magic gourd, and above the chatter of the dusky rabble, incantations were sounding loudly, when my eyes, turned purposely from the horrible sight, suddenly caught a glimpse of an object slowly-moving over the roof of plantain-leaves that covered one of the huts. Again I looked, with eyes strained into the dark night, and distinguished the figure of a man, lying full length upon the roof, creep cautiously along and peer over at the weird scene. Suddenly another dark head appeared against the night sky, and as I glanced around at other huts, I saw a man lying flat upon the roof of each.

Almost before I could fully realise that the operations of the cannibals were being watched so narrowly, a red flash of fire showed where the first mysterious figure was kneeling, followed by the report of a gun, and next second the chief fell forward from his stool, dead—shot through the heart.

Startled by the report, the whole village was instantly in confusion, but ere they could discover whence the shot was fired, a withering volley was poured into them from the roofs of the huts, by which many fell dead and wounded. Then we became aware that the village was the object of attack, and, by the flashing of the guns on every side, knew it was surrounded. The ivory horn was sounded, and the Avisibba responded with alacrity to the call to arms, but volley after volley was poured into the centre of the place, and bullets were whistling about us and tearing their way through the foliage overhead.

The first shot had been well aimed, but although their chief was dead, the warriors, shouting defiance in loud, strident tones, seized their spears, shields and bows, and commenced to shoot their poisoned arrows wherever a flash betrayed the position of an enemy. Who, we wondered, were the assailants? Their possession of guns told us nothing, as many of the cannibal tribes near the Congo possess firearms. Nevertheless, the attack would probably result in our lives being spared, therefore we pressed ourselves as closely as we could to the trees to which we were bound and awaited the result.

For fully five minutes our mysterious assailants kept up a rapid rifle fire. The air was filled with the uproar of the shouts, as the mass of noisy, lusty-voiced cannibals defended their homes with arrow and spear, but, finding that each volley maimed or killed some of their number, they at length swarmed out of the roughly-made wooden gate of the village to repel the attack in the open, leaving their women and children behind.

The great fire burned low, but upon the platform I could distinguish the inanimate form of the Arab, stretched as it had been left, and the body of the cannibal chief was still lying where it had fallen, his plumed helmet having been assumed by his son. Beyond the stockade enclosing the rows of huts, the din of heavy firing increased, and the yells of the savages rose louder as the fight continued, until, at length, one or two wounded natives staggered back to their homes and fell to earth, each being quickly surrounded by a chattering crowd of excited women. At length the savage shrieks outside sounded fainter, the firing seemed to recede, as if the natives had taken to the forest, and their assailants were following them, when suddenly, from the roofs there dropped a dozen men, wearing white gandouras, firing their guns indiscriminately at the women, in order to frighten them into submission as prisoners, and, as they did this, about two hundred others swarmed in from the opposite direction, having entered by the gate.

I stood staring at them—amazed. They were shouting in my own tongue!—they were Arabs! To two of the men who rushed past us, I cried in Arabic to release me; and, finding I was one of their race, and that Tiamo was my slave, they quickly drew their *jambiyahs* and severed our bonds.

Delighted, we both dashed forward, and regained freedom. A dozen of our rescuers were trying to resuscitate their unfortunate tribesman lying on the planks, and were so far successful that he was soon able to stand. The attack had been delivered just at the right moment; had it been delayed another instant his limbs would have been shattered by the heavy mace. Meanwhile, into the village there continued to pour large numbers of Arabs, with their negro allies, and, while some secured and bound the women and children as slaves, the remainder entered and looted the huts of everything that was considered of value. Once or twice, men near me received wounds from the arrows of a few cannibals lurking around corners, therefore, I deemed it prudent to seize the gun and ammunition bag of a dead Arab, an example imitated by Tiamo.

Up to this moment we knew not the identity of our half-caste rescuers, for all were so excited that we could learn nothing. Presently, however, when the women and children had been marched outside to join the warriors who had been taken as prisoners, I gave one of the Arabs "peace," and expressed thanks for my timely rescue.

"It is Allah's work, O friend. Thank him," he answered, piously.

"Of what tribe art thou? Whence comest thou?" I inquired, eagerly.

"We come from the Kivira (forest). We are the men of Tippu-Tib," he answered.

"Tippu-Tib!" I echoed, dismayed, well-knowing that these ferocious bandits were the ivory-raiders whose sanguinary and destructive marches were common talk, even in Omdurman. Tippu-Tib was, according to rumour in the Soudan, the uncrowned king of the region between Stanley Falls and Tanganyika Lake, for thousands of Arabs had flocked to his standard, and his well-armed caravans were dreaded everywhere throughout the Great Upper Congo Forest. In their search for stores of ivory they had, I afterwards learnt, levelled into black ashes every settlement they entered, enslaved the women and children, destroyed their plantain groves, split their canoes, searched every spot where ivory might be concealed, killed as many natives as craft and cruelty would enable them, and tortured others into disclosing where the treasure was hidden.

These bandits were now marching through the Great Forest for the sole purpose of pillage and murder, to kill the adult aborigines, capture the women and children for the Arab, Manuyema and Swahili harems, and seize all the ivory they could discover. In the wholesale slaughter that preceded the burning of the Avisibba village not a man was spared. The fight ended in a ghastly massacre. Some escaped into the depths of the forest, but the others were shot down to the last man. Then the fighting-men and slave-carriers searched every nook in the village until at length the chief's store of ivory, consisting of over eighty fine tusks, was discovered secreted in a pit beneath one of the huts, and being unearthed, amid much excitement was distributed among the carriers. Afterwards the village was burned to the ground. Truly report had not lied when it attributed to the men of Tippu-Tib the most revolting, heartless cruelty and wanton destruction.

We had been rescued from a horrible death, but swiftly indeed had the curses of the man whose limbs had been so brutally crushed fallen upon the savage chief; swiftly indeed had Allah's wrath fallen upon the village. Both our fellow captives had, I learned, been scouting at dawn on that day, and been seized by the Avisibba. Tippu-Tib was not present in person, preferring to remain away in the far south, near Ujiji, while his men gathered wealth for him; his head men, it was said, being rewarded with all ivories weighing from twenty to thirty pounds, all over that weight belonging to him, and those under being kept by the finders. By this arrangement every man in the caravan was incited to do his best, and it is little wonder that they should descend upon villages without mercy, each fighting-man and slave seeking to obtain the largest share of slaves, ivory and other loot. It is not surprising either that the very names of Tippu-Tib, Kilonga-Longa, Ugarrowwa, Mumi Muhala, Bwana Mohamed and other ivory-raiders, should be held in awe by the natives of the great tracts of primeval forest and grassland, covering thousands of square miles, between the country of the Niam-Niam and Lake Kassali and between Lake Leopold II and the unexplored Lake of Ozo.

There was delay in distributing the burdens among the carriers, delay in securing the sorrowing band of Avisibba women and children, delay in packing up the loot for transportation, and in cooking and eating the fowls, plantain flour, manioc and bananas which had been found in the huts.

Therefore it was not until the shadows of the trees, creeping on as the sun passed overhead, reminded the raiders that the day was wearing on, that they left the smouldering ashes of the village to resume the march.

During the great feast that followed the fight, I had explained to Ngalyema, the half-breed headman, that I was an Arab from the north, and related how I and my slave had been seized in the forest and brought to the village as captives. When he had listened intently to my story, he said, laughing, —

"Allah hath willed thy release. Join our expedition and share the ivory with us, for assuredly we have been favoured on our journey, and have secured many tusks and hundreds of slaves," and he lolled upon his arm and pulled apart a piece of fowl with his fingers. Finding I was a true-bred Arab, he had placed me on a social level with himself, and spoke openly.

"Whither goest thou?" I inquired.

"Eastward, up the river to Ipoto, where our headquarters are at present established. Thence we shall continue to ascend the Ituri to Kavalli's, and afterwards to the grasslands that border the Albert Nyanza. But what mission bringest thou hither from the far north, without fighting-men?" he asked, looking at me sharply.

"I am in search of a spot, the direction of which none knoweth save Allah," I answered, it having suddenly occurred to me, that perhaps, in the course of his wanderings, he might have obtained the knowledge of which I was in search.

"What is its name?"

"It is a wondrous black crag, and is known to those who live in the deserts as the Rock of the Great Sin."

"The Rock of the Great Sin!" he slowly repeated, gazing at me in astonishment. "Thou, O friend, art not alone in seeking to discover it?"

"Not alone?" I cried. "Who seeketh it beside myself?"

"A white man who came to Uganda by smoke-boat across the Victoria Nyanza."

"What was his name?" I asked, eagerly.

"I know not. He was a Roumi of the English, and one of Allah's accursed."

"Didst thou have speech with him?"

"Yea, he sought me at Masaka eight moons ago, and knowing that I had led my master's caravan across the forest may times, asked me whether I could direct him to the Rock of the Great Sin, and—"

"And didst thou guide him thither?" I demanded, breathlessly.

"Nay. He offered two bags of gold and ten guns to any who would guide him thither, but unfortunately neither myself nor any of my followers knew its whereabouts."

"Why did this tou bab (European) desire to discover it?" I asked.

"He did not reveal. I told him that within the rock was the place of torment prepared for unbelievers, but my words only increased his curiosity and anxiety to find it," and the thick-lipped headman grinned.

"Then thou canst give me absolutely no information," I observed, disappointedly. "Hast thou, in the course of thy many journeys afar, learned nothing of its existence beyond what the wise men and story-tellers relate?"

"Since I left Masaka I have, in truth, learned one thing," he answered, his capacious mouth still full of food.

"What is it? Tell me," I cried.

Ngalyema hesitated for a moment, then answered,—

"Three moons ago, during a raid upon one of the villages of the Wambutti pigmies, three days' march into the forest from Ipoto, one of the dwarfs of the woods who fell into our hands told me he knew the whereabouts of the rock, and that it was far away, many, many days' journey in the forest, and quite inaccessible."

"In which direction?"

"I know not," the headman answered. "The dwarf had been wounded by a gunshot, and pleaded for the release of his wife. I kept him while I settled a dispute which had arisen about some ivory we had discovered in the settlement, intending to question him further, but when I returned to where I had left him he was dead."

"And his wife? Did she know anything?"

"No; she had heard of the rock as the dwelling-place of some pagan spirit that they feared, but knew not where it was situated."

"Then, whither dost thou advise me to search for information? Among the pigmies of the Wambutti?"

"Yea. It is evident they are aware of its existence, though apparently they regard it as a sacred spot, and guard the secret of its existence jealously.

The manner in which the dwarf appealed to me, declaring that he would disclose the secret if I released his wife, showed that he believed he was imparting to me information of the highest importance. What is hidden there I cannot tell; but it is strange that both the white man and thyself should desire to rest thine eyes upon it."

"I have taken an oath to a woman to endeavour to discover it," I answered, simply. "I will accompany thee in thy return towards the country of the pigmies and continue my search among them."

"If thou goest among them, may the One Merciful grant thee mercy," Ngalyema said.

"He alone can guide the footsteps and reveal that which is hidden," I added. "Onward to Ipoto will I journey with thee, and strive to learn the secret of the forest-dwarfs. Of a verity will I follow the clue thou hast given unto me. Allah maketh abundant provision for such of his servants as he pleaseth. He knoweth whatever is in heaven and earth."

Chapter Twenty Seven
Ngalyema

There is much truth in our Arab saying, that a day of pain appears everlasting if one does not dream of the bright to-morrow. A life's unrest, indeed, seems but a day's if one looks to the calm that Allah has promised shall be the reward of Believers. Beyond the pain and weariness is a white dawn, reunion and peace. Life with the fierce brigands of Tippu-Tib, the ivory king, was full of vicissitudes and horrors, as along the narrow native track, through the gloomy forest, we pushed forward.

Owing to the large number of rapids, it was impossible for the raiders to use the native canoes to ascend the Aruwimi on their return to Ipoto, where they had temporarily established themselves; therefore, in order to secure more ivory and slaves, Ngalyema had decided to take a route which ran into the forest, six days' journey from the river, and which the guides assured us would follow the course of the Ituri and pass through a district where many settlements might be raided.

Compelled to travel in single file, our journey through the dark, endless Forest of Perpetual Night was slow, tedious and hazardous. At almost every step we were retarded by stumps, roots, climbers, convolvuli and green-scummed pools, while, by the absence of light, we were chilled and depressed, and the poisonous odours arising from the decaying mass of vegetation sickened us. Here and there, where the interlaced foliage overhead allowed the sunshine to struggle through, flocks of parrots screamed and whistled gleefully, and the tall tree-trunks looked grey and ghostly in the pale light; but our progress, creeping among the dense undergrowth, and climbing over fallen patriarchs of the forest, was full of anxiety. Plantains grew everywhere, therefore there was no lack of food; but the brutality with which the raiders treated their slaves caused a number of deaths ere we had been a dozen days on the march.

At length, one morning, the scouts, consisting of the two native guides, and about twenty Arabs, who were some distance ahead, rushed back with the news that they had come upon a large clearing, and that we were evidently approaching a village. The order to halt was immediately given, and Ngalyema himself, with a small force, went rapidly forward with the scouts to reconnoitre. In an hour they returned, stating that there were several villages in close proximity, and, with my gun ready, I accompanied the fighting-men in their dash forward. Passing across the clearing, where every plantain-stalk bore an enormous bunch of the fruit which filled the air with its odour, and where corn and sugar-canes were profusely cultivated, our pioneers suddenly came across a number of poisoned skewers, artfully concealed in the path, and these having been carefully picked out, we crept along, past a heap of bones of slaughtered game, to surround the settlement.

It was exciting work. We knew not whether the alarm had already been raised and the natives were lying in ambush. Each moment we expected to be greeted with a flight of poisoned arrows from the concealed defenders; but as we got within sight of the huts it seemed that our approach had been unnoticed.

Suddenly, however, the white garments of the raiders attracted attention, and in a few moments the village was in a tumult of apprehension. Without hesitation, our thick-lipped headman ordered the raiders to disperse into the jungle and surround the village, and as they dashed away and I took up a position behind a tree at a little distance from Tiamo, we could hear loud blasts being blown upon a horn.

In an instant the raiders opened a galling fire. A number of my fellow-marksmen had clambered up the adjacent trees, others were concealed in the dense undergrowth, while a small body still remained in the rear, prepared to charge when commanded. A few seconds after the alarm had been raised, the black warriors, armed with bows, arrows, shields and long spears, poured out of the stockade, yelling and brandishing their weapons, but so well had the attack been planned, that each volley of the Arabs felled dozens of the blacks.

Finding that we had got into ambush so cleverly, they retired immediately within their stockade, and from their cover launched flights of poisoned arrows in every direction. The missiles, the merest scratch from which would produce tetanus and death, swept through the foliage above us and stuck in the trunks of the trees in our vicinity, nevertheless wherever a black head or savage head-dress showed above the high stockade, it was picked off with unerring precision by our sharpshooters.

The rattle of musketry, however, had alarmed the neighbouring villages, and almost before we were aware of it we were attacked in the rear by a crowd of yelling savages armed with clubs and bows. For a few minutes our position appeared exceedingly critical; but this contingency had not been overlooked, for suddenly I noticed a number of our men, who had been left to guard the slaves, were drawing off the defenders' reinforcement, and shooting them down with a cool recklessness that was surprising.

For half-an-hour the fierce fusillade continued, until at length Ngalyema gave the signal to charge. To this the Arabs quickly responded, and in a few moments had stormed the stockade and were inside, swarming over the huts, and fighting the savages hand-to-hand. The *mêlée* was exciting, but against guns savage weapons proved to be of little avail, and ere long a ruthless massacre of the unfortunate blacks became general. The very air was halituous of freshly-shed blood. As at Avisibba, the women and children were secured, the place looted, and every nook and corner searched, to discover the secreted tusks. None, however, could be found.

Ngalyema had evidently good cause for belief that a considerable amount of ivory had been collected, and after his men had proceeded to the three other small villages in the immediate vicinity, thoroughly searched them, and captured the defenceless portion of the inhabitants, the chief of the Avejeli, whose life had been spared, was brought before him. His name was Yakul, a stalwart savage, of proud bearing, wearing a loin-cloth of goatskin and a conical shaped head-dress ornamented with a swaling crimson plume, while upon his arms, wrists and ankles were four bangles fashioned from *matako*, the brass rods imported by white traders on the Congo.

Through one of the guides, who spoke the Monvu tongue, the headman of the raiders put a question, asking where his ivory was concealed. On hearing the inquiry, even before it was fully translated, he drew himself up, looked keenly into Ngalyema's face, and answered, —

"Thou hast killed and enslaved my people, and thou mayest kill me. Thou art the friends of Tippu-Tib, against whom our wise men have long warned us. Finish thy dastardly shedding of blood. Kill me, and go."

"We have no desire to kill thee," the headman answered, with a smile. "Indeed, thou shalt regain thy liberty, and thy wives shall be returned unto thee if thou wilt disclose the hiding-place of thine ivory."

"Thou hast destroyed my people. See now! Thou hast already applied the fire-brand unto my village!" he cried in fierce anger, shaking both his black fists. "Go. May the curse of the Evil Spirit who dwelleth in the darkness of the Great Forest, follow thee until death."

"Pick out thy wives," the other said, pointing to the large group of trembling women and children. "They are free, and likewise thyself, but the men of Tippu-Tib depart not hither until thou hast led them unto the place where thou hast concealed thy treasure."

The chief's fierce black eyes flashed with angry fire, as, waving his hand with a gesture of impatience, he replied, —

"Already have I answered."

His four wives, however, watching the progress of the negotiations, and overhearing the offer of Ngalyema, dashed forward and flung themselves before their master, beseeching him to save his own life and theirs by disclosing the secret.

But he waved them aside with regal gesture, and folded his arms resolutely.

Then, one of the women rose, and turning to the Arab headman, said, —

"To save our lives I will reveal the spot unto thee. Come, it is but an arrow's flight distant!"

The chief heard the words and sprang straight at her throat, but ere he could reach her the Arabs pulled him down. She stood erect and queenly, a splendid specimen of savage womanhood.

"Follow me," she cried, wildly, and twenty of the raiders, myself included, sprang forward and accompanied her a little distance into the jungle until we came to a great ironwood-tree. For a moment she halted, with her back towards it, apparently taking bearings by a cottonwood-tree with silvery bark, and then, counting thirty paces in its direction, told us to search.

In a few minutes the dead leaves and fallen boughs were cleared, revealing a floor of hewn wood, and this being torn up the coveted treasure, consisting of more than a hundred magnificent tusks, was discovered beneath.

Shouting with glee, the raiders rushed back to their leader, announcing the news, and triumphantly dragging the chief's wife back with them. Her three female companions cried loudly to the headman to release them, but he only laughed brutally, and ordered the Arabs around him to put them back with the other slaves. Then, finding to their dismay that the headman's promise would not be fulfilled, the whole of the captured women made the forest ring with howls of execration, and heaped upon the raiders the most terrible curses their tongues could utter.

Meanwhile, the ivory was being pulled out of its hiding-place, and allotted in burdens to the slave-carriers. The flames, now spreading from hut to hut, leaped, roared and crackled, and a thick black smoke ascended, drifting slowly over the tops of the giant trees.

Turning to the proud chief of the Avejeli, the headman, through the negro interpreter, exclaimed, —

"I gave unto thee a chance to escape, but thou wouldst not accept it, even though the liberty of thy wives depended upon thy word."

"The word of a follower of Tippu-Tib, like water fallen upon sand, is never to be found again," Yakul answered.

Ngalyema bit his lip in anger, and waving his hand to those around him, exclaimed in Arabic, —

"Bind him. Let the son of offal die!"

In a trice cords were slipped around the ankles, wrists and neck of the unfortunate wretch in such a manner as to render him utterly powerless. Then the Arabs asked, —

"Speak, O leader, in what manner shall the pagan's life be taken?"

"Take him yonder into the forest, and find a nest of red ants at the foot of a tree. There bind him, smear upon him some plantain juice, and let the insects devour him."

"Thou hast spoken well, O leader!" the brigands cried, exultingly, and before he could realise the horrible fate that awaited him, the unfortunate chief, whose only offence was the strenuous and gallant defence of his home and his people, was hurried away into the jungle by the joyful rabble.

The shouting of the men executing the brutal Ngalyema's orders could be heard away in the forest, while the remainder of the bandits proceeded with their work of relentless destruction. Not content with levelling the villages to ashes, they cut down the plantain grove, trampled down the corn, and destroyed the manioc, afterwards refreshing themselves with draughts from a trough of banana wine found in the village.

When the party returned from securing the chief in a position where he would be quickly eaten alive by the pests of the forest, the whole of the fighting-men reassembled, apparently beside themselves with delight at the complete mastery they had obtained over the savages. Piteous appeal availed the unfortunate slaves nothing. They were beaten, cuffed and tied together—two who attempted to escape, including the chief's wife who had divulged the whereabouts of the ivory, being shot dead, and their bodies kicked ruthlessly aside.

At length the raiders, headed by one of the captured women, who was promised her liberty if she would act as their guide, moved forward along a narrow track leading into the depths of the forest, enriched by one hundred and thirty tusks, and nearly two hundred slaves.

As the men marched, onward, goading on the slaves with revolting brutality, I lingered behind for a moment to pick up a curiously-shaped axe that had apparently been forgotten. As I did so a loud, despairing shriek fell upon my ear.

I glanced around. The last of the rear guard of Tippu-Tib's brigands had disappeared along the dark track. I remembered that the register of the actions of the righteous is in Illiyyûn, the book distinctly written: those who approach near unto Allah being witnesses thereto.

Again the piercing shriek was repeated, and I knew that the unfortunate wretch, bound to a tree, was being tortured to death, and literally devoured by a myriad insects. The injustice of his sentence caused me to hesitate, and a second later I resolved to release him.

I had but a few moments in which to accomplish it, for I well knew that, if discovered, my own life might be taken by the wild, bloodthirsty horde, who were indeed companions of the left hand, whom Allah had cut off, and over whom was the arched fire. Nevertheless, I dashed into the jungle, axe in hand, and guided by the condemned man's cries, found him lashed tightly to a tree, and already covered from head to foot by the pests.

In an instant my axe severed his bonds and he sprang forward, and falling upon his knees, gratefully kissed my feet, uttering many words of thanks which I could not understand.

But I had not a moment to linger, therefore I gave him "peace," and speeding back again to the smouldering ashes of the village, plunged into the forest depths down the dark, narrow path my merciless companions, the ivory-raiders, had taken.

Chapter Twenty Eight
Pigmies of the Forest

On every hand on their march eastward my companions spread destruction and death. The raiders' track was marked by blood and ashes, for almost daily they shot down natives, burned villages, and added to the number of their slaves.

The horrors of that journey through the eternal gloom were endless, and the many cruelties and butcheries perpetrated in cold blood sufficient to send a thrill of horror through the most callous heart. Through all my varied experience with the hordes of the Mahdi and the Khalifa, I had never witnessed such scenes of fiendish brutality. Tiamo, whose savage nature had at first rejoiced in being one of this lawless band, was soon sickened, and often shuddered and expressed disgust.

Yet through all I had one goal in view, one object to attain—the discovery of the mystic spot where the Secret of the Asps might be revealed. The dreams that waved before my half-shut eyes were ever of Azala. Ever uppermost in my mind was the thought of her imprisoned in that great palace, surrounded by every gorgeous luxury, yet not allowed to participate, and patiently awaiting my return. Each day, when darkness set in, I thought of her opening her lattice, praying for Allah's favour and breathing words of love to be borne afar to me upon the sunset wind. When should we again meet, I wondered. Perhaps never.

But the story of my strange journey, stranger than man had ever before undertaken, slips away from me as I think of her.

The notches on Tiamo's gun, which he fortunately recovered before leaving Avisibba, showed that the day arranged for the attack upon Kano by the Dervishes had long passed, for already we had been absent five moons. If Ayesha had not delivered my warning, or if the Sultan had disregarded it, then the Empire of Sokoto was doomed. Of what dire consequences would result from the non-delivery of my hastily-scrawled message I feared to contemplate, for I knew that if the Ansar entered Kano, the woman I loved would most certainly be seized and carried away to grace the harem of the brutal Ruler of the Soudan.

But, trusting to the guidance of the One Guide, I strove to assure myself of her safety, and with a stout heart pushed forward, determined to overcome every obstacle that beset my path. Bitten and stung by numberless tribes of insects, including a beetle so small that it could not be detected with the naked eye, but which burrowed deeply into the flesh, producing most painful sores; continually on the alert against the many green, gold and black snakes, puff-adders, pythons and other deadly reptiles, we went forward, week by week, until the wretched slaves, half-starved and brutally ill-used, became mere shrunken skeletons of their former selves, disfigured by terrible ulcers caused by the insects, while the fighting-men themselves became lean, pale and weakened. Through a suffocating wilderness of arums, amoma and bush, over damp ground that exuded foetid, poisonous vapours, we struggled onward, until one day we were startled to hear on before us the sound of muskets, loud, wild shouting, and the violent beating of tam-tams.

Ngalyema and his men halted quickly to listen. The sounds approached.

"Thank Allah!" the headman cried in delight when, in a few moments, a strange, half-bred Arab pushed his way toward us, giving us loud and profuse greetings. "Our guides have not deceived us. We are at last at Kalunga!"

Pushing forward, our scouts had apprised the raiders' settlement of our approach, and the wildest excitement at once prevailed. My companions, with one accord dashed onward, and on accompanying them I found myself in a great, open clearing around a strong stockade, within which stood a number of well-constructed huts. Here, once again, after a perpetual gloom lasting nine weeks, we saw the blessed light of day, the cloudless sky and the brilliant sun, and breathed the pure air laden with the sweet perfume of many flowers.

We were, I discovered, actually in the country of the Wambutti pigmies, some of whom, sleek little people, about the height of a sword, and of the colour of yellow ivory, I saw among the Arabs. Kalunga was an out-lying station established by Tippu-Tib's brigands in order to extend their raids deeper into the Forest of Perpetual Night; and it was Ngalyema himself, who, a few hours later, suggested that from the curious race of forest-dwellers in the vicinity I might possibly obtain knowledge of the whereabouts of the Rock of the Great Sin. He even suggested that one or two of his own fighting-men should accompany me on my lonely journey south in search of the pigmies, but knowing that he desired to obtain for himself knowledge of the spot, I firmly declined his offer, declaring that I felt less open to attack accompanied only by Tiamo than if his slave-raiders bore me company.

During two days I remained at the Arab settlement, watching the manner in which the slaves were secured previous to deportation to the headquarters at Ipoto, on the Ituri river, forty days distant; then, with my trusty companion, El-Sadic, I left the place at dead of night, in order to escape Ngalyema's vigilance, and again we plunged into the forest depths along the narrow, winding, half-effaced track which had been pointed out to me as running south to the distant villages of the mysterious race of dwarfs. In that impenetrable darkness our progress was slow, but when day dawned above, just sufficient light struggled through the dense foliage to enable us to pursue our way. It was a lonely journey, full of terrors and anxieties, for were we not approaching the tribe, of all the people in the Forest of Night the most hostile? Ever on the alert lest we should receive the poisoned shaft of some hidden dwarf of the woods, or tread upon a poisoned skewer, we struggled still onward. Day succeeded day until we kept no count of them. Tiamo, who had borne the fatigues of our long journey without a murmur, and bravely faced the perils to which we had continuously been exposed, now appeared to have grown despairing and gloomy. The eternal twilight was certainly not conducive to high spirits, but my dwarf companion seemed overwhelmed by some strange precursor of evil.

As deeper into the forest we penetrated, food became scarcer, and hunger consumed us daily. We were subsisting on wood-beans, occasional plantains, bananas and some wild fruit, but as not a gleam of sunshine gladdened our eyes, or breath of pure air refreshed us, it was scarcely surprising that my slave should give vent to his innermost thoughts. One morning, in the dim, grey hour when things were just creeping out of darkness and everything was colourless and unreal, he appeared unusually gloomy, and when I inquired the cause, answered, —

"In the night, O master, I had a dream. The future was revealed unto me," and he shuddered perceptibly. "Verily, I believe that our quest is futile; that death is nigh unto us. I have a presentiment that the eyes of the beauteous Lalla Azala will never again be gladdened by sight of thee, and that mine own bones also will be stripped by the scavengers of the forest."

"Let not such gloomy apprehensions find a dwelling-place within thee, Tiamo," I answered, forcing a smile. "Relinquish not thy brave bearing. For aught we know we are, even at this moment, on the point of a discovery."

"The men of Tippu-Tib assured me that the dwarfs of the Wambutti resent the intrusion of strangers, and murder those who dare approach them except in force," he exclaimed, gloomily.

"Did we not set forth to seek the Rock of the Great Sin, and didst thou not express thy readiness to accompany me whithersoever I went?" I asked.

"I did, O master," he answered. "But I knew not that we should seek to penetrate the country of the man-eaters."

"Allah,—may he be glorified!—counteth them as flies, but extendeth unto us his guidance and protection," I said. "Put thy faith in the One Guide, and he will comfort and preserve thee."

Mumbling some mystic words in his own tongue, the meaning of which I knew not, he fumbled with his amulets and raised his open hand above his head, as if imploring the protection of his pagan gods. Then, rising to his feet, and with a look of renewed energy, he exclaimed,—

"Of a verity thy lips utter the truth. We may be even now near unto the shore of the Lake of the Accursed, and upon the verge of discovering that which is weirdly mysterious and unknown. I will abandon fear and continue to seek with diligence for that of which we are in quest."

"We have both promised," I said, solemnly. "We have travelled afar, and are but fulfilling our duty towards the Lalla Azala, thy mistress."

"True, O master," he said. "Pearls of wisdom fall ever from thy lips as rain upon a thirsty land. I am ready. Let us move forward."

At the bidding of my apelike companion I rose, and again we started along the disused track, rendered almost impassable by trailing creepers, vines, and thick undergrowth. During that day we struggled forward, passing through a village that had apparently been burned by the Arabs some months before, and, continuing our way still southward, we entered a path that had been so widened by elephants that we could walk side by side and converse, when suddenly, without warning, the earth beneath us gave way and we were both precipitated headlong into a deep pit that had been artfully concealed by leaves, twigs, and a thin layer of earth. My knee was bruised severely, but in a moment I struggled to my feet to gaze around. I raved to and fro, screaming and crying upon Allah and Eblis, for I was dismayed to discover that the pit had been dug so deeply, with sides slanting inwards, that to escape was utterly impossible.

We had been caught by one of the elephant-traps, in the arrangement of which the pigmies display so much ingenuity and cunning. We had fallen into an abyss of doom.

"Alas, O master! this misfortune hath shackled our footsteps!" the dwarf exclaimed, rubbing his abnormally large woolly head where he had struck it. "I dreamed that we were dying."

No word passed my lips. In vain I searched frantically for some mode of escape, but could discover none. My companion's words, were, alas! too true! We had nothing left, but misery! The heart of night, and the forest's heart were tranquil in primordial silence. The mishap was worse than a misfortune, for it meant either capture by the malicious little denizens of that weird realm of perpetual darkness, or a lingering death from starvation.

To endeavour to reach the surface, I mounted the dwarf upon my shoulders, but my heart sank when I saw that the point to which he could stretch his hands was still fully a spear's length below the ground. Had he been a full-grown man and not of dwarfed stature, it was possible that we might have escaped by this means, but all schemes that we devised proved impracticable, and we were compelled to walk backwards and forwards within the dark, deep hole, awaiting the arrival of our exulting captors, who would, no doubt, believe that in me, an Arab, they had caught one of their arch enemies—the raiders of Tippu-Tib.

The gloom grew deeper, the birds far above ceased their chattering, a fact which told us that it was the hour of the *maghrib*, when, suddenly in the silence, we heard leaves rustling, and twigs broken as by footsteps.

Next second, a black head appeared, cautiously leaning over the pit looking down upon us, and a voice uttered a loud cry in a language neither of us knew.

My heart leaped, and beat quickly.

The savage's face seemed to smile in mockery of my dismay; his scream of delight was the death knell of all my hopes, and, as the sinister head was withdrawn, I stood breathless, unarmed, wondering in what form death would come to us, and praying to Allah that we might die swiftly and painlessly, for I dreaded the horrible, revolting tortures I had so frequently witnessed.

I remembered it was the hour when Azala, in the far-off city of the Sultan, was wafting to me, from her high lattice, a fervent message of comfort, of peace and of love. There came before me the pale image of those hours of enchantment. Upon the successful accomplishment of my strange mission depended all our future, all our happiness. I struggled to look the circumstances fairly in the face, to see the folly of my wild frenzy, and to reason with myself.

But a profound sense of loneliness, helplessness and despair had settled upon me. I became seized by an excessive dread.

Chapter Twenty Nine
Facing Malec

Above, in the dimness, there moved again a grotesque, spectral shadow. The savage was peering into the pit, but it occurred to me that he was unable to distinguish us in that rayless obscurity.

He shouted in a hoarse voice, and I saw that in his hand he carried a long spear. Neither of us replied or moved a muscle. We watched in silence, waiting with drawn breath. Everything, except the hole above where the unkempt head showed as a round, black projection, was profoundly dark, and when I looked up again it had disappeared. A deep stillness fell, broken only by the distant trumpeting of an elephant; then suddenly we heard a noise like the breaking of sticks and the tearing of foliage. With our eyes riveted upon the hole through which we had fallen, we were, a few minutes later, startled by the appearance of a curious glare, as if a fire had been lighted, and suddenly the black denizen of the forest appeared at the hole, holding above his head a roughly-made torch. Its fickle light shone down upon us, but at the same time illumined the black, savage face of the man who held it.

Involuntarily I gave vent to a loud ejaculation of surprise. In an instant I recognised the sable features. The man who had discovered us was none other than Yakul, the fearless chief of the Avejeli, whom I had rescued from death!

"Peace, O friend!" I cried excitedly in Arabic, remembering that although he had been questioned by Ngalyema in the Monvu tongue, yet he nevertheless understood the language of the Desert.

"See!" shouted the dwarf, in despair, unaware that I had released him from his tortures. "See! It is the chieftain that the raiders condemned to die. He will assuredly seek revenge upon us!"

I saw him, and even through the mask of my madness I knew him again, and terror took hold of me. But our anxious apprehensions were in an instant dispelled, for Yakul, recognising me, waved his torch, shouting in very indifferent Arabic,—

"Nay, do not be surprised, O my rescuer! Truly am I thy friend. Be patient, and ere long thou shalt both escape."

And as the weird, black figure uttered these reassuring words in a shrill tone, he placed the torch upon the ground and left. Reappearing in a few moments, he shouted, and commenced to lower a long wreath of climbing plant that he had cut from a tree, and when he had secured the end to a neighbouring trunk he bade us ascend with care.

Thankful for this sudden and unexpected deliverance, Tiamo clambered up first, and I followed, finding myself a few minutes later standing beside my pagan ally, expressing fervent thanks for our timely rescue.

"If thou hadst not severed my bonds, the scavengers of the forest would long ago have cleaned my bones," the tall, keen-eyed savage answered, leaning upon his spear. The fine goatskin he had worn as a mark of chieftainship had been replaced by a strip of common bark-cloth, and he no longer wore his curiously-shaped helmet, with its swaling plume. His village had been burned by the fiendish brigands of Tippu-Tib, nearly all his people had been murdered or enslaved, his treasure-stolen, and he was now a homeless wanderer. Briefly I explained to him the accident that had befallen us, at the same time expressing a fear that the pigmies might discover us.

"Fear not that," he answered. "I have ever been an ally of the dwarfed people of the Wambutti, and in my company not a hair of thine head shall be injured."

"Art thou on thy way to them?" I inquired.

"Yea, and nay," he answered. "Since thou didst release me, I have followed closely thy footprints."

"Followed me!" I echoed, remembering how many days he must have journeyed.

"Since the raid of the destroyers I have been ever behind thee, and have ofttimes watched thee and thy companion unnoticed."

"For what reason hast thou sought to thus keep observation upon me?" I asked, puzzled. The small fire he had lit still threw a faint glow, sufficient to reveal his dark and not unhandsome face, and Tiamo stood by, speechless and wondering.

"I desired to ascertain that thou wert journeying along the right path," the chief replied, mysteriously.

"The right path? What meanest thou?"

"An Arab dareth not to journey with one slave through the Kivira, unless he hath some definite object in view," he said, with a low, rather harsh laugh. "At risk of thy life thou didst release me from a certain and horrible death, and in return I have secretly watched thy progress towards thy goal."

"My goal!" I cried. "What knowest thou of my goal?"

"Already have I told thee that, since my rescue, I have been as thy shadow. I followed thee to Kalunga, and there overheard thy conversation with the brutal headman Ngalyema, in which thou didst tell him of thy search, and he, with consummate craftiness, offered to send his armed men with thee. As I lay hidden, I heard thee tell him of thine anxiety to reach the Rock of the Great Sin, because upon the success of thy mission depended the happiness of the woman thou lovest. My life was in thine hand; therefore I determined at once to assist thee."

"To assist me!" I exclaimed, breathlessly. "Knowest thou where the Rock of the Great Sin is situated?"

"I do, O my friend," he answered solemnly, still leaning upon his spear, with the other hand resting upon his hip.

"And canst thou direct us thither?"

"In order to accompany thee unto the rock, I dogged thy footsteps, determined not to make my presence known if thou couldst obtain from others the information thou seekest. Until sunrise to-day thou didst travel in the direction of the abode of evil, but after last night's sleep thou didst turn off from the right track, and hence I found it imperative to make my presence known and give thee warning, so that thou mayest turn back and again strike the right path. In consequence, I sped forward, expecting to find thee settling down for the night, but instead I discovered thou hadst fallen headlong into a trap set for elephants. Thou hast been, however, extricated—"

"Thanks to thee," I interrupted, laughing. But he continued,—

"Extricated by one whose life thou hast saved for no other reason than because the condemnation was unjust," and he paused. Then, looking round, he added, "Come, let us be seated at yon fire; let us eat and sleep that we may be refreshed for to-morrow's journey."

All three of us walked to the fire, and seating ourselves, the pagan chief produced some ripe bananas and some wild fruit, which we ate ravenously while he chattered on unceasingly.

"Have thine eyes ever gazed upon the Rock of the Great Sin?" I asked presently, when he had described how he had followed the men of Tippu-Tib for many days at imminent risk of detection.

"Yes. Once, years ago, I gazed upon it from afar, but dared not to approach it."

"Why?" I inquired.

"Of a verity the spot is sacred. He who endeavoureth to ascertain its secret, will assuredly be smitten by a terrible pestilence—the hand of the Evil One who dwelleth therein, will strike swiftly, and the adventurous investigator will wither like a rootless flower beneath the sun."

Tiamo, silent, with eyes opened wide, hugged his knees and drank in every word Yakul uttered. My curiosity was also thoroughly aroused, and I urged the chief to relate to me all he knew regarding the strange, unexplored spot. Its mystery had been deepened by each superstition or legend I had heard regarding it, yet it was curious that nearly every popular belief asserted that some strange deity of good or evil dwelt therein, or in its vicinity. But at length I had now discovered one who had actually gazed upon it with his own eyes, and knew the way thither. There was no longer doubt of its reality; it actually existed, rising lonely and solitary from the dark waters of the Lake of the Accursed, just as it had been mirrored in the heavens.

For the first time during our long and fatiguing search, sometimes across great tracts of virgin forest wherein man had never before set foot, we now at last heard it described minutely from the lips of an eyewitness. Eager and elated, we both felt that we were on the point of a discovery, and were prepared to risk the strange pestilence so dreaded by the pagans and the touch of the unseen evil hand, in order to explore the dark and gloomy crag, where it had been asserted by Azala the Mystery of the Asps remained hidden.

Yakul, as he munched his bananas, told us how, eight years before, when assisting the Iyuku and Indebeya peoples against the Manuyema, there had been severe fighting, and with his warriors he had followed a host of the invaders south through an unknown part of the Great Forest, until at length he had driven the enemy into a natural trap, for, on account of the Lake of the Accursed and the range of inaccessible mountains beyond, they were unable to retreat further, and being compelled to again fight, they were completely wiped out by the Avejeli.

During the battle in that little-known region he discovered they were within actual sight of the Rock of the Great Sin, but of the whole of his brave warriors not a man dared to venture nearer on account of the declarations of their wise men, that if any attempted to approach the forbidden spot a terrible pestilence and total destruction would inevitably fall upon the tribe. In consequence of this he had stood afar off and viewed the rock and the unknown and unapproachable land beyond, fearing lest, by going nearer, he should invoke the wrath of his pagan gods, or cause revolt among his warriors, who had become cowed and terrified at discovering themselves in the shadow of the dark rock, which was the seat of the dreaded Evil Spirit of the Kivira.

While within sight of the Rock of the Great Sin, they declared the air was deadly. They began to suffer from joint aches, he told us; their knees were stiff, and pains travelled through their bodies, causing them to shiver and their teeth to chatter, after which their heads would burn and the hot sweat would pour from them, so that they knew no rest. During the two days they remained there life was but one continuous ague, and they left the country declaring it to be bewitched.

Chapter Thirty
A Prophecy

"Fearest thou to return?" I asked the chief of the Avejeli, when he had concluded his interesting description of the overthrow of the Manuyema.

"If thou desirest me to bear thee company, I will guide thee until thine eyes can discern the black rock, and the poisonous waters surrounding it," he answered. "Then, if thou art fully determined to approach it, I will remain until thou returnest."

"I cannot sufficiently thank thee for thy promise, O friend," I answered. "For many moons have I wandered with my slave, over the desert and through the endless and terrible Kivira, in search of some one who could direct me unto the spot I seek. Now that thou hast given me thy promise to conduct me thither, thou hast of a verity revived my hopes with the refreshing shower of thy good favour."

"Are we not friends?" Yakul asked. "Already thou hast shown, in manner plain, a boundless generosity towards me; therefore gladly will I conduct thee to the sacred place thou seekest."

"Indeed thou art my friend. May the most perfect peace ever rest upon thee, and may wisdom always distinguish thee above thy fellows," I answered, adding, "Thou hast spoken of the rock as the seat of the Evil Spirit of the Forest. Tell me, why do thy people of the Avejeli regard it as sacred?"

"Because, beyond the rock is an inaccessible and mysterious tableland which none have ever gained. Some believe it to be a country filled to overflowing with bananas, yams, manioc, corn, honey and fruit, and peopled by a strange race of monkeys, who live in huts like ourselves, and are armed with bows and spears. Others declare that the plateau, though covered with grass at the edge, where visible, is nevertheless a glaring, barren, and uninhabited wilderness of endless extent."

"And what is the name of this unknown country?" I asked, curious to know whether the pagan tribes entertained a belief similar to ours.

"It is called the Land of the Myriad Mysteries, because, to the dwellers on the edge of the forest, the first flush of dawn appeareth always like a mysterious blood-red streak from behind the rock. By our wise men it is said that away there dwelleth the great Evil Spirit, whose invisible myrmidons lurk in the silent depths of the forest, ever ready to bring destruction and death upon those they may seize."

"Believest thou that the Evil Spirit hath power supreme?" I inquired.

"Yea, most assuredly. Once, many years ago, the Good Spirit, who dwelleth in the sun, reigned supreme in the Kivira, until a rivalry arose between the god of Life, and the god of Destruction, and they struggled fiercely for the mastery. At first, the Good Spirit was the most powerful, for into the bright light which he shed the Evil One dared not venture. But at length the god of Darkness, with considerable ingenuity, invoked the aid of the trees of the forest, and they, obedient to him always, raised high their spreading heads, interlaced their giant branches, and shut out the sun's light, thus allowing their master, the Evil Spirit, to obtain complete control of the earth. It was then that he took up his abode in the Land of the Myriad Mysteries, placing between his seat and the dwelling-place of mortals a lake, the water of which will, it is said, poison arrows dipped into it, and a chain of mountains, unapproachable by reason of the death-dealing odours exhaled from the swamp in the deep valley at their base."

The chief paused, hugged his knees, and gazed gravely into the dying embers.

"Hath no man ever been able to penetrate into the mysterious abode?" I asked.

"Many lives have, it is said, been lost in foolhardy attempts by the curious," he answered, slowly. "None has, however, successfully braved the wrath of the One of Evil, who dealeth death with aim unerring. Our wise men have said that when, generations ago, the Evil Spirit conquered his rival, entrance was gained to his kingdom by a remarkable cave in the rock, and that in the cave there lived a hideous wild beast with eight legs, whose tusks were each the length of a spear, whose claws were each an arrow's length, whose eyes were like flaming brands, and whose breath was as the smoke of a camp fire. The god's attendant spirits were forbidden to pass beyond the zealously-guarded portal, but one day a spirit, more adventurous than the rest, managed to escape into the abode of men. His spiritual form enabled him to cross the poisoned waters without a canoe, but as he was passing rapidly over the plain his absence was detected by the god of Darkness, who, in his wrath, suddenly turned him into a human being, and doomed him to wander the earth as an outcast forever. He is wandering now, for aught we know. Truly, the wrath of the King of the Land of the Myriad Mysteries is to be feared, and death cometh swiftly to those who offer him not offerings of flesh, and arouse his anger by expressing disbelief that he ruleth the earth."

"Then, according to thy belief, the Good Spirit is powerless?" I said.

"Yea, he hath, alas! been vanquished, and the god of Darkness holdeth supreme sway over men," he answered. "Among mine own people I have witnessed more than one case where a man expressed disbelief in the One of Evil at dawn, and ere darkness hath fallen he has come to a violent and unexpected end. The punishment of the sceptical is always death."

"And the dwelling-place of the Ruler of the World is that high land, towards which, at sunrise, we shall be pushing forward to discover?" I said.

"Yea. But have a care of thy life, O friend," he urged, in a tone of consternation. "Thou mayest gaze upon it from afar, but to approach it will be to encompass thine own end."

"When we reach within sight of it I shall decide how to act," I laughed, amused at the pagan's apprehensions. "Strangely enough we have, in our land, a legend very similar to thine, which telleth how one adventurous man escaped from the mysterious region, after which the cave became closed and all entrance and egress barred. The mystery fascinateth me, and I am determined at all hazards to seek its solution."

"Dost thou think thou wilt succeed where valiant men for ages past have failed?" he asked, in a tone of reproach.

"I may fail also," I said. "If thou wilt lead me thither, I will make at least an effort."

The black chief did not reply, but sat silent and motionless, still hugging his knees, and gazing with thoughtful, heavy expression into the fire. Perhaps he was trying to devise some scheme whereby I might be deterred from committing an act which he considered sheer folly. But I was determined to keep the promise I had made to Azala, and seek some explanation of the mystic marks upon our breasts. It was strange that every tribe—followers of the Prophet and pagans alike—possessed some curious legend regarding the unapproachable country; strange, also, that so many of the quaint beliefs coincided in two facts; namely, the escape of an adventurous spirit and the subsequent disappearance of the cavern. These legends had apparently been handed down through so many ages that they had now become bound up in the quaint and simple religious belief of the pagans, proving the great antiquity of the original incident or story upon which they were founded.

That some extraordinary mystery was therein hidden, I felt instinctively, and longed for the days to pass in order to stand before the gigantic rock and examine it closely. Tiamo, much impressed by what Yakul had said, was likewise eager to view the spot; but the chief's declaration that it was the dwelling-place of the Evil Spirit caused him considerable perturbation, for, as a pagan himself, he believed implicitly in the existence of Jinns, and in the One of Evil, which he constantly declared lurked in the most gloomy depths of the Forest of Perpetual Night. Once or twice on our lonely journey he had been terrified at seeing in the darkness some mysterious object moving, but it generally turned out to be a monkey, a leopard, or some other animal startled by our sudden invasion of his domain.

At such times I laughed at his dread of darkness, but I confess that more than once in that weird and terrible wilderness of trees I, myself, had become infected by his abject fear, and stood in readiness to witness some uncanny being advance towards us. Now, however, my little apelike companion expressed a profound belief that the seat of the Evil Spirit was actually beyond the Rock of the Great Sin, and that the story, as related by Yakul, was the most sensible solution of the mystery he had yet heard. I could not reprimand him, because I did not wish to cast doubt upon the belief of the grateful savage who had proved our sincere friend. Therefore I held my peace, declaring that I would express no opinion before I saw the spot.

Yakul laughed when I thus made reply to my slave, and turning to him, said, —

"Thy master acteth with discretion. Ofttimes, we trip in the hurry of the tongue. They are wise who speak not before examining a matter themselves."

"For many moons have we journeyed in search of the Rock of the Great Sin," the dwarf answered, "and, even though I may fear him who dwelleth therein, yet I, like my master, will not be deterred from approaching it closely."

"Then, thy life will pay the penalty of thy rashness," the chief observed, slowly nodding his head to emphasise his words.

"The result of any folly will be upon us alone," Tiamo said, in a resentful tone. "Lead us thither, and leave us to our own devices."

"Such is my intention," answered the chief of the Avejeli. "If thou hadst searched through the Forest of Perpetual Night, thou wouldst not have obtained a guide, even though thou hadst offered him a sack of cowries, or an ass's load of brass rods."

"Why?" I inquired.

"Because the secret of the existence of the seat of the Evil Spirit in our midst is carefully guarded by the forest tribes, and to lead a stranger thither is an offence punishable by death. Our prophets have for centuries urged upon us the necessity for keeping the whereabouts of the rock secret, declaring that some day a stranger will come from the north, and seek to penetrate the mystery. If the stranger is successful, then the vengeance of the Evil One will descend upon all forest-dwellers in whose keeping the secret remaineth, and sweep them out of existence by means of a terrible scourge of leprosy. Therefore, the tribe of pigmies holding the country near the rock are deadly hostile towards those who approach them, and none, save the Manuyema, have ever been permitted to go near, and even they were all quickly massacred by us, not one being spared to spread the news among his compatriots."

"Then, in acting as our guide, thou art running a risk of death?" I exclaimed, in surprise.

The chief nodded assent, adding: "It is the only means by which I can repay thee for giving me my life."

"If our efforts are satisfactory, thou wilt assuredly receive ample reward," I said.

"I want none," he replied. "But bring not upon our people the doom that hath so long been prophesied," he added, with earnest fervency.

"I may be the stranger whose coming hath been foretold," I observed, laughing.

El-Sadic, the dwarf, grinned from ear to ear, and rubbed his thighs, while Yakul moved uneasily, and, taking up a stick, slowly stirred the fire.

"I trust not," he said, in a harsh tone. "It would be better that I had died where the murderers of Tippu-Tib bound me, than I should be instrumental in leading the destroyer of our race unto victory."

"Destroyer of thy race!" I echoed. "I have no desire to destroy either the pigmies of the forest, or the stalwart dwellers of the river banks. My campaign is not one of conquest, but of curiosity. In searching for the rock I am but redeeming a pledge to the woman I love. Therefore, have no fear as to my intentions;" and laughing again, I added, "Whatever may occur, thou wilt assuredly be remembered."

"But the prophecy, it is—"

"Heed it not, be it what it may," I urged, interrupting him. "Be thou our guide, and give us thy protection through the country of the pigmies. Assuredly wilt thou be fitly rewarded."

"I take no reward from one to whom I owe so much," he answered, proudly. For a few moments he hesitated, then added: "I have promised to direct thy footsteps unto the mysterious region of the Evil One, and will do so, notwithstanding the prophecy. The pledge of Yakul is never broken. Therefore, trust in me, and within twelve days thine eyes shall be gladdened by the sight of the gloomy rock for which thou hast so long searched."

I thanked him, assuring him that by such an action he would repay my small service a thousandfold, and he accepted my expressions of pleasure with that calm dignity which had held him exalted above all others of his tribe.

"Then let us rest," he said. "To-morrow we must retrace our steps one march, and then strike in the direction of the sunrise. Yakul shall lead thee, but if thine adventurous expedition shouldst cost thee thy life, let it not be upon my head, for already have I given thee full warning of the dangers that must beset thee."

"Thou art exonerated from every blame, O my friend," I answered. "Of our own free desire we go forward unto the Land of the Myriad Mysteries, and we are ready that the consequences rest with us."

"Well hast thou spoken, O master," my slave exclaimed. "Wheresoever thou seekest for truth, there also will I bear thee company."

"Then let us refresh ourselves by sleep, and let us proceed at sunrise," said the chief of the Avejeli; and soon afterwards, having made couches of leaves, we stretched ourselves around the embers of our fire, the flickering of which cast weird, grotesque shadows upon the boles of the giants of the forest.

How long I slept I have no knowledge, but the crackling of wood awakened me. Opening my eyes quickly, without moving, I saw the flames had sunk and sleep had stolen over my two companions. Tiamo lay on his side, his hand on his *jambiyah* at his waist, while Yakul snored and rolled as if he did not like the ground to lie upon. The single ember that blazed threw its light upon some dark bushes within my line of sight.

Suddenly I thought I detected a small object moving in the deep shadow, and strained my eyes into the gloom. Yes! I was not deceived! Another dark form moved, then another and another, and as one crept out on tiptoe from the thick undergrowth, I saw it was a tiny, half-naked dwarf, wearing a curious square head-dress, advancing noiselessly, a small poisoned arrow held in his bow ready to fly at the first sign of our awakening.

The one creeping towards us did so with evil intent, for there was a keen, murderous look in his tiny, bead-like eyes. During the first few moments of this discovery I remained spellbound, allowing our adversaries to creep forward until within two spears' length of us.

Then I sent up a loud shout of alarm that rang through the great forest and came back again with strange, almost sepulchral echo.

Chapter Thirty One
On the Horizon

Instantly the tiny people of the Wambutti, none of whom reached higher than my waist, scampered back into the undergrowth, startled by my unearthly yells, but at the same moment Yakul jumped to his feet in alarm, an arrow in his bow.

"Why hast thou given warning?" he cried, glancing at me. "What hideous shape hath frightened thee?"

"See! in yonder bushes, the pigmies are lurking," I gasped in alarm, pointing to the spot where they had concealed themselves.

"How didst thou detect their presence?" he inquired.

"I watched them."

Turning towards the thick bushes, the savage chieftain shouted some words in a tongue unknown to me, and next second the impish little denizens of the forest depths sprang from their hiding-places, and recognising their friend, came crowding around, dancing and greeting us effusively.

Briefly Yakul explained our position. His eyes were fire; his passion for his slaughtered and enslaved race, and his passion for revenge, were as the lode-star of his life. After consultation, the hunters of the Wambutti relit our fire by rubbing two sticks together, and squatted around it, laughing and chattering in their strange language until the grey light, glimmering through the tall trees, told us that dawn had come. Times innumerable had the Avejeli assisted the dwarfs against the raiding dwellers on the grasslands and on the river banks. The yellow-complexioned pigmies, dwelling as they do deep in the impenetrable depths of the boundless Forest of Perpetual Night, are formidable enemies, for they conceal themselves so cleverly that their arrows and spears pierce the intruder before he is aware of their presence. As hunters, these little-known men stand first among the pagan tribes of Central Africa, and in return for food and bark-cloth supply the neighbouring tribes with quantities of ivory, and the deadliest of arrow-poisons. Their complexions are much lighter than the dwellers by the river or on the plains, and their villages are mere collections of tiny huts that appear like little straw-covered mounds placed in the centre of a forest clearing.

At first our weird little friends seemed inclined to regard me with considerable distrust, but on Yakul's assurance that I was no ally of Tippu-Tib's, their distrust gave place to curiosity as to my purpose in travelling through the forest. Yakul reminded them of the promise of assistance they had many times given him, and told them of my mission; whereupon, after consultation with their headman, they consented—not, however, without some reluctance—to guide us towards the Land of the Myriad Mysteries; and after re-arranging their elephant-trap into which we had fallen, our fire was extinguished and we struck camp, turning our faces in a north-easterly direction. Through a great, gloomy tract of primeval forest, where the foliage was so dense that scarcely a ray of light could struggle through to illuminate our weary footsteps, we passed over marshy ground, where poisonous vapours hung undisturbed by the faintest breath of air, and where neither animals nor birds could live; on over the decaying vegetation of centuries; on, day after day, now scrambling over fallen giants of the forest, and ever and anon sinking knee-deep in quagmires of foetid slime. Often we struck an elephant track which assisted us, but were always compelled to leave it very soon in order to continue our course. Thus through many dreary hours we pressed forward in the dull, dispiriting gloom.

Confident in the knowledge that each bivouac brought us nearer the spot for which I searched, I heeded neither fatigue nor peril, and judge my satisfaction, joy and eagerness, when at last we suddenly emerged from the forest gloom into the blessed light of day. Halting, I inhaled the first invigorating breath of pure air I had breathed for many weeks.

The dwarfs raising their hands above their heads, gave vent to some cabalistic utterances; then, trembling with fear, stood, not daring to proceed further into the country forbidden. Yakul called us to witness that our friends had guided us in the right path, and Tiamo, turning to me, cried excitedly in Arabic,—

"Of a verity, O master, soon will our eyes be delighted at the sight of the great rock. The chief Yakul is assuredly as sincere a friend as if he had made blood brotherhood with thee."

Facing towards the holy Ka'aba, I thanked Allah for his deliverance, and recited the Testification with some verses from the book of Everlasting Will.

Under a brilliant noonday sun the open country spread wide before us, a beautiful plain, covered with grass of freshest green, and stretching away into the far-off horizon, where a range of mountains rose blue, misty and indistinct.

"Behold!" shouted Yakul, pointing with his spear to the distant serrated line a moment later. "Behold, yonder peak that standeth higher than the rest, and is shaped like the prow of a canoe, is the spot which thou seekest. Lo! it is the Rock of the Great Sin!"

My eyes, strained in the direction indicated, could just distinguish the point where one mountain rose higher than its neighbours, its summit apparently obscured by the vapours that hung about it.

"Art thou certain that yonder crest is actually the rock we seek?" I asked, shading my eyes with my hands, and eagerly gazing away to the blue haze that enshrouded a mystery upon the elucidation of which my whole future depended.

"Of a verity the grassland beneath thy feet is the same field whereon my people gained the signal victory over their enemies. Behold! their whitening bones remain as relics of that fight; and yonder, afar, lieth the forbidden Land of the Myriad Mysteries."

"Let us hasten thither, O master," urged Tiamo, who had been standing agape in amazement, eagerly drinking in every word uttered by the sable chieftain.

"In short space shall we reach the shore of the wondrous Lake of the Accursed," Yakul exclaimed. "By to-morrow's noon our faces shall be mirrored in its waters."

"Let us speed on the wings of haste," I said; and then, remembering Yakul's confidence in the non-success of my strange mission, I added, "Each hour is of serious moment. Already have I tarried too great a space on my way hither, and must return more quickly than I came. How I shall journey back to Kano I know not."

"Thou needest not retrace thy footsteps along the route thou hast traversed," answered the chief. "Due north of yonder rock there runneth a track which leadeth through the Great Forest to Ipoto. Thence, crossing the Ihourou river, the way leadeth on through the desolate country of the Mbelia unto the mountain called Nai, whence thou canst journey in six marches to Niam-Niam, and onward unto thine own desert land."

Our friends, the dwarfs, had grouped themselves under the shadow of the trees on the edge of the forest, conversing seriously. None summoned sufficient courage to wander forth upon the verdant land, where flowers grew in wild abundance, and where herds of buffalo grazed undisturbed.

This strange land, unknown to all except themselves, they held in utmost awe. They dared not approach it more closely, lest the dreaded pestilence that had been prophesied should fall and sweep them from the face of the earth.

Yakul approached their headman, urging him to accompany us and explore the mysterious rock, but the tiny man only shook his head, and drawing himself up, answered,—

"Verily, we are thy friends, O friend, but seek not to cause us to invoke the wrath of the Destroyer, lest the pestilence should fall upon us. He who resteth his eyes on yonder rock will assuredly be smitten, and his entrails withered by the breath of the Evil Spirit of the Forest that scorcheth like the flame of a burning brand. To pass over yonder grassland is forbidden."

"We go forward in search of the Land of the Myriad Mysteries," the chief of the Avejeli explained.

"Then assuredly thou goest unto certain death," the dwarfs replied, almost with one accord, shaking their heads and shrugging their narrow shoulders.

"Be warned," their headman added. "The Destroyer is mighty; he ruleth the Great Forest and its people. Assuredly he is swift to punish!"

"He who will bear us company unto the Lake of the Accursed, let him stand forth, or if he dare not venture, then let him hold his peace," said Yakul, standing erect, spear in hand.

But not a dwarf advanced. All feared to pass across the fertile plain, and investigate the mysterious country beyond.

Then, after much parleying and many solemnly-uttered warnings on the part of the pigmies, my two companions and myself left them, setting our faces resolutely towards the sacred lake, the approach to which was prohibited to all.

The grass was soft beneath our feet after the difficult march through the untrodden forest; the sight of flowers, of animals and of birds refreshed our eyes after the eternal silence and appalling gloom in which we had existed through so many weary days; and as the sun sank in a sea of crimson behind us, and our shadows lengthened across the grass, I halted for a few moments to repeat the sunset prayer, remembering that there was one afar off who had opened her lattice and breathed upon the hot, stifling desert wind a fervent message of love.

Within sight of the entrance to the mysterious Land of the No Return I wondered, as I strode forward, what the result of my mission would be;

whether, by good fortune, I should be enabled to reach the Rock of the Great Sin in safety; whether the explanation of the mysterious Mark of the Asps upon my breast would ever be revealed; whether the true-hearted woman I loved so dearly still stood in peril of the vile intrigues around her; whether the Khalifa's plot had been frustrated, and whether, by Allah's grace, my feet would ever again tread the well-remembered courts of the luxurious Fada at Kano.

The traditions of the sons of Al-Islâm and those of the pagans were alike so ominous that, as the dark mountains gradually became misty and indistinct when the night clouds enveloped them, I became filled with gloomy apprehensions, fearing failure, and the fulfilment of the strange, terrifying prophecies of the dwarfs.

Chapter Thirty Two
The Great Sin

Hastily we sped forward early next morning, our eyes eagerly riveted upon our goal.

The saffron streak of dawn showed behind the great, gloomy range of blue and grey, and as the fleecy clouds lifted, we saw that the higher peaks beyond were tipped with snow. The lofty crests were tinted with an unusual blood-red light. Truly the country beyond had been justly named by the pagans the Land of the Myriad Mysteries.

Soon we ascended a knoll, and at its summit were enabled to distinguish, straight in front of us, a pool of dark water which, at that distance, seemed only a leopard's leap in width, lying immediately beneath the Rock of the Great Sin.

"Behold!" cried Tiamo, who had sped forward a few paces and gazed around. "See! O master! Yonder must be the Lake of the Accursed, the poisonous waters that all men fear!"

Even as I gazed, the sun shone forth from behind the mountains which Yakul called the Jebel el-Mantar (Mountains of the Look-out), and the shadow cast by the dark, towering rock fell across the black, silent pool. We quickened our pace, each of us breathlessly eager to investigate the mysterious spot. A great golden eagle came from his nest on the summit of the rock, soaring high above us, while a crowd of grey vultures hovered around with a persistency which seemed precursory of death.

"Alas! The birds of evil follow us," exclaimed Yakul, observing them; but neither Tiamo nor myself answered, for we were both too full of our own thoughts, fearing lest our mission should prove abortive. My slave fingered his amulets, uttering many strange exhortations, while my companion, the chief of the Avejeli, raised his long, sinewy arms towards the rock and cried aloud to the Evil Spirit, humbly acknowledging that he had broken the commandment, and earnestly craving forgiveness.

Nevertheless, we still hurried forward, and, half-an-hour before the sun reached the noon, were standing at the shore of the black pool, upon the unruffled surface of which the high, inaccessible face of the rock descending sheer into the water was faithfully reflected, with every detail of colour and form.

The scene was exactly similar in every particular to that which, from the lattice in the palace of Kano, I had seen reflected upon the sky. The mirage, though inverted, had been an exact reproduction of the wild, gloomy landscape.

With wondering eyes I gazed around, seeking to discover some clue to the mystery, but was at a loss how to commence.

The width of the Lake of the Accursed, from the spot where we stood to the base of the rock, was about a gunshot, and it extended on either side along the bases of the mountains as far as the eye could reach. The Rock of the Great Sin rose, a wall of dark grey stone devoid of any vestige of herbage, towering rough and rugged to enormous height, and overhanging in such a manner that it could not be scaled. Like the giant mountains and rocky pinnacles around and beyond, it was utterly inaccessible. Even if the water had not formed a natural barrier no man could ascend its precipitous face or climb its rugged, overhanging crags; while all around a chain of impassable rocks and mountains reared their mighty crests between us and the mysterious Land of the No Return. Suddenly I felt in my throat a strange sensation as of asphyxiation. Violent fits of coughing seized both my companions, while my own throat seemed to contract strangely, until I could only breathe in short, painful gasps.

Just at that moment my eyes fell upon the long, narrow pool, and I saw, wafted slowly along its glassy surface, a thin blue vapour. Bending, I placed my hand in the water; it was just tepid, and strongly impregnated with sulphur. Then I noticed that, within an arrow's flight of the shore, not even a blade of grass grew. The Lake of the Accursed was evidently fed by a large number of hot springs, and the strong sulphurous fumes given off exterminated life in every form. The assertions of the pigmies were correct. Those who approached the waters were in imminent peril of death.

Finding ourselves in this critical position, we all three sped away to the zone where the grass grew abundantly, and there found that we could again breathe freely. Without approaching nearer to the Lake of the Accursed, we proceeded to investigate the rocks to right and left. Apparently these high, grey crags flanked the bases of the giant, snow-capped mountains that beyond, in the unknown Land of the No Return, reared their heads to the cloudless heavens; but though we searched throughout the long and brilliant day, we were unable to discover any means of approach to the unknown and unexplored plateau that lay behind. As far as we travelled east or west the poisonous waters and soft, slimy swamps formed a natural gulf that precluded any attempt to scale the dizzy heights forming the outer, impregnable limits to the strange, rock-girt realm.

Times without number I stood gazing up at the dark mysterious rock, the spot held in awe alike by pagans of the Forest of Perpetual Night and true Believers. It had remained for me to discover that which for generations my kinsmen had sought and failed. So far, indeed, Allah had allowed me to be successful, but the promised elucidation of the mystery seemed as far off as ever, and as evening fell and the gigantic mountains, magnificent in their wild ruggedness, became crimsoned by the fiery afterglow, I began to realise the utter impossibility of obtaining from that grey, frowning wall any explanation of the Mark of the Asps, or of gaining the Land of the No Return, whereon the foot of man had never fallen.

When the plain was flooded with roseate radiance, we held earnest consultation together, and agreed that to remain nearer the lake for any length of time would prove fatal. Even Tiamo, who had been so sanguine of success, now expressed a fear that, with the exception of discovering the rock, our journey could have no further result. Yakul endorsed the dwarf's opinion, as, sitting upon his haunches, hugging his knees, he repeated a prayer to the Evil Spirit whose vengeance he feared.

Night came soon, and the mountains were silver with moonlight. The waters of the lake glittered in the white beams; the silver moon queened heaven amid her court of silver stars. What was there beyond that impassable barrier? A world all purity, all peace; a blanched world, bleached of blood and shame; a world of mystery, so fair it seemed to wait for some ethereal being, tall and radiant, winged with light, to path its unknown valleys. Sleep came not to my eyes. By some strange intuition I felt that at that spot some weird mystery remained hidden, and having travelled thus far, and actually discovered the Rock of the Great Sin, the spot that had remained a mystery through ages, I was determined that nothing should deter me from exploring further.

Yakul and the dwarf were eating their morning meal as I strolled alone at the edge of the zone, beyond reach of the poisonous, insidious vapours. Once again I gazed up at the weird, precipitous crag in abject wonderment. With its towering summit standing out boldly against the vault of cloudless blue, and its delicate tints of brown and grey faithfully reflected upon the still waters, it rose, a barrier between the Known and the Unknown— mysterious, marvellous, magnificent.

With arms folded and chin upon my breast, I surveyed its inaccessible base, seeking for the hundredth time to discover some means of gaining the land beyond, when suddenly my eyes were attracted by a portion of the rock close to where the waveless waters lapped its enormous base. In its aspect there was nothing very remarkable, yet my eyes, on the alert for the slightest clue, detected that for a short distance the black strata of the rock ran at an entirely different angle to the remainder, as if at some time or other the base had been disturbed by some violent upheaval. Covering my mouth with my hand to exclude the suffocating vapours, I rushed down to the edge of the lake, straining my gaze in its direction. At about a spear's length above the surface, this strange inequality extended, but apparently the rock above had remained undisturbed by the volcanic action.

The legend alleging that the savage serpent, which ages ago guarded the entrance to the Land of the No Return, had smote the rock in his wrath, and that its rocky portals had instantly closed, recurred to me. Could that spot have been the actual entrance to the Unknown Land? Might not the zealously-guarded gate have closed and sunk beneath the surface of the unfathomable waters?

I held my breath, feeling myself on the verge of a discovery. Yet to investigate seemed impossible, for we had no wood from which to construct a raft, and the very air was poisoned by noxious vapours that wafted in serpentine gusts across the surface with the faintest zephyr.

Yakul shouted, but I heeded him not. I was gazing fixedly at the Rock of the Great Sin, striving to devise some means by which to reach and examine the disturbed portion of its base. It occurred to me that, by diving into the water, I could perhaps swim across and return without becoming asphyxiated, therefore I walked back to where my two companions were squatting, and amazed them by announcing my intention to cross the Lake of the Accursed.

"But are not its waters fatal? Thou wilt, of a verity, be poisoned!" cried Tiamo, springing to his feet and clutching my arm in alarm.

"Unto the Lalla Azala I gave my pledge that I would strive to elucidate this mystery," I answered, calmly. "I shall plunge in yonder, and strike towards the rock. If I fail, return quickly unto her and tell her in what manner I died. Tell her that for many moons have I journeyed until at last I discovered the Rock of the Great Sin, and that, in seeking what was hidden, I was brought unto Certainty. But, by the grace of the One Merciful, who hath guided me by the sun of his favour, I hope to find strength sufficient to make my investigation, and return hither in safety. In case I should not," I added, removing one of my amulets from the little string of talismans, sewn carefully in soft leather, that I had worn always next my skin ever since I could remember, and handing it to him, "in case I should fail, take this to the Lalla Azala, and tell her that my last thoughts were of her."

"Truly I will, O master," answered the dwarf, grasping the small golden circle, and feeling it with nervous, trembling fingers.

"Is it not folly, O friend, to trust thyself in yon sacred lake? There is death in its breath," Yakul urged, regarding me with a strange look of pitying suspicion, as if fearing that I had taken leave of my senses. To him the very suggestion seemed preposterous. He had feared to approach the waters, and my resolution to desecrate them by plunging in filled him with awe.

"It cannot be avoided," I answered. "I seek that which I desire to find, and am determined to make the attempt if Allah—whose name be exalted!—willeth it."

"And if thou failest?" he asked.

"Allah alone knoweth the hearts of men. He leadeth me, and I am not afraid," I answered.

"Alas! I fear thou wilt find naught," the savage chieftain exclaimed. "Yon mystery is hidden from man, and vengeance falleth upon him who seeketh to tear aside the veil."

"I know," I said. "A hundred times hath the same words been spoken unto me. Each man to whom I mentioned the object of my journey prophesied failure, yet their prognostications have, up to the present, proved untrue. I stand here, before the rock which followers of the Prophet have sought for ages, but could not find, and I tell thee I am resolved to investigate further."

"Have a care of thy life, O master," cried my slave. "Think, the Lalla Azala, who loveth thee, could live no longer if thou wert dead."

"It is to aid her, El-Sadic, to fulfil my pledge, to gain that which she hath said will bring us together never to part, that I essay this attempt. I go. If I fail, act as I have spoken. May Allah accord thee his favours."

Convinced of the fruitlessness of any effort to deter me from diving into the poisonous pool, the pagan dwarf bowed his head, while Yakul drove his spear viciously into the ground and turned from me with a gesture of impatience. Addressing Tiamo, I asked him to accompany me, and we walked along the edge of the grass to a point opposite where the strata of the rock had apparently been disturbed. Then, halting a few moments, I gave him a further message of affection to deliver to my enchantress in case my strength should fail. Overcome with emotion, the faithful slave again and again pointed out the perils of such a rash attempt, urging me to abandon it, but I was determined, and quickly divested myself of a portion of my clothing.

Aloud I besought the Omniscient One to bear me on the strong arm of his aid, and shouting a word of encouragement to my alarmed companions, I dashed across the strip of parched, barren ground, holding my breath, throwing myself upon the mercy of the One Merciful—then, a moment later, I plunged headlong into the reeking, malodorous waters.

The strange sensation of asphyxiation seized me as I rose to the surface, but, determined not to turn back, I struck out boldly for the opposite side, where the rock descended sheer into the lake. Keeping my mouth well closed I took long, bold strokes, each of which brought me nearer to the precipitous face of the giant rock. The shouts of my excited companions broke upon my ears, but I swam on, striving with all my might.

Exerting every muscle, I clave the waters, propelling myself towards the point that had been disturbed by the singular upheaval. Very soon, however, my breathing became shorter and more difficult. The surface of the water seemed gloomy and ominous in the shadow cast by the sacred rock, and although I had long considered myself a strong swimmer, yet the difficulty of gaining breath paralysed my muscles, and a strange cramp that I had never before experienced seemed to seize me in iron grip.

In the centre of the dreaded Lake of the Accursed I felt my strength fast ebbing.

With set teeth I struggled against the fate that threatened each moment to overwhelm me, and, after resting a few seconds, struck out again straight towards my goal. As I neared it I was astonished to find that swimming was much easier, and my pace increased. Then suddenly I became aware that a current was carrying me swiftly towards the very spot I desired to reach. The dark rock rose before me, bare and imposing, and the black strata, that from the shore had appeared like lines thin as bow strings, now showed wide, rugged and distinct. My satisfaction at being thus assisted by a current, the existence of which I was ignorant, was quickly succeeded by a fear that froze my blood, as suddenly I noticed, right under the disturbed portion of the rock, a great eddying whirlpool, towards which I was being swiftly carried.

To enter those circling waters meant certain death. With all my might I fought and struggled, endeavouring to turn back, but, alas! found myself utterly powerless, being carried helplessly forward towards the funnel-shaped depression in the centre of the whirlpool, where all objects that entered were sucked down into its deep, unfathomable depths. When in

England, I read of fatal circling currents in the sea, but the discovery of one in a still lake dismayed me.

Onward I was swept, the current gaining greater rapidity every moment. Knowing that no hand could be outstretched to rescue me, I cried farewell words to my companions. But my voice, thin and weak as a child's, could not reach them. For life I fought desperately, but all effort was futile. Like a mere chip of wood floating upon the surface I was drawn into the fatal circle, and carried round the outer edge of the strange whirlpool with such terrible velocity that my head reeled, and a sickening dizziness overcrept me.

So near I passed to the mysterious rock, that in order to steady and save myself, I clutched at its smooth, gigantic base with both hands. But only for a second. Over the pale yellow slime with which the stone was covered my frantic fingers slipped, and falling back powerless into the eddying waters, I was again swept into the fatal, ever-narrowing circle.

The eddying current whirled me round and round with amazing swiftness for a few moments, until suddenly I reached its centre, and felt myself being sucked down by an irresistible force. An instant later I knew that the black waters had closed over me. Confused sounds roared in my ears like the thunder in Ramadan, but ere my sensibility became utterly obliterated I knew I was being carried deep down into a darkness that, even in my critical state of breathless half-consciousness, filled me with an all-consuming terror and chilled my heart.

Chapter Thirty Three
Where Dwelt the Devourer

In the appalling darkness that overwhelmed me, I fought, blindly beating the water with frantic hands. As I struggled to extricate myself from the power of the whirling current my arms suddenly struck against stones on either side. With desperate effort I put out my hands, and to my amazement found myself being carried onward, by a rushing flood, through what appeared to be a narrow tunnel in the face of the rock, deep below the lake's surface. Though but half-conscious, I remember distinctly reflecting that the whirlpool had no doubt been caused by this violent outrush of water descending to feed some subterranean river, and that the chasm had probably been caused by the volcanic disturbance that had first attracted my attention. Half suffocated, and powerless against the roaring torrent, I was sucked downward, deep into the fathomless chasm.

Suddenly my fingers came in contact with a projecting ledge of rock, which I gripped with all my might, just managing to steady myself, and so arrest my further progress. Drawing breath, I was amazed to find that my head was above water, although the wild roar of the flood was deafening, and in the total darkness I could distinguish nothing. With set teeth I strained every muscle, and after several futile attempts, at length succeeded in scrambling over black, slime-covered stones beyond reach of the roaring torrent rushing down to mysterious subterranean depths. Strangely enough, the air seemed fresher than outside in the lake, for here, in the heart of the rock, there appeared to be ventilation. This discovery renewed my hopes. The aperture that admitted air would prove a means of egress from that dark, loathsome place, if only I could discover it. Though still giddy from the effects of the whirling waters, I rose slowly to my feet, and found that I could stand upright. With eager fingers outstretched before me I felt my way carefully onward over the rocks, rendered slippery by the sulphurous deposits of ages. In fear and trepidation lest I should slip and fall into some yawning fissure, I nevertheless groped on up a steady incline until suddenly my eyes caught a faint but welcome glimmer of grey light.

Towards this I stumbled on, falling once upon my hands and severely grazing them, but taking no heed of the accident in my breathless eagerness to discover some means of escape. I stood facing the mute darkness, all mystery, and gloom.

Clambering on over some rough boulders, and passing between the great rocks that had fallen so near to one another that it was with difficulty I squeezed between them, I at length found myself in an enormous cavern, from the vaulted roof of which depended gigantic stalactites, while high up, and inaccessible, was an aperture that admitted light and air, but, in front of me, all was a black, impenetrable darkness. The great place had, undoubtedly, been formed by the action of the water, but the process had involved an enormous length of time, and now the course of the subterranean stream had been diverted by some upheaval.

With the evil-smelling waters dripping from my ragged gandoura, I stood gazing around the great, natural chamber in wonderment. Was this the cavern described in the legends as the entrance to the Land of the No Return? the dwelling-place of the savage reptile that acted as janitor? My eyes were fixed upon the Cimmerian gloom beyond, for I feared to come face to face with some unknown and uncanny tenant of that chamber, where my timid footsteps echoed away into the impenetrable blackness, in which every sound became exaggerated, and every object weirdly distorted.

The sides of the cavern were apparently of rough, black granite, but in the grey light that fell across the place, the long crystals of fantastic shape glistened and shone with the brilliance of diamonds, and the floor, rough and uneven, was formed of huge boulders, that had evidently been tossed hither and thither by the violent volcanic eruption that had altered the angle of the strata outside. Little rivulets flowed over the floor, cutting deep channels in the stones, where blind and colourless crayfish of enormous size, and of unknown type, slowly crept, while, disporting themselves in the water, were strange, finny denizens of the subterranean river. On examination, I found they had no eyes, and had lost the colouration characteristic of their outer-world relatives, by reason of passing their whole time in total darkness. There were also great, grey toads, and fat, slowly-moving lizards, alike sightless and uncanny. From where I stood, the distant, roaring waters sounded like the continual, monotonous moaning of the storm-wind, and it was with failing heart that I proceeded with my explorations, for I well knew that to reach the exit high above was utterly impossible.

Without food or fresh water, I had been drawn into that great cavern by the whirlpool and entombed. Tiamo and Yakul, watching for me to rise to the surface, and finding that I had utterly disappeared, would, I knew, conclude that I had been drowned; and the dwarf, acting upon my instructions, would return to Kano, bearing the sad tidings to Azala. Alas!

I could not communicate with them. In my helplessness I cried aloud unto Allah, the Most High, to show me the right path, but my wild wail only echoed through the hollow cavern, like the mocking voice of Azrael.

Under the great opening, that was overshadowed by a huge boulder, but into which blew fresh air in stormy gusts, showing that near the spot the rocks were open to the sky. I stood in full consciousness that could I but climb to that altitude I should be enabled to enter the forbidden land. Yet all thought of gaining that exit had to be abandoned. Even if I could scale the steep wall of the cavern, to reach the opening in its roof was impossible.

Here was yet another barrier between myself and the unknown.

Having carefully surveyed the cavern to right and left, I went forward at last, clambering over great, sharp stones that hurt my feet and grazed my elbows, and splashing into deep black pools, until, passing beyond the circle of light towards the portion of the strange place that remained in total darkness, my eager eyes suddenly caught sight of a portion of the black wall of the cave that had evidently been rendered flat and smooth by the hand of man, and upon it, deeply graven in the stone, but now half-obliterated by Time's effacing finger, was a wall-picture, the extraordinary character of which held me amazed, petrified.

" OVER THE STRANGE, FANTASTIC OUTLINES MY EYES TRAVELED."

The Eye of Istar | 189

Over the strange, fantastic outlines my eyes travelled, deciphering the ancient scene it was intended to represent. An exclamation of amazement involuntarily escaped my parched lips, for it furnished me with the first clue to the mystery I was striving to elucidate. It told me of things of which I had never before dreamed.

Truly, I had struggled through the natural, and hitherto impassable barrier between the known world and that unknown, and was now actually on the threshold of a land of a thousand wonders.

The earnest, appealing words Azala had uttered, when requesting me to seek the truth, recurred to me, and, as I gazed upon these outlines, limned upon the rock-tablet by hands that ages ago had fallen to dust, I felt myself on the verge of a discovery even more extraordinary than any my wildest thoughts had ever framed.

The detail of the mysterious picture was amazing. Its art was unique— the art of a cultured, luxurious civilisation which had long been forgotten, even in the age when our lord Mahomet lived—but in it was one feature so curious and remarkable that its sight held me breathless, agape, transfixed.

The tablet, fashioned from the solid rock, was of great extent, with life-sized figures in bas-relief, sculptured with consummate skill, and as soon as my eyes caught sight of it I recognised its great antiquarian value. The study of forgotten nations had always attracted me from boyhood. Indeed, I had followed the example set by my father, who was perhaps the best-known antiquarian among the Arabs of Algeria, and was frequently sought out by travellers interested in the relics of bygone ages. While I was still a lad, he, at that time living in Constantine, met an Englishman named Layard, who came to examine the inscriptions at the Bab-el-Djabia and the ruins at Sidi Mecid, and subsequently embraced the opportunity of accompanying him through Kurdistan and Mesopotamia as interpreter. Afterwards, he assisted in the excavations on the sites of ancient Babylon and Nineveh, where many wonderful archaeological treasures were brought to light. He was present when the great winged bull was discovered beneath the mound of Nimroud, and on account of the keen interest he took in the various sculptures unearthed, and his ability to sketch them, he was promoted to be one of the Englishman's chief assistants. Thus, from the first great discovery of Assyrian remains, my father had been enabled to study them, and when he returned home four years later, he brought with him many copies of strange cuneiform inscriptions, and drawings of curious sculptures, all of which interested me intensely. From him I thus derived my knowledge of the inscriptions of Babylonia, imperfect though it might be, but yet of sufficient extent to enable me to discern the Arabic equivalents of the strange lines of arrowheads graven upon this rock, and forming part of the picture I had so unexpectedly discovered. While at college in Algiers, I had eagerly devoured the few books in French, explaining the monuments of Babylonia, and in London had continued the study, by that means adding to the knowledge I had already gained under the tuition of my father. Few sons of Al-Islâm are archaeologists, but, as with my father, so also with me, the study had been a hobby, and on many occasions the French professors had expressed surprise at the extent of my knowledge of that strange language known as cuneiform.

By the dress and physiognomy of the figures portrayed upon the rock-tablet, I at once discerned they were not ancient Egyptian, as I at first believed, but Assyrian. The general arrangement of the picture showed it to be a record of similar character to those found in the wonderful buried palaces of Nineveh and Babylon.

In the faint glimmer of light I stood straining my eyes upon this silent record of a forgotten age. The first object I distinguished was a winged circle at the right-hand corner; the emblem of the Babylonian supreme deity. Below, in a chariot drawn by three handsomely-caparisoned horses, were three warriors in coats of mail, one being in the act of discharging an arrow at the enemy, one driving, and the third shielding his companions. The trappings of the horses, and the decorations of the chariot itself consisted of stars and other sacred devices, while at the side was suspended a quiver full of arrows, and the helmets of the warriors showed them to belong to the early Babylonian period. Following the chariot was a eunuch on foot, with a bow over his shoulder, a quiver slung behind, and bearing in his hand a kind of mace.

He was represented attired in a dress ornamented richly with gold and heavy fringe, while his upper garment was apparently a golden breastplate, across which showed the band by which the quiver was suspended. He wore no head-dress, and his feet were bare, but his position and bearing denoted that he was the servant of a monarch. Behind him there was depicted a chariot, not so gorgeously decorated as the first, drawn by two horses and led by two men, probably eunuchs. Over the horses' heads rose high plumes, three in number, tassels fell over their foreheads and hung around their necks, together with rosettes, engraved beads and the sacred star; their tails were bound in the centre by ribbons, and suspended from the axle of the chariot was a large tassel. Standing behind, as if already passed by the expedition, the sacred tree was elaborately and tastefully portrayed, the tree bearing a large number of those mystic flowers that are so prominent a feature in early Babylonian decoration, showing that the dwellers within that wonderful city were possessed of highly-refined taste. Below was a picture of two scribes, writing down the number of heads and the amount of spoil, while the tablet behind them was occupied by many lines of graven arrowheads.

Underneath was pictured, in graphic detail, a peaceful, religious procession of gods, borne on the shoulders of warriors. Each figure was carried by four men: the first was that of a female seated on a throne, holding in one hand a ring, in the other a kind of fan, and on the top of her square, horned cap was a star. The next figure was also that of a female, wearing a similar cap, seated in a chair, and holding in her left hand a ring; she was also carrying something in her right hand, but its form I could not distinguish. The third figure puzzled me considerably; it was much smaller in its proportions than those preceding it, was half-concealed in a case or box, and had a ring in the left hand; while the fourth was that of a man in the act of walking, holding in one hand a thunderbolt, and the other an axe, evidently the Babylonian deity, Belus or Baal. Upon the identity of the other gods I was undecided, but in the right-hand corner of the tablet was sculptured a figure of the goddess Istar, the Assyrian Venus, draped and standing erect on a lion, crowned with a mural coronet, upon which was a star, denoting her divinity. In one hand she was represented as bearing the moon, and the other grasped two objects which had first attracted my attention and riveted my gaze. She was holding out two serpents, entwined in such a manner as to form the puzzling device with which my breast was branded—the Mark of the Asps!

Taking a small, flat stone, I stood on tiptoe and carefully scraped away the dirt of ages from that portion of the sculpture, finding underneath the two serpents engraven in minute detail. Then I scraped the dress of the eunuch and found the same symbol there depicted. Save in one or two instances, the ages that had passed since the great rock-tablet had been hewn had left it untouched. The deeper portions of the picture were, however, filled with dark grey moss and the accumulated dirt of centuries, but with the aid of the stone I commenced to scrape the inscriptions and very soon succeeded in so far cleaning them that the lines were decipherable.

It was apparent that the intention of the sculptor had been to portray, at the base of the picture, the procession of gods being carried into the Temple of Istar, or Astarte, but the reason she bore in her hand the entwined serpents was a mystery inscrutable. Upon the walls of the palaces at Nimroud, many representations of the goddess, bearing in her hand a single serpent, had been discovered, but never before had she been found pictured with the mystic symbol that had been the problem of my life.

I stood before the dark face of rock, speechless in wonderment, for here, as Azala had predicted, I had actually made a discovery, amazing and bewildering. The mark that we both bore upon our breasts had for ages remained engraven there, a symbol of forgotten deity, a device, no doubt, held in reverence and awe by a civilisation now vanished.

That vast, weird cavern, filled with the monotonous roar of tumbling waters, inhabited by blind, unknown animals and reptiles, yet rendered almost fairylike by its wonderful stalactites, which glittered whenever a shaft of pale light caught them, was indeed peopled by ghosts of the past. By whose hand had those marvellous pictures been chiselled? By whose order had that tablet been prepared? The dark, gloomy place was, indeed, well named the Gate of the Land of the No Return. Was I not actually within the Rock of the Great Sin? What, I wondered, was the nature of the great sin to which the rock had remained a mute witness?

With arms folded, I stood gazing upon the sculptured stone, long and earnestly, thinking, with affection, of the graceful, trustful woman who loved me, and for whose sake I had struggled to set foot upon ground that for ages had remained untrodden by man. Even at that moment I knew, alas! that her slave, Tiamo, would be on his way back to Kano to impart the news of my death, and I myself was powerless. To return was impossible. I was compelled to proceed.

But if I failed to discover any exit? The dread thought chilled my heart. Perhaps, after all, I had been entombed, and my fate would be death from starvation.

With only an impenetrable darkness beyond, the outlook was by no means reassuring; nevertheless, I struggled desperately to stifle my apprehensions, determined to decipher, as far as my knowledge served me, the cuneiform inscription, which I anticipated might explain the mystery of the symbol borne by the goddess Istar, whose worship formed such a historical feature in the religion of Babylon.

As I gazed around the dull, dispiriting, natural chamber, there crept over my heart a terrible sense of loneliness, such as I have never before experienced. Seized by an appalling, indescribable dread, I shuddered.

Next second, however, I set my teeth firmly, arguing within myself that upon my coolness my escape might depend, and then commenced a careful study of the parallel lines of chiselled characters. For fully an hour I was engaged in scraping and deciphering each word, finding their study so fascinating, that I actually forgot that I was alone in that wonderful natural prison. A considerable time elapsed before I could discover the commencement of the inscription, but having done so, I found that, with the exception of one or two small places, where the action of time upon the stone had caused it to fall in scales and thus efface the words, I could decipher it sufficiently well to ascertain its purport.

The words I read caused me to stand aghast. The statement, quaintly expressed and sometimes vague, staggered belief. Commencing about the centre of the tablet, it read as follows:—

"Ruler of the World and Builder of Babylon, the City of Cities, I, Semiramis, daughter of the Moon-god, Sin, who conquered the hosts of my enemies, who is never triumphed over by my foes, who put my captives to the sword and offered sacrifices, caused this record to be written by Nebu-sum-Iskum, my scribe, in the month Elul, day 18th, year 25th. Semiramis, Queen of Babylon.

"*The record of my warriors, the battle-shout of my fighting, the submission of enemies hostile, whom Anu and Rimmon to destruction have given, on this my tablet and my foundation-stone have I written. The tablets of my father duly I cleaned; victims I sacrificed; to their places I restored for future days, for a day long hereafter, for whatsoever queen hereafter reigneth. When the temple of Anu and Rimmon, the gods great, my lords, its walls grow old and palaces decay, their ruins may she renew, my tablets and my foundation-stones duly may she cleanse, victims may she slay, to their places may she restore, and her name with mine may she write. Like myself, may Anu and Rimmon, the great gods, in soundness of heart and conquest in battle bountifully keep her. He who my inscriptions and my foundation-stones shall conceal, shall hide, to the water shall lay, to the fire shall burn, in dust shall cower in a home underground, a place, not seen for interpretation shall set, the name written shall erase and his own name shall write, and an attack evil shall devise; he also, from the world I have left, who seeketh to enter this my kingdom called Ea, the Land of the Lord of Wisdom, may Anu and Assur, the gods great, my lords, strongly injure him, and with a curse grievous may they curse him. May* he wither beneath the touch of Niffer, lord of the Ghost Land, his kingdom may the gods dissipate, and may he be rooted up and destroyed from out of his country; the armies of his lordship may they devour, his weapons may they break, the destruction of his army may they cause; in the presence of his enemies wholly may they cause him to dwell; may the Air-god with pestilence and destruction his land cut off; want of crops famine and corpses against his land may he lay; against the sovereignty of his full power may he speak; his name, his seed in the land may he destroy.

"To extend my empire I left Ninyas, my son, to govern Babylon, and went forth with my legions into the land of the Ethiopians, and there overthrew mine enemies, of captives taken forty thousand, and of oxen twenty thousand, and much spoils of gold and silver and precious stones. And the number of the slaughtered men amounted to thirty thousand. Even while my warriors were counting their great spoils came there unto them news astounding, that over Babylon my son, Ninyas, had proclaimed himself king, whereupon my army that I had led rose up against me, their quern, and marched northward, through the land of the Egyptians, to the banks of the river where I built Babylon and constructed my gardens that overhang and are unsurpassed. May they enter the regions of corruption, the dwelling of the deity Irkalla: may dust be their food, their victuals mud; may the light they not see, and in a terrible darkness dwell. Of my legions and my slaves as many as have remained loyal unto me, numbering twenty thousand, renounced their citizenship, and after wandering and fighting for twenty moons, accompanied me unto this place, the road whose way is without return, to the house whose entrance is without exit, there to found a country that I have named Ea, and raised up my throne in a city which standeth from this Rock of Sin, the Moon-god, fifteen marches towards the sunrise... Here have I offered sacrifices to the Sun-god and to Anu, and set up this my record. To this, my land, none may enter and none may leave on pain of a death terrible and swift. Upon him who breaketh this my commandment may the wrath of the Air-god most avenging fall, may he be smitten with pestilence, may his limbs rot and drop asunder, and may he fall captive in the hands of the great Devourer of the Living... Lo! I am Astarte, worshipped by men in the temples of Babylon, and the star is set upon my head. This my commandment have I written here, at the Gate of the Land of the No Return, which is the only entrance to the country without exit; the country in which I have raised the city called Ea, the gates of which are of brass, and the magnificence of which surpasseth even Babylon which I built, and upon which my curse hath now fallen. These are the words of Semiramis, the queen whom men call Istar, daughter of the Moon-god, the conqueror of all enemies, who founded the Kingdom of Ea, to which men from the world we have left may not enter, neither may a single man, woman or child among my subjects leave. Verily, this my kingdom is the Land of the No Return, and I, Semiramis, who ruled *over Babylon, and who, as Istar, ruleth all men throughout the world, have here built my palace and established my foundation-stones and set up my monuments. This throne have I, the goddess-queen of the world and of the heavens, erected. He who seeketh to enter my forbidden kingdom, to tear it out or overthrow it, so shall he and his family be torn out and be overthrown, and from his place shall he be uprooted. And I have set up this throne in the strength of the Sun-god Shamas, lord of light, and driver away of evil, to whom I have offered sacrifices and burnt-offerings abundant. These words I speak."*

Thrice I deciphered this strange record from beginning to end, to reassure myself that my eyes did not deceive me, until at length I became convinced that I had elucidated its meaning correctly; that I was actually on the threshold of the Land of the No Return; that could I only escape from my subterranean prison, I might actually discover the hidden, unknown and mysterious Kingdom of Ea, founded by the great queen, who, ages ago, built the most wonderful city of cities.

I stretched forth my hands above my head, and with a loud voice implored the aid, protection and guidance of the One. But my words only came back to me from the dark, damp recesses of the cavern, deep, distinct and dismal. There was no exit.

Chapter Thirty Four
The Land of the No Return

With strained eyes and failing heart, I gazed around the gloomy, sepulchral cavern. High above, a faint grey light glimmered far beyond my reach, while before me was only an impenetrable darkness, wherein I feared to venture, lest I should fall into some abyss. The curious wall-picture looked weird in the faint rays, and the long row of warriors, bearing the figures of their strange gods, presented a fantastic, but dismal, appearance. Once again I stood gazing at the strange sculpture, fascinated by the device of the asps, the strange symbol that had linked Azala's destiny with mine, and the meaning of which it was my sole object to discover.

Beyond, in the undiscovered Land of the No Return, an explanation might await me, if only I could reach that mysterious region; but, as again I gazed about me, I could not rid myself of a horrible presage that the rushing, poisonous waters had drawn me to my doom. I had taken in every detail of that scene sculptured in the black rock with such minuteness that, if called upon, I could have made a drawing of it with accuracy, for therein lay the first clue to the mystery. This remarkable record of Semiramis, besides putting an end to the doubts which for ages had existed regarding her deposition as Queen of Babylon, also announced the establishment of a new colony, of which the world, up to that moment, had gained no knowledge. Historians, antiquarians, professors, imams and wise men of Al-Islâm had for centuries been puzzled by the strange legends, but had never penetrated the veil of mystery. It had remained for me to unearth a record of the highest interest, which for ages had lain hidden within its natural tomb. Deciphering those chipped lines of curious arrowheads, I felt myself on the threshold of a world unknown, and trembled lest I should encounter any uncanny or undreamed-of object in that wonderful chamber below the earth.

As I stepped across the sulphur-stained rocks, in order to examine the opposite wall of the cavern, my foot caught some object, and stooping, I picked it up. It was a short, straight sword of very ancient pattern, still in its scabbard, with a wonderfully wrought crosshilt of gold thickly encrusted with dirt. I endeavoured to draw the weapon, but failed, for the blade was firmly rusted in its sheath, therefore, finding it useless and only an encumbrance, I was compelled to cast it aside.

From where I stood I gazed upon the curious monument of a momentous but forgotten period, and the sight of the strange symbol brought vividly to my mind my faithful promise to Azala, and my dead mother's injunction to prosecute the search after truth. I remembered that upon the result of my mission Azala's happiness, perhaps even her life, depended; therefore, with sudden resolve, I saw that to escape by the way I had entered was impossible; to penetrate the rayless darkness beyond was the only chance remaining to me.

At first I shuddered at the suggestion, not because I entertained any foolish superstition, but the place was altogether so weird and extraordinary that I deemed it more than probable I should witness some terrible sight, or encounter some strange being unknown to our world. Unarmed, clothed only in a wet and ragged gandoura, but with my little string of charms I had worn since childhood still around my neck, I stood breathless in hesitation.

For Azala's sake I had plunged into the Unknown, and I decided that to secure our mutual happiness I must face the consequences, which meant the exploration of that dark, sepulchral pit. Already Tiamo was on his way to her to impart news which I knew would cause her despair. Dire consequences might follow. Therefore I knew it was imperative that I should, in order that her grief might not be unduly prolonged, lose no time in seeking the truth and returning to her. Thus, at last, after considerable trepidation and hesitation, I strove to overcome my fears, and decided to proceed with my investigations, and search in the darkness for some exit.

Many were the perils I had faced fearlessly during my adventurous career as one of the Ansar of the Khalifa, and through the tedious journey in search of the Land of the No Return, but never in the darkest hours had I experienced such abject, indescribable fear as now froze my heart and held me inanimate and powerless. I clenched my hand, and, turning my eager ear towards the invisible portion of the great natural chamber, listened. But I could detect no sound beyond the roaring of the torrent; then, with a sudden determination to penetrate and explore the place, I strode forward into the very bowels of the earth, entering a darkness that could almost be felt, as impenetrable, indeed, as that to which our holy Korân tells us the tormented dwellers in Al-Hotama are doomed.

On, with both hands outstretched, I groped, now tripping in the fissures cut deeply in the rock by the tiny rivulets which seemed to traverse the floor of the cavern in every direction, now floundering through a quagmire of slush which emitted an unpleasant, sulphurous odour, often cutting my feet upon the sharp, jagged rocks, and frequently grazing my knees and elbows. But I was too excited to notice pain. Of the size or extent of the place I had no idea, but, having ventured therein, I was compelled to proceed, and continued my explorations, penetrating deeper and deeper into the tunnel-like cave. At first I had proceeded very slowly and with great caution, but soon, anxious to ascertain whether exit were possible, my feet hurried, and I stumbled quickly onward, eager to discover the extent and nature of the honeycombed labyrinth, fearing lest, after all, it might be merely a *cul-de-sac*.

I was actually in the very heart of the giant base of the Rock of the Great Sin, the wonderful black, towering crag which had only existed in the morning mirage of the desert and in the legends of the story-tellers throughout the Soudan. Over ground that foot of man had not trodden for ages I stumbled, seeking the unknown alone, unarmed, and in darkness appalling and complete. Reflection brought with it a sense of impending danger, an evil presage that, strive how I would, I could not get rid of its depressing influence. Yet the calm face of Azala, with her dark, serious, trusting eyes rose before me, and the thought continued to recur to me that for her sake I had striven, and, so far, been successful. Once again the knowledge of her passionate love held me to my purpose; once again I pressed forward blindly to seek the knowledge that for all time had been withheld from man.

On I went through the everlasting gloom, clambering over the rough, uneven rocks, then sinking knee-deep in the slimy deposits left by the rivulets. In the impenetrable darkness of the noisome place, strange noises startled me as blind, unseen reptiles escaped from my path, plunging into the water with a splash, and great lizards scuttled to their holes beneath the stones.

Between giant boulders, which had apparently fallen from the roof, I squeezed myself, climbing over high barriers of stone and creeping on all-fours through crevices that were all but impassable, I had proceeded for more than one hour. I shouted, but the distant echoes above and around showed that the extent of the gloomy place was bewildering, and so complete was the darkness that the terrible dread oppressing me became intensified. Nevertheless, one important fact gave me heart, causing me to persevere, namely, the atmosphere was not poisonous, showing that somewhere in that wonderful grotto air was admitted. Where there was air there must be light, I argued, and where light, then means of exit. Therefore I proceeded, with eyes strained in the blackness before me, hoping each moment to discern some welcome glimmer of the blessed light of day. But, alas! although my wandering footsteps took me deeper and deeper, no welcome ray was I enabled to detect. Had I but a torch, my progress would have been more rapid, for I could have avoided sinking into those sloughs of icy-cold slush, and could have stepped across the water-courses instead of stumbling clumsily into them. Half the horrors surrounding me would have been dispelled if my path had been lighted; but when I had stood before the graven picture I had sought carefully, but in vain, for wood that I might ignite by rubbing, and so construct a flambeau. Compelled to plunge into the impenetrable gloom, without light or means to defend myself, I was truly in unenviable predicament.

With dogged pertinacity of purpose, engendered, perhaps, by the knowledge that to escape from that subterranean chamber was imperative if I did not seek starvation and death, I kept on until my legs grew weary and almost gave way beneath me. My feet were so pained by the sharp stones that I at last tore strips from my gandoura and tied them up, obtaining considerable relief thereby. Then, starting forward again, faint and hungry, I plodded still onward towards the dreaded unknown. Some knowledge of the enormous extent of the place may be gathered from the fact that for fully three hours I had proceeded, when suddenly an incident occurred which caused me to pull up quickly and stand motionless, not daring to move.

Beads of perspiration broke upon my forehead as I realised an imminent peril. In walking I had accidentally sent some pebbles flying before me, and my quick ears had discerned that they had struck and bounded down into some abyss in the immediate vicinity. Instantly I halted, and it proved a stroke of good fortune that I did so, for on going upon my knees and carefully stretching forth my hands, I was horrified to discover myself on the very edge of a yawning chasm, the depth or extent of which it was impossible to determine.

Here, then, was an impassable barrier to my further progress! For three long hours I had struggled to penetrate the horrible place, but now, in despair, I told myself that all had been in vain.

My eager fingers felt the jagged edge of the abyss before me. Then, lying full length upon the damp, slimy rock, with head over the great pit, I shouted in order to ascertain its depth. My voice, though echoing above, sounded hollow and became lost in the depths below. Groping about, I discovered a stone the size of my fist, and hurling it over, listened, with bated breath. The minutes passed, but no sound rose. Again I threw down another piece of rock, but, as before, I could detect no noise of it striking the bottom. The chasm was unfathomable.

Again, taking some small pebbles worn smooth by the action of the water, I flung them a considerable distance into the darkness. Apparently they struck the rocks on the opposite side of the terrible pit, for I could hear them bounding down from crag to crag until the noise became so faint that they were lost entirely. Once more I shouted, but my voice echoed not in that vast, immeasurable abyss that had evidently been caused by the same great upheaval which had, ages before, closed the entrance to the cavern, and formed the dreaded Lake of the Accursed. Might not the exit have been sealed in the same manner as the entrance? The suggestion crossed my mind and held me appalled.

Finding myself unable to proceed further, I crept, still upon my hands and knees, along near the edge of the chasm for a considerable distance, until at last I found, to my delight, that it extended no further, and by the exercise of constant caution I crawled onward, length by length, until I discovered, by casting pebbles about, that I had passed it. Then gladly, with a feeling of apprehension lifted from my heart, I rose again, and with renewed energy continued my way.

After this incident I took every precaution, consequently my progress was slow and painful. The thought of how narrowly I had escaped a horrible death caused me to shudder, nevertheless my eyes were eager to discover some welcome gleam of light and hope. During yet another hour I struggled forward over ground that rose gradually, then descended again so steeply, until I began to fear that another chasm lay before. My fears, however, in this direction proved groundless. Yet, as I proceeded, the little stream seemed to increase in volume, and there was a damp, noxious smell about the noisome place which gave rise to a belief that, after all, there was no exit, and that the cavern, like the forbidden land, was a place whence, if once entered, there was no return. Just as that conviction was forced strongly upon me, I also discovered another more startling fact, which rendered my despair complete, and told me plainly that in that dwelling of the Great Devourer I should find my grave.

My progress had been arrested; my hands had come into contact with a wall of rock which stretched before me on either side. I shouted, and the unseen rock gave back my voice, proving that I had gained the extreme end of the cavern.

Determined to thoroughly investigate this abrupt termination of the place before seeking an exit in another direction, I crept forward, feeling the rough, rocky wall with eager, trembling hands. Having proceeded for some distance, my heart suddenly bounded with excitement as I discovered another outlet beyond, and eagerly stumbled forward, still in impenetrable gloom. All the strange legends and tales of the story-tellers I had heard related regarding this weird place surged through my mind, and, as I pressed forward, I admit that I was in constant fear and trepidation lest I should meet, face to face, the legendary tenant of this limitless subterranean labyrinth, the terrible being referred to on the tablet of Semiramis as the Great Devourer, or Guardian of the Gate of the Land of the No Return.

But the entrance to the forbidden land, if thus it proved to be, was difficult enough, and guarded by horrors and pitfalls sufficient without the necessity of a janitor such as that described so luridly by tellers of strange romances in the desert-camps. Stumbling on up a steep incline I was at length compelled to halt to regain breath. Weakened by the desperate fight I had had for life amid the roaring torrent which had sucked me down, fatigued by the struggle to penetrate the deep recesses of the cavern, I rested for a few moments, my head reeling and my legs trembling as if unable to support my body. Suddenly a loud, shrill cry caused me to start, and next second a gust of air was swept into my face by the flapping of enormous wings. For an instant I felt the presence of some uncanny object near me, but in a moment it had gone, and when I recovered from my sudden alarm, I knew that it was some great bird which probably had its nest in some deep and secret crevice. Its shrill, plaintive cry echoed among the vast recesses, but grew fainter as it flew on before me. My sudden terror was quickly succeeded by feelings of satisfaction, for the presence of the bird was sufficient proof that there was an exit in the vicinity.

With heart quickened by excitement I once again moved forward, gained the summit of the incline, clambered quickly over some gigantic masses of fallen rock, and at last, when I had mounted to the top of what at first seemed an impassable barrier, my eyes were gladdened by a sight which caused me to cry aloud with joy.

Far below me, so distant as to appear like a mere speck of grey, the light of day was shining.

Its approach was by a rough and exceedingly steep descent, but I hurried on with foolish disregard of the perils which beset my path, on account of the slippery deposits on the stones. Once or twice I nearly came to grief. In places the descent was so abrupt that I had to turn and crawl down, steadying myself with my hands and knees; but I heeded nothing in my frantic eagerness to escape and gain the dreaded Land of the Myriad Mysteries.

As I neared the opening, I discovered it was not large, and half choked by masses of rock that had either fallen or been placed there to bar the entrance, while about them were tangled masses of profuse vegetation, which no doubt hid the existence of the cavern to any who should chance to pass it outside. In the high roof near the exit, hundreds of birds of brilliant plumage had their nests, and were flying in and out, singing and uttering shrill cries, while in the light and air, moss, plants and giant ferns grew in wild profusion. Great green snakes, too, lay curled beneath the stones, and I was compelled to be wary, lest I should be bitten. Even on arrival here my escape was barred by a huge mass of stone three times higher than myself, and so wide that it entirely filled up the exit. Nevertheless, I managed, after considerable difficulty, to scale the rocky obstacle, and pausing on its summit for a moment, I ascertained that a dense forest lay beyond. Then I descended through the tangled bushes and creepers to the ground outside, and once more stood free in the fresh air, with a brilliant, cloudless sky above.

I had actually set foot in the forbidden Land of the No Return!

But it was already the hour of the *maghrib,* and the fast dying day showed that the time I had spent in the wonderful dwelling of the Great Devourer, was longer than I had imagined. Remembering that at that hour Azala had opened her lattice and breathed to me her silent message of love, I sank upon my knees, and turning in the direction of prayer, went through my sunset devotions with an earnest fervency which I fear was unusual, thanking Allah in a loud and thrice-repeated Fatiha. Rising, and lifting my hands to heaven, I uttered the words that pilgrims repeat before the Black Stone in the Holy Ca'aba: "There is no God but Allah alone, Whose Covenant is Truth, and Whose Servant is Victorious. There is no God but Allah without Sharer; His is the Kingdom, to him be Praise, and He over all Things is potent."

Then, having kissed my fingers, I made a meal from bananas I plucked from a neighbouring tree, and having slacked my thirst at a tiny stream, the water of which was as cool as that of the well Zem Zem, I skirted the forest for a considerable distance, but finding my further progress barred by a wide river, that, emerging from the wood, ran in serpentine wanderings around the base of the high, inaccessible mountains, I was compelled to plunge into the forest. Upon the tablets of Semiramis, it was stated that the unknown city of Ea had been built at a spot fifteen marches towards the sunrise, therefore in that direction I proceeded.

At first, the forest was rendered dark and gloomy by the entangled bushes, but the trees soon grew thinner, yet more luxurious. Many of them were in blossom; many bore strange fruits that I had never before beheld; while the ground was carpeted with moss and an abundance of bright-hued flowers. Everywhere was an air of peaceful repose. Birds were chattering before roosting in the branches above, the rays of the sinking sun gilded the leaves and fell in golden shafts across my path, a bubbling brook ran with rippling music over the pebbles, and the air was heavily laden with the subtle scent of a myriad perfumes. Presently, when I had penetrated the belt of forest and emerged into the open grassland, I stood in amazement, gazing upon one of the fairest and most picturesque landscapes that my wondering eyes had ever beheld.

The country I had entered was the dreaded kingdom of the Myriad Mysteries; yet, judging from its fertility and natural beauties, it appeared to me more like the paradise our Korân promises for our enjoyment than a land of dread. Indeed, as I stood there in the cool sunset hour, amid the fruitful trees, sweet flowers and smiling plains, bounded far away by ranges of purple mountains, I doubt whether it would have surprised me to have met in that veritable garden of delights the black-eyed houris which the Book of Everlasting Will describes as dwelling in pavilions, among trees of mauz and lote-trees free from thorns. Such, indeed, I thought, must be the dwelling-place prepared for the Companions of the Right Hand, for are they not promised couches adorned with gold and precious stones, under an extended shade, near a flowing water, and amidst fruits of abundance which shall not fail nor shall be forbidden to be gathered?

Slowly turning, I gazed back upon the Rock of Sin, the Moon-god, the name of which in the centuries that had passed had been so strangely corrupted by Arabs and pagans alike, and noticed that although from where I stood its summit looked similar in form to its aspect from the other side of the Lake of the Accursed, yet it was not so lofty here, and evidently this hitherto undiscovered region was considerably higher than the countries surrounding it, although even here the mountains forming its boundary were of great altitude, many of their summits being tipped with snow. Dark, frowning and mysterious, the rock rose high among the many peaks of the unknown range, while behind the giant crests to the left the western sky was literally ablaze, and the sun, having already disappeared, caused them to loom darkly in the shadows.

Out upon the plain I passed, keeping still to eastward, but soon the light blue veil of the mountains before me became tinted with violet and indigo, and finally settled into leaden death. Then night crept on, and the stars shone bright as diamonds in a sultan's aigrette. During several silent hours I could discover no sign of man, but at length, when I had crossed the plain, with the moon lighting my footsteps like a lamp, I approached, at the foot of a hill, a wonderful colonnade of colossal stone columns, some of which had broken off half-way up and fallen, while across the quaintly-sculptured capitals of others there still remained great square blocks that had once supported a roof. Here and there in the vicinity were other columns, singly, and in twos and threes, while the intervening ground was covered with *débris*, over which crept a growth of tangled vegetation, as if striving to hide the ravages of time.

The great ruin, apparently of an ancient palace or temple, stood in desolate grandeur, ghostly in the white moonlight, while behind rose verdant hills, steep and difficult of ascent. Approaching close to the columns, through a mass of fallen masonry and wildly-luxuriant verdure, I examined them, and was struck by the enormous size of the blocks of stone from which they had been fashioned, and the curious and grotesque manner in which they had been sculptured with figures. The art was of the same character on these monoliths as upon the tablet of Semiramis, the beautiful and brilliant queen who was worshipped as a goddess. There were many representations of the Assyrian deity, and in places lines of cuneiform writing, but the suns and rains of ages had almost obliterated them, and had also caused much damage to the sculptured figures.

In the silence of the brilliant night I stood beneath those amazing relics of a forgotten civilisation and pictured the departed magnificence of the wonderful structure. There remained portions of an enormous gateway, with giant winged human figures carved out of huge blocks of stone; and on examining one of these I found a portion of an inscription, in long, thin lines of arrowheads, easily decipherable in the full light of the moon. After a little difficulty I succeeded in reading it as follows:—

"In the beginning of my everlasting reign there was revealed to me a dream. Merodach, the Great Lord, and Sin, the Illuminator of Heaven and Earth, stood round about me. Merodach spake to me, 'O Semiramis, Queen of Babylon, with the horses of thy chariot come, the bricks of the House of Light make, and the Moon, the Great Lord within it caused to be raised his dwelling.' Reverently I spake to the lord of the gods, Merodach, 'This house, of which thou speakest, I will build, and the temple shall be the dwelling of the Moon-god in Ea'."

What a magnificent pile it must have been in those long-forgotten days when the legions of Semiramis marched, in glittering array, through the long colonnade to worship the Moon-god, Sin, beneath the statues of illustrious Babylonians! or when their luxurious ruler, enthroned a queen in the hearts of her people, and dowered with charms that inspired to heroism, flashed through those great corridors in her gilded chariot, surrounded by her crowd of martial courtiers and fair slaves! or when, with bare arms and golden helmet on her head, with all the pomp of war, she sallied forth on her fleet steed, caparisoned in crimson and gold, to review and harangue her warriors on the plain.

Allah had destroyed it because it was ungodly.

No trace of the presence of living man had I discovered, and I began to wonder whether, after all, this Land of the No Return was uninhabited; for was it not likely that in the ages that had passed since its discovery by Babylon's queen, the colony, like the once-powerful race beside the Euphrates, had dwindled away and become entirely extinct! There were no signs of these ruins having been visited, no trace of any recent encampment, or the dead ashes of the fires of recent travellers. Upon the stretch of bare, stony ground, before the half-ruined gateway which would have served as a good camping-ground, I searched diligently, but discovered nothing that proved the existence of inhabitants; therefore, wearied and footsore, I at length threw myself down at the base of one of the giant monoliths, and with part of my gandoura over my face to shield it from the evil influence of the moonbeams, sank into heavy, dreamless slumber.

Chapter Thirty Five
A Visitant from the Mists

Day had dawned fully three hours ere I arose. The great ruins, revealed by the brilliant morning sun, were much more extensive than I had at first believed. For fully half a mile mighty columns rose, here and there, like gigantic, moveless giants; many had fallen, and their walls of enormous blocks and their prostrate pillars looked up piteously to the day. Time alone had worn down their rigid strength, and swept the capstones from the towers. Time, too, had clad some of them in a disintegrating mantle of green.

There was not one of the hundred columns and monoliths in which did not lurk some tale, or many tales, of loyalty, or treason, or despair. There was not one of the five great gates I could distinguish whose portal had not swung open wide for processions of triumphal pageantry, of exalted grief, of pagan pomp, or military expedition. Thick as the leaves of the climbing plants, festooning crevice, niche and broken parapet, must be the legends, traditions and true tales that enwrapped those walls if man still inhabited that land. Upon the stones, chipped with surprising neatness and regularity, were many uneffaced inscriptions; the pompous eulogies therein contained being the only epitaphs the long-dead founders of the Kingdom of Ea possessed. This prodigious pile, useless centuries ago, torn by earthquakes and half levelled by time, was indeed a fitting monument to the great Semiramis, the self-indulgent Queen, the conqueror of all lands from the Indus to the Mediterranean, and builder of Babylon, the most extensive and wonderful capital in the world.

At last, turning my back upon the desolate scene, I went forward and commenced to ascend the steep hillside. It was a stiff ascent, but, on gaining the summit, I looked down upon a panorama of beauty impossible to adequately describe. Streams, forests and verdant valleys stretched out below, bounded far away by a range of fantastic mountains rising in finger points in all directions. Proceeding in search of the mysterious, unknown city, which, according to the inscription, lay in the direction of prayer, I descended the steep hill, passed through vast entanglements of jungle in the valleys, suddenly coming across a delightful stream watering a narrow valley with precipitous walls of rock on either side, and densely filled with all kinds of tropical vegetation. I ate some bananas, revelled in the luxury of a bath, and then continued my journey towards the sunrise by plunging into a forest of quol-quol trees, some of which reached to the height of sixty feet, stretching out their weird arms in every direction. The quol-quol is an uncanny-looking tree, exuding a poisonous, milky gum, which is exceedingly dangerous. The Dervishes, in making their roads around Khartoum and Omdurman, had much difficulty with this tree, for the milk from it, if it squirts into the eyes when the tree is cut, produces blindness. Beneath the trees were flowering, rich-coloured gladioli, long, hanging orchids, sugar plants, and many thorny trees of a species I had never before seen.

Lonely, and half convinced that I had entered a land uninhabited and forgotten, I threaded the mazes of this veritable poison forest, at length emerging into a clump of gigantic baobabs, and thence into a slightly undulating district, sparsely clothed with thorns and euphorbia, and teeming with game. At last I found myself crossing a beautiful, park-like track where herds of buffalo grazed undisturbed, and at sundown came to a rich, fertile country, dotted with clumps of pine-trees and large patches of forest, abounding in pretty glades and glens of mimosa brush full of beautiful blue birds and monkeys.

That night I sought sleep under a huge sycamore, and next day continued my tramp towards the distant range of mountains, over the crests of which showed the first rosy tint of dawn. Compelled sometimes to wade streams, and often climbing and descending precipitous rocks, passing through narrow, romantic gorges, and coming now and then upon beautiful and unexpected cascades, I toiled onward through that day, and although I passed some ruins, apparently of a house, half hidden by wild vegetation, yet I discovered no trace of the existence of living man. Never before had I experienced such a sense of utter loneliness. I had the bright sun and cloudless sky above. I was free to wander hither and thither, and around me grew fruits that were the necessaries of life; but I was alive in a region which, as far as I could observe, had remained untrodden for many centuries. Again I spent the night beneath a tree, my head pillowed on a fallen branch; and again I set forth to reach my goal, as recorded on the rock-tablet of Semiramis. Forward, ever in the direction of the Holy Ca'aba across grass plains, through rocky ravines and shady woods bright with flowers, and as sweetly scented as the harem of a sultan, I trudged onward, in my hand a long, stout staff which I had broken from a tree, in my heart a feeling that I alone was monarch of this smiling, unknown Land of the No Return that I had discovered.

Yet I remembered that, after all, I had not yet elucidated the mystery of which I was in search—the reason of the Mark of the Asps; and although I had discovered it in the hand of the Assyrian goddess, yet such discovery only increased its mystery. So I kept on my toilsome path, stage by stage, still pious, still hopeful, still believing that the secret of the linked reptiles would eventually be explained.

Never swerving from the direction of the sunrise, and each day at the *maghrib* making a mark upon my staff with the sharp stone I carried, I continued in search of the city of Semiramis. Up the almost inaccessible face of one of the great mountains of the range I had seen afar I toiled many hours, until, stepping from sunshine into mist and drizzle, my feet were upon the snow that covered their summits, and the intense cold chilled me to the bone. Higher yet was I compelled to climb, until, as if by magic, I passed through the belt of mist into brilliant sunshine again. The effect was one of the most curious I had ever witnessed. Below was a sea of crumpled clouds, extending as far as the eye could reach, out of which peered high mountain peaks like islands in a sea of fleecy wool. During two whole days I clambered, half-starved and chilled, across this vast, towering range. The air was health-giving and invigorating. In the early morning everything was clear and bright; as the day advanced the clouds would gather from the plains and gradually roll up the mountain side, enveloping the lowlands and valleys in a dense mist; occasionally, towards sundown, this mist would roll over the edge and envelop a little of the high plateau in its clammy folds, but it quickly dispersed as the sun went down, and the morning would again break bright, with hoar frost sparkling everywhere.

At the foot of the mountains the ground was swampy and enveloped perpetually in a white mist, so dense that, for a further period of two days, I wandered over the marshes, not knowing the direction in which I was travelling, but trusting to the keen natural instinct with which men of my race are endowed. So dense was this mist hanging over the trackless, pestilential bog that I could distinguish nothing a leopard's leap distant, and my gandoura was as soaked with moisture as if I had waded a river. Judge my surprise, however, when suddenly I found that the vapours had veiled from my eager eyes another more inaccessible and still higher belt of mountain than the first.

Darkness was already creeping on when I made this discovery, therefore I resolved to rest and sleep before attempting to climb the rugged heights before me. It was necessary, in order to discover the direction of the mysterious city, that I should climb above the belt of impenetrable mist and take bearings in the clear atmosphere. Fortunately I had found a banana-tree a few hours previously and carried some of its fruit with me, therefore I ate my fill, and afterwards threw myself down to snatch a few hours' slumber.

How long I lay I know not, but I was startled by feeling a soft, clammy object steal slowly across my breast. It was as icy cold as the hand of a corpse. Opening my eyes quickly, I was dazzled by a brilliant light shining into them, but in an instant the bright flash disappeared and an unearthly and demoniac yell sounded about me. In the impenetrable darkness, caused by night and the dense mist combined, I could distinguish nothing, but, starting up, held my breath in alarm, listening to the echoing yells receding in the distance. They sounded like three loud shouts in the same strain, followed by a long, plaintive wail.

At first I endeavoured to reassure myself that my breast had not been touched by the clammy snout of some wandering animal which had been startled by my sudden movement, but try how I would I could not convince myself that those yells proceeded from any but a human being. Again, as I felt my gandoura, I discovered that it had been unloosened with care, evidently for the purpose of closely examining the mark I bore upon my breast! The bright light, too, was an undeniable fact which pointed conclusively to the presence of human inhabitants of this mist-enveloped ravine.

Sleep came no more to my eyes, for through the long, dreary night I kept a watchful vigil. Strange noises, as if of some one moving cautiously in my vicinity, sounded about me, but in which direction I could never detect with certainty, for both shadows and sounds became distorted by the thick vapours by which I was surrounded. Several times I heard the same mysterious, mournful cry, now close to me, and again sounding afar, as if in answer to the plaintive call. Scarcely daring to move, I patiently awaited the light of day, which came at last, spreading gradually at first, but soon causing the darkness around me to fall, and the white, choking vapours to become more dense and bewildering. There was the same strange, sulphurous odour that I had experienced when swimming the Lake of the Accursed, and I began to fear that the poisonous gases exuded from the swamps would cause asphyxiation. As soon, therefore, as the light grew strong enough to enable me to see where I placed my feet, I started forward to face the huge mountain. I had not taken three paces before my eyes, keeping careful watch upon the ground, detected something which caused me to involuntarily utter a cry of surprise.

At my feet was lying a short, straight sword, in a scabbard of beautifully-chased gold, with a magnificently jewelled cross hilt. It was attached to a leather girdle, the buckle of which was thickly set with fine emeralds, and the bright condition of the scabbard, and the keen, unrusted appearance of the blued-steel blade told me that it had not remained there many hours. Then it occurred to me that the weapon was similar in design to the ancient one I had found in the Cavern of the Devourer, and that it must have been dropped by my mysterious visitant. It was plain that, after all, I was not the only human being in that mysterious Land of the No Return; equally certain, also, that my intrusion had been discovered.

Was this the Land of the Myriad Mysteries, that region dreaded by my clansmen of the deserts from the Atlas to the Niger? Was this weird, misty gorge, devoid of herbage, and exuding a death-dealing breath, the actual entrance of the territory of all-consuming terror?

I paused, examining the weapon curiously, wondering who might be its owner. Fearing, however, to remain there longer, I buckled the girdle about my waist, and aided by my staff, commenced the steep and toilsome ascent.

An hour's hard climbing took me above the heavy vapours into the brilliant light of day, and I then discovered that the mountain I was negotiating was of greater altitude than any of the peaks of my native Atlas. At first the slopes were grass-covered, and mimosa bushes grew plentifully, but as I went higher there were only patches of stunted herbage, and higher still no herbage grew. As hour by hour I toiled upward, in places so steep that I had to use both hands and knees, I gradually neared the region of eternal snow. Soon after noon I halted, seating myself upon a rock to rest. Gloomy thoughts oppressed me. Below was nothing but a sea of vapour; above a sky brilliant, without a cloud.

Being compelled to pass through that curious gorge of grey, eternal mist, I had lost my bearings entirely, and knew not in what direction I was now journeying. For the past two days I had been travelling through a shadowy and inhospitable region, wherein I had seen not a beast of the field nor fowl of the air. The action of the mysterious visitant puzzled me. If it were a man, as I supposed, why should the mark upon my breast have such attraction for him? In his hurried flight he had lost his sword, and apparently feared to return to seek it. The enigma puzzled me, occupying my thoughts during the whole of that fatiguing and perilous climb.

Having rested for nearly an hour, my eye suddenly caught the notches upon my staff. I picked it up and carefully counted them.

They were already fourteen. On this, the fifteenth day, I ought, if credence were to be placed in the rock-tablet of Semiramis, to reach the mystic city of Ea.

Eager to gain the summit and gaze upon the land beyond, I rose and once more plodded onward with dogged pertinacity. Upwards I strode, until the perspiration rolled in great beads from my brow, and my matted, unkempt hair became wet from the same cause. As I gained a kind of small plateau, covered deeply by untrodden snow, an icy blast chilled me to the marrow, causing me to wrap my rags closer about me; but heeding not fatigue, I sped rapidly over the small plain and commenced the final ascent to the lowest crest over which I could pass. This occupied me fully two hours, for the ascent was the most difficult I had yet encountered; but presently I found myself upon a stretch of comparatively level ground, with snow lying thickly everywhere, and the surface frozen so hard that my feet left no imprints. Beyond this plain was only the sky, therefore I knew that I had at last reached the highest point.

In order to regain breath I was compelled to halt for a few seconds, but those moments were full of intense eagerness. What lay beyond I feared to ascertain. Whether I had travelled in the right direction I was unaware; but if I had, then it was time that I should reach the goal for which I had so long and so arduously striven.

The iron of despair was entering my soul, but next second, shaking if off, I dashed forward at full speed to the edge of the lofty plateau, and gazed with wondering, wide-open eyes into the land beyond.

The panorama below held me speechless in wonderment. Dumbfounded, I stood open-mouthed, rigid, rooted to the spot.

Chapter Thirty Six
The Torture-Wheel

The scene which burst upon me was so unexpected and startling, that at first I found myself doubting my own senses, and was inclined to believe that it was merely a mirage, or some fantastic chimera of my own imagination. As I continued to gaze upon it, taking in all the details discernible from that distance, I was compelled to admit that the objects I saw existed in reality, and to congratulate myself that I was actually within sight of my longed-for goal.

Behind me the sun was fast declining, but deep below, there stretched on either hand a broad river, winding far away into the distant, purple haze. At the foot of the giant mountain whereon I stood was a great stretch of grassland, across which ran a road paved like those the Franks construct in Algeria, and straight as a spear shaft, leading to a most wonderful and amazing city.

Surrounded by stone walls of colossal size and enormous height, houses extended as far as the eye could reach, and even from where I stood I could detect that the thoroughfares, running at right angles to each other, were all broad and handsome. The architecture, as far as I could distinguish, was such as I had never before seen, and the houses, built upon a great hill rising abruptly from the plain, rose tier upon tier to the summit, which was crowned by an enormous palace with a roof of burnished gold, which glistened with blinding brightness in the brilliant rays of the declining sun. Close by, from the extreme summit of the hill, rose a square tower of such colossal proportions that it seemed to reach to such a height that the building, at its summit, was in the gathering clouds of evening. The highest portion of the tower was of silver, then, counting downwards, it was blue, then pale yellow, then bright gold, red, orange and black. Each of these stages, I knew, represented one of the chief heavenly bodies—the silver being that of the Moon, the blue Mercury, the yellow Astarte, the gold the Sun, the red Mars, the orange Jupiter, and the black Saturn. I had read long ago, in the records of Babylonia, of the similar temple tower that Nebuchadnezzar built at Birs-i-Nimrud, and, glancing in other directions, saw similar edifices dotted everywhere.

The great palace on the hilltop was so extensive that its buildings and gardens stretched away into the blue distance, and its walls and colonnades were, like everything within that wonderful place, so enormous in their proportions as to be amazing. Through the centre of the palace gardens ran a beautiful river, spanned by many bridges, and as it wound away, it branched out into another stream that meandered through the city. Upon the very summit of the hill, in close proximity to the temple tower, and within the impregnable walls of the palace, rose a pavilion, the walls of which appeared to be constructed entirely of gold.

But it was not only there where the eye was dazzled. The hundred enormous gates in the strong walls that girt the city were of gold, and even as I looked I saw a cavalcade of horsemen crossing the plain, the sun's rays slanting upon the breastplates of polished gold, giving the well-drilled band the appearance of a broad, glittering thread.

At each entrance to the city were high watch-towers whereon soldiers stood ever-watchful night and day, and the wonderful walls, that even Time could not throw down, were evidently used for promenading, for I could distinguish many objects, like tiny, black specks, moving over the broad thoroughfare formed thereon. On either side, as far as my keen vision could penetrate, nothing presented itself but a colossal and magnificent city of villas, palaces and temples, of pavilions of red and silver, of beautiful, shady gardens, and wonderful structures in tiers of various colour, of temple and tomb towers, of square, solidly-built, flat-roofed residences, of bridges of polished marble and alabaster, and wonderful brazen gates. The proportions of its buildings, even though I could only obtain but a bird's-eye view, were marvellous, the wideness of its thoroughfares astounding; its thousand towers and pinnacles beggared description; its extent so great as to cause me to stand aghast.

This, then, must be the majestic city of Ea, the wonderful capital, founded by the beautiful but frail woman who had constructed it in imitation of Babylon. While the latter city had ages ago fallen to decay, and sunk forgotten beneath the earth's surface, this magnificent place, with its ostentatious display of wealth, even in its very gates, had remained through a hundred generations; the same amazing, impregnable citadel of the great queen's faithful followers; the same collection of palaces of bewildering luxury; the same time-defying stronghold of a warlike race, the same stupendous centre of incredible extent; the same unapproachable capital of an unapproachable land, as when Semiramis herself, surrounded by her lovers and courtiers, entered its brazen gates with pomp and splendour, amid the clash of cymbals, the beating of drums, and the flourish of trumpets.

Her great temple, with its unequalled colonnade, which I had passed some days ago, had, for some reason unaccountable, been allowed to crumble and fall away, but here, in this marvellous city of a thousand wonders of imposing forms and harmonious outlines, the memory of one of the most notable of queens was perpetuated. And I was the first man from the outer world to gaze upon this one glorious and unique monument of a long-forgotten past!

I stood leaning upon my staff, lost in astonishment, watching agape the incredible scene. Fascinated and stupefied by its magnificence, I contemplated it in bewilderment, while the afterglow, shedding a ruddy light upon its wonderful towers, caused the burnished gates and roofs to shine red as blood. Soon it died away, and when the sun sank in the mists behind me, a sudden gloom fell, and chill night crept rapidly on. As the stars appeared in the heavens, a million lights shone everywhere in the city, the broad streets of which seemed bright as day. Great sacrificial fires threw an uncertain light from the summits of some of the taller towers, and from the wonderful fabric on the summit of the hill one single light of intense whiteness shone brilliant as a star.

An hour sped by, yet still I remained lost in astonishment. The myriad lights gave the strange city a curiously weird aspect, and I feared to meet any of its denizens. Were they, I wondered, of the same form as my fellows of the outer world, or were they veritable giants in stature, that they should build structures of such incredible proportions?

Though I dreaded to meet them, yet I longed to be able to pass those ponderous brazen gates, to tread those wondrous streets, to enter those curiously graduated temple towers, and wander in those shady gardens beside the running waters.

With my bejewelled sword and girdle strapped over my dirty, ragged gandoura, should I be enabled to pass those gates and enter the city forbidden to those outside the rock-girt boundary of this unknown kingdom? This question I asked myself a hundred times, compelled to doubt whether such attempt would not result in my arrest and perhaps execution as a spy. I had faced without fear the thousand perils of my journey from the City of the Mirage; but to encounter the guards of mighty, mystic Ea would, I knew, require all the courage of which I, as an adventurer, was possessed.

When, however, the moon shone out, I began slowly to descend towards my goal. With exceeding difficulty I let myself down over those slippery, snow-covered rocks, treading ofttimes on perilous ledges, where a false step meant instant death on the crags beneath. Naught cared I of the risks I ran in descending so rashly, but, eager to set foot upon the plain, I stumbled on, now jumping, now crawling, until I gained a grass-grown slope where progress was not fraught by so many dangers.

Suddenly I came to a rocky gorge, down which roared a broad, swift torrent, and, as it came into view, a scream of pain and despair broke upon my ear. The sound seemed suddenly smothered, then, a few moments later, echoed again. I listened, and found that it sounded with regularity above the roaring of the waters. Whence it proceeded was a mystery, but, as I followed the stream in my descent, I suddenly encountered a great chasm in the earth, before which was an enormous wooden wheel, revolved by the current which flowed beneath, and then disappeared to feed some subterranean river.

As I watched it in the full moonlight, puzzled as to its use, the scream startled me again, and, at the same moment, I perceived something white upon the moss-grown wheel flash above for a moment, and then plunge beneath the water. Again it rose, and was again plunged in. A third time it rose, and my eyes, now on the alert, caught the form of a man, who, tightly-bound to the wheel, was being every moment plunged into the icy stream.

Then I knew that the wheel was used for one of the most horrible forms of torture and death. Alone, the wretched victim was slowly dying, dreading every moment to meet the water, and each time, as he rose in the air, awakening the echoes by his despairing cries for rescue. He passed me so closely that I could touch him with outstretched hand where I stood, but so swiftly that, although a dozen times I strove to cut his cords with my sword, I failed. The manner in which the wheel could be stopped I knew not, and was thus compelled to stand and see the poor wretch die before my eyes. Apparently he recognised that my efforts to release him had been unavailing, and swooned, his unconsciousness being quickly followed by suffocation.

Even as I stood watching, I heard footsteps, and, slinking back in the shadow behind a great rock, saw approaching four tall men of fine physique, wearing shining breastplates, bearing between them the frail, inanimate form of a woman. They were followed by two other men, who, by screwing down a block of wood on the axle of the wheel, raised it above the raging torrent. With a few swift strokes of their swords, the men severed the bonds that held the body of the victim, and, as it fell with a splash into the whirling stream, it was speedily engulfed, and swept down the chasm into the bowels of the earth.

The men, who spoke a tongue unknown to me, laughed roughly among themselves as it disappeared, and then, tearing from the woman her golden ornaments, they bound her upon the wheel. While doing so she recovered consciousness, and, recognising her impending fate, gave vent to a shrill, heart-rending scream. But her cruel captors merely jeered, and, having ascertained that she was secure, again lowered the wheel, which immediately began to revolve.

For a few moments the soldiers watched the monotonous punishment, then, in response to a word from the one apparently in authority, descended the path and were lost to view.

As soon as they were out of hearing I emerged from my hiding-place, and, acting as I had seen the men act, succeeded at length in raising the wheel, and, grasping the trembling form of the woman, severed her bonds and dragged her from her perilous position, afterwards lowering the terrible wheel and allowing it to again revolve.

Taking her in my arms I bore her some little distance, and, after some effort, restored her to consciousness. Her hair, which fell to her knees, was like golden sheen, and her complexion as pale as those of the women of the Infidels who come to see the Desert at Biskra, or seek renewed health from the waters of Hamman R'hira. Indeed, the people of Ea all seemed white-skinned, for the brutal soldiers had in their faces no trace of negro origin.

When the woman I had rescued opened her eyes there was a terrified look in them, but on finding that I was supporting her head and endeavouring to bring her round, she uttered some words. Not being able to understand her, I shook my head. Again she addressed me with like result. Then, sitting up, she suddenly asked me yet another question, but again I shook my head.

Springing to her feet as if electrified, she gave me one look of abject fear and fled away among the bushes, screaming, leaving me standing in mute astonishment. Was it my ragged, unkempt appearance that had caused her such terror? She had apparently been seized with a sudden insanity; but whether the horrible torture of the wheel had unhinged her mind I knew not.

Retracing my steps to the torture-wheel, I followed the path which the soldiers had taken, and in half-an-hour reached the plain.

Then I hesitated, undecided whether to walk forward and inspect the walls and closed gates of the gigantic city, or wait until its brazen portals were opened at dawn. It occurred to me that, if detected by the watchmen, I should be seized as a spy, therefore I decided to snatch a brief rest and wait for morning.

Finding a great tree at the foot of the mountain, I made a pillow of leaves and was soon dreaming of weird adventures and tortures applied by fiendish captors. I had evidently been more fatigued than I had imagined, for suddenly I found myself roughly handled by two soldiers of colossal stature, wearing curiously-fashioned robes, reaching nearly to the ground, and was surprised to discover the sun shining brilliantly.

They addressed to me a question which I could not understand; then, next second I found myself surrounded by men with drawn swords as my arms were quickly pinioned by a dozen eager hands, then amid loud shouts of triumph I was dragged across the plain towards the brazen gate, to enter which had been my sole desire.

My courage failed me. Had I not read on the tablet of Semiramis that no stranger was permitted to enter the Kingdom of Ea on penalty of death? It was plain that my fierce-bearded captors had discovered I was not of their world, and as they hurried me towards their mysterious stronghold I felt that, by my own recklessness in sleeping within an enemy's camp, I had sought my doom.

Chapter Thirty Seven
Ea

As across the plain my captors hurried me, I was amazed at the strength of the colossal walls of the mysterious city. Approaching one of the great brazen gates, flanked on either side by gigantic, sculptured figures of human-headed monsters, I saw that the walls were fully two hundred feet in height, their base being constructed of huge blocks of a polished stone full of shells, and their upper portions of sun-dried brick, cased with great slabs of granite cemented with bitumen. They exceeded in thickness any I had previously seen; the ramparts, used as a promenade and drive, being fully eighty feet in breadth, and surmounted by hundreds of high watch-towers, each bearing a huge sculpture of an eagle-headed monster, apparently the national emblem.

Even from beneath the shadow of these enormous, unbreakable walls the crowd standing thereon, watching our advance, looked small as a swarm of bees, and as we neared the open gate an excited, strangely-attired mob came forth to meet us, leaping, yelling and pressing round my captors, as if eager to obtain sight of me. All were of pale complexion. The men, tall and muscular, were dressed in flowing linen robes reaching to the feet, over which were garments of wool and short white, or crimson, cloaks with embroidered edges, while those who who were not soldiers each wore a cylindrical seal suspended from the neck, and in their hands bore staves, the head of each being carved with an apple, a rose, a lily, or an eagle. The women, mostly handsome but all dark-haired, were invariably attired in white, their bare, finely-moulded arms loaded with ornaments, and their waists girt by broad double girdles of leather or gold set with gems. Rich and poor alike had apparently turned out to view me. The men, many of them gilt-helmeted warriors, drew their swords and flourished them, yelling imprecations in their unknown tongue, while the women, some of whom were evidently the wives and daughters of wealthy citizens, hurled execrations upon me, and took up stones as if to fling at me.

Mine was indeed a hostile reception. The people of this race I had so strangely discovered seemed notable for their extraordinary tallness and grace, their handsome, clear-cut features, and their artistic mode of dress.

The wealth of the city must, I thought, be immense, for the women of the lowest class were plentifully adorned with gold ornaments and jewels, and the raven locks of the men of the upper classes were curled and perfumed, as if aping a fashionable effeminacy.

Arrived at the gate, I was struck by its stupendous proportions. The great human-headed lions standing on either side of the entrance were fully a hundred feet in height, while the road itself between the two sculptured colossi consisted of a single slab of black stone, whereon was an inscription in the cuneiform character, the signs of which had been filled in with copper kept bright by the hurrying sandals of the inhabitants.

As I passed through and entered the city, teeming with a civilisation forgotten by the world outside, I was enabled to judge better the great thickness of the impregnable fortifications which had, ages ago, been raised by blows of the lash. Of such gigantic proportions were they that I marvelled how they had ever been constructed. The moment we entered the city fifty trumpets blared forth in all directions, soldiers in helmets of gold and bronze, alarmed by the warning note, seized their arms and dashed to their posts, while behind us the great gate quickly closed, and guards scrambled to the walls and watch-towers in such numbers that they appeared like swarms of ants.

Held secure by a dozen sinewy hands of armed warriors, and surrounded by a yelling populace, I was hurried forward along great thoroughfares of enormous houses, any of which would, in my own world, be termed a palace. All were great, square, solid structures of stone, constructed in three tiers, with broad terraces adorned with fine sculpture, and mostly painted in bright blues, reds and greens. One feature, however, struck me as curious; there were neither windows nor lattices. There were a few apertures, these being mostly closed by silken hangings or squares of talc. The great paved thoroughfares, through which handsome chariots, drawn by three horses abreast, passed and re-passed, were entirely different from any I had previously seen.

A clamour had been raised. The people understood; consternation ensued; then an immense rage possessed them. Each residence was surrounded by a high wall, enclosing shady gardens full of great, ancient trees and cool, open-air baths, while from the terrace of nearly every house women, white-robed and anxious, gazed down upon me with evident curiosity, while their slaves beside them fanned or shielded them from the sun.

The magnificence of the city was unequalled. There was an air of strength in every stone, and wealth in every residence. Armed warriors were everywhere; and as we proceeded, the crowd increased and the excitement rose to fever heat. Patricians left their palaces, tradesmen their shops, women abandoned their children. The report of my discovery and capture had apparently passed rapidly from mouth to mouth, and those responsible for the defence of the great city had alarmed the guard, and closed its hundred gates, fearing lest spies should enter or leave.

As we passed through one handsome street after another, the multitude following, straining their necks to catch a glimpse of me, acted in a manner that aroused my curiosity. The girls and women, after gazing into my face, turned westward to where, high upon the hilltop, the huge, handsome tower, painted in many colours, loomed against the bright sky, and raising their right hands towards it, they placed their left upon their heads, crying aloud some strange, cabalistic words. Their actions puzzled me, but subsequently I ascertained that the tower towards which they turned was the temple of Astarte, and that they invoked upon me the curse of the goddess, to whom they were by law each compelled to make sacrifice once in their lives. The men also lifted their hands to the temple of Rimmon, the Air-god and Destroyer, the tower of which rose on the opposite side of the great city, and from their thousand brazen throats cried maledictions upon me, and called forth the most terrible vengeance of their gods.

Many rushed towards me with uplifted staves, and even the soldiers themselves shook their naked blades at me threateningly, but any such hostile demonstration was promptly suppressed by my escort pressing closely around me, guarding me from the irate mob, yet, at the same time, looking upon me with suspicious dread.

With closed gates the city was agog, the guards watchful, the excited populace on their housetops and terraces, wringing their hands in sheer desperation, straining their eyes to catch sight of my ragged, unkempt form; while the surging, turbulent crowd about me went mad with rage. What treatment I was about to receive at the hands of my captors I dreaded to contemplate, but remembering the ominous words engraven on the tablet of Semiramis I felt that the penalty for being found in the precincts of that forbidden region was death; for was I not in the Land of the No Return? Yet, ignorant of this strange tongue, I could neither appeal for clemency nor make explanation; therefore, forced to keep the seal of silence upon my lips, I took in every detail of the extraordinary scene, the magnificence and architectural wonders of the city, and the dress and habits of this newly-discovered race.

At a distance of about half a league from the gate whereat we had entered we passed through a second brazen portal of equal dimensions to the first, guarded, as before, by a colossal winged monster in black stone on either side. The single slab placed between the two figures was, in the same manner as that at the outer gate, inscribed with many lines of half-obliterated arrowheads, but above, suspended from a great chain stretched between the stone monsters, was a large figure of the human-headed lion in burnished copper. Here again the walls, fully a hundred feet in height, were of enormous thickness, and as we entered the great paved court the ponderous gates were closed in face of the howling, execrating mob.

Warriors of Ea in their bright helmets and shining breastplates, bearing glittering spears, swarmed everywhere, and as I was hurried across the open court they pressed around, as eager to view me as if I were, of some unknown species. A magnificent war-chariot, the sides of which were of beaten gold, with quivers full of arrows hanging in readiness in the front, was standing. The four splendid white horses harnessed to it champed their bits and pawed the ground ready to start, and the driver, with shield and spear in hand, held the reins, prepared to step in and drive on through the opposite gate at any instant.

The man craned his neck as I passed, but my face was more eagerly scanned by a richly-dressed woman in gold-embroidered robes who stood beside him. The look of abject terror in her eyes caused me to give her a second glance, and next instant I recollected her features.

It was the woman who had been placed upon the torture-wheel, and whose bonds I had severed. Who was she? What was she? I wondered. Our eyes met, and she started. The colour left her face when she saw I had recognised her. Then turning from me in the direction of the temple of Astarte, she raised her long, white arm, and with her hair falling to her waist, gave utterance to that unknown invocation that fell from each woman's lips.

A moment later I lost sight of her, being conducted up a gradual incline and through many gates, strongly guarded by soldiers, whose arms flashed and gleamed in the brilliant sunlight. The blare of brazen horns and the clash of cymbals echoed everywhere among the great windowless buildings ranged around the courtyard, until suddenly we came to yet another gate, which was closed. Thrice a trumpeter blew long, deep blasts, and when at length it opened there was revealed, standing alone, an aged priest, whose snow-white beard swept to his waist. Attired in white robes of gold-embroidered silk, with a strange head-dress of gold, fashioned to represent the sun, he uttered some unintelligible words in a deep voice, slowly raising his arms as if in supplication to heaven.

As he did so a dead silence fell upon my captors, who, impressed by his presence, halted and bent their heads, mumbling strangely. For a few minutes the old priest remained calm and statuesque, then, with a few final words, he walked slowly aside and was lost to view, while we continued our way across a court where the exteriors of the buildings were beautifully sculptured, and where there were many shady trees and sweet-smelling flowers. These people were a nation of Infidels, who knew nothing of Allah, or his Prophet, and who bowed before images of wood and stone. They had faith in the sun, moon and stars, and consulted them. When good or evil befell them, they ascribed it to their celestial gods being favourable or unfavourable. The worship of these gods was directed by the priests, who were guided in their turn by soothsayers and magicians.

Half-way across this open space, however, my captors pulled up before a wide door, guarded by two recumbent figures of winged monsters similar to those at the outer gates, and entering a long, dark, stone corridor, the walls of which were formed of strange bas-reliefs, they led me at last down a flight of steps to a spacious, dimly-lit apartment with walls, roof and floor of stone.

When they had left me, and their receding footsteps and strangely-hushed voices had died away, I started to examine the cell. It was a large place, air being admitted by a door of strong iron bars that led into a kind of paved and covered patio. Towards the door I strode, and with my face against the bars was peering out into the gloomy place beyond, when suddenly a deep roar, that made the very walls shake, startled me, causing me to draw back.

I did so only just in time, for at the same moment a great, shaggy body hurled itself against the bars, bending them, causing them to rattle, and for an instant shutting out the faint glimmer of grey light. Then, as it fell back, gnashing its teeth, lashing its tail and roaring with rage at having lost its prey, I saw, to my horror, that it was a great lion, a veritable king of the forest.

With its snout against the bars it stood, rolling its eyes, lashing its tail from side to side and glaring at me, while I shrank back trembling, for I now knew the intention of my captors was to cast me to the lions to be torn limb from limb.

What I had at first imagined to be a courtyard or patio was, in reality, part of the lion-pit, above which were ranged many tiers of seats for spectators who came on holidays to witness the helpless victims being devoured by the beasts. The cell in which I was confined was where captives were kept in readiness for the entertainments, for on examination I found that the iron door could be raised from above, the beasts being thus admitted to my cell without the gaoler running the risk of entering to admit the animals.

Many inscriptions were rudely scratched upon the walls; but although I endeavoured to decipher some of them, the only signs I could, in that dim light, distinguish were, *"Li-ru-ru-su lu-bal-lu."* These oft-repeated Assyrian words, scratched and engraven by many hands, meant, "May the gods curse her, may they devour her!"

Slowly the hours crept on, but the fierce animal, crouching at the door of my cell, held himself in readiness to pounce upon me if I should emerge. He never took his fiery eyes from me. My every movement he watched, silent and cat-like, scarcely moving for an hour together. I knew that sooner or later I should be torn asunder by those cruel teeth the beast displayed as he yawned widely in contemplation of appeasing his hunger, and upon me there fell a settled despair. Alone and helpless I paced the stones, worn smooth and bright by the nervous tramp of thousands of previous victims, longing for the end. Death was preferable to that terrible, breathless suspense.

Presently, when I had been there fully three hours, I heard the sounds of reed instruments, clashing cymbals and rolling drums outside, followed by the hum of human voices, at first low and distant, but, as another hour wore on, increasing in volume. Shouts and light laughter reached me, and, by the excited manner the dozen lions paced and repaced before my cell, I felt instinctively that the great amphitheatre was now filled with eager spectators.

Each moment seemed an hour. Awaiting my doom, I stood with my back against the heavy-bolted door by which I had entered, with bated breath, striving to meet my end with fortitude. Hoping against hope, my strained eyes were watching the iron bars that separated me from the hungry beasts, dreading each moment that they would be lifted.

Suddenly, as I stood thinking of Azala, wondering how she had fared, and whether Tiamo had yet reached Kano with news of my death, one of the shaggy beasts sprang past my bars, and next second a dull roar of applause and the loud clapping of hands broke upon my ear.

A dead silence was again followed by the wild plaudits of the multitude.

Again and again this was repeated; then there seemed a long wait. Apparently I was considered a valuable prize, and it was probable that my turn was next.

At that moment one of the lions slunk past my cell to his lair, his tail trailing on the ground and bearing between his teeth some object.

There crept over me a strange faintness such as I had never before experienced. Yet I strove against it, supporting myself against the wall, and knowing that my fate could not be much longer delayed.

Those moments were full of breathless horror. From where I stood I could hear the animals crunching bones between their teeth. They were preparing themselves for another victim. My blood froze in my veins.

The fatal moment at last came. A loud, grating noise sounded in the roof of the cell, and slowly the iron bars were lifted bodily, removing the barrier between myself and death.

I stood paralysed by fear. Another moment and I should cease to live! Yet in that brief instant a flood of memories surged though my turbulent brain, and the thought of my terrible doom was rendered the more acute because I had actually succeeded in gaining the Land of the No Return when all others had failed.

But before me was only a death most terrible, and I had no means by which to defend myself.

One of the beasts, slinking slowly across the pavement some distance away, espied me. Turning, he sniffed quickly, crouched, and with an exultant bound sprang towards me.

In that instant, however, by what means I know not, the iron gate fell with a metallic clang into its place, and the animal, thus frustrated, crashed against the bars and tumbled back with a terrible roar of rage.

It was a hairbreadth escape. For a moment I was saved.

Seconds, full of breathless suspense, passed. Horror-stricken, my eyes were fixed upon those iron bars, fearing lest they should rise again, but it seemed that by design, and not by accident, the gate had fallen. Time after time the shouts of the assembled multitude rent the hot air as the prowling beasts pounced upon the captives. Still the iron bars of my cell rose not again, and at last, when the animals had slunk into their lairs to sleep, and the spectators had departed, I cast myself into a corner of my cell to rest and think.

Darkness crept on apace; the quiet was broken only by the low, uneasy roar of the lions, and at length a single streak of bright moonlight fell across the paved court outside. In order to occupy my thoughts, I tried to decipher some of the engraven inscriptions by feeling them with my finger-tips. This, however, was not successful, because the unfortunate wretches confined there had possessed no proper tools with which to chip the stone. At length, however, footsteps resounded outside, the bolts of the heavy door grated in their sockets, and as I started up, four soldiers, two of whom bore lighted flambeaux, entered, ordering me, by signs, to accompany them.

Eager to escape from the lion-pit! Waited not for a second invitation, but hurried with them away up the steps, along the echoing corridor and out into the moonlit court. All four grinned sardonically at the eagerness with which I left the dreaded cell, but directing my footsteps across two magnificent courts, we came to a great open space, in the centre of which rose the enormous temple tower of Astarte, before the entrance of which a fire-altar burned. The high tower, which I had seen from afar, was, I found, erected in seven square stages, each smaller than the other and coloured differently, rising to such an enormous height that its summit seemed almost beyond human gaze. The base was of stupendous dimensions, and as we skirted it two clean-shaven eunuchs, in flowing robes of bright crimson, guarded its alabaster portals, while others stood beside the fire-altar, silent and motionless. Over the great entrance to this temple of the Seven Lights, approached by a broad flight of marble steps, was an enormous representation of the circle, in which was the winged figure of a man in the act of discharging an arrow, but having the tail of a bird. This symbol, denoting time without bounds, or eternity, the image with its wings and tail of a dove showing the association of Astarte, was the sacred emblem of Baal, and I therefore knew that this magnificent and wonderful temple was devoted to the supreme deity Belus, the altar of which stood ever ready for the sacrifice. Women, in soft, clinging robes of white and gold, flitted in and out like shadows, while others wandered in pairs under the great trees, chatting, laughing and enjoying the cool, bright night.

Presently we came to yet another huge gateway, consisting of two colossal female figures carved from the solid rock, rising to a terrific height, and bearing upon their heads the enormous block of stone forming the top of the imposing entrance. The stupendous proportions of the gate amazed me, but facing us, as we passed through, was a wonderful structure, more extensive and more imposing than I had ever seen, rising high above us and approached by a flight of a thousand stone steps of great width. Upon each step stood two spearmen, one on either side, so that the approach to the magnificent entrance to the royal palace was guarded day and night by no fewer than two thousand armed men, standing there, veritable giants, mute, silent, and ever-watchful.

The scene was weird and imposing. As we stood at the foot of the steps we gazed up between the files of warriors armed with shining steel. Above, on either side of the giant portal, great fires leaped from enormous braziers, the red flames illuminating, with a lurid brilliancy, the wonderful, massive sculptured façade, and shedding a fitful glow upon the lines of statuesque warriors.

Having passed through the gateway, we started to ascend the steps, but ere we set foot on the first, our passage was barred by two thousand glittering spears meeting one another with a ringing clash, and presenting an impassable barrier of steel. Our progress thus arrested, we halted, and at the same time one of my conductors shouted some strange words, producing from the leathern pouch suspended at his side a small hollow cylinder of grey baked clay, which he held above his head. In a moment two stalwart men, evidently officers, wearing breastplates of beaten gold, advanced and eagerly scrutinised the cylinder. Having carefully read some words thereon inscribed, they examined the impression of the seal. Both men having satisfied themselves that our credential was genuine, regarded me with mixed curiosity and awe, then shouted an order which caused the long lines of guards to withdraw their spears with a clash at the same moment, almost as if they were one man.

The great steps were high and steep, and the ascent long and tedious. Once or twice we halted to regain breath, then panting on again, climbed higher and yet higher towards the most gigantic and wonderful palace in the world. Half-way up I turned, and saw the immense city of Ea, full of bright lights and gaiety, lying deep below, while beyond was a background of towering, snow-capped mountains, looking almost fairylike under the brilliant moon.

So extraordinary was the scene, and of such colossal proportions was the palace, that I felt inclined to doubt my own eyes; yet it was no dream. I was actually in Ea, approaching a structure, the mere, fantastically-sculptured façade of which was of such height and magnitude that, even though my eyes were dazzled, I marvelled at the many slaves who had doubtless been engaged in its construction.

At last, gaping and bewildered, I stood upon the great paved area before the gigantic entrance, on either side of which were colossal winged bulls sculptured from white alabaster. Ere we were allowed to proceed we were compelled to again exhibit the strange clay cylinder, and then were permitted to pass between the enormous bulls, finding ourselves in a vast hall lit by flaming braziers. Upon the alabaster walls were the sculptured records of the empire. Battles, sieges, triumphs, the exploits of the chase, the ceremonies of religion were there portrayed, delicately sculptured and painted in bright colours. Beneath each picture was engraved, in characters filled up with bright copper, inscriptions describing the scene represented. Above these sculptures were painted other events—monarchs, attended by eunuchs and warriors, receiving their prisoners, entering into alliances with other monarchs, or performing some sacred duty. The emblematic tree, similar to the one I had discovered upon the tablet of Semiramis, winged bulls and monstrous, eagle-headed animals were conspicuous among the ornaments of the coloured borders enclosing these strange wall-pictures. At the upper end of the hall was a colossal statue of a queen, evidently Semiramis herself, in adoration before the supreme deity, her robes being adorned by lines of arrowheads, groups of figures, animals and flowers, all painted in brilliant hues, a group of white-robed women praying before her. Several doorways, formed by gigantic winged horses and lions, or human-headed monsters, led into other apartments, in each of which were more sculptures, while the alabaster slabs upon which we trod each bore an inscription recording the titles, genealogy and achievements of some monarch of past ages.

It was indeed an entrance of amazing magnificence, with ceiling of massive beams of dull gold, but mere stupendous still were the many vast apartments through which I was ushered. Elegant women of the court, unveiled, reclining on couches, and attended by slaves who slowly fanned them, gazed at us languidly as we passed, and from some of the great chambers there came sounds of stringed instruments and cymbals where women were revelling and dancing. At each door were stationed four warriors, wearing breastplates of gold, and standing motionless, with drawn blades, while above the entrances the brazen sign of the deity was invariably suspended by a chain.

The palace was bewildering in magnificence, amazing in extent.

At last, turning suddenly to the right, we entered a small chamber crowded by courtiers, soldiers and slaves, who, however, spoke only in hushed tones. Here our appearance caused the utmost consternation, and the men drew back, as if fearing that my touch might contaminate them. Two courtiers, however, emerged from the crowd, and, having held a conversation with my guides in an undertone, they produced under-robes of linen, a rich outer garment of green silk, and sandals such as they themselves wore. By signs they commanded me to assume them, and when I had discarded my old, dirty and tattered gandoura, and attired myself in their strange dress, I paused, wondering what strange adventure would next befall me.

Great curtains of yellow silk, upon which hideous monsters had been embroidered, hid the opposite entrance, which was guarded by a body of twelve armed men, whom I knew to be eunuchs by their clean-shaven faces and curious, golden head-dresses.

Suddenly four trumpeters—two stationed on either side—raised their enormous horns of gold, and with one accord blew three ear-piercing blasts, at sound of which all present bowed low in the direction of the curtains, an example which my guides motioned me to follow.

As we did so the great silken hangings slowly parted, revealing a scene so unexpected and dazzling that I stood agape in stupefaction. It was marvellous, incredible, astounding; its brilliancy caused my bewildered eyes to blind; its striking splendour filled me with amazement. I stood lost in wonder; held in fascination.

Chapter Thirty Eight
Istar

The great apartment was very lofty. Innumerable openings pierced its vaulted ceiling, through which the bright stars were visible. Upon the walls of alabaster, half hidden by rich hangings of purple silk, were portrayed winged priests or presiding deities standing before the sacred trees, armed men and eunuchs following their queen, warriors laden with spoil, leading prisoners, or bearing presents and offerings to their gods. The pavement, highly polished, was encrusted with gold, mother-of-pearl and glass; the ceiling was of ivory, and in the knots of the gilded beams were set great turquoises and shining amethysts.

At every step in this wonderful temple and palace combined, an increasing immensity had surrounded me, and now, as the veil was withdrawn, revealing this most gorgeous and luxurious apartment, I knew not how to act. An incertitude intimidated me.

With body still bent, like those of the crowd of courtiers and eunuchs among whom I stood, I nevertheless raised my eyes. Beyond the pearl and golden pavement before me rose twelve semi-circular steps of silver, leading up to a great throne of glittering crystal, which, in the bright white light shining upon it from four apertures in the ceiling, gleamed with an iridescent fire. Upon this couch, the supports of which were four winged bulls, fashioned from solid blocks of flawless crystal, the back consisting of an enormous crystal representation of the winged figure in the circle, the supreme deity, and adorned with the heads and feet of the lion and the ram, a lion's skin was spread. Reclining upon it in graceful abandon, the rings of her wavy hair tumbled about her in such abundance that she appeared actually to lie on a mass of golden sheen, was a woman of exquisite beauty. Attired in a loose, white robe, sparkling with diamonds from neck to foot, her waist girt by a wide girdle of wonderful emeralds, her bare neck, arms and ankles loaded with magnificent jewels, the effect under the bright rays was absolutely dazzling. The crystal throne shed all colours of the spectrum, but its bejewelled occupant at every movement seemed to flash and gleam with a thousand fires.

She was of amazing beauty, with white, delicately-moulded limbs, tiny hands and feet, eyes half-closed, and as her dimpled chin rested upon her bejewelled arm her clinging robe indistinctly defined the graceful outlines of her form, and her breasts rose and fell slowly as she breathed.

Two gorgeously-attired priests, on either side of the great crystal throne, stood with crossed hands, silent as statues. In strange, high head-dresses, surmounted by silver stars, and attired in robes of silver, they gazed down upon us without moving a muscle. Near the throne, three gigantic negro slaves in leopard-skins, cooled the reclining beauty with great fans of flamingoes' wings, while, grouped around, ready at any moment to execute their mistress's slightest wish, stood a hundred waiting-women, eunuchs and slaves. The vapours of exquisite perfumes floated everywhere.

As we halted, with bent heads, before the wonderful throne, its occupant slowly stretched her white arm beyond her head, and, opening her eyes, her gaze fell upon us. Two female attendants immediately advanced and encased her tiny, bare feet in slippers of serpent skin.

When they had returned to their places she slowly raised herself upon her elbow, and, with her chin upon her palm, raised her right hand, pointing upward. Instantly there appeared, high upon the wall above the crystal throne, where the signs of the deity were sculptured, in letters of fire the height of a man, an inscription in the cuneiform character. As it appeared, priests, eunuchs, slaves and attendants surrounding her sank upon their knees, and, in awed silence, pressed their brows to the pavement.

Lifting my bewildered eyes to the fiery lines, I gazed beyond the wondrous medley of inshot colours and precious stones, and read,—

"I am Istar, Supreme on Earth and in Heaven, Ruler of the Present and the Hereafter, who holdeth the lives of all men in the hollow of my hand. Every man is my slave: every woman shall sacrifice unto me in the House of Lustre. Those who break my commandments Anu and Rimmon, the gods great, shall destroy and devour. Thus I speak."

Thrice the Queen of Ea raised her slim hand, and thrice the lines of enormous arrowheads glowed red and fiery like living coals, each time disappearing and leaving no trace upon the wall. The silence was complete, broken only by the crackling of the herbs as they burned in the great, golden perfuming-pans, but, as the letters of fire died away for the last time, the beautiful woman, with tranquil eyes, slowly placed her foot upon the bare backs of the two women who were lying upon their faces, forming a footstool before the throne, and, with languorous grace, rose and stood upon their prostrate bodies. Then, outstretching her arms, she stood gazing upon us, as if giving us her blessing, and next second my companions, raising themselves, shouted with one voice, "*Istar sa-la-dhu yusapri. I la-tu nahdu nemicu banat sini makhri naku ci nasu-sa-eni!*"

These words, in the ancient language of Babylon, I was able to understand. Outside the palace a corrupted tongue was spoken, but here, before the Queen, worshipped as goddess, only the original tongue was heard. The words uttered by my companions were,—

"Lo! Istar, the Ruler, is revealed! Thou art the glorious Lady of Wisdom, beauteous daughter of the Moon-god, Sin. Before thee our wives and our daughters make sacrifice, and to thee we, thy suppliant slaves, raise our eyes. Thou art our deity!"

As their echoing voices died away, the Queen, fanned by her sphinx-like attendants, slowly re-seated herself upon the crystal throne. A languid expression settled upon her features, and, with her foot upon the neck of one of the women before her, she lounged, one hand thrown carelessly over the crystal, human-headed monster that formed the arm of the gorgeous seat of royalty, and the other toying with the emeralds in her girdle.

From the crowd surrounding me, there stepped forward upon the pavement of pearl and gold, a tall, white-bearded man in a breastplate of green serpent skin, denoting that he was a high-priest, on either side of him standing a trumpeter. Thrice their loud blasts awakened the echoes of the chambers around, then Istar, casting an inquiring glance towards the man, commanded him to speak.

He hesitated, his trembling hand resting upon the bejewelled hilt of his sword, and the little gold bells, sewn at the hem of his robe, tinkling musically.

"Speak! O Rabbani, son of Nabu-ahe-iddina. Why demandest thou an audience in this my dwelling-place? Why goest thou not unto the temple to make sacrifice before the golden image?"

"Let not anger consume thee, O Queen of All the Gods," cried Rabbani, lifting his hand in supplication, and falling upon his knees. "We have ventured into this Everlasting House, passed the Gate of Glory, and entered into the House of the Raising of the Head, because there is one evil-doer among us, with whom thou alone in thy majesty and power canst deal."

A smile crossed the face of the living goddess, and at the same moment a tame lioness, walking past the silent priests of Istar, halted before its royal mistress, who, with her soft hand, patted its sleek back, as a woman caresses a spaniel.

"I am in no mood to decide what punishment shall be meted out to evil-doers. I leave that to my judges," she answered, with a quick gesture of impatience.

"Lend us thine ear, O Queen, whose name we dare not utter beyond these walls, whose tongue is unknown, save to thy priests, eunuchs and courtiers, and to whom every woman maketh sacrifice. Cast us not forth from thy presence, for assuredly thy slaves are faithful and bear the information which, though it be of amazing character, yet, nevertheless, the truth must be told, and that quickly."

"'O QUEEN OF EARTH AND HEAVEN! O PEERLESS AMONG WOMEN! THE DREADED DAY HATH DAWNED!'"

"Then utter it, and be gone," Istar said, glancing at him sharply.

"Know then, O Queen of Earth and Heaven, O Peerless among Women, the dreaded day hath dawned! The Great Destroyer is in our midst!"

Istar, pale and startled, sprang to her feet, clutching her jewel-laden breasts frantically, as if to stay the beating of her heart.

"The Devourer!" she gasped, white to the lips. "Speak! I command thee! Speak quickly, son of Nabu-ahe-iddina, or thou shalt be cast for ever into the realm of Niffer, lord of the Ghost Land."

"I speak, O Mighty One," he answered. "Would that my tongue had been torn from its roots, and my lips sealed by the seal of the Death-god, ere it should have been my duty to make this my announcement. The Devourer from the outer world hath been discovered wandering upon the mountains. How he gained this land, which is without entrance and without exit, no man knoweth. The wise men believe that he came hither like a fowl of the air."

Istar, trembling, clutched the glittering arm of her crystal throne for support, while a dark, sinister expression settled upon her flawless countenance. The crowd about me, awe-stricken and hushed in expectation, awaited her words breathlessly.

"Lo!" cried the high-priest of the Temple of the Seven Lights, suddenly stepping back and dragging me roughly forward, "Lo! O Beauteous Queen of all the Gods, he is here, in thine holy presence!"

I lifted my face. Our eager eyes met.

Her tiny hands were so tightly clenched that the nails were driven into her palms, her breasts heaved and fell quickly, her brows knit in a fierce anger, but in her eyes was a look of unutterable dread.

For a moment she covered her face with her hands, as if to shut me out of her gaze, but next instant she raised her narrow eyebrows, her blanched lips parted, and she turned upon the high-priest in a sudden outburst of fury. Extending her bare arm towards him she cursed him.

"Knowest thou not the writing upon my foundation-stones, offspring of Anu, defiler of the holy Ziggurratu?" she screamed in rage.

The aged high-priest uttered a cry, as if he had been struck a blow. But he answered not.

"Knowest thou the words graven upon the great image? Speak, accursed one. Speak!"

"I do, O Queen," he faltered.

"Then, malediction upon thee. Vengeance and hate, sorrow and torture of the flesh. May the Air-god rend thee; may Shamas, the lord of Light, hide his face from thee for ever; and may Niffer, lord of the Ghost Land, take thee for his slave! May Ninkigat, the lady of the great Land of Terrors, strangle thee, and may the other—whom I dare not name—fill thy vitals with molten metal and consume thee!"

"Mercy!" cried the wretched man, falling upon his knees, and grovelling upon the polished pavement. "Mercy, O Istar, Queen of Ea, and ruler of all creatures! Have mercy upon thy servant!"

"Nay, unto me thou hast shown no mercy, accursed spawn of a scorpion; thou shalt receive none," she answered. Then, lifting her hand towards the file of soldiers that lined the walls, she commanded,—

"Abla, Nabu-nur-ili, Akabi-ilu, forward quickly, ye guards of our majesty. Take this son of Nergal forth to the top of the steps and cast him down with force like a dog, so that his bones be broken and his body mutilated. Then, with his blood, let the words graven upon the image be re-written on the lintel of the Temple of the Seven Lights, so that all may remember. Away with him. Let his body be cast into the lion-pit," she added, with a majestic sweep of her white arm. "I have spoken."

"Have compassion, O Istar! At least, let me live!" cried the aged priest; but ere he could utter the last sentence the soldiers had dragged him forth, with the dreaded Queen's imprecation resounding in his ears in multiplied echoes.

In the full fury of her ungovernable rage this beautiful goddess of the Mysterious Land, at first so graceful and languorous, looked magnificent. With her unbound hair falling about her shoulders and reaching below her girdle, she raised her arms in mad rage, pouring forth a string of curses so terrible that those surrounding her visibly shuddered.

"And thou!" she cried, suddenly turning and gazing intently upon me with eyes sharp as arrows. "So thou art the stranger!"

The people around me were full of passionate anger and abject terror. Behind, before me, everywhere, I saw only glaring eyes, strained wide-open as if to devour me, defiant faces, eager hands fingering sword-hilts, and heard the gnashing of teeth between threatening lips.

"So thou hast dared to accompany that viper Rabbani, and enter my presence!" she cried, in a second outburst of indignation. Her strange terror had been succeeded by rage and defiance terrible to behold. The veins in her brow stood out like blue cords as she spoke, and her soft, perfumed cheeks were suffused by anger.

"I was brought before thee by thy people, O Queen," I answered, endeavouring to appease her. "I knew not thine high-priest, ere I entered thine House of Lustre."

"I have spoken; and he shall die," she snapped, apparently thinking I was making an appeal on the aged man's behalf. "Ascend to me, so that I may see thee more closely."

Thus commanded, I crossed the inlaid pavement and ascended the broad, silver steps leading to the great throne of crystal, before which she now stood upon her prostrate women, erect and queenly. Gaining the pavement of gold whereon the throne was set, I was drawing nearer, when two great eunuchs sprang forward, motioning me not to approach her further.

"Arrest thy steps," they cried, frantically. "The person of Istar, our ruler, is sacred. None but dwellers within this, her temple, may look upon her."

"Retire," she cried to the eunuchs. "I commanded him to approach me."

The men slunk back to their places in chagrin, and as they did so I advanced yet another couple of paces, and dropped upon one knee before her. Her beauty was amazing. The sweet perfumes that exuded from her ample draperies filled my nostrils.

"Whence comest thou?" she asked me in calm, serious voice, gazing upon me with her huge, wonderful eyes.

"From the world that lieth beyond the impregnable limits of thy kingdom, O Queen," I answered.

"Who art thou, that thou shouldst speak our sacred tongue?" she inquired quickly, in surprise.

"I am but a wanderer," I replied. "The language of ancient Assyria hath been recovered by our wise men from the monuments of Nimroud and of Babylon." Her surprise found echo in the murmurings of the eager, excited crowd; but a moment later she asked, —

"How camest thou hither?"

"By an entrance which I followed. It led me through the Valley of Mists, until I came hither unto this thy city."

"An entrance!" she cried, in alarm. "Then thou earnest not as a bird of the air!"

I replied in the negative, and was about to explain the extraordinary manner by which I had gained access to the mysterious Land of the No Return, when she turned upon me with clenched hands, in a paroxysm of rage so sudden that I was startled.

"Then thou art actually a pagan from the unknown land beyond," she cried, trembling with anger. "Be thou accursed! accursed! accursed! May the celestial triad cut thee off, and may Rimmon tear and devour thee!"

A murmur of approbation went round those assembled, and at the mention of the dreaded god all bowed, while the priests in their horned caps raised their arms and lifted their deep voices in adulation.

Speechless, I stood before her while she poured out upon me the vials of her uncurbed wrath. I trembled, fearing lest she should condemn me to a similar doom to which the aged high-priest had been hurried for what appeared to be a petty offence. In her anger she stamped her tiny foot upon the neck of one of the prostrate women, causing her to writhe. But the half-nude pair acting as her footstool uttered no cry. They were worshipping the goddess and sacrificing themselves to her.

"Thou accursed son of the Unknown!" she cried, addressing me. "Thou hast dared to enter this my forbidden land, therefore thou art my captive, my slave, my servant!" She had folded her arms with an air so terrible that I was immediately as one rooted to the golden pavement.

"Kill him, O Istar!" the people cried. "Suffer not his baneful presence to contaminate us! Suffer not his unclean hand to touch the hem of thy sacred robe! Kill him! Let us witness the lions tearing him!"

At the raising of her white, bejewelled hand there was complete silence. She looked at me, crushing me with her haughty beauty.

"He came hither," she said, addressing her courtiers and slaves, "in order to feast his eyes upon what is forbidden, to discover that which for a hundred generations hath been hidden from the pagans of the other world. He therefore shall, ere his soul is given unto Rimmon, witness that which he desireth. He is my captive. My name shall gnaw him like remorse. I will be to him more execrable than the pest, and he shall feel every moment, until the day he is cast into the lion-pit, the chastisement of a goddess."

Ghastly, and with hands clenched, I quivered like a stringed instrument when the over-tense strings are about to snap. Words choked me, and I bowed my head before her.

"My slave thou art," she cried, turning suddenly upon me. "Thou shalt ever grovel in the dust before me; thou shalt take the place of those women who have prostrated themselves before me, and are from this time forth absolved. In future thou shalt be as my footstool. Neither by night nor day shalt thou leave my presence. In my waking hours my heel shall be upon thy neck; in my hours of slumber thou shalt still be wakeful. Whithersoever I go there also shalt thou go, placing thyself as rest for my feet, and thus be ever in my sight. If thou attemptest to fly, I will draw the bears from the mountains, and the lions shall hunt thee, even unto the ends of the earth."

Stepping from the women, upon whose quivering bodies she had been standing, she commanded them to rise, and at signal from her the eunuchs tore from my shoulders the robe in which I had been attired. Then, although struggling vainly in their iron grip, I was cast, face downwards, upon the pavement before the throne, and a moment later the mysterious Queen of Ea stood with her feet upon my back. Her weight crushed my breast, causing my breathing to become difficult; but, applauded by her subjects, she remained in that position addressing them, cursing me for daring to enter her kingdom, and assuring them that ere long they should be entertained by my death beneath the claws of the lions.

"I heed not the graven lines upon the foundation-stone," she exclaimed, in conclusion. "Three hundred thousand soldiers are ready day and night to do my bidding, and if men fail me, I will call down the wrath of the gods most terrible. I will overthrow this my city and burn its temples. Not a single tower, nor tree, nor wall shall remain, and the galleys shall float on streams of blood. I fear not this slave beneath my heel. I would kill him now, with this my poniard; but ere he dies he shall feel the chastisement of Istar. I am thy ruler, and his punishment is in my hands."

"Wisely hast thou spoken, O Goddess, whom we worship with one accord, and to whom we sacrifice those of thy sex. Thou art indeed our just ruler, at whose word mountains tremble and rivers stand still. Thine armed men shall ever be faithful unto thee, and beneath thine heel we leave the wanderer from the Unknown."

"Then go; let the veil fall," she answered. "In my temple, before the graven lines upon my foundation-stone, let full thanksgiving be offered at moonset for our discovery of this wanderer, who is safe in our hands, and thus prevented from escaping back unto his own execrable, accursed race."

"We obey thee, O mighty Istar!" rose from the throats of the assembled multitude as, with one accord, they moved back towards the ante-chamber, still keeping their faces towards the beautiful woman they worshipped. Confusion spread for a few minutes, but at last all retired, save those grouped around the throne, and the great yellow curtain fell, leaving the brilliant Queen in ease and semi-privacy.

Wearied, she threw herself upon her great crystal lounge, lying gracefully back, with the toes of one bare foot just touching me, while her women crowded about and attended her at her elaborate toilet.

Chapter Thirty Nine
Foretokens

Istar's white-robed women brushed out her hair, which fell about her like a cascade of rippling gold, bathed her face in a golden bowl filled with perfume, and gently washed her white hands. Then, when her toilet was complete, they retired at a sign, leaving me alone with her.

When all was silent she lifted her tiny foot from my neck and commanded me to rise.

"Tell me, whence comest thou?" she inquired, in a hard rasping voice, when I stood before her.

Our eyes met. Hers were of that unusual tint—almost violet. They held me in fascination.

"I came from the desert land two moon's march beyond thine," I answered, noticing, at the same moment, that her shapely hands trembled. "I entered thy dominion by the gate known to us as the Rock of the Great Sin, the secret way that no man hath before penetrated."

"Thou hast discovered it!" she gasped excitedly, half rising from her crystal seat of royalty, gleaming with its thousand iridescent fires. "Tell me, in which direction doth it lie?"

"Far north, beyond the Mountains of the Mist, beyond the ruins of the wondrous temple thine ancestor raised to Sin, the Moon-god."

"But tell me the exact position of the rock of the great god Sin," she demanded, eagerly. "It is a spot which existeth in the sayings of the priests, but it hath been lost to all men in the mazes of legendary lore."

"Its exact position I cannot accurately describe," I answered. "Since passing through it and deciphering the rock-tablet of Semiramis, I have travelled many days in forest and over plain and mountain."

"Couldst thou not guide me thither?" she asked, eagerly.

"I fear I could not, O Queen," I answered.

"Thou art, indeed, the Destroyer; the man who is my bitterest enemy," she observed, in a deeply reflective tone.

"How?" I inquired. "Surely I have done thee no wrong!"

"Since the day of Semiramis, the founder of Babylon and of Ea, it hath been told to each generation by our sages that a dark-faced stranger from the north shall one day enter our impregnable kingdom and approach its ruler," she said, hoarsely. "His entry shall be the curse that Anu, god of Destruction, hath placed upon our land, and this our city, with walls unbreakable, shall be overthrown and crumble into dust. When Semiramis founded this our land of Ea, she made not sufficient sacrifice unto Anu, therefore the dread god overthrew her colossal Temple of the Sun, and laid a curse upon the city, saying that he would one day direct hereto the steps of a man from the world beyond, and that this man should be the Destroyer. Thou art the one sent by Anu."

She had fixed her brilliant eyes upon me, holding me transfixed. There was in her face a strange look of combined terror and hatred.

"Well," I said, after a pause, "believest thou that I am the prophesied doer of evil?"

"Assuredly thou art," she answered. "All is evil in thine accursed world beyond."

"And thou, the goddess Istar, believest that I am capable of working evil against this thy giant city!" I observed, smiling. "Thou fearest that I am possessed of the evil eye."

"Thy coming fulfilleth the prophecies of our priests through ages," she answered, in a low, harsh tone. "Thou art mine enemy. I, my people and my land are doomed."

"This, then, was the reason that I was cast into the lion-pit," I observed.

She nodded in acquiescence, adding, "It was proposed that thou shouldst be devoured by the wild beasts as recompense for thine intrepidity; but I rescued thee because—because, I wished to hear thy story from thine own lips."

"Already have I told thee all," I answered. "This thy land is known to the world beyond only by vague legends and the unwritten romances of story-tellers. When I return, I will tell my fellows of the wonders I have witnessed within thy brilliant kingdom."

"No," she answered, rising with true regal dignity, yet trembling with anger. "Thou shalt never go back, for to thee, as to all men, this is the Land of the No Return. To kill thee will only hasten disaster upon myself, therefore, thou shalt remain my slave, and lest thou shouldst attempt to escape, thou shalt never leave my side, either by day or by night. I hold thee in servitude irrevocably. When the Day of Destruction, foretold by the prophets, cometh, then shall thine heart be torn out whilst thou art still alive, and given to Ninep, my tame lioness, to devour at a mouthful."

I bowed, smiling bitterly; but no retort escaped my lips. Her strange, weird manner held me spellbound.

"At least it shall be known," she cried, angrily, "that I hold in bondage, as my personal slave, the man who hath entered our land to bring evil upon us. Attempt not to escape, or assuredly will I slay thee with mine own hand," and she drew from her girdle of emeralds a short, keen knife, with hilt fashioned like a winged bull, which she kept therein concealed.

"Thou appearest to consider me as harbinger of ill," I answered, with knit brows. "I have no design upon thee or thine. Love of adventure and a secret quest have led me hither."

"A secret quest!" she cried. "What was it?"

"I had heard stories of wonders within thy land, and sought its whereabouts," I said, ambiguously.

"Then, thou didst discover the secret entrance; the mystery that hath remained hidden through an hundred ages?"

"I did, O Istar," I replied. "Long I toiled in the darkness beneath the foundations of the rock of thy Moon-god, and emerged into thy wondrous country, with its city more amazing than any mine eyes have ever beheld."

"Art thou dazzled?" she asked, smiling for the first time.

"Indeed I am, O Queen," I replied. "The magnificence of thy city, the splendour of this thy palace, and the beauty of thy face entranceth me. Of a verity thine is a world apart, and thou art goddess and queen in one."

She fixed her clear, wonderful eyes upon me, and her breast, covered with jewels, slowly heaved and fell. In her gaze I noticed, for the first time, a curious expression, and her manner was undisguisedly coquettish.

"Then, why dost thou desire to leave our land of Ea? Why not remain here in happiness and contentment?" she asked, raising her pencilled brows, and toying with the long, gold pendant hanging from her ear.

"Because," I answered, frankly, "because I am pledged to a woman who loveth me."

"Who loveth thee!" she cried, fiercely. "Who is the woman?"

"Azala, daughter of the Sultan 'Othman, of Sokoto," I answered.

She was silent for a long time. Her white, well-formed hands twitched nervously.

"Azala," she repeated slowly, in a hollow voice. "And thou desirest to return because thou lovest her?"

I nodded.

"The penalty for thine intrepidity is death," she continued, gravely. "For the present I spare thee, but thou shalt die when it pleaseth me. I am Istar, the ruler who holdeth her enemies in the hollow of her hand."

"I am not thine enemy," I protested.

"Thou art!" she cried, with flashing eyes. "Thou, son of Anu, art the Destroyer whose coming hath been foretold."

"I am prepared to serve thee, and to prove to thee that I have entered thy land without evil intent," I said.

"Be it so," she answered, drawing herself up suddenly. "Thou shalt serve me as slave, and attend me everywhere; but while I have breath thou shalt never return unto thy master Anu, the god of Destruction, who dwelleth in the land afar."

Her agitation was intense. In her excitement she stood beside her great crystal throne, grasping with both hands one of the human-headed monstrosities which served as arms, while her pale face had assumed a haggard look, and around her eyes were large, dark rings. This woman who, as Queen of the ancient realm, was also worshipped by every man and woman as Istar, the Goddess of Love, possessed an extraordinary personality. In features, in manner, in her luxurious mode of life, she was remarkable; while, as I had already had illustration, she was cruel, quick-tempered and relentless, overlooking no fault, and holding her unique position as some supernatural ruler of earth. The legend current throughout Ea, prophesying the appearance of a visitant and the downfall of the city, was extremely unfavourable to me, I knew; nevertheless, I recollected my pledge to Azala, my long and adventurous journey thither, and now that I was actually at last in Ea I was more than ever determined to fathom the mystery that my well-beloved had alleged would be revealed unto me. The strange life about me held me entranced with wonder. Everything was upon a scale so colossal and extravagantly luxurious that I gazed about lost in wonder. The dwelling-place of the beautiful woman who held me captive, a palace and temple combined, was, indeed, a magnificent pile of amazing proportions and was well named the House of the Raising of the Head, for it was full of marvels at every turn. Istar's firm determination that I should not leave her side was certainly disconcerting; nevertheless the Korân telleth us that by patience much can be accomplished; therefore, I decided to stifle the voice of protest, endure my lot, and bow to the woman who had held me humiliated as slave in sight of her brilliant court.

Again, with eyes flashing, she heaped fierce curses upon me, declaring that my life should be made a burden; that ere a moon had passed I should long for death; and that my face should never again be brightened by the eyes of the woman I loved. In the midst of a string of epithets bestowed upon me with a terrible volubility, two heralds, in golden breastplates and white-plumed helmets, entered the chamber, and raising their great brazen horns blew three loud blasts, whereat Istar, the words of reproach dying on her lips, sank among the cushions of her throne, while, almost at the same instant, the great silken curtains again parted, revealing the assembled multitude of soldiers, courtiers, eunuchs and priests, who had apparently remained awaiting their Queen's pleasure. Erect, I stood beside the gleaming throne gazing upon the brilliant court of this curious monarch, while Ninep, the tame lioness, walked slowly past, sniffing inquiringly at her mistress, then stood licking her soft, bejewelled hand, the hand that she declared would strike me dead if I attempted to return to the world outside. Impetuosity was one of her many peculiarities. One moment so fierce was she that she would herself assassinate any who hesitated to obey her wish; the next she would smile good-humouredly, as though she knew not a moment of anger, and malice found no resting-place within her heart.

Suddenly she raised her hand, and a silence, deep and complete, fell upon the gorgeous, perfumed multitude. Ninep yawned, stretched herself at her mistress's feet, and placing her head upon her paws, blinked lazily at those below the steps of polished silver.

"Know," she said a moment later, in a clear, not unmusical voice, "this son of Anu beside me is indeed the Destroyer whom our fathers have expected for ages, and whom the prophets have told us will bring evil upon Ea."

"Let him be given as food to the lions!" they shouted. "Kill him, O Istar, that he may not betray us into the hands of those who seek our destruction! Anu hath set his seal upon Ea, and our city must be overthrown, but let the spy be killed so that he may not furnish report unto those who sent him hither."

"He shall die," Istar replied, briefly.

A roar of approbation instantly broke forth; but next instant, again raising her hand to command quiet, the queen-goddess continued,—

"He shall die when, as my slave, he hath served me."

"Let him die now, O Istar!" they shouted. "Gladden our hearts by letting us see the lions tear him limb from limb. He is the Destroyer, the visitant against whom the sages have warned us. Through him will the vengeance of Anu, the dread god, descend upon us. Let him die!"

"No," she answered, both hands resting upon the crystal arms of her glittering throne. "I have spoken. He is my personal slave, bound to my side by night and by day."

"Dost thou not fear to have a son of Anu as thy body-servant?" asked an aged priest, with flowing white beard and high head-dress of shining gold, surmounted by a star, the emblem of Istar. "He may wreak vengeance upon thee."

"I am Istar, and know not fear," she answered, haughtily. "Men bow to me, and women make sacrifice in my temple. For those who incur my displeasure, Merodach, the protector of mankind, will not mediate."

Then the queen-goddess nodded towards a man of tall stature, attired in a robe of dead black. Again the trumpets sounded thrice, as signal for her captains to come forward and present their reports. They came, one by one, advancing to the foot of the steps, bowing upon one knee, and obtaining the sanction of their sovereign upon various matters.

At last, when about twenty had been received and dismissed, a man older than the rest, and wearing a breastplate in which rubies were set in the form of a great star within a circle, advanced, knelt before the bewitching Queen, and mumbled some words that I could not catch.

Istar inclined her head slightly in approbation. Then, bidding the white-headed warrior to rise, said aloud, —

"Know, Larsa, this stranger that is within our gates hath discovered the Rock of the Moon-god, and entered into our presence thereby. The curse of Anu, the Progenitor, who changeth not the decree coming forth from his mouth, hath fallen. Go with thine hosts far beyond the Mountains of the Mist even unto the confines of Ea, and there search long and diligently, so that thou mayest discover and defend the secret way. Let not the feet of those of evil defile our land, for assuredly the sign is set upon us, and destruction threateneth. Thy valiant hosts must avert it."

"Thy will shall be done, O divine patroness," the old man answered, bowing low till his beard almost swept the pavement. "I will haste to do thy bidding."

"May Merodach encompass thee with his shield that none can penetrate," she exclaimed, as, turning, he went forth to lead his soldiers in search of the strange, natural gate by which I had entered.

For an hour the queen-goddess continued to receive those who craved audience, giving advice, hearing petitions, and dispensing justice. Then her brows knit, she grew tired, and at her command the great apartment was cleared of all except the twelve slaves whose duty it was to cool her with their huge fans of flamingoes' wings.

"Thou hast not told me thy name," she exclaimed, suddenly turning upon me.

"Thy servant is called Zafar," I answered.

"So be it," she said, glancing at me quickly, with sinister look. She paused a moment, then, rising languidly from her seat, slowly descended the steps, followed by all her retinue, including myself.

"Depart not from my sight," she commanded, turning towards me. "Where I go, there shalt thou go also."

Through the great hall she led the way into a smaller apartment, hung with gorgeous stuffs, where, in an alcove beyond, was a great couch supported by four lions in silver, with curtains of purple worked with silver. In the centre of the chamber was an upright conical stone, black, with many lines of arrowheads engraved thereon. It was, I afterwards learned, the symbol of Baal, the ruler and vivifier of nature.

Her women, priestesses of Istar, attired in loose robes of pure white, with their unbound hair secured by a golden fillet, unloosed her heavy girdle of emeralds which confined her waist, removed her little slippers of snake skin, and again bathed her face with some delicate perfume. Then they tenderly laid her to rest upon the couch, and while four men-at-arms, with drawn swords, took up their positions as guards, two at head and two at foot, they threw themselves down upon the lion-skins spread about. Before the alcove, wherein reclined the queen, a veil of silver sheen descended, for already her wondrous eyes had closed, and, tired out, she had fallen into a light slumber.

I, her slave, sat upon the floor, hugging my knees, deep in thought, and waiting, with the silent guards, until the dawn. Truly my position was a remarkable one. I had found that which all men before had failed to discover. I was actually living in a world unknown.

Chapter Forty
The Festival of Tammuz

But one desire possessed me—to return to Azala.

In the many days which followed the first night of my captivity I witnessed innumerable marvels. The pageantry in the palace, known to all as E Sagilla, "The House of the Raising of the Head," was of amazing brilliance; and in the great city, sixty English miles in circumference, and built with extreme regularity, with broad, straight streets crossing one another at right angles, the sights which met my gaze filled me with astonishment. Though the dwellers in that long-forgotten kingdom possessed many inventions similar to those I had witnessed in London, yet their religion, manners and customs were the same as those which existed four thousand years ago, when the all-powerful Semiramis caused her record to be engraved in the foundations of the rock she consecrated to her supposed father, the Moon-god, Sin, "the lord of the waxing and the waning." The buildings were on colossal scale, with towers reaching to a far greater height than any I had seen in European cities, and the display of gold, silver and gems, mostly brought there ages ago by the notable woman who founded Babylon and conquered Ethiopia, held me in constant wonderment. In the great courts of the temple-palace I watched the sacrifice of rams upon the triangular fire-altars, attended by long-bearded priests of Gibil, the Fire-god, in robes whereon were embroidered fir cones, apt emblems of fire; and everywhere I noticed symbols of the celestial deities, while power was typified indiscriminately on every hand by colossal figures of winged, human-headed, and sometimes eagle-headed, lions and bulls.

Through one whole moon I had been slave of Istar, and scarcely left her side for a single instant by night or day, hourly witnessing sights that were amazing, and occupying my leisure in deciphering the profuse cuneiform inscriptions graven on almost every wall or door-lintel by hands that ages ago had crumbled to dust. From them I learned much regarding the history of that wondrous kingdom; how, before the death of Semiramis, she was worshipped as Istar, Goddess of Love. In some inscriptions I found her referred to as "Queen of the Crescent Moon," "Queen of the Stars," and "Queen of Heaven"; in others as "Queen of War and Battle," "Archeress of the Gods," and "Queen of all the Gods;" but it was distinctly stated in several of the colossal wall-pictures that, before she died, she decreed that her daughter should be ruler of Ea, and that all should worship her as Istar. Each Queen should remain unmarried until the age of forty, and should be worshipped as Goddess of Love, and each King should be known as Hea, and should place his daughter upon the throne in preference to his son. Through four thousand years this wonderful kingdom had existed in all its magnificence, in defiance to Anu, the god of Destruction, and during that period the dignity of queen-goddess had been handed down from generation to generation, its bearer dwelling within that great temple raised by the autocratic Empress who founded Babylon. Those giant walls, with their sculptured feasts and victories, had remained intact, black and polished like iron, colossal monuments of Assyria's greatness, and as in the silence of night, when I watched while Istar slept, I gazed upon them and reflected, wondering whether Allah would ever allow me to escape to tell the world of my amazing discovery of this mysterious, unknown realm.

Many were the feasts held within that colossal palace, but chief among them was the Festival of Tammuz, "The only-begotten son of Dav-Kina, the lady of the earth." This, held about one moon after my captivity, was upon a scale of unsurpassed magnificence, the feasting, drinking and merry-making continuing throughout seven days and nights. The court of the garden of the palace wherein Istar feasted the people of Ea was fitted up with white, green and blue hangings, fastened with cords of fine linen and purple to silver rings and pillars of marble; the couches of the female guests were of gold and silver upon the pavement of red, blue, white and black marble. Men sat in high chairs of ivory, and drank wine from golden vessels, slaves served them with various fruits and viands, and each hour the guests were entertained with music and dancing. Of musical instruments there were but two kinds—a drum, and a sort of triangular lyre with ten strings, held in the left hand, and struck with a plectrum held in the right. Exalted upon her dais, in the centre of the beautiful garden, sat Istar, with queenly hauteur gazing down upon the animated scene. Every house throughout the city was illuminated, for the Festival of Tammuz was celebrated by all, and many were the magnificent banquets given by high officers and notabilities. Twice Istar drove through the streets in her gilded chariot, drawn by eight milk-white stallions, I, her slave, sitting at her side. She did this, no doubt, to publicly demonstrate to the populace the fact that she held me captive, for as we passed along the straight, broad thoroughfares she was greeted by the wild plaudits of the multitude, while upon my head curses most terrible were showered.

When on the last night of the great festival the music had been silenced, the guests had left their couches, the dancing-girls had retired, and we were alone together in the silent, moonlit garden, she sighed deeply, glanced at me for an instant, and rose. Her heavy anklets of gold clinked as she descended the silver steps of her throne, and, as mutely I followed, I saw that high above us still shone the single shaft of intense white light from the summit of the towering Temple of the Seven Lights. It was, I had learned from one of the priests, known as The Eye of Istar, a light that had shone forth, night and day without ceasing, ever since Semiramis herself made the first sacrifice in that high temple tower of seven coloured stories, consecrated to the Goddess of Love. On the summit of that tower every woman was bound by the law of Babylon's founder to make sacrifice to Istar, and it was the duty of the white-robed vestal virgins to keep the light burning incessantly, to remind the people that Istar watched over them and was their ruler. Ofttimes I had been seized with curiosity to ascend that tower where all women, rich and poor alike, were compelled to prostrate themselves at least once in their lives, and it was with satisfaction that I now saw my royal mistress slowly approach the entrance to the temple tower. As we crossed the great court the huge crowd that had assembled bowed in silence. At the portals twelve fair-haired girls, in robes of pure white, greeted her with great ceremony; then, headed by a wizened old priest, with snowy beard and horned cap of gold, surmounted by a star, we commenced to climb the wide flight of winding marble stairs. The ascent was long and toilsome. At each stage we halted, and a prayer was recited to the god to whom it was dedicated, until at length we reached the great domed pavilion that formed its summit.

From above, the unquenchable light shone down upon the gigantic city, while the roof of pale blue, decorated with golden stars, was supported by twisted columns of gilded marble. Ibises, the sacred birds of love, flitted in and out at will, and in the centre, raised upon a silver pedestal from the pearl and ebony mosaic pavement, stood an undraped statue of Istar herself. Its sight entranced me, for in her right hand she was represented as holding two asps entwined, the same symbol as that branded upon my breast!

Around the image of the Goddess of Love, a crowd of young women and girls from the city were kneeling. Some had their lips pressed to its feet; others were lounging upon skins gazing away out upon the brightly-lit city. The scene was indeed a striking one. The bright moon shed her light full upon the statue, causing it to stand out in bold relief, while the golden braziers, here and there, burned perfumes which filled the air with a delicious, intoxicating fragrance. When we entered all was silence, but the instant it became known that Istar herself was present, with one accord the worshippers rose, struggling with one another to kiss the hem of her gold-embroidered robe.

Once each year, at the conclusion of the Festival of Tammuz, Istar herself ascended to pass the night within the temple, and pose in the flesh as the Goddess of Love. Hence, on that night, great crowds assembled to see her enter the tower, and the unmarried women of Ea, who had not before made sacrifice, congregated at the summit. The scene was strangely impressive. Surrounded by her white-robed priestesses, she stood before the image in the ekal, or main nave, and raised her bare white arms to heaven.

When all her votaries had kissed her robe, and ranged themselves around her, a dead silence fell. Suddenly, in clear, musical tones, her hands still raised above her head, whereon was fixed the golden star, she commenced to chant the beautiful hymn to the Moon-god, Sin, —

"Merciful one, begotten of the universe, who foundeth his illustrious seat among living creatures. Long-suffering father, full of forgiveness, whose hand upholdeth the lives of mankind. Lord, thy divinity is as the wide heavens, and filleth the unknown seas with its fear. On the surface of the peopled world he biddeth the sanctuary be placed—he proclaimeth their name. The father, the begotten of gods and men, who causeth the shrine to be founded, who established the offering, who proclaimeth dominion, who giveth the sceptre, who shall fix destiny unto a far-distant day, look down upon this our House of Lustre, and let it never be cast down."

Then the women, casting aside their outer garments of silk and purple, knelt and prayed long, invoking the indwelling spirit of life, called "Zi," following it by a supplication to Mul-lil "lord of the night sky," and concluding with an appeal to Istar herself, crying,—

"In heaven, who is supreme? Thou alone art supreme! On earth, who is supreme? Thou alone art supreme!"

It was a curious and weird form of adoration and worship. The Goddess of Love stood erect and statuesque, without moving a muscle, as each worshipper, advancing, paid her homage. Some kissed her finger-tips, others her bare feet, each making declaration that they were henceforward her slaves. Meanwhile, the priestesses, all young women of extreme beauty, chanted softly strange hymns to the great Baal, head-father and creator of the universe, and with the moonlight streaming full upon her, Istar looked, indeed, one of entrancing beauty, yet cold as an icicle. Above her head the statue, its stone arm outstretched, held the strange symbol that Azala and I bore upon our breasts, and as I stood watching I saw with what intense devotion the women worshipped her. Unseemly rites were undoubtedly connected with the worship of Istar, the Babylonian Venus, in the time-effaced city of Sardanapalus, but here there were no degrading symbols; indeed, the surroundings in this elevated temple showed considerable purity of taste and feeling, and the sacrifices were in the form of gold, jewels, food and wine.

At length, after many prayers and supplications to each of the gods of the celestial triad, Istar turned, and, accompanied by her priestesses, slowly moved away, her votaries still remaining prostrate upon their faces.

Behind the ekal in which she had been standing was a veil of golden thread, which, being drawn aside, disclosed the sacred seat or couch called the papakha, the holy of holies of the Goddess of Love.

When we had passed beyond the veil, it fell behind us, and the priestesses, having attended Istar at her elaborate toilet, she reclined with languor upon the purple velvet cushions of her soft couch. Meanwhile, the votaries were leaving, and, when the veil was again raised, the ekal was deserted. But only for a moment. An aged man, in long, black gown, came forth from the darkness, and, standing on the spot where the goddess had stood, raised both hands towards her. His appearance was evidently part of the annual custom, for it was apparent that the priestesses and slaves, cooling their mistress with their great fans, had expected him.

Scarcely, however, had he opened his mouth, when Istar, springing from her couch, stood glaring at him with threatening gesture. Her hands trembled as words escaped her, "Ah! I had forgotten! Forgotten!" she wailed. Unsteadily she swayed forward for a moment, then sank back again upon her couch with blanched countenance.

"Lo!" cried the aged prophet, in a croaking voice, "through three-score years have I uttered warning!—the same warning, that since the day of the founder of Ea, hath been spoken at the conclusion of each Festival of Tammuz, son of the Lady of the Earth."

"Yea, I know! I know!" gasped Istar. "Loose not thy tongue's strings. Each year thou hast repeated thy prophecy; spare me its recital to-night!"

"Semiramis, our great queen, commanded that it should be uttered, therefore seek not to stay my words," he answered reproachfully, in a grave voice. "Thus saith Anu, god of Destruction, 'Semiramis, when she built Ea, made no sacrifice, because she feared me not. Behold, I will direct unto Ea a stranger, who shall enter within its gates, and the day of whose coming none shall know. He shall be as a sign unto you that I will bring upon Ea a king of kings from the north, with horses and with chariots, and with horsemen, and with companies, and with much people. He—'"

"No!" cried Istar, covering her haggard face with her hands, while the tame lioness stood watching, her tail sweeping the ground. "I know thou art the skeleton of the Feast of Tammuz, but spare me thy disconcerting words."

The prophet, however, continued, heedless of her earnest supplications.

"'He shall kill the daughters of Ea in the field; and he shall make a fort against thee, and cast a mount against thee, and lift up the buckler against thee. And he shall set engines of war against thy walls, and with his axes shall he break down these towers. By reason of the abundance of his horses, their dust shall cover thee; the walls of Ea shall shake at the noise of the horsemen, and of the wheels and of the chariots, when he shall enter into thy gates, as men enter into a city wherein is made a breach. With the hoofs of his horses shall he tread down all thy streets; he shall put thy people to the sword, and thy strong garrisons shall be against them as a weak reed. And they shall kill thee and send thee to the city of Ninkigat, ruler of the great land of evil, whose palace walls are clothed in dust, the inhabitants thereof wearing robes of feathers like birds. And they shall make a spoil of thy riches and a prey of thy merchandise; and they shall break down thy walls and destroy thine houses; and they shall root up thy foundation-stones, and lay thy timber and thy dust in the midst of the water.'"

Istar set her teeth. For an instant she glanced at me, the stranger foretold by the prophet; then her eyes were turned upon the man who had prophesied her downfall. I saw in their violet depths a steely glitter, as with one hand she fondled her pet Ninep. Almost as the last word left the old man's lips she rose to her feet, and, with a word to the lioness, she pointed to the aged man who had dared to incur her displeasure. Ninep crouched at the feet of her mistress for a single instant, then, flying through the air, fixed her deadly fangs in the sage's throat.

One loud scream of agony sounded as man and beast rolled over in deadly embrace. Next second I saw the polished pavement was defiled by blood.

Obedient to the call of her mistress, Ninep trotted back and licked her hand, leaving the prophet mangled and dead. Slaves quickly removed all evidences of the tragedy, and while they did so Istar sank back, her fair face buried among the cushions, a single sob escaping her.

Chapter Forty One
The Temple of Love

That night, in gloomy mood, Istar reclined dreamily upon her soft papakha, dismissing all her priestesses and slaves, so that I remained alone with her. With my back to one of the golden pillars supporting the roof, I sat silent in thought, scarce daring to move, for fear of the dozing lioness. Istar had fallen into a troubled sleep, and lay tossing upon her couch with tumbled tresses.

A sudden murmur from her caused me to glance in her direction, when I saw her lying, still asleep, ghastly pale beneath the light of the moon. Her robe was disarranged; her delicate chest, that slowly heaved and fell, had become revealed. As I looked, I discerned, to my amazement, that it bore the device of the entwined asps, identically the same as had been branded upon me; the same as appeared on the rock-tablet of Semiramis!

Azala had spoken the truth. So far had the Mystery of the Asps been revealed. The strange link that joined me with the daughter of the Sultan 'Othman joined us both, in some unaccountable manner, to the goddess-queen of this ancient land of marvels. I rose, and, creeping nearer, minutely examined the mystic mark upon her chest. It was seared as deeply, and presented a blemish as hideous, as my own. Lying, as she was, in graceful abandon, with one arm flung over her head, her chest rose and fell each time she breathed, but suddenly she drew a long, deep-drawn sigh, and her eyes opened.

I started back, but already she had detected me. "Well?" she exclaimed, regarding me with dreamy glance through her half-opened lashes, slowly readjusting the white silken robe that had come apart at the neck. "Why hast thou approached me?"

"Thou hast slept uneasily," I answered, "and a hideous mark upon thy breast became revealed."

Languidly she raised her head upon her arm, and with eyes still half-closed, like Ninep, her dozing lioness, she said,—

"Come hither, Zafar. Come to my side."

Obediently I approached her couch. Her breast rose, causing her diamonds to sparkle. During the past few days I had not failed to notice in her manner an entire change. She accorded me more liberty; she no longer placed her spiteful heel upon my neck as sign of triumph, and seldom she spoke to me with wilful gesture. Once, the amazing thought had flashed across my mind that she actually loved me, but at such absurd notion I had laughed and placed it aside.

"What seest thou in the Mark of the Asps to amaze thee?" she asked, when I had drawn nigh to her, and Ninep sniffed my legs inquisitively.

"It is as a strange mark," I answered. "I was wondering what its meaning might be."

"Ah!" she sighed. "Its meaning none can tell, save that those who bear it are the doomed."

"The doomed!" I gasped. "Why?"

"Upon his accursed Anu setteth his mark. Hence it is that I bear it," she answered, gravely. "Thou art mine enemy, Zafar," she added, after a slight, painful pause. "To-night have I sent away my women, so that I may speak with thee, the stranger whose coming hath been prophesied for ages. By all men in Ea I am supposed to hate thee, yet—yet—"

Again she paused, looking at me intently with eyes in which burned the unmistakable light of love.

"Yet thou canst not bring thyself to cast me into the lions' pit," I observed, smiling bitterly. "Better that thou shouldst give me my liberty, and allow me to depart."

"Never," she cried, starting up. "Thou shalt never leave me. If I am doomed to die, thou shalt die also."

"Why?" I asked. "I have wrought thee no ill."

"Thou hast struck the chord of affection within my heart, Zafar," she said, passionately.

"Already have I told thee that Azala, daughter of the Sultan 'Othman, is betrothed to me," I answered, not in the least surprised at this passionate declaration.

"Heed her not," she cried. "Already I know that Anu, though he sendeth thee hither as sign of the overthrow of Ea, hath, nevertheless, placed upon thee also the Mark of the Asps."

I started. I had no idea that she had ascertained the secret hidden beneath my robe of crimson silk. Some slave must, at her bidding, have examined my chest as I slept.

"And if so?"

"Then thou wilt assuredly meet with a violent end." I smiled, and she regarded me with knit brows.

"If thou art my friend," I said, "then thou wilt release me."

"No. None departs from or enters the Land of the No Return," she answered. "Since the foundation of Ea one man only escaped into the outer world. It happened ages ago. He never returned hither, for on the day the calamity befel us Anu was wroth, a great earthquake occurred, and the gate by which he made his exit became closed for ever."

Already had I heard a similar legend during my long and eager search for the Rock of Sin, the Moon-god, the "illuminator of the earth and lord of laws."

"Who was the man who escaped?" I inquired.

"Legend saith his name was Nebo," she answered. "Knowest thou any of that name?"

In the negative I replied, reflecting upon the strange story of the escape of this man beyond the confines of Ea, and wondering what adventures befel him.

Then she went on to relate how, on many occasions, there had appeared in cloud-pictures, or mirages, inverted pictures of the unapproachable world beyond; and I, in turn, explained how the Rock of the Moon-god and the Mountains of the Mist appeared frequently in the desert mirage in far-off Kano.

"Hast thou ever seen Ea mirrored on the clouds?" she inquired.

"Never," I answered. "Thy city is unknown, hence my speechless amazement at its discovery."

"Why desirest thou to return to thy land of evil?" she asked, stretching forth her hand and softly stroking Ninep's sleek back.

"Because of the woman I love."

She bit her lip to the blood, and glanced at me with an evil glint in her bright eyes.

"Thou carest naught for me," she observed, reproachfully, regarding me sharply with narrowing brows.

"I am but thy captive," I responded. "As Queen of Ea thou mayest not allow love to enter thine heart until thou growest old. Why dost thou taunt me?"

Mention of the rigid law of her great ancestress, Semiramis, caused her to frown.

"So be it," she answered, hoarsely. "If thou wilt not renounce thy love for this woman who dwelleth in thine accursed land, then thou art still my slave."

"I am content," I said.

"Thou hast chosen?" she inquired, slowly rising to her feet and standing erect before me.

"I have chosen." "Then to-morrow the lions shall rend thee in full gaze of the assembled people of Ea, who shall make sport of thy supplications, and thy cries shall be as music unto their ears," she burst forth, in a sudden fury of passion. "Anu shall rend thee, Nergal, lord of death, shall seize thee, and thou shalt be accursed by the Fever-god, and cast into the dread kingdom of Niffer. Baal shall show thee no mercy; Adarmalik, lord of the noonday sun, shall hide his light from thee; Shamas shall blind thee, and thou shalt exist for ever in the torments prepared by Ninkigat in the burning land where all is dust. Thou hast disdained the favours that I would have bestowed upon thee, despised me, and flung back the love that I would have given thee. Therefore shalt thou die. I, Istar, ruler of Ea, have spoken."

Her beautiful face was distorted by fierce, uncontrolled passion, vituperation fell from her lips with a rapidity which almost choked her, her mass of dead gold hair had escaped from its fillet and fell in profusion about her shoulders, while her white, filmy robe, open again at the neck, disclosed the hideous, mysterious blemish scarred dark red upon the white flesh—the mark that was branded upon the woman I loved as well as the queen-goddess who had condemned me to death.

My dogged silence enraged her. It seemed as though during the weeks of my captivity she had unconsciously grown to regard me with affection, and held me as slave of her caprice. Yet my thoughts, ever of Azala, were so full that I had never before actually realised the position in which I now suddenly found myself.

"Thou utterest no word!" she cried. "Thou art still defiant. To-morrow wilt thou crave mercy at my feet, but I will show thee none. Thou hast sneered at my power, set at naught my good-will, and refused to abandon all thought of return to thy land of evil, and the woman who holdeth thee entranced. Thou shalt never look upon her face again!"

I turned away from the irate beauty, whose hands were clenched within their palms until the nails drew blood, and without replying, slowly crossed the polished pavement of the temple, passing over the spot whereon the hapless prophet had fallen beneath Ninep's deadly claws, and advancing to the sculptured parapet of alabaster, whereon I leaned in thought, gazing down upon the gay, brightly-lit city, and the great buildings and courts which comprised the wonderful House of the Raising of the Head. Ninep uttered a low growl. The moon shone brightly, lighting up the extensive view on every hand. Below lay the well-remembered flight of steps, brilliantly illuminated, with their double row of guards in shining breastplates. Beyond the palace walls the lights of the streets showed in long, straight lines. Above, the shaft of intense white brilliance, the inextinguishable Eye of Istar, still streamed forth upon the wondrous city of Ea, lighting up its terraces, its obelisks and colossal temples like day, while, far away in the distance, the snowy, serrated crests of the Mountains of the Mist showed high, ghost-like, mysterious.

Beyond lay freedom and Azala. Already had I witnessed that Istar, quick-tempered and passionate, was capable of any cruelty or treachery, even towards her most trusted friends. This woman, worshipped as Goddess of Love, was, indeed, full of grace, beautiful in form, with a face almost flawless; but the cruelties she practised almost daily were revolting. To incur her anger meant death, either upon the torture-wheel or in the lion-pit, and ofttimes, while standing beside her, I had noticed the exultant pleasure with which she condemned men and women to torture or to the grave. The people of Ea called her goddess; I thought her a fiend.

As over the parapet I gazed aimlessly away across the gigantic capital of this world-forgotten race, it became impressed upon me that, to save my life, I must at once seek means of escape. But how? As Istar's personal slave, it seemed impossible to elude her vigilance; even if I escaped outside the city my way back to the Rock of the Moon-god was uncertain. I recollected also that within the gloomy cavern there existed an utterly impassable barrier between myself and the world I had left—that roaring inrush of water descending to feed the subterranean river. Times without number thoughts of freedom had possessed me, but on each occasion I had been forced to abandon hope, resign myself to the galling captivity in which I existed, and possess my soul in patience.

Now, however, I had become desperate. The moon, while I stood watching long and earnestly, became obscured by a dense black cloud shaped like a falcon's wing, which left only a patch of green sky half round its disc. On either side of the city the great plain stretched dark and wide. The shapes of the mountains could not be discerned, but showed like a heavy cloud bank against the horizon. My strained eyes could discern a speck of light afar off, which, as it was too low for a star, could only mark the existence of some house on the distant mountain side. The silence could be felt.

The day of feasting and mad gaiety had, it seemed, exhausted all the voices of nature as well as those of men.

At length I turned towards the papakha. Istar had sunk back upon her purple couch, wearied by the continuous gaiety of the festival, and forgetful of her wrath, had again fallen asleep, her head thrown back upon a great, tasselled cushion of rose silk. One of her slippers had fallen off, disclosing her bare foot, with its heavy, bejewelled anklets, while near her Ninep had stretched her long body, with her snout between her paws. Between us stood the life-sized statue upon its pedestal, the image of Love, before which all women of Ea bowed and made sacrifice. Ghostly it looked in the pale half-light with the symbol of the entwined asps held within its right hand, and as I advanced towards it I touched its base. The stone had been worn smooth as glass by the lips of priestesses and votaries who had worshipped at that shrine through all the ages since Semiramis; the feet and legs were worn hollow and out of symmetry by the osculations of the millions of women who had ascended that tower to the gorgeous Temple of Istar to prostrate themselves. The image stretched forth its arm over me ominously, and the perfumed smoke from the braziers, whirled up by a breath of the night wind, wrapped around me a subtle, almost suffocating, fragrance.

Istar slept on with heaving breasts. One chance alone remained to me—a dash for liberty.

Advancing cautiously a few paces I craned my neck to satisfy myself that her slumber was not feigned; then, with a last look upon her, I turned and crept silently away into the shadow where the stairs descended.

I had just reached them, when a faint rustling behind me caused me to glance quickly round. In an instant I recognised the truth. Istar had followed me. With a cry of rage she sprang upon me, her poniard gleaming in her hand. Long ago she had vowed to kill me if I attempted to leave her side, and it was now her intention to carry out her threat. One fierce blow she aimed at my heart, and in warding it off the blade gashed my arm. At the same moment, however, I wrested the weapon from her hand, and held her tightly by the wrists.

To free herself she struggled violently, but I held her powerless, when suddenly there was a low, ominous growl, and Ninep, in defence of her mistress, pounced upon me, her great claws fixing themselves in my left shoulder. Instantly I recognised the ferocity of my second adversary, and releasing Istar, I plunged the long, keen knife full into the eye of the lioness.

Fortunately my aim proved true, for in a few seconds the great brute, her brain penetrated, fell back helpless and dying.

Again Istar, with the fury of a virago, rushed upon me, declaring that I should not escape. My first impulse was to kill her. Indeed, I confess I raised my knife to plunge it into her breast, but next second gripped her by the throat, and hurled her back upon the pavement where she lay huddled in a heap, stunned, motionless, and unconscious.

With a final glance at her inanimate form, I secreted the knife within my silken girdle, then dashed down the stairs—down, down, through the six deserted temples, tier on tier, until I reached the silent courtyard, which I hastily crossed and went to Istar's private apartment, whence I took a small tablet of sun-dried clay whereon a message had been impressed. This I placed in my pouch, and, taking a staff, set forth to gain my freedom.

In fear each moment lest Istar should regain consciousness, and raise the alarm, I hurried on through the great apartments with their colossal sculptures, where scribes and courtiers, officials and soldiers, were slumbering after the week's festivities, and at length gained the head of the brilliantly-lit flight of steps, the one way by which the royal palace could be approached.

As soon as I drew near to the head of the broad stairs the lances of the guards were interlaced from top to bottom. My passage was barred until I had explained to the two officers that I was bearer of an urgent message from Istar, and exhibited to them the tablet bearing her seal. Then only was I allowed to proceed. At each of the seven gates between the actual entrance to the palace and the brazen gate of the city, I presented my credential and was afforded free passage. In trepidation I approached one of the great doors of polished brass that closed the entrance to the city, and again drew forth the tablet. The officer of the watch scrutinised it long and carefully by the aid of his lantern, then, finding everything satisfactory, gave orders that the gate should be opened to pass out a messenger of Istar.

One of the ponderous doors creaked at last, and groaning, slowly fell back just sufficiently to allow me to pass.

"May Merodach guard thee, messenger," shouted the officer as I went forth.

"And thee also," I answered, as out upon the plain I sped quickly in the direction of freedom. Behind me the shaft of white light still streamed from the summit of the Temple of the Seven Lights; before me were the half-obscured Mountains of the Mist.

Once I glanced back upon the wonderful centre of a civilisation unknown to the world, then resolutely I set my face towards the pole-star, determined to put as great a distance as possible between myself and those who would undoubtedly pursue me ere the first saffron streak of dawn showed the direction of Mecca.

Chapter Forty Two
Crooked Paths

Full of increasing anxiety were the days following my escape from Ea. At dawn, while high in the shadowy Mountains of the Mist, I heard the alarm beaten in the distant city below, and could just distinguish, through the cloud of vapour, troops of horsemen leaving the brazen gates to scour the country in search of me. Istar had, no doubt, recovered, and, perhaps, had declared that I had made an attempt upon her life. A determined effort would, I knew, be made to secure me; therefore, having found the path I recognised as having before traversed, I pushed onward, day by day, until I reached the ruins of the great temple which had held me in wonderment when first I had entered that mysterious realm; then, striking due north, through forest and fertile, park-like country, I came to a river which I remembered was not far-distant from the small, half-concealed hole whence I had emerged. Proceeding along its sedgy bank at early morning, I came round a sharp bend, espying, to my amazement, a cluster of tents before me, and held back only just in time to escape detection. Already my pursuers were ahead of me! Nevertheless, taking a circuitous route, and sleeping in a tree that night, my eyes, after long and diligent search, were gladdened by the sight of the spot I sought.

As I stood before it, I reflected that, although I had defeated the evil design of Istar, I was still in a position equally as perilous as before, because of the raging, foaming torrent, which, descending from the Lake of the Accursed through its funnel-like aperture, formed a natural and insurmountable barrier to my freedom. Ea was indeed the Land of the No Return.

I had eaten my frugal morning meal, and was about to leisurely enter the long, natural chamber beneath the rock, and there decide upon some plan of action, when suddenly the bright gleam of arms through the greenery attracted my attention, and a moment later I found myself confronted by two of Istar's soldiers, who had evidently been watching me.

They called upon me to surrender, at the same time shouting to their comrades; but, without an instant's hesitation, I evaded their grasp and scrambling up into the hole, plunged into the dark fissure and sped quickly along over rocks and stones, heedless of where I went. Hurrying footsteps sounded behind me, the voices of my eager pursuers echoing loudly through the place, causing the flock of bats and birds nesting there to fly out into the sunlight in a dense, screaming crowd, while I, dashing onward, fled like a rat before a ferret.

The chase in the pitch darkness was long, wearying and desperate. It was a race for life. By their voices I could distinguish that the soldiers were gradually gaining upon me; yet, struggling on, now and then falling and cutting my knees as I scrambled over the sharp rocks, being always compelled to keep my hands stretched forth lest I should stun myself against the rough sides of the natural passage. Still, I was determined to hold out until the last, although not a single ray of hope glimmered through the dispiriting gloom. Istar had told me that, as bearer of the Mark of the Asps, I was doomed. Although I struggled forward I had been compelled to abandon all hope of returning again to Azala.

Close behind me were my pursuers, yelling like fiends. The place sent back weird, unearthly echoes from its uneven, vaulted roof, yet, in the utter darkness, they could not see me, but only pressed forward, eager to run me to earth and ascertain the extent of the strange, unknown grotto.

Suddenly I held my breath, feeling myself treading for an instant upon air, and uttering a loud shriek when I realised the truth. I had forgotten the great chasm into which I had so nearly fallen when last I had passed there, and had now plunged headlong into it! Down, down, I felt myself falling, until the fearful velocity with which I descended rendered me giddy. Those moments in mid-air seemed an hour, until, after dropping a long distance, I felt a sudden blow on the back that drove the breath from my body and held me paralysed. I knew then that I was lost.

When, a few minutes later, I again became conscious, I heard excited voices far above uttering words of caution. My shriek had evidently been noticed by my pursuers, who, surmising that some evil had befallen me, halted, and feeling their way carefully forward, had discovered the wide chasm which I had believed unfathomable. I was lying in soft dust which, preventing any of my bones being broken, had also deadened the sound when, long ago, I had cast stones into the pit to ascertain its depth. Slowly I struggled to my feet, and finding myself uninjured, began groping about in the darkness to ascertain the accurate dimensions of the abyss. Half choked by the fine dust, I stumbled about, with outstretched hands, but could discover neither sides nor roof, when suddenly a soldier's robe, which had been saturated in some oil from a lantern and was flaming, tumbled down upon the spot where I had fallen. My pursuers had done this to ascertain the depth of the chasm.

The welcome light revealed to me that, instead of being in an abyss, I had been precipitated into a lower and larger cavern, the roof of which was hung with huge stalactites, glittering with prismatic fire, and of dimensions so enormous that the fitful glare did not reveal its opposite extremity.

Fortunately, in my efforts to discover the extent of the weird place, I had advanced some little distance from the bottom of the pit, therefore my pursuers saw me not.

"He hath vanished!" I heard one man cry. "Of a verity he is the Destroyer, the son of Anu, whom to attempt to capture is as futile as the endeavour to make water run up hill."

"He sprang into the gulf, and disappeared like a spirit," cried another, as he peered over into the yawning chasm. "It was his intention that we should follow and be dashed to pieces on the rocks. His cry alone saved us."

"Come," I heard another voice exclaim, "let us leave this noisome abode of Anu, or his hand may wither and destroy us as it destroyed the Temple of Sin."

Soon the light died down to glowing tinder, and the voices, growing fainter, were quickly lost in distant echoes.

I knew I was entombed. To search for any exit seemed hopeless. Nevertheless, with a supplication to Allah to lighten his servant's burdens, I tore a strip from my robe, unravelled it, and by blowing upon the glowing tinder, obtained a light for my torch. Then, having improvised several more torches in case of necessity, I started forward. On every side was a cavernous blackness, so large was the natural chamber into which I had fallen. Still I strove on, determined at least to ascertain its true dimensions.

Presently I raised a loud shout, and listened. In a thousand distant echoes my voice came back, showing that the cavern was of wondrous extent. The ground was not uneven, though here and there were large masses of rock, thrown up, as if by the same earthquake as had formed the Lake of the Accursed, and, hurrying forward, I gazed about me to discover something in the impenetrable blackness on every hand.

One fact alone gave me courage. The air was good, showing that somewhere was an outlet to the world above.

Thus, with frantic effort, I struggled on, lighting a second torch, and keeping straight ahead, until at last, to my dismay, I was confronted by the damp wall of rock that formed the end of the cavern. Turning at right angles, I walked beside this wall to ascertain the width of the chamber, when, having proceeded about thirty paces, I discovered a fissure, or tunnel-like passage of considerable width, which led away into the deep gloom beyond.

Determined, at least, to explore its length, I plunged into it, holding my torch high above my head. At first it descended slowly, then rose with gradual ascent, sometimes narrowing, at others widening, until I again came to a blank wall of rock.

I had been deceived. It was a mere fantastic *cul-de-sac*.

A moment's pause, then, turning with sinking heart, I retraced my steps a considerable distance until, just before I emerged into the great cavern again, I became aware of a second grotto leading out of the natural tunnel wherein I stood. This I had not before noticed, therefore, with eager steps, started forward to explore it. Here again the ground rose, but the cavern was spacious, and leading out of it was another grotto rising gradually and leading to a third, slightly narrower, through which I toiled for fully half-an-hour, burning the whole of my outer robe as torches, until by accident my light became entirely extinguished. Unable to rekindle it, I was plunged in darkness that could be felt. Striving on undaunted, however, my eager hands came at last in contact with a wall of rock before me; but, scarce had I made this dismaying discovery, ere I found that the subterranean burrow took a sudden turn at right angles, and again ascended sharply.

To my surprise the rocky roof above me became just distinguishable. A grey light showed ghostly and indistinct. Then, a moment later, as I mounted the steep ascent, I saw, straight before me, the blessed light of day, and uttered a loud cry of relief and joy.

In eagerness I sped forward, rushing out of the cave, the mouth of which was half choked by brushwood and brambles, to find that I had actually passed beneath the Lake of the Accursed, and was beyond the confines of the Land of the No Return.

Only by a miracle had I escaped death. Of a verity Allah maketh abundant provision for such of his servants as he pleaseth, therefore I knelt to return thanks for my deliverance.

My exit had been made at the edge of the forest, within actual sight of the towering Rock of the Moon-god, and having riveted its exact position upon my memory, I plucked some bananas and ate them, afterwards setting my face to the north on my long journey back to Kano.

Following the directions given me by my lost friend Yakul, I searched for the track which he had told me ran through the great forest to Ipoto, and after some little difficulty discovered it; then, traversing it for many days amid the forest gloom, I at length reached the town he had named. To detail my journey northward is unnecessary. Ever pressing forward, and without meeting with much adventure, I swam the Ihourou river, and joining a party of traders, crossed the rocky country of the Mbelia, passing beneath the snow-capped summit of the mountain called Nai, eventually arriving at Niam-Niam. Here I was fortunate enough to fall in with a caravan bound for Katsena, within the Empire of the Sultan 'Othman; and three moons after my escape from Ea I experienced the delight of seeing the minarets and cupolas of Kano rise dark against the blood-red sunset.

News I gained in Katsena, however, had caused me most intense anxiety. Although, as far as I could learn, no conspiracy against the Sultan had been attempted, yet I heard from Arab traders in the market-place that Azala, my beloved, was to be given as bride to the Khalifa, in order to further cement the friendship between Sokoto and the Eastern Soudan. It had been arranged months ago, before the Khalifa's return to Omdurman, and the date of Azala's departure for the east was already past. Therefore, in fear lest the woman I loved should have already left, under escort, to become bride of the brutal autocrat, I spurred forward over the desert to Kano.

My first breathless question of the guards at the gate was of Azala. She had not left, they answered, but preparations were complete, and she would go forth, with a large armed escort, at noon on the morrow. Then I made sudden resolve, and entered the great Fada to boldly seek audience of the Sultan 'Othman, the ruler who had forbidden me to re-enter his Empire on pain of death.

While passing beneath the high, sun-blanched wall of the harem, on my way to the Hall of Audience, I came face to face with the dwarf Tiamo, who, on beholding me whom he thought dead, stood petrified. When I had reassured him, he briefly explained how he had returned to Azala with news of my tragic end; how, overwhelmed by bitter grief, she had become careless of everything, even of her betrothal to the Khalifa. Hastily I scribbled a message of reassurance in Arabic to my well-beloved, and the impish little man hobbled away with it secreted in his gaudy sash, while I continued my way to crave speech with the autocrat. After many formalities, I was allowed to approach the divan, where he sat in his green silk robe, calmly smoking; but as I advanced his keen eyes recognised my face, and his brow darkened grimly.

"Well?" he exclaimed in anger, as I bowed the knee before him. "What seekest thou? Have I not already expelled thee from this my kingdom?"

"Yea, O Sultan," I answered. "But I would have a word with thee in private. I desire to impart unto thee a secret."

"Of what?" he inquired, with a quick look of suspicion.

"I have witnessed that which the eyes of men have never before beheld," I answered, "I have discovered the Land of the No Return!"

The Sultan started up at my words, and the greatest sensation was created among his assembled court. For a moment Azala's father regarded me keenly; then, uttering a word, waved his hand, signifying his desire to speak with me in private. Instantly the crowd of courtiers, slaves, eunuchs and soldiers retired, and a few minutes later we were alone.

"Well?" he exclaimed, pulling at his bejewelled pipe thoughtfully. "Explain unto me thy discovery."

Seated on the mat before the royal divan, I told him the whole story; how Azala had rescued me; how I had reached his daughter a second time, and my strange quest at her instigation.

When I mentioned the latter his brows knit severely, and displeasure was betrayed upon his dark face. Then I related the conversation between the two conspirators who were plotting to bring about the overthrow of Sokoto, explained how I had discovered the Rock of the Great Sin, and described the magnificence and enormous wealth of the kingdom of Ea. I told him of my adventures within the mysterious realm, of my captivity in the hands of Istar, and of the strange wall-picture of Semiramis.

During an hour we conversed together; then, at last, I referred to Azala's forthcoming journey to Omdurman, and hazarded an opinion that she should not be united to one who was an enemy of his Empire. Upon my words he pondered deeply, slowly stroked his full, dark beard, but made no response. Then, not without trepidation, I offered a suggestion. It was that, in return for Azala's hand, I would lead his hosts by the secret way into Ea, and conquer that wealthy country, which could then be annexed to Sokoto.

He reflected, apparently doubting my ability to lead an expedition of such magnitude; but after I had explained my previous experiences as a Dervish soldier, he at last accepted the terms of my offer, and very soon we had arranged the details. He would give me, he promised, twenty thousand men, armed with European rifles, together with all the cannon which had been captured in a recent campaign against the French, and the four Maxim guns and ammunition sent to him as a present a few months before by the Royal Niger Company. One condition I laid down was, that I might hold converse with Azala ere I set forth upon the hazardous undertaking. To this he raised no voice of dissent, therefore, later that evening, I spent a joyous hour with my well-beloved in the room I knew so well.

To describe our meeting is unnecessary. Suffice it to say that, when she set eyes upon me, she burst into a torrent of tears. Long ago had she mourned for me as one who had lost his life in attempting to fulfil her wish, and could scarce believe her eyes when Tiamo had given her the scrap of paper with my message. I explained my discoveries, my ambitions, and the generous promise of the Sultan. Then, after a protracted interview, I bade her farewell until such time as I could claim her, and departed with her fond kiss warm upon my lips.

That she watched the preparations hourly from her lattice I knew, but at sunrise, three days later, all being ready, I set forth at the head of the Sultan's army. Tiamo again came with me as body-servant, our journey over the deserts being of a far different character to when we had fled like thieves from Kano. With our green standards flying, and our bright arms and accoutrements glittering in the sun, ours was a brilliant cavalcade, every man intensely eager to view the mystic, unknown land of which story-tellers had told through countless ages.

By forced marches we reached, within six weeks, the Rock of the Moon-god, our army augmented by thousands of black followers from Niam-Niam, and, on making careful reconnoissance, I soon discovered the natural, tunnel-like passage whence I had emerged on escaping from Ea. Taking with me a strong pioneer party, we thoroughly explored the huge caverns below, fixed lights in various parts, placed ladders against the wall of rock over which I had tumbled, and above, at the edge of the chasm, suspended strong ropes and pulleys for raising cannon, horses, and heavy material. This work occupied us four days, but when at length everything was complete, we found the entrance to the gallery too small to admit horses and guns. We therefore blew away the rock with some dynamite, procured long ago from the Niger traders, and without many mishaps passed through, and at last gained the fertile Land of the No Return.

The eagerness of the soldiers of Sokoto and our pagan followers, who had joined us out of curiosity, to penetrate this strange, legendary land, knew no bounds, and the excitement on the first night we encamped upon the grass plain rose to fever heat.

I had sent forward trusty scouts, attired in the garments of citizens of Ea, copied from my own, lest we should fall into an ambush, and already had watchers secreted on the Mountains of the Mist, in full view of the city we were preparing to surprise.

Well I knew the colossal strength of Ea, "the place with walls unbreakable," and when addressing the army after we had recited the sunset prayer that evening, I disguised not the fact that the struggle must be desperate.

All were, however, undaunted. Each man announced his readiness to go forward, bent on conquest.

Chapter Forty Three
Doom

Our assault upon Ea was sudden and unexpected. Under cover of night we cautiously advanced on our last march, and having placed our guns in position, halted in readiness. From the high summit of the Temple of the Seven Lights the unquenchable Eye of Istar still streamed, white and brilliant. The giant city was ablaze with lights, as if for another festival, and at first sight of this colossal centre of a forgotten civilisation the soldiers, awe-stricken, feared that our expedition against such a gigantic fortress was foredoomed to failure.

Before commencing the attack, however, I urged them to valiant deeds, repeating those words from our Korân which have given heart to Moslem armies ever since the days of the Prophet—"If there be a hundred of you that persevere with constancy, they shall overcome two hundred; and if there be a thousand of you they shall overcome two thousand, by the permission of Allah; for Allah is with those who persevere. It hath not been granted unto any prophet that he should possess captives until he had made a great slaughter of the infidels in the earth. Allah is mighty and wise."

After many bows and genuflections, my companions rose, and, mounting, spurred forth, in readiness to their posts. In silence half-an-hour went by, when, by prearranged signal, six of the French guns loaded with explosive shell suddenly crashed forth, at the same instant, sending their deadly missiles right into the centre of the city, almost as far as Istar's palace. We listened. The sound of the explosions echoed weirdly among the misty heights above.

With such infinite care had we approached that this signal was the first notification received by the people of Ea of the presence of enemies. The instant the cannons had roared forth, our great storming parties spurred across the plain to certain of the city gates, armed with engines for battering them in, and charges of dynamite for blowing them into air. So well guarded, however, were those gigantic walls that, ere our squadrons could reach the gates, they were assailed by withering showers of arrows and spears. Indeed, a moment after we had sent our first shells into the city, the high, frowning battlements seemed alive with defenders. Volleys of stones from ancient catapults were showered on every hand, while bowmen, from the slits in the flanking towers, discharged upon us a deadly arrow storm.

Our black contingent, with their long bows and poisoned arrows, quickly turned their attention upon the archers of Ea. Expert marksmen these pagans were, and at this moment proved themselves of the utmost value. Each soldier who showed himself upon the high walls was picked off with an aim unerring by our archers, behind whom were the well-drilled soldiers of the Sultan making careful shots with their rifles, and away upon the high ground at the rear the cannons kept up their thunder, each shell bursting and spreading terrible devastation within the city. The constant explosion of shells and firearms appalled the defenders beyond measure, for this was their first knowledge of the art of modern warfare, and, as I afterwards learned, it was believed that because gunpowder was used by us that Anu himself, the dread god of Destruction, was directing us, and against him they were powerless. Nevertheless, the pugilistic spirit was still fierce within the hearts of those descendants of the valiant hosts of Semiramis, and they fought desperately for the defence of their capital and their goddess-queen. In the lurid glare, shed by the fires caused by our shells, we could discern huge, cranelike machines mounted on the walls, discharging at us arrows and volleys of stones, while other ancient mechanical contrivances emptied upon our scaling parties great caldrons of boiling pitch or water.

Throughout that well-remembered night we kept up a continuous and galling hail of lead upon the city, but with little effect save that, time after time, we swept away hundreds of soldiers from the walls and caused conflagrations in every quarter, the majority of our force remaining safely beyond the narrow zone of the defender's fire. As dawn crept on, times without number our scaling parties attempted to fix their ladders of rope and cane, but on each occasion were hurled back, leaving many of their number dead or dying. The sun rose. Arrows and javelins fell thick and fast, while, from plain and hill, we poured a continuous and deadly shower of death-dealing missiles over those ponderous, time-worn walls. The hundred enormous brazen gates resisted every attempt of those of our men who dashed forward to batter them in. Their thickness and strength were colossal. Whole parties of the young and dauntless, who rushed across the plain up to the very walls, dark-faced and determined, were sometimes swept into eternity even to the last man, by the frightful showers of jagged arrows and sharp flint stones discharged from catapults.

Noon came. The breathless hours passed but slowly. Hundreds of our soldiers and pagan followers were stretched dead, yet, with the exception of causing a few alarming conflagrations within the city, we seemed to achieve but little progress towards victory. Our ability to project our missiles to far greater distance than the defenders was of greatest advantage, and our losses in these earlier hours of the siege were never serious.

Towards sundown, after a long and toilsome day, we decided to make a sudden and vigorous assault, with our advance covered by artillery in our rear. The military tactics of the soldiers of Sokoto were perhaps primitive as compared with European standards; nevertheless, our men, at the roll of the war drums, dashed forward in force to make a strenuous and frantic endeavour to enter the ancient, mysterious capital. Yet we met again an opposition so terrific that some of our squadrons fell back appalled, while others were literally riddled by arrows from the battlements. Long and valiantly we fought to batter down the gates or scale the walls, but without avail. Stones, bullets, spears and boiling liquids fell in showers upon us from every point. Many fell dead or mortally wounded upon the sand, and it appeared as though the remainder would be wiped out, until, with one accord, they beat a hasty retreat, followed by the cheers and yells of the defenders.

This reverse almost disheartened us.

Each moment the conflict increased in vigour. Although the soldiers of Ea possessed no firearms, the defence they made was of a character desperate and remarkable. From every point our guns blazed away with monotonous regularity, and our rifles flashed everywhere, yet we seemed not to effect the slightest impression upon that city of colossal strength. Every turret, every battlement, shed showers of arrows and sharp stones which inflicted terribly painful wounds, while, in reply, our pagan allies let loose their flights of poisoned darts with unerring and deliberate aim.

Once an arrow struck me in the forearm, but, fortunately, inflicted only a slight wound; yet almost at the same moment Tiamo, who was standing beside me, unfortunately received another dart, which caught him full in the throat and stuck quivering there. Instantly I recognised the terrible nature of the wound, and knew it must prove fatal, as, alas! it did ere our savage assault terminated. Now that we had advanced within the range of the defender's fire, our loss of life was becoming serious. By the tragic end of the dwarf I had lost a sincere and genuine friend, and Azala a devoted slave. I had, however, but short space to keep beside him, as my presence was urgently required elsewhere. Therefore, with a few words of comfort, I was compelled to leave him and ascend to where the guns were thundering.

The afterglow was burning in the sky, when, looking forward, I discerned, standing upon the wall, Istar herself, white-robed, with streaming, unbound hair. Her arms were upraised as if in the act of encouraging her men, and directing the defence.

I chanced to be standing beside one of those deadly, rapid-firing guns captured from the French, and, as I looked, our gunners sighted their weapon.

"See!" cried one. "That woman there! A little lower. Now!"

Instantly the gun crashed forth. Next second there was a flash of fire upon the battlement where Istar had stood, and when the dust and smoke cleared a few moments later a breach in the wall showed that the shell had blown to atoms everything within its reach.

It seemed absolutely certain that the woman who had held me captive must have been killed instantaneously. If she had escaped, it was little short of marvellous.

Daylight faded, evening crept on, still our bombardment continued with unceasing vigour. None of us had appeased our hunger since long before dawn, and few had been able to snatch a draught from their waterskins. Darkness fell, and the stars appeared through the choking smoke clouds, clear cut as gems, when suddenly, to the astonishment of all, the long shaft of white light, kept burning night and day at the summit of the Temple of Love, increased in brilliancy, streaming over the city and plain. Our enemies now used it as a search-light, such as I had seen on the battleships in the bay of Algiers, and thus were they enabled to narrowly watch our movements.

Nevertheless, we were able after considerable effort to outwit them, for, the fire from the walls having slackened as darkness prevailed, we sent a large body again forward, our reinforcements standing formed up in a huge square in readiness. The squadron sent as pioneers were all picked men, who, like myself, had seen battle in many parts of Africa, and were determined to bring matters to a crisis. Quickly and noiselessly they sped forth, and were lost in the darkness. While our main body harassed the defenders and kept them fully engaged, these men worked their way silently towards the great gate through which my captors had led me when I had been taken prisoner. Fully half-an-hour elapsed without a sign. Standing, with eyes strained in the direction they had taken, I began to fear they had met with disaster. Indeed, I had already given orders to two scouts to ride forward and bring back report, when suddenly there was a bright, blinding flash. The very earth was shaken by a terrific, deafening explosion, followed instantly by a second report which awakened the echoes of the mountains far and wide.

Almost the next moment a great tongue of flame shot up behind the city wall, revealing the reassuring fact that the gate, with its huge flanking towers manned by hundreds of the defenders, had been entirely demolished, and that a great fire had been started. Loud, exultant shouts rose from every throat when this truth became realised. Our war drums rolled loudly, our heavy guns were silenced, and instantly, ten thousand well-armed and valiant men dashed forward to spring through the breach and enter the gigantic city. I headed them, but at the ruins of the gate we found that half the number of the brave ones who had so effectively used the dynamite had been slaughtered, and that a huge, compact body of troops had massed within, determined to resist our advance. Hence we were compelled to fight hand-to-hand, while engines of war, like the ancient mangonels and ballistae, worked over our heads, laying us low by dozens. A hundred stratagems we had already practised, but to no avail, therefore, we determined upon taking the city by sheer force. In numbers, we were vastly inferior to the defenders, but sight of our firearms held them terrified.

The *mêlée* among the heaped ruins of that ponderous gate was frightful. Bigotry, revenge, love of loot, and all the voices that unite to hurry men to evil, pressed us forward at this crisis time. Veterans, who had fought in all the desperate battles with the French towards the Niger bank, and away beyond Lake Tsad, were not to be disheartened. They were desperate and furious.

Still the defenders held out. Their ranks presented the appearance of a wall of lowered spears.

While we strove on, fearing that this last bold venture might fail, a loud rattling like musketry sounded in front of us. Instantly I knew the truth. One of our Maxim guns had at last been brought into play.

The effect of that most deadly of modern weapons was appalling. Thrice it spat out its leaden hail, sweeping along the lines of spearmen from end to end. Then, with loud, fierce yells of triumph, we poured into the city over the heaps of bullet-riddled bodies, fighting amid a chaos of writhing limbs, gashed faces and bleeding, trampled humanity.

Thus, we at last passed the high masses of Babylonian masonry, which had once seemed so dark, sheer and impregnable, and dashed forward into the mystic capital of Ea, engaging the defenders hand-to-hand in every hole and corner, while our comrades, having witnessed our success, sped on after us great bodies of reinforcements, against whom it was impossible for either citizens or soldiers to struggle. The darkness of night was dispelled by the red glare of the fires, as the incendiary's brand was applied to wooden structures, while the curses of the vanquished mingled with wails of the dying and shouts of the victors.

The carnage was frightful.

After an hour's desperate street fighting, during which time my garments were torn from off my back in shreds, the defenders began to cry for quarter, but, although we granted it, our black allies, drunk with the frenzy of battle, refused to show mercy, and hundreds of those who had defended their homes so bravely were impaled by spears, or laid low by poisoned darts. Many were the ghastly scenes I witnessed, as, amid that terrible massacre of the vanquished, we pressed on in force towards the dazzling House of the Raising of the Head. Again we met with a determined opposition, which cost us considerable loss ere we could break it down and ascend the long flight of steps to the palace itself. On gaining the top, I rushed forward, at the head of the storming party, into the great pavilion, with its sculptured walls, and was amazed to find it deserted.

Alone, I dashed away across court after court, until I reached the entrance of the great hall, wherein stood the crystal throne. Without ceremony I tore aside the heavy curtain and entered.

Istar, who had, by some almost miraculous circumstance, escaped destruction on the city wall, was lounging upon her seat of royalty, her beautiful face pale as death, her teeth firm set, and in her eyes a look of unutterable dread. All her brilliant court had deserted her and fled, leaving her alone to face her enemies.

As I entered, her gaze met mine, and she rose to her feet with slow hauteur. I advanced to seize her, but, raising her shapely, trembling hand, she screamed, "Stand back, thou son of Anu! Stand back!"

"Thou art now my captive!" I shouted, halting an instant before ascending the steps of polished silver.

She clenched her teeth, held her breath, and trembled. With a quick movement, she raised her left hand and placed it against her velvet cheek. Next instant, I saw a tiny streak of blood trickle down upon the strings of jewels which adorned her neck.

Then, horrified, I noticed that in her hand there writhed a small black asp of the most venomous species. She had placed its flat head against her cheek and deliberately allowed it to bite her.

"What hast thou done?" I cried, aghast.

"I, Istar, will never be taken captive!" she answered, with imperious gesture. "Thou hast brought thine accursed hosts within my kingdom, broken down my walls, burnt the Temple of Baal, and entered this my palace to sack it and break down the foundation-stones of my fathers. Therefore thou shalt, at least, have no satisfaction in securing me."

She swayed slightly, and from her grasp the small reptile wriggled and fell upon the polished pavement, hissing viciously.

I knew she was doomed, and made a movement to ascend the steps.

"Ah! don't touch me!" she shrieked wildly, her wealth of unbound hair falling in profusion about her shoulders. "Canst thou not see that the asp's poison is fatal?" she gasped hoarsely, her face, with its ugly streak of blood, a ghastly hue. "Anu hath seized my kingdom. Merodach hath forsaken me. See!" she cried with difficulty, reeling and clutching for support at the arm of her glittering throne. "See! I leave thee! The word of the prophet—is fulfilled!"

Her thin, blanched lips moved, but no further sound escaped them. Her face was drawn and haggard, her limbs were convulsed by icy shiverings, and her bejewelled fingers, hitching themselves in her filmy garments, tore them in a paroxysm of pain as the deadly venom throbbed through her blue veins.

She glared at me with a ferocity that showed how desperate she was.

But only for a moment. Her nerveless hand refused to support her, and, staggering forward unevenly, she suddenly threw up her shapely arms, with a wild, shrill shriek, and fell heavily forward upon the pavement before the ancient throne of Babylon's queen.

I dashed up to where she had fallen, and, bending, raised her fair head and placed my hand upon her white scarred breast.

Her heart had ceased its beating. Istar, the direct descendant of Semiramis, the beautiful woman worshipped as goddess and queen, was dead.

I rose and stood gazing upon her lifeless, prostrate form. Horror held me dumb. Yet I was conqueror of the most ancient and remarkable city in the world.

Chapter Forty Four
The Talisman

With lightning speed the news of Istar's death spread from mouth to mouth throughout Ea, and all opposition to our occupation quickly ceased. Priests, eunuchs, populace and soldiery regarded our entry, and the death of their goddess-queen, as the fulfilment of the dreaded curse of Anu, and openly declared that to fight against the decree of the great Destroyer, supreme on earth, was utterly futile. Hence the Moslem hosts, acknowledging me as leader, poured into every part of the once-impregnable city, and proceeded to seek suitable quarters in the best residences and in the House of the Raising of the Head, the wonders of which held them entranced.

During the first few hours the soldiers of the Sultan, with that inborn love of loot which has characterised every Arab man-at-arms since the days of the Prophet, sacked the houses of the wealthy, and would have wrecked the palace of Istar had I not taken precautions, threatening that any discovered pilfering would be cast into the lion-pit without ado. By dint of most strenuous exertion I thus managed to preserve the palace intact, but our negro allies, on entering the city, intoxicated by success, had at once become entirely beyond control, and I fear that many citizens and their property fared badly at their pagan hands.

As soon as I had arranged for an efficient guard in every hall throughout the great palace, and had taken precautions to confine the soldiers of Ea in one quarter of the city, lest they should return to resume the defensive, I ascended to the Temple of Love, and there, in presence of three of my chief officers, extinguished that great light called the Eye of Istar, as sign of my complete conquest of Queen and people.

The seething populace of Ea, when they saw that the light which had burned uninterruptedly for ages no longer shone, regarded its failure as sign that Shamas and Merodach had for ever forsaken them, and that city and people had, by Istar's death, been given over to the designs of Anu, the dreaded, and his evil hosts. They remained inert, cowed, trembling. The luxurious Temple of Love, with its worn statue of the goddess, presented the same appearance as it had done on that memorable night after the Feast of Tammuz, when the Queen slept while I had watched in silence. Her couch, with its purple cushions, was tumbled, as if she had recently lain there, and the fresh offerings of food and wine at the foot of the statue showed that votaries had recently ascended to prostrate themselves in conformity with the rigid law of Semiramis.

Leaning over the balustrade, I stood gazing down in wonder at the magnificence of the city I had conquered, and watching the breaking of the dawn. Paper being brought at my command, I sat down and wrote a report to the Sultan, urging him to come and witness his mysterious, newly-acquired possession, and at the same time claiming Azala's hand. To my well-beloved also I wrote a message of affection, and these I dispatched in charge of six trusty messengers, who had acted as scouts, with orders to speed on the wings of haste back to Kano.

As I again looked down upon the terraces and courts an imam from the Fada at Kano came forward, and placing himself at my side, raised his arms and uttered, in a firm, loud voice, our call to prayer.

Thus, for the first time in the history of Ea, was the Temple of the Seven Lights used as mosque, and the name of Allah uttered from its high minaret. Thrice he shouted, with all his might, those well-known words which cause the Faithful to bend the knee towards the Holy City wherever they may be, and the soldiers lounging about the courts below, hearing it, prostrated themselves and recited their thanks to the One Merciful with heartfelt fervency. Verily Allah is endued with indulgence towards mankind; but the greater part of them are not thankful.

At first, as representative of the Sultan, there was much to occupy me; but the people, finding our rule unoppressive, quickly became well-disposed towards us, and soon, the defenders being disarmed, my task was rendered easy. Then day followed day—bright, sunny, indolent, never-to-be-forgotten days of waiting in patience for the coming of the Sultan.

The high-priests of the Temple of the Seven Lights undertook the obsequies of their dead Queen, which they carried out with great pomp and ceremony, the body being carried by twelve vestal virgins to the summit of the tower and there cremated, the ashes being afterwards cast to the winds amid the singing of hymns to the Moon-god and much weeping and wailing. Still, the fact that upon my breast was a mark exactly identical with the one she had borne puzzled me, and during the long period of waiting for the arrival of the Sultan 'Othman I used every endeavour to discover some elucidation of the mystery. Soon I grew impatient, and ofttimes wandered alone through the magnificent courts, plunged deep in oppressive thoughts. The non-arrival of the Sultan caused me serious apprehension that, during our absence, the Khalifa had attacked Kano. If so, I feared for the safety of Azala. To distract my attention from the one subject which occupied me both by night and by day I applied myself diligently to the study of the gigantic wall-sculptures and inscriptions, and succeeded in deciphering some exceedingly interesting records of the luxury in which lived Semiramis and her successors.

The treasures we discovered within the palace were enormous. Jewels of great price, which had belonged to the founder of Babylon herself, golden ornaments of every kind, many of that antique design shown in the wall-pictures, dishes and drinking-vessels of gold, golden armour, bejewelled breastplates, and swords with hilts set with magnificent gems were stored in great profusion in the spacious vaults below the palace, while the ornaments worn by priests, priestesses and high functionaries in the daily exercise of their religious duties, were all of amazing worth. Besides these treasures of gems and gold, we discovered a vault filled to overflowing with the records of the dead monarchs of Ea, cylinders and square cakes of sun-dried clay, with cuneiform inscriptions impressed upon them by the hands of scribes who had lived three thousand years ago. In later centuries it appeared that a kind of papyrus had been used by the inhabitants of this world-forgotten kingdom, nevertheless, all the earlier records had been impressed upon clay or chipped on stones in like manner to those discovered beneath the mounds where once stood the giant cities of Nineveh and Babylon. Through many weeks I occupied myself with them, the result of my investigations having been recently given to the world in the form of two substantial volumes published in Paris.

One day, while engaged in translating a record of the historic victory of Semiramis over the Ethiopians, neatly impressed upon a hollow cylinder of white clay, the commander of the guard entered hastily with the glad tidings that the cavalcade of the Sultan was actually within sight, and half-an-hour later I received the great 'Othman and his daughter in the glittering throne-room where first I had encountered the Queen whose beauty had been amazing.

The Sultan's reception was wildly enthusiastic. War drums rolled, the conquering green banners of Al-Islâm waved in the brilliant sunshine, and the soldiers of Sokoto, who had fought so valiantly, were cheered again and again by the great escort of their autocratic ruler. Even the vanquished citizens of Ea lost their sullenness, and having found our rule beneficent and devoid of the harsh oppression they had anticipated, united in applauding the conqueror.

Amid ringing cheers he entered the magnificent hall wherein the luxurious Istar had held sway, and, greeting him at the steps of the throne, I motioned to him to ascend to the royal seat of prismatic crystal. This he did, and in obedience to his desire, Azala and myself followed, standing by him at either hand.

Then, when quiet had, with difficulty, been restored, he addressed those present in congratulatory terms, thanking Allah for the success of our arms, and turning to myself, publicly declared me worthy the hand of his daughter Azala.

This announcement was followed by thunders of applause. Outside, firearms were discharged, cannons roared, and news of our betrothal spread away into every corner of the city.

When again the Sultan could obtain a hearing, he added that, having discovered this mysterious kingdom hitherto unknown, it was but just that its rule should be given into my hands. Henceforward, he said, I was Governor of Ea, and as soon as arrangements could be made for fitting marriage festivity I should be wedded to Azala. Advancing to the woman I loved, we clasped hands joyously, and her eyes met mine with an expression full of tender passion. Then, turning to the Sultan, I acknowledged his gracious bounty, and declared that now I had Azala at my side I would spend the remainder of my life in his service as Governor of this new, far-removed portion of his Empire.

Azala, too, in musical voice, trembling slightly with emotion, declared that I had successfully fought a fight that few would have attempted, and others united to heap praise upon me of so laudatory a character that I confess to entertaining a desire for its cessation.

After a protracted audience, the Sultan made sign that he wished to be alone, and when all had withdrawn, except my betrothed and myself, he turned to me, saying—

"Of a verity, Zafar, thou hast fought a valiant fight. Strange it is that thou returnest to that which is thine own."

"How?" I inquired, puzzled at his words.

"Thou bearest the Mark of the Asps," he answered.

"The same symbol was borne by Istar," I said. "I discovered it while she slept."

"Upon my breast also is the mark," Azala observed.

"The mysterious emblem hath, of course, puzzled thee," the Sultan said, smiling as he addressed me. "Azala hath ofttimes asked its meaning, but I have rendered no explanation until now. Because thou art betrothed unto my daughter, it is but fitting that I should make explanation. Thou hast witnessed the symbol upon the foundation-stone of Semiramis, and I have to-day learned that Istar, as represented in image at the summit of the Seven Lights, beareth in her hand the asps entwined. The Mark of the Asps is the Babylonian sign of royal sonship, the symbol with which the first-born of every ruler since Semiramis hath been branded."

"But how came I to bear the mark?" I inquired, eagerly.

"Thou hast heard the oft-repeated story of the man who, long ages ago, before the great earthquake, succeeded in eluding the vigilance of the guards at the Rock of the Great Sin, and escaped into our world."

"Yea. I have often pondered deeply over that legendary tale," I replied.

"It was no legend," he asserted. "One man did actually escape from Ea. He was son of the reigning queen, and bore upon his breast a mark identical with thine. Far and wide he travelled over the Great Desert, and obeying the injunction of his ancestor, seared with a white-hot iron the mystic symbol upon his eldest son. Thus through many generations was the Mark of the Asps placed upon the breast of the eldest child of either sex, until a legend became rife that ill would befall the family if that mark were not impressed. For ages the practice, descended from father to child, until it came to thy father, who branded thee."

"My father!" I cried. "Surely he was not a lineal descendant of the Queens of Ea!"

"He was. Thy father and myself were brothers, but early in life we parted in Constantine, I to the south, where I met with many adventures, becoming commander-in-chief of the army of Sokoto, and subsequently being placed upon the royal divan as Sultan. Some years after parting with thy father I heard that he was dead, and, unaware that he had a son, I, desiring to perpetuate the family legend, impressed upon the breast of Azala the mark that thou hast witnessed."

"Then it is now easy to account for thine amazement at finding the mark upon the breast of myself, thy captive in Kano," I observed, smiling.

"I had never dreamed of thine existence, and as it was alleged that evil would accrue if the mark of royalty were placed on any but the person entitled to it, I banished thee, in fear, from my kingdom," he replied. "After I had sent thee out of Sokoto I became seized with regret, and used every endeavour to rediscover thee, but without avail. Meanwhile, it seemeth that thou wert beloved of thy cousin Azala, and wert striving to elucidate the mystery. Thine efforts have at last been crowned by success, and assuredly the expressions of good-will I have uttered towards thee are genuine."

"I accept them," I answered, amazed at this unexpected revelation. "Thou art brother of my father, and I thy nephew."

"It is but just that thou shouldst rule over Ea," Azala said, laughing joyously, after she had explained that the marvels she had revealed in Kano in order to impress me were produced, as I had suspected, by mechanical means. "The mark was branded upon me under the misapprehension that thou didst not exist. But in thee, the Unknown, I have found a husband; and Ea, thine estate by right, a conqueror and ruler."

"Hast thou still an amulet thy father gavest unto thee before his death?" the Sultan asked, presently.

"I have," I answered, placing my hand beneath my silken robe, and drawing therefrom the small bag of soft kid-skin I had worn for years suspended, with other talismans, about my neck.

"Open it, and let us gaze upon it."

I obeyed, and drew from the well-worn charm-case a small, cylindrical seal of chalcedony. It was of ancient design, like those discovered by Layard, the Englishman, in the mounds at Nimroud, about the length of the little finger, semi-transparent and blue almost as the morning sky, drilled from end to end with a hole, to allow its suspension from the neck.

"Yea," said the Sultan, taking it from my hand, and examining it with greatest care. "Thou hast truly preserved intact the relic which hath been in our family through countless generations. Now will I reveal unto thee its strange secret."

"What secret doth it contain?" I asked, glancing at it eagerly.

"Upon it are words," he answered, "but so minute is the inscription that only by placing it in the sun's rays, and watching the shadows, can the inequalities of its surface be detected. Come hither."

He rose, and we followed him across the great, empty hall to where the sunlight streamed full through an aperture in the high, gilded roof. Then, placing the cylinder upon a small, golden stool, inlaid with amethysts, that Istar had used as a table, he told me to examine it and say what words were thereon inscribed. At first I could detect nothing, but presently, by placing it at a certain angle, I could detect that its surface was entirely covered by an inscription in cuneiform character, so minute that none would dream of its existence. Only by allowing the sun's rays to fall at a certain angle across the blue stone could the tiny rows of arrowheads be deciphered, but after a long examination, with the Sultan and Azala eagerly gazing over my shoulder, I was at length enabled to gain the knowledge it imparted.

The first portion of the ancient inscription was a brief supplication, in the picturesque language of Assyria, to Istar, Goddess of Love, followed by a statement that the stone itself was the talisman of Semiramis, founder of Babylon, who had decreed that her son should bear the royal mark upon his breast in such a form as should be indelible, and that the first-born of the royal line should be branded in the same manner by an iron heated until it glowed white. There was a tiny sketch of the symbol, together with full directions as to the manner in which the flesh must be seared, and the whole concluded with an exhortation to Merodach to preserve the bearer of the talisman, and a fervent prayer to Baal, head-father and creator of the universe. At the end was the signature of some scribe, and appended the seal of Semiramis herself.

This strange historic talisman had, I recollected, been carried by my father in all his travels, and on his deathbed he had bequeathed it to me, with strict injunctions never to part with it, as it secured its wearer immunity from disease or violent death. Around my neck I had carried it through all the fights against the English in the Soudan, and during all the long and toilsome journeys which I have related. Now it had explained to me a secret so strange that, without its unimpeachable evidence, I could never have credited the truth.

Again and again I re-read the curious inscription, graven by a hand that must have crumbled into dust more than four thousand years ago; then, witnessing Azala's great interest in it, I tenderly placed my hand around her jewel-begirt waist and kissed her.

The Sultan smiled benignly, and telling me to mount the steps, and seat myself upon the crystal throne that was my birthright, he gave orders for the curtains to be drawn aside so that those assembled might witness the high position to which I had been exalted.

The Sultan, again mounting the steps of polished silver, addressed the brilliantly attired crowd, explaining briefly that I was the direct descendant of the founder of that kingdom; that upon my breast I bore the mystic Mark of the Asps; and that, in my hand, I held the long-lost talisman of Semiramis, which ages ago had been carried away to the outer world by the adventurous son of Istar who made his escape and never returned. It was, he declared, but meet that I should occupy the crystal throne whereon had lounged the languid, luxurious queens through so many centuries, a statement which won the loud and long-continued plaudits of the multitude.

Chapter Forty Five
Conclusion

That night I wandered through the ancient, gigantic palace, hand-in-hand with my well-beloved, pointing out its many marvels, explaining the curious inscriptions upon its colossal foundation-stones, and, taking her to the summit of the Temple of the Seven Lights, showed her the giant city by night. Happy were we in each other's love; yet happier still when, seven days later, amid feasting and merry-making, that was continued throughout a whole moon, we were made man and wife. Our rule has, I believe, found favour with the people. We fear not invasion nor rebellion, because our impregnable country is still the Land of the No Return, at any moment when we choose to block the one single gate by which it may be entered.

As Prince of Ea I have complete control of its ancient treasures, and at Azala's instigation have sent many wall-sculptures, and other relics of interest, to various national museums in the European capitals. To Paris I sent a colossal block of black stone, strangely sculptured, representing the great feast held by Semiramis after she had built the walls of Ea, which she declared unbreakable. To Vienna we dispatched the stone, triangular altar of the Fire-god, Gibil, which stood at the entrance of the House of Lustre. To Berlin went a conical stone, bearing a beautiful hymn to Baal in well-preserved cuneiform character; and to the British Museum, in London, an institution to which my father had sent many relics he had collected, I presented a collection of ancient gems, among them being the little chalcedony cylinder, in order that all should be enabled to inspect the strange heirloom, the possession of which led to the discovery of a long-forgotten civilisation.

The visitor to England's national collection of antiquities may discover it in the Assyrian Room, reposing upon its tiny cushion of purple velvet, fashioned from the papakha of the Goddess of Love, the couch of Istar, a mute relic of one of the greatest monarchs the world has ever known. Before it a neat black tablet, with gold lettering, gives a translation of the injunction regarding the placing on the breast of the first-born the device known as the Mark of the Asps, together with a statement as to its date. Many, perhaps, have seen it during the past twelve months, but none know its real history, which I have here written for the first time. After reading this record they may possibly linger before the case containing it a trifle longer, and reflect upon the curious chain of incidents which caused the ragged, wandering Dervish, who carried it forgotten in his charm-case, to become ruler of a land the existence of which was hitherto unknown, and to secure as wife the sweetest woman his eyes had ever beheld.

With Azala as my wife, mine is a life of happiness unalloyed. Of a verity ours is a rose-garden of peace. The only murmur of discontent ever heard within our kingdom is because the shaft of white brilliance no longer shines to remind the vanquished of the cruel but beautiful queen they idolised as Goddess of Love, and to give them promise of freedom from the Moslem yoke. But the light that had shone on uninterruptedly through forty centuries has never burned since that memorable night when I quenched it, and never will again.

Its extinguishment was emblematic of my complete conquest of the Land of the No Return. I have closed for all time the ever-vigilant Eye of Istar.